A WOLF IN SHEEP'S CLOTHING

SAM HALL

A Wolf in Sheep's Clothing

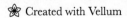 Created with Vellum

Stalk me!

Stalk me!

Facebook author group: Sam's Hall of Heroines
Facebook page here
Newsletter sign up here
Instagram here
Book Bub here

Author Note

This book is written in Australian English, which is a weird lovechild of British and American English. We tend to spell things the way the Brits do (expect a lot more u's), yet also use American slang and swear more than both combined.

While many people have gone over this book, trying to find all the typos and other mistakes, they just keep on popping up like bloody rabbits. If you spot one, don't report it to Amazon, drop me an email at the below address so I can fix the issue.

samhall.author@gmail.com

Trigger Warning and Structure Explanation

If you've read Ahead of the Pack:

I previously published the first seven chapters of this book in a free novella that has since been unpublished. While I did tweak things a bit and it has been edited, you could easily skip to Part 2 and continue reading.

Trigger warnings:

Brief mention of parental death due to illness.

Some discussion of fertility issues of minor characters.

Some discussion of mental health issues.

Part I

Ahead of the Pack

Chapter 1

It was tough being a beta in a world full of alphas and omegas, but never more than during adolescence.

There I was, like every other weekday morning, cooling my heels at the bus stop, waiting for it to turn up and take me to school, when just like clockwork, they arrived. I didn't sense them, didn't scent them like an omega would, not until they were almost upon me.

"There you are!"

Big, strong, masculine arms went around me, grabbing me tight, fingers digging into my ribs. I stiffened, then bucked within his grasp, but that was a big mistake. I was acting like prey. A low growl came in response, his grip growing tighter.

"Trying to get away from me, little beta?"

That should've scared me, and if it were any alpha other than him or his brothers, it might've, but instead, I drove my elbow backwards, slamming it into his ribs.

"Oof!" he said, recoiling.

I grabbed my bag and slung it across my body as I turned to face him, his brothers ranging around him as he made a great show of being wounded before straightening up, a lazy smile spreading across his face.

"Can't even get the drop on a beta, Fen," one of them said, giving his shoulder a shove.

Fen.

The name I'd scrawled inside a million love hearts on scraps of paper I'd burned, screwed up, and tossed away with a violence I shouldn't have felt. I was supposed to be a calm, rational, reliable beta, and I reminded myself of that when his hand went to my hair.

"How're you doing, Red?"

My hair was ruffled like you would a dog's or a young child's, forced to fall in my face, obscuring my gaze. But when I looked up at him from behind the scarlet curtain of my hair, just inspecting him before I swept my unruly mane back behind my ears, I had to tell myself the same thing I always did.

Fen touches everyone like this.

He's casual with his affection.

He's an alpha, you're a beta.

He's Alpha Vanguard's son and, therefore, way too good for you.

And the last one—the most painful one.

You're not an omega.

"I'm fine," I replied belatedly, picking up my books and holding them to my chest, and that was my second mistake. It was a defensive gesture, and nothing got a wolf's attention like when you were trying to hide something. All five of them clustered closer now, those easy smiles fading. I watched their nostrils flare, their eyes taking on a silvery cast as they inspected me much more thoroughly.

But for no reason. I had literally nothing to offer them. I was a beta, I couldn't shift, I had no wolf and I also had no—

As if to make sure to interrupt my thought processes, the bus chose to turn up then, the pump of the air brakes alerting us to its presence. The door swung open, but as I went to climb in, a strong hand slapped down on the folding door.

"Sit with us, Red."

Fen's voice was a low buzz in my ear, one that made me want to shake my head to dislodge it, but I resisted. He stood there, the bus driver being oh so patient when faced with the alphas' sons at play, because Fen didn't give a shit about how long this was taking or the fact that everyone in the bus was watching us. His eyes were like chips of jade that almost glowed against the deep tan of his skin, and now they were beginning to twinkle. He saw my irritation, smelled it too as he breathed in big lungfuls of my scent, and that just made him smile wider.

Eyes do not twinkle, I told myself grumpily. *That's a biological impossibility.* I raked my hair back and stomped up the bus stairs, trying to scurry down the aisle and find an empty seat, when I heard them come behind me.

You always knew where Fen and his brothers were, because that was where the sound, the energy was, and today was no different. Every single person on the bus would have turned the moment they got on, like flowers following the sun. Hands would have reached out to be high-fived, fists to be bumped, obsequious comments made as they passed. It should've been enough to make me hate them.

But it wasn't.

I found an empty seat towards the back. Not too close, as that's where all the omegas and alphas sat and making yourself a target wasn't smart. Not too near to the front either, as that was where the younger kids were. The equivalent of social suicide for a year twelve student. I went to sit down so I could slide across the vinyl seat, nestle up against the window and stare out of it, counting down the days until I was done with this place. Bye, bye, Bordertown, hello big city and university.

Of course, that didn't happen though, did it?

Another hand reached across me, gripping the back of the seat, and in case that message wasn't made clear, a voice said, "Uh-uh…you know where you sit."

"Ryan…" I hissed out the name of Fen's second-in-command. He was an alpha too and so close to Fen in strength, his brother might have to face some dominance fights in the council ring in future, but that wasn't what mattered now. He was also my former childhood playmate, now the bane of my existence.

"Seriously?" I snapped, and the kids closest to us looked away abruptly. If I was dumb enough to take on the strongest pack in the town, I was doing that on my own. "You guys take that shit Dad said too fucking far."

"Or not far enough, depending on how you think about it."

Another voice, and this time, the owner of it pushed past me, forcing me to press against Ryan, resulting in a snicker. Haze Vanguard, Bordertown's resident bad boy, complete with piercings and full sleeve tattoo he'd gotten the moment he turned eighteen. He looked me up and down with eyes the colour of ice, his dark hair falling in his eyes.

"You bitch about it every fucking time," Haze said, "but you know where your spot is. Don't want to make a big fuss?" He opened his arms wide, and now every kid was watching what was going down. "Just go to your seat like a good little fucking beta."

"Only for two more weeks," I said, grinding the words out. I couldn't keep my opinions to myself, something that had always had my dad shaking his head, right up until he died of cancer. "Then I'm out of this dump."

"Sit the fuck down, beta."

And then there was Blake. Blake was the biggest of Fen's crew, with muscle upon muscle few teenage boys could achieve, meaning outsiders would have thought he was the contender for head alpha of the town. He didn't pull his punches, ever, and right now, he didn't hold any of his alpha bark back. My legs moved of their own accord, and I found myself sitting in the same spot they redirected me towards every day.

Usually, I didn't fight it. Usually, I just let myself be herded where the nice alpha boys wanted me to be, sat wedged between the bodies of men with the minds of teenagers, listening to their commentary about the omega girls and boy. Usually, I was just a nice little compliant beta, like most of the others on the bus, and right now, as I perched my books on my knees, I tried to be like that, I really did.

"I'm sitting with the beta," Fen said, throwing himself down beside me, the hot, heavy weight of his arm going across the back of my seat.

Not you, I told myself furiously. *This has nothing to do with you.*

"Fuck, I know we're animals, but do we have to act like it?"

And with that came the last of them, Colt. Pushing past a smirking Ryan and Haze, he was an unlikely member of their pack, and he knew it. He looked like he was made of whipcord and hardened leather, possessing a sinewy build rather than bulky, meaning people often mistook his designation. He was quick to remind them, with his words, then his fists, but the irritated look he shot the others spoke volumes. No easy confidence for him. He was the wolf that no one saw coming, and he wasn't afraid to flash his fangs when he did.

"You OK?" he asked me, sitting down on my other side. I nodded. "You get all your applications in on time?" I glanced sharply up at him to see his hazel eyes were intent. He'd have my answer, just like the others. I nodded again. "Still thinking about studying medicine up in the big city?"

"Out of state," I corrected him. "I need to get away…"

I didn't finish the sentence because he winced slightly, then grit his teeth, the others filing past him or Fen, taking their place across the big broad seat that spanned the width of the bus.

"We good to go?" the driver asked, and Fen waved lazily, a gesture that would not have looked out of place on a king in his throne room. The bus engine roared into life, and then finally, we started moving.

"Only two more fucking weeks of school…" Fen hissed as we watched the streets of the town we were all born in whizz past. "Then freedom."

I was counting on that, more than he could possibly know. In the city, there were more betas than alphas or omegas. In the city, I could get ahead with my wits and smarts, show the world what I was capable of. No one would care about my designation or my family or anything. All they'd want to see would be what I could do.

And this was why.

Some of us beta girls theorised that Cheryl and her clique got on at one of the later bus stops past her house to make sure there was a captive audience when they got on the bus. Whether that was true or not, they certainly got it. The three of them, the town's precious omegas, sauntered up the stairs and down the aisle. Two girls and a guy, but each one was a picture of dewy skinned perfection. Eyes the colour of jewels, hair as soft as silk, the girls had those insanely proportioned bodies that just didn't seem real to the rest of us. Lush tits and hips and wasp-like waists, they were like caricatures of feminine power. And then there was Cyrus.

"He's a grade A twink," my friend, Nikki, had said, and she was right.

High cheekbones, impossibly full lips, big luminous eyes, and a lean musculature that just screamed *touch me*. There'd be hell if you did, though. I'd seen him take someone who didn't show him due deference down in a series of lightning fast moves, leaving them lying bleeding on the floor as he strolled away. Omegas were made for mating, our biology teacher had told us, and so they displayed exaggerated secondary sexual characteristics to make that clear, just like a bird might have bright feathers or a deer, a rack of horns.

Well, Cheryl was putting her secondary sexual characteristics right in Fen's face as she bent down, the already deep scoop neck of her top revealing even more.

"Is this seat taken?"

Her voice was soft and breathy with just a hint of smokiness, and she smiled like this was all too delicious, right up until she turned and placed her well rounded behind on Fen's lap…

And he shoved her off.

"Riley sits with us," he told her flatly when she glared up at him from the floor, hissing her displeasure. "You know that."

"And you know you need to find a mate, and soon. Once school finishes, when Alpha Vanguard calls a conclave…"

I let her words and her bullshit wash over me, allowing it to become some mildly annoying background noise, because none of this had anything to do with me.

My father had been a beta enforcer to Alpha Vanguard's pack, almost an uncle to the boys that surrounded me. His job, like the other enforcers, had been to smooth things over, ensure the ruling pack's orders were followed to the letter, and he had done so admirably. When we were little, they used to joke about the boys and me, as the alpha's pack had sons, and Dad had only a daughter. I was going to grow up to be an omega, their omega, and they would be my pack, treasuring me, protecting me, mating…

I'd gone along with the idea for a while, feeling something inside me that tugged at the mention of it, and Dad had been sure that was an early sign that I had an animal. And so, on his deathbed, he'd made the boys promise to look after me when he couldn't. But after a respectable mourning period had passed, Alpha Vanguard had taken me to one side and spelled out the way things had to be.

"We always planned for you to mate our sons," he'd told me. "But Mother Nature, she has her own ideas." His eyes had raked down my much more modestly curved beta body, one just like my mother's, and he'd shaken his head. "A pack of alphas need an omega. Even if we could support your relationship with them—"

His tone was soft, as gentle as he could make it, and there was real sorrow on his face. Didn't lessen the blow though.

"The first time an omega goes into heat around them, they'll leave me," I'd said woodenly, reciting the received wisdom of the pack.

Alphas and omegas, they went together like peas and corn. They just made sense, but alphas and betas? We served them, helped them. In the old days, we would have ensured the pups survived, working hard to provide food and shelter. But now?

Now I was getting out.

Cheryl focussed all her ire on me, her perfectly contoured face screwing into an ugly expression, her eyes flashing.

"You lay a fucking finger on her," Ryan rumbled, the threat resonating throughout the whole bus, "and I'll make sure you regret it, Cheryl."

This was what I'd miss—Ryan's cheeks flushing under his deep tan, his eyes shifting from blue to silver, his dark hair scraped back with a hasty hand, all humour gone. Dad had meant for the best, trying to ensure his baby girl made it into adulthood in one piece, but he never knew what he'd done to me, making these boys promise to look out for me.

It put a target on my back, that was one thing, because Cheryl's rule as queen bee of the school was not going to be fucked with by anyone, let alone some beta. The second was it didn't allow me the anonymity of my natural place in the pecking order. Some betas dealt drugs to get in with the different alpha groups, some procured free alcohol. Others left clothes behind with complete abandon, not caring in what context they got to touch the golden alphas, just that they did. But most were like me—just content to skate by, be productive, and part of the community.

In my case, it wasn't going to be this community.

The worst thing about Dad's promise wasn't that though. It was being forced to watch all five of them lean forward, a picture of masculine menace in my defence. That was what fucking killed me. We'd been as close as kin, the six musketeers, right up until they revealed as alpha and I'd...

The reveal of my designation was nothing major, just a tiny little blip of a thing, as sometimes was the case with betas. There was no massive surge of hormones for us, like there were with alphas and omegas. Cheryl had been a plain little stick of a girl before she developed, becoming some kind of sex goddess overnight, whereas I was just me—the girl they'd be forced to leave behind, because they couldn't keep pushing the omegas away. They wouldn't want to.

"I can't wait until my first heat," Cheryl said, picking herself up and dusting off her skin-tight jeans as a means to draw attention to her curves. "I'm going to make you beg for a piece of this, Ryan Vanguard, and then I'm going to tell you what I should've all this time. Fuck off!"

She flipped him off with one perfectly manicured finger, then reshuffled the other beta kids, shooing them off seats until she and her crew were happy with the arrangement before the bus driver could finally put the vehicle in gear. I sank down, feeling the omegas' eyes on me, wanting the bus seat to just swallow me up and hide me.

Two more weeks, I said over and over. *Two more weeks.* That thought fused with the sound of the bus engine, repeated over and over, until we got to school.

"C'MON," Colt said, the bell ringing the minute we got off the bus. We should have been here ages ago, but the delays of the morning had us here right as school started. He wrapped his arm around me and steered me towards the door. "I'm walking you to class today."

Chapter 2

"Riley, can I have a quick chat before you go?"

The bell had gone for recess, but Ms Thornton, my physics teacher, looked up from her desk, a bright smile on her face, before she waved me over. Blake appeared at the doorway, frowning when he saw me walking towards the desk, not out the door. They took the directive to keep me safe seriously, but that didn't necessarily extend to spending precious break time in class.

"Ah, sure," I replied to the teacher. "Is everything OK?"

"Better than OK." She was positively beaming. The sound of a cleared throat had both of us looking at the doorway. Blake pulled away to allow the principal and the careers advisor into the classroom. "We've got some amazing news. Come in, Blake," she said to the alpha. "No point hovering in the doorway."

Was it his dragging feet or was it the purposeful bustle of the teaching staff that had me on high alert?

"So, you know how you sat the UCAT test back in July?"

The UCAT was a test sat by students wanting to study medicine in Australia. On top of having to get damn near perfect score in all your year twelve work, you needed to ace the test as well to ensure a place. My palms were instantly coated in sweat now, my heart racing from a standing start. I just nodded belatedly in answer to her question.

"Well, the test results are released to universities in September, and they match the scores with student applications for medical degrees and…" Ms Thornton squealed then. The tall, lean, almost butch physics teacher squealed like a little girl, and I just stared.

"Not only are you the first student at Bordertown High to attempt the UCAT," the principal said in that cheerfully authoritative way he used at most assemblies, "but…" Everyone leaned forward, including me, but the responses were all different. The teachers were all excited, Blake was scowling, his arms crossed over his broad chest, and me? I was terrified. They obviously thought the news was good, but was it actually? Was it what I wanted? Would it give me a way out of this fucking town?

Apparently, the gods were kind, because the answer was a resounding yes.

"The premier university in the state is offering you a scholarship with a generous stipend to cover living expenses. You'll have free accommodation, your meals provided for…"

I wanted to hear what they were saying, the details were so, so important, but my head filled with this white staticky noise, followed by a high-pitched whine. I was too young to experience first-year medical student syndrome, but right now, I felt like I was having a bloody heart attack. My pulse was racing, my heart felt like it was bouncing around in my chest like a basketball, and the muscles across my torso seemed too tight for me to take a full breath. The pressure inside me was building, building…

"It's OK, beta." Blake's deep voice cut through everything, creating calm where there had only been insanity. And when I took my first real breath in, nothing felt better than that rush of sweet, sweet air. Of course, that was when reality snapped back abruptly.

"Riley, are you OK?" Ms Thornton said, reaching out, but she dropped her hand when Blake shot her a censorious look.

His arm went around me, and he pulled me in close, something we hadn't done since…

"She's just overwhelmed," he told them. "This is some amazing news, but… This is what her dad wanted for her."

No, it wasn't. He wanted this—me plastered against Blake's big body, leeching his strength, him stepping up and looking after me, all of them doing that. As if summoned by my thoughts, I heard the sound of heavy footsteps, and then the rest of the pack all came running in.

"What the fuck happened?" Fen asked Blake, not waiting for an answer as he lifted my chin, staring into my eyes. "Some shit go down? The omegas attack you again?"

"Mr Vanguard," the principal said stiffly. "Language, please."

"We'll use all the appropriate language you like, as long as you tell us what happened to Riley," Haze drawled.

"She's as white as a ghost," Colt snapped, peering down at me, then glaring at them. "What fucking happened?"

The principal stood tall then and gave the alphas his most perfect beta smile. He might have to recognise their authority in all other things, but not here.

"Riley has been given a full scholarship with incredibly generous conditions to study medicine…"

I couldn't seem to hold on to the details, my head whiting out the minute people started talking. Instead of the glimpse into my future, all I heard was the frantic rattle of Blake's heart, one whose pace matched mine. Finally, people stopped talking, the guys steering me out of the room, and for once, I was glad for their overprotective bullshit. They got me out of the building, downstairs, and over to the table we always sat at. My books were removed, my bag placed beside them, then a bottle of Coke and an unwrapped salad sandwich were set before me.

"Eat, Riley," Fen said, using the slightest touch of alpha command to prompt me to do what I needed. I took a sip of the Coke, the caffeine and sugary goodness helping resettle me, then grabbed the sandwich and took a bite.

"Good girl," Ryan said, his voice even and calm, so then I was too.

This was why alphas were so important. They could guide and steer the emotional state of a community, ensuring calm, well regulated towns or creating frightening despotic regimes like we'd studied in history. *They would be so good as town leaders*, I thought as I chewed. *If they showed everyone the same care as me…* Ryan watched my every chew, nodding encouragingly, while Colt slotted in beside me, putting his arm around my back. Haze sat cross-legged on the table, picking at his beat-up Converse sneakers, and Blake continued to scowl. But as always, we turned to Fen.

"So you're going?" he asked, smiling then, but it didn't reach his eyes. Instead, they were big and green, wide open and transmitting everything he was feeling, like they had been when Dad died. "Fuck, Riley…"

"You did good," Colt said, giving me a squeeze. "We'll keep drilling you every night until exams—"

"God, how I wish we were actually drilling her," Haze said with an exaggerated sigh, then winked at me. "You could pretend to be our omega, like we used to when we were kids. Once more for old time's sake, though with considerably less—"

"Shut the fuck up, Haze," Blake rumbled. I didn't want to meet his eyes, those dark depths flashing now with so much I knew he'd never say. "So you're gonna take this scholarship?"

"I have to," I replied. "This is it. What I've been working for since…" I swallowed. "Since Dad died. I've got no future here. You're going to take one of the omegas as a mate…" I glanced behind me to where Cheryl and her posse all sat, ostensibly completely oblivious to us. "And I don't have it in me to be someone's bitch."

"Fuck, could you imagine?" Fen said, now with an honest-to-goodness smile. "Remember when Viviane was the first omega to reveal and started throwing her weight around and Riles—"

"Put her on her arse for beating up the year seven kids," Blake said with a snort. "That was fucking glorious."

I shook my head, finding myself smiling against my will, but that didn't last for long. When I looked up, regarding each one of them, I said, "I can't put the ruling omega on her arse, no matter who she might be. Your beasts won't let that happen, for one. They'll know her, your fated mate, and you'll do anything to protect her. Anything. Friendships from the past…" There was a low rumble at that. "They won't matter, and you know this."

We'd all seen what we thought were rock-solid relationships fracture and disintegrate when people found their fated mates. While people revealed as alpha, beta, or omega at puberty and alphas and omegas shifted into wolves at some point in early adulthood, true mates came after. The bond was so intense, so complete, that loyalty, friendship, anything that was incompatible between mates was set aside, and I knew none of the Border-town omegas would tolerate me around.

"This is why you've been pulling away from us," Fen said in a low, dangerous tone, a growl rising in the others. "This is why you don't want us around."

"I'm just trying to meet my destiny head-on," I said, getting to my feet, wrapping the sandwich up, ready to throw the rest away. "Yours is here, with one of the omegas, and mine is in the city."

"Sit down and eat, beta," Ryan said, and my knees buckled, my arse slamming down on the concrete bench.

"This is not what Dad wanted for me when he spoke to you," I said, trying to fight his command but failing miserably. As if in support of his highhanded bullshit, my stomach rumbled in response. "He didn't want you bossing me around, making me your little beta slave."

"Oh, Riley…" Haze purred. "If we did that to you, you'd be putting something else entirely in your mouth."

"Fucking shut up, brother," Blake said, slapping Haze up the back of the head.

But I unwrapped the sandwich, biting down and chewing, working methodically through it as they all watched, like it was the most satisfying thing in the world.

"What do you know about what your dad asked of us?" Colt asked with a sidelong look. "We had a lot of conversations with him, close to the end."

I set the sandwich down now, three quarters eaten, but nothing they would be able to do would get me to eat more. I stared at him, his longish light brown hair falling in his eyes, and those hazel depths bore into mine, neither of us able to look away.

But I was saved by the bell, the familiar *ding, ding, ding* cutting through their compulsion and allowing me to make my escape. I grabbed my gear, dumped my rubbish, and then hurried off to class, hoping to ditch all five of them this time.

"Running, beta?" Haze's arch voice spoke almost directly into my ear, his arm linking with mine. "Please do. You know what it does to my instincts."

His eyes flashed silver then, showing me how close to the surface his beast was, and when he grinned, I saw that his fangs were sharper, longer.

"Haze…"

"He likes it when you run." His head tipped to one side as we stood in the middle of the busy hallway, students and teachers weaving their way around us, like we were rocks in a stream.

"Haze!"

I tried to jerk my arm free of his grip, but his fingers closed tighter, making me feel the prick of his claws through the light fabric of my shirt.

Oh shit.

Haze was funny, sarcastic and completely inappropriate, but his wolf? That was a whole other ball of wax.

"Haze, it's OK," I said in a much calmer, much more soothing tone. "I need you to come back to me now. Just take a breath and focus on my voice." I couldn't compel him like his brothers or his fathers could, but I could coax him. I'd done it when he was younger, not long after he revealed. "Today's not the day, Haze. You don't want to wolf out in front of the whole fucking school, force your dads to come marching down here and get you in order."

He bared his fangs then, a terrible silent snarl forming. I swallowed hard, taking a deep breath and then reaching out, pushing my fingers into the silky feathers of his hair, stroking a thumb across the top of his cheekbone, just like I used to do before.

"Come back to me, Haze."

He blinked then, the silver receding, his mouth closing, a small frown forming, as if he couldn't work out what the hell was happening. Those blue eyes flicked around the hallway now, as if seeing it for the first time.

"What the fuck are you doing, beta?" Valerie, one of the omegas, spat, wandering closer, her hands on her hips. "Groping alphas like some pathetic little omega wannabe?"

For a second, I was worried Haze was going to relapse and that his beast would come rushing back to the surface, but it was pure male aggression, not wolf, as he snarled at her.

"Fuck off, Valerie! Honestly, if I had any interest in anything you might have to say, I'd let you know."

"Oh you'll be interested…" she said with a sultry smile. "I revealed first, so it's likely my heat will come on first, and then you'll be—"

Haze took my hand, marching us up the hall and finding my English lit class with unerring accuracy, but he didn't leave me at the door. He followed me in, then sat the both of us down at the back of the class.

"Mr Vanguard?" Mr Whiteley, my English teacher, looked up from the class text he was reading from, peering across the room at us. "Have you joined my class this late in the year and I wasn't notified?"

"Joined? No," he replied, to the sound of titters from the betas in the class. "But I'll be here for the rest of the term. A very quiet, very well-behaved visitor."

"Well, that will make a lovely change from your usual behaviour in my communications class," Whiteley said, turning back to the class. "If you wish to sit through preparation for the English literature exam, I won't oppose it. Now, if everyone can get their notebooks out…"

I went to get my book out but was hampered by Haze's hand sliding under the desk and grabbing mine, his thumb rubbing against my knuckles. I shot him a shocked look, but his gaze was firmly fixed on Whiteley and his discussion of the different character arcs of the main players in *Hamlet*.

"Haze, I need to take notes," I whispered.

My hand was released, that arm going across the back of my chair, his fingers now contenting themselves with playing with the no doubt split ends of my hair, so I got my book out and a pen and started scribbling down important points as Whiteley spoke.

"Congrats, Riles," he said under his breath. "You worked fucking hard for this and you got it. You deserve every damn scholarship they can throw at you."

And that was when I hated my father, just a little.

If he hadn't put this pressure on the boys, if he hadn't made them feel personally responsible for me, we wouldn't be in this position.

Haze should be in Valerie's or Cheryl's or even Cyrus' class, playing with their hair, not mine. While they would be able to start finding their true mates when their beasts revealed themselves, putting in some human legwork first helped smooth that process. Instead, they were wasting their time with me.

This was what I wanted to study when I got into medicine— the way omegas and betas and alphas actually worked, not just the half baked folk science that currently passed for our understanding of designation. I wanted to know what drew the six of us together, even though it shouldn't be the case. Alphas frequently ditched childhood friends when they revealed, so why hadn't they? Was it just their vow to Dad or…? I chanced a sidelong look at Haze, and he stared right back, a small smile forming then, full of all that mischief he'd brought to our gang as kids.

"So can anyone tell me what role Ophelia plays in *Hamlet?*" Whiteley asked, jerking my attention back to the room. "Don't tell me 'crazy ex-girlfriend.' I don't need to know what she was, I need to know why she was written into the play. Shakespeare used her for a specific reason. Anyone?"

I raised my hand then, glad at least in this respect, I had an answer.

Chapter 3

Two weeks later.

I laid my pencil down, sucking in a breath, then letting it out before glancing up at the clock. I had half an hour before the exam ended, my final exam. I straightened my spine, turning my answer book back to the start, ready to review my answers, but I knew. I couldn't tell you how or why, but I knew. There was a feeling, a burning sensation, that just told me when I'd aced something, and right now, that flared hot inside me. Every answer I cross-checked validated that. *Tick, tick, tick,* I could imagine the marker going as they read my submission, then my fingers shook slightly.

But what if they didn't?

The scholarship was awarded based on the assumption I'd kill my exams, so I scoured each response, the words of my teachers ringing in my ears as I made minor corrections until finally someone said, "Pencils down, please." I laid mine down, collected my booklets up, and put them together on my table. Then when we were given leave, I stood up and walked out in a daze...

Right into them.

"Riley…" Colt could only say my name, frowning as he searched my face. We'd sat up for hours last night, going over my notes, drilling the information into my brain.

"Fuck, tell us you killed it," Fen said. "You did, right? You killed it?"

"It's not the end of the world if she didn't," Ryan told the others. "There are other options."

"Options here?" Blake asked with a grunt.

"Yes, I for one would like to explore local options as well," Haze said with a nod.

"I killed it…" I barely whispered the words, but they all stilled, facing me. "I mean, I think—"

I gasped as I was swept up in a suffocating embrace, and I couldn't tell who, not until my hand slid down his back. *Ryan*, my brain supplied, having managed to develop an encyclopaedic knowledge about the Vanguard brothers, along with all the hot and cold running bullshit of year twelve.

"Stop hogging her and give her here."

The words were delivered in a terse way. *Blake*, I recognised instantly. For a big guy, he could hold me oh so gently, caging me in his arms but still letting me breathe. At that, I went limp in his grip, daring to rest my head on his shoulders.

"You did it, babe."

"We still have to wait—"

"You did it."

He didn't say many words, which pissed the others off, as it meant people paid more attention when he did, and right now, I was as willing to surrender to that certainty as I was to his embrace. It felt like I let out the first real exhalation of breath that I'd been able to all day, muscles I hadn't realised I was holding tight slowly uncoiling.

"C'mon, we're going up to the point tonight," Fen said, interrupting the moment.

"The point?" I pushed away from Blake, stepping free of him, of them. "I'm not going up there."

MacDonald's Point was a notorious make out place and not somewhere I was going with anyone, but they all just grinned.

"There's a big year twelve party being held up there with a bonfire and everything. People are burning their old school books, getting on the piss…" Fen said with a challenging smile. "Last chance to carouse with your fellow classmates before you ditch this popsicle stand."

"Ah…sure," I replied, my hand going to my hair, then my clothing. "But I need to go home and—"

"Grab everything to be burned? We are here to help," Colt said in a rueful tone. "I want to burn that physics textbook personally."

"I'm not burning my bloody textbooks. They're expensive, so I'm donating them to the school at least."

"Ughhh, stop being so fucking practical and just come run amok with us tonight," Haze said with a growl, but that slowly transformed into a smile. "This is the end of something and that needs to be marked in the customary tradition."

"Shitty pizza and goon bag wine?" Ryan asked.

"Shitty pizza and goon bag wine," Haze confirmed.

"ARE you sure this is a good idea?"

Mum stood in the doorway of my bedroom as the guys ransacked it, grabbing loose-leaf paper and notebooks before stuffing them into a garbage bag.

"Is what a good idea?" I asked her.

"Going to the point with the Vanguard boys." Her eyes darted from the chaos in my room to me, then back again. "Riley, you're not an omega."

"I am well aware of that."

"There's no future—"

"There's no future." I repeated her words back to her in a much more matter-of-fact tone. "Results come through in January. I'm going to be working in Aunty Rose's café most days to make as much money as I can before I go. My use by date is rapidly approaching." I looked back at the guys, wincing at the mess they'd made of my room, knowing I'd have to sort that out.

Later, my brain whispered seductively, because right now, checking out for a few hours was incredibly appealing. My results were in the lap of the gods now. I'd done everything I possibly could to ensure I'd aced the exams, but… For just this night, I could live in the moment, not thinking about past or future, just now.

And shitty goon bag wine would help that eminently. I'd message Nikki, see if she and her boyfriend, Paul, wanted to join us, and then just celebrate having met a crucial milestone.

School was out for summer. I was done. I was no longer a year-anything student. I was eighteen, legally an adult, and I was about to take my first step into adulthood by getting heinously drunk, then vomiting in the bushes as my best friend held my hair back. Then the two of us could whine some stupidly maudlin shit about never forgetting each other before passing out in the back of someone's car. It was an Australian rite of passage. I said something of the effect to Mum, minus some of the more sordid details.

"We'll make sure Riley comes back in one piece," Colt said, taking up position by my side. "I'm not drinking tonight." Keys came flying through the air, and he caught them without even looking. "So no harm will come to her."

This was, of course, the point where she weakened. Typical beta, but also typical of this household. Dad had loved the Vanguard boys like they were his own sons, and he would've moved heaven or earth to look after them and me, so that became the deciding factor.

"Well, if you're sure."

"Scout's honour," Colt said, doing a salute. Not the Scout one, but no one cared. Mum nodded then and stepped away from the door, just in time for the guys to walk out with bags of my crap in tow.

"I just need to get changed," I said.

"Why? You look awesome in what you're wearing," Fen said,

letting his eyes rake down my body. And there was Mum's frown back.

"I need something comfortable if we're gonna hang out at the point," I said. "And anyway, these have exam germs on them."

"Wanna toss them in the bag to be burned as well?" Haze asked with a wide grin.

"Just go out to the car. I'll be ready in five," I said.

I shut the door on Mum, knowing she had more to say, and rushed to my drawers to pull out a loose cotton singlet and a pair of cut off denim shorts—cool, comfortable, and most importantly, not school clothes. I slipped on my checked Vans and then I stopped before the mirror, consulting my reflection.

In some ways, I was glad I was a beta. While I was wearing a bra, I didn't have to if I didn't want to. I could get away with loose clothes like these or short shorts, because really, I was just all long legs and arms like a spider monkey. The only thing I could take any pride in was my hair.

Long, deep scarlet red and just like Dad's, without the requisite freckled skin. I knew girls who worked damn hard to dye their hair my colour, and I didn't need to. I pulled the thick mane back, then wove it into a quick French braid, using a hair tie on the end. Then I was on my phone, sending a text to Nik.

R: *Coming to the point?*

N: *Y! You?*

R: *Guys got my shit, ready to burn.*

N: *Damn, girl, omegas gonna get hissy! Meet me at the top carpark.*

I shoved my phone in my pocket and then walked out.

"Riley…" Mum said, pushing herself away from the wall in the hallway, but as she looked me up and down, taking in my slapdash attire, something seemed to settle. She forced herself to smile, then walked down to the kitchen, grabbing her bag and finding some cash before handing it over. "Eat something before you drink, so you've at least got something to line your stomach. Might mean you don't vomit later."

I grinned, then bounced over, pulling her in a hug.

"Thanks, Mum. I'll talk to you later."

"Stay safe!"

HER VOICE RANG in my ears as I walked out to the front of the house, the big black SUV the boys had been gifted idling on the side of the road.

"Hey, baby," Fen said with a sharp grin. "Wanna ride?"

"I get shotgun?" I asked, opening the passenger side door and sliding in. "Who the fuck gets the bitch seat?"

This was one of a row of much smaller, foldable seats in the rear compartment of the car.

"We scissors, paper, rocked that shit, and Hazel lost!" Ryan replied with a cackle.

"Shut the fuck up," Haze said. "You're riding in here on the way home."

That quickly devolved into the kind of raucous bickering they were all known for, only Fen keeping out of it.

"You ready?" he asked me, those green eyes shining as he stared at me.

"Let's do this shit," I said. "Time to get my goon on."

Chapter 4

"Oh my god, food baby," Nikki said, flopping backwards and into Paul's arms as she nursed a small bump at her stomach. The beta wrapped his arms around her, nuzzling his face into her neck. Nik and Paul were intending to stay in Bordertown, get jobs, maybe move in together… Something sweetly domestic. The scene they painted right now kinda tugged at me, so I drank down a mouthful of wine.

If I stayed here, someone would be found for me, the alphas would make sure of it. Ensuring the happiness and harmony of the town was their highest priority, and if that entailed match-making betas, they'd do it. Or rather, their omega would. But I'd never had a chance to experience this, to be held, to be nuzzled. Well, almost never.

"C'mere," Fen said, hooking his arm around my waist and pulling me onto his lap before retrieving my drink and filling it back up from the cardboard cask of shit wine we'd bought, then presenting it to me. "I've got the cure for what ails you."

It wasn't the overly sweet white wine I was sensing as I took another mouthful, but the guys' eyes on me. Giving and taking food and drink from wolf shifters was a big, big deal, but not now, not here. I forced my muscles to relax, to settle back against Fen's solid chest, to ignore the spicy, woody, masculine scent of him and just pretend like this was old times. When we were just kids, falling all over each other like a pile of puppies. When drawing me close, passing me around, holding me like this was all innocence.

Because right now, it wasn't just his scent I was getting. His arm was loose around me, his voice strong and confident as he talked shit with his brothers, the stories and the crap becoming more and more convoluted the more wine was consumed. Well, all but Colt. He sat quietly at the edge of the group as he often did, watching all the bullshit go by, except this time, it appeared I was the bullshit. Those eyes of his slid over his brother and me, making me shift uncomfortably on Fen's lap, which just made Fen's hand slap down on my leg, holding me still, right where he wanted me.

It wasn't just the warmth of Fen's body or the sound of his voice or the feel of his breath riffling the little baby hairs on the back of my neck. Something hard rose beneath me, pressing into my bony arse, making clear exactly how the man of my dreams was responding to me.

I chanced a look over my shoulder, those green eyes meeting mine, his shit-eating grin only softening slightly, but his pupils? I caught the moment when they expanded, a slight silvery cast covering his iris as his wolf looked out at me. The grin faded, becoming something much lazier—the way a wolf looks when it opens its jaws to pant, catching its breath after the hunt. Or was it before? I jerked my eyes down belatedly, knowing how rude it was for a beta to stare at an alpha, although alphas weren't constrained by the same rules. When I finally looked up, Colt stared without a hint of regret, his eyes shining bright, bright silver.

"Ugh, I should've known you were here, hanging out with these losers." A sharp, feminine voice had all of us groaning, and me more than anyone. Whatever tension had been building dissipated, so my groan was more from relief than anything.

Cheryl and her crew looked down at the lot of us, casting a censorious eye over the mess of pizza boxes and shitty wine. "We just came by to tell you the Williams boys are here tonight."

Alpha packs were born at least a year or so apart, often in clusters, and the Vanguards and the Williams were two of the three packs in their cluster. This meant that they'd all been raised knowing one pack would rise through the ranks, taking over as the ruling pack in Bordertown when the boys' dads stepped down. The others could either live under their rule, as the Williams boys' dads did, or they could bugger off to some other town, challenge the existing alphas there, and hope they won. Until that was settled, their ability to coexist was a shaky one.

"What the fuck are they doing here?" Ryan snapped, his eyes flashing silver and the omegas simpered at that. "They graduated a few years ago."

"Maybe they're here for us," Cyrus said with a sharp look at the alphas. "Did you think about that?"

"Then you better run along then," Haze said with a dismissive wave. "Wouldn't do to keep the mighty Williams boys waiting."

This wasn't going to the omegas' plan at all, and I kind of felt sorry for them.

Omegas were raised a certain way—to expect to be pampered and fought over, to inspire unholy levels of lust in alphas, and to use what power they had over their bigger, stronger mates to ensure their needs were met.

It was actually an area of our biology that fascinated me. Theories abounded as to why things were this way. Firstly, it was assumed it was an evolutionary thing. Alphas were just so much stronger than the rest of us, particularly omegas, so what was to stop them from snatching them and raping them over and over? There was some prehistoric evidence that this was the case in the distant past. But since then, it had become a chase, the hunting instincts and natural competitiveness of alphas leading them to perform greater and greater gestures to try and win the unruly omega to their pack, because that was the other thing.

The Vanguards might win in a dominance fight against the other young packs and come out supreme, but if they didn't take an omega, they wouldn't last long. Alphas were all about legacies —taking a territory and holding it, then caring for everyone in it and providing stability in the form of the next generation of alpha sons, who'd do the same. No omega? No babies, no future, no leadership. A community didn't rise up against their alphas often, but that would definitely be grounds for it.

So for the three omegas, this should've been the most glorious time of their lives. All three packs should've been vying for each one of their hands, the three of them treated like queens or a king, but instead…

I pushed Fen's arm away, his muscles tightening too slow for him to stop me as I clambered to my feet.

"Where are you going?" Fen asked in a low growl, he and his brothers beginning to rise to their feet.

"I need a piss," I shot back. "Cheap wine and my bladder aren't friends. Nik, you coming?"

She nodded belatedly, giving Paul a long kiss first before following behind me, both of us turning our backs on the disgruntled omegas, and that was a fucking mistake.

I thought I was doing the right thing by getting out of their way and letting the omegas spend some time with the alphas that were their birthright, removing the weird obstacle of obligation and habit that I'd turned out to be.

Of course, it couldn't be that simple, could it?

"Hey!"

Both Nik and I stopped halfway across the carpark with the toilet cubicle just in sight. So damn close. The two of us turned around to see Cheryl and her omega buddies standing there, fairly spitting with rage, if their silvery eyes were anything to go by.

"What the hell do you think you are doing?"

"Going for a piss," I drawled, Nik smothering a snort of laughter.

"Before that," she insisted. "You know you have no future with them."

"With them, with this town, with anything to do with Bordertown, including you, Cheryl," I said. Nik let out a little gasp, which let me know that perhaps the wine was doing the talking, but I charged on. "This is your town, one of you will take those guys as mates. You'll rule this place."

I watched the three of them flutter their eyes at that. I fought the urge to laugh because it was just so damn easy to disarm them.

"You're damn right we will," she insisted, but her words sounded hollow, even to me.

"I don't know if you've heard, but I'm going to the city for university in a very short period of time. I'm done with this town. Nik is so in love with Paul, it makes me slightly nauseous."

"Hey!" My friend punched me in the arm, but I didn't really feel it. Damn, I was drunk.

"No one here is a threat to you," I finished up, then turned to go, really needing to go to the loo now.

"As if you could be, beta bitch."

I froze then, my muscles locking down, a completely un-beta-like impulse to grab this fucking bitch and pound my fist into her smug little face rising, rising, and then falling as I considered the consequences of that. Hurting an omega came with an auto-matic expulsion from the community, no questions asked, and I wasn't going out like that. Of course, my self-restraint couldn't be respected, could it?

"You need to keep the hell away from the Vanguards," Cheryl spat out. "They're not for you."

"Riley…" Nik said, placing a placating hand on my shoulder as I spun around.

"I know that. I've always known that," I ground out between clenched teeth. "I've told them that a million times, and I've tried to keep them the fuck away from me but…"

My words faded away as I peered over the tops of the omegas' heads, to where a familiar group of guys began to emerge, eyeing the situation here with eyes that shone like the moon.

"Why don't you tell them that?" I snapped, and then jerked my finger in the pack's direction.

My tone, my message, they were enough to bring a shitstorm raining down on my head, but I'd picked my words well, because the three of them spun around, the lure of alphas much more important than putting down a mouthy beta. They turned towards the pack just like everyone did, like the guys were the sun and the rest of us were just little satellites, orbiting them endlessly.

But not this fucking planet. I stomped on over to the no doubt spider infested toilet block, shone my phone torch around the cubicle meticulously before doing what I needed to, then emerged to find a white-faced Nik waiting for me.

"Holy shit, Riley…" was all she could say.

"Message Paul to meet us at the bonfire," I said. "I'm not going back there to watch Cheryl and her omegas play hide the sausage with the guys."

"But they—"

"It's just biology, Nik," I said, washing my hands all too vigorously. "And we need to get the hell out of the way of it. Unless you've got a little biology you want to work on tonight?"

I waggled my eyebrows at her with exaggerated emphasis, and she cracked up as a result.

"Maybe we might slip away later," she said, elbowing me in the ribs as we walked out. "But first let's find you someone to slip away with."

But that had never happened before, something that filled me with an irrational shame. I knew why. The guys' overprotective crap kept suitors away. But part of me couldn't help but long for some beta to come forward, so inflamed by my beauty that he would insist on a place by my side. I snorted at that, recognising it for the bullshit it was, but… My hands rubbed at my arms, as if that might help. I touched myself because no one else did, no one but them.

"Riley!"

I heard my name being called faintly, but that just helped my feet move faster.

"C'mon," I said, "let's find that bonfire."

Chapter 5

I watched the flames burn higher and higher, feeling some kind of connection to the destructive blaze. Cheers went up as more books, more pencil cases, folders, even novels were tossed on the bonfire. Shit, that bit made me wince. All the paraphernalia of our school years was burned up, reduced back down to ash, the stink of burning plastic filling the air. But my bottle of beer was cold. Shit, and slipping through my fingers! I clenched my fingers tight, just in time to stop it from smashing down on the concrete below. Which reminded me, time for another swig.

"You're pissed!"

This was announced with a strange kind of triumph, and I glanced owlishly up at the deliverer of this statement. He was a tall, shadowy figure, one it took me a moment to recognise. Ready laugh, easy lope as he walked through the halls, played basketball…

"Clayton!" I said, jubilant that I remembered his name. He seemed equally as pleased. He sidled in close, then pushed my plait off over my shoulder, tracing a finger down the line of it before turning to me.

"Want to come for a walk?"

I knew what this meant, the social rituals of high school discussed fervently in classrooms, the yard, and over social media all the time. Just like that, with no lead-up, no courting, he wanted to know if I wanted to go and make out. My lips fell open, and he seemed to catch every second of that, unable to look away until I pursed them.

I shouldn't. I barely knew the guy, had probably shared maybe ten words with him in all of high school, and what? I was gonna share spit with him now? I thought of the omegas and their hostile glares and then of the boys they stood in front of, blocking access to. I couldn't keep hanging around the Vanguards like some kind of moth-eaten mascot, passed around, petted, stroked, scented whenever they felt like it. They mated for life, whereas betas? We could enjoy all the casual sex we liked, and right now, I wanted at least a taste of that.

"Sure," I said, smiling, and he smiled with me.

"Well, c'mon then."

HE DREW me away from the fire, the cool night air soothing my skin, right up until he took my hand in his.

"I've always thought you were so fucking pretty, Riley." I paused at that, and Clayton turned, looking down at me and smiling at my obvious look of shock. He stepped closer then, his hand sliding up behind my neck, just stroking the skin there. "So many of the guys do. You're so hot, with those amazing legs and this fucking red hair…"

This, I needed this weirdly crude, harshly breathed ode to my charms more than anything else tonight, and as a result, the guy had my complete attention. He smiled then, his cockiness a pale echo of theirs, but I didn't care. He was a beta, he was here, and he was telling me I was pretty. He was exactly what I needed. I had to respond in some way but I had no experience with this, so I just tilted my head, grazing his arm with my cheek, but that seemed to be enough.

"I really want to kiss you right now," he said, before swooping in and doing just that.

I'd heard plenty of horror stories from other girls, of wet sloppy kisses or tongues seeking to do interdental work, but I considered myself lucky here. Clayton's hands surged around me, tugging me close until I felt dwarfed by his long, lanky body. He seemed to know what he was doing, claiming my mouth as his, then moving slowly in these little nipping movements, ones I could anticipate and meet before they teased my mouth open. Then his tongue slid against mine, sending a bolt of something intense shooting through me, making me shiver, right up until he pulled away.

He saw my breathlessness, my wide eyes, and he just smiled, then took my hand again.

"My car's over here."

"We're not driving anywhere, right?" I asked, some moment of self-preservation forcing me to remember that drunk driving equals bad.

"No, we're not going anywhere." As if to illustrate that, he unlocked the rear door of his car, ushering me into the backseat, only to follow me in.

Oh, I thought as he loomed over me, his mouth seeking mine and finding it like two magnets snapping together. Kisses, searing kisses set me alight, making me wonder why the hell I hadn't done this sooner.

Oh right, I remembered why.

No! my conscious brain snapped, or was it my subconscious? Whichever one had the wheel, I leant into this, into him, into the sharp whistle of Clayton's breath, the desperate clawing of his hands through my hair, loosening my braid until my hair fell in a heavy curtain around me.

"Fuck, Riley…" He stopped right then, even as I leaned in for more, his eyes raking over me like I was some sort of goddess or something. "I wasn't going to say anything. I wanted to play it cool, but shit… You're leaving?"

"Yeah, I'm going to the city. I got a scholarship."

He smiled then, but it was a pained thing, an expression I knew well, I'd just never seen it on another person's face, especially when it came to me.

"I've been crushing on you so fucking bad. Have since middle school. Look, I know this can't go anywhere, but…" He swallowed, then shook his head, a complete change from the confident basketball player I'd seen in the hallways. "Would you go out on a few dates with me before you leave?"

This, I had hoped for, dreaming that this would start once school was over, once I got the hell out of town, but to have opportunity come knocking that much earlier than expected? I admit to feeling a selfish flush of satisfaction at that. I knew I was smart, I knew I was hard-working, but as a woman? Most of us were marinating in great soups of self-doubt, but it felt like I had even more to worry about. Few friends, no boyfriends, no dates, no offers, nothing. I was a modern woman. I wanted to kick arse at uni *and* be validated sexually.

"We can't have anything long-term…" he continued nervously in the face of my silence, but I leant forward to quiet him.

"Yes."

"Yeah?" That smile was back, and how had I never seen how bright it was? It felt like it lit up the entire darkened interior of the car. "Yeah?" This was said much more teasingly as he pulled me closer, our mouths finding each other's again.

"Yes, please…" I gasped as I felt his lips on my neck, nipping the sensitive skin, then soothing it with kisses.

"Fuck, Riley…" he groaned, hauling me up and onto his lap, forcing my arms to wrap around his shoulders or fall back. "Riley…"

He kept saying my name between kisses, then again as his mouth explored the column of my neck, making me squirm, then once more as he kissed all the skin revealed by my tank top. But at some point, we were either going to stay as we were, or things were going to take a step further.

If I hadn't been drinking, we probably wouldn't have.

Clayton probably wouldn't have tried. But we were invincible right now, walking away from school as survivors, moving on to a bright new future. So when his hand closed over my breast, a question in his eyes, I nodded. There was no point in taking it slow. I was going, he was staying, but right now, we had this, a kind of electrical charge that seemed to build and build inside me, and he seemed to sense that.

"Fuck…" he hissed as he slid one strap off my shoulder, then my bra strap, his lips covering every inch of ground he took. Another questioning look as he moved to pull the cup down and reveal my breast to his eyes, his mouth, his tongue.

I was overheated, burning from within, and that was all focussed on the aching nipple he was centimetres away from. Alcohol swam in my blood, making me aware of the way my pulse raced and my body responded, locking me down to the here and now. This Riley, Riley now, wanted to know what it would feel like for those full lips to close over my nipple, his thumb moving now to swipe across the cloth, giving me a hint.

Like Eve taking the apple from the snake in Eden, that was all it took to sign my downfall in my hometown. I nodded, just a tiny thing, but Clayton's entire focus was on my responses, and that was heady. He peeled the cup of my bra down, my nipple pulling even tighter in the cool air, his eyes still on me right up until his lips brushed against the tight bead.

"Shit!" I hissed, my fingers digging into his hair, raking along his scalp as he flicked his tongue across it, then sucked it into his mouth.

I knew how to get myself off, having developed the ability to stealth orgasm in my bedroom and the shower without alerting Mum, but oh my god. Someone else's touch added a whole other dimension to things, my pussy pulsing helplessly in time with his sucks. Then, just when a good rhythm started, he'd pull away, tracing the sensitive spot with his tongue, before sucking me in again. My hips rocked in response, his hand sliding down to press on my butt, forcing me to grind against his hard length.

Fuck, fuck, fuck… This was all happening way too fast, but drunk Riley didn't give a shit, did she? She was chasing pleasure and fun and just being a normal fucking teenager, thinking she was going to end her school career with a truly explosive bang, when the door was wrenched open.

"What the fuck do you think you're doing?"

The question was growled in an inhuman voice, because the owner wasn't one hundred percent in human form right now. Clayton was torn away from me, dragged out onto the concrete, the five of them ringing him, dark monstrous shapes. Their eyes blazed moon bright in the darkness, but that wasn't all. As their teeth were bared, I saw the flash of actual fangs.

"What the fuck do you think *you're* doing!"

My shout echoed throughout the carpark, would no doubt draw an audience, which considering my tits were out, wasn't ideal, but I couldn't seem to find the capacity to care. I stood over Clayton, a wolf protecting her mate, and that was exactly the wrong thing to do.

"Riley?" Colt's voice shifted between growly and deep and his normal one, a world of questions there.

"Did he do this to you?" Ryan stepped forward, his body vibrating with restrained power, his eyes sliding down.

"Shit!" I said, scrambling to resituate my bra and top, when I was shoved back against the car, my hands knocked away.

"Oh no…" Haze said, cocking his head to one side, that same toothy smile there but ten times wilder. "Don't do that on our account."

"Fuck's sake, Haze…" Blake went to step in, but as soon as he got close, his nostrils began to flare, his eyes joining his brothers. "Jesus…"

"So beautiful…" Haze's hand rose, shaking, his claws forming, then receding as he reached out.

Which should not fucking happen.

We were all schooled on the way alphas and omegas shifted. They had wolves, we didn't, and as a result, we had to be careful about pushing them. Not only could they shift into bloodthirsty animals at a moment's notice, but their self-control was weakened when they were provoked, so we learned not to antagonise them.

But this was my life, my body, and it had nothing to do with any of them anymore, so I pulled my hands in, jerked my clothes back where they were supposed to be, and then I stood tall, facing down their collective gaze—one which was going to be added to in moments.

"What the fuck…?" Ryan came closer, then Colt, and the four of them blocked out whatever was happening behind them, and for good reason.

I jumped when I heard a dull thud, quickly followed by a yelp of pain, then another.

"No," I said, but it made no fucking difference. Fen Vanguard was beating the shit out of Clayton, and for what? "No," I said, much more firmly, shoving at their chests, clawing at the wall of muscle that kept me pinned where I was. "No!" I raked my nails across skin, slashed at clothes, becoming a wild thing now, because each cry of pain felt like my own, even as I felt a rush of guilt because Clayton was the one hurting, not me. "Fen!" I threw all of my breath, spirit, power into my voice. "Fen Vanguard, you got a problem, you sort it out with me!"

"What an excellent idea," Haze rumbled, grabbing my wrists, showing me exactly how fucking powerless I was. He stretched them up over my head, gripping them in one hand as he took in the way my body was forced to elongate.

"Why does she smell like that?" Ryan asked, his head tilting, his voice completely transfigured, as were his mannerisms. He sniffed the air the way the neighbour's dog did when a bitch went into heat.

"Fuck…" Colt hissed, shoving his way closer to the sound of his brothers' rumbles of discontent. "Riley…" He sucked breaths in with rapid pants, but that just made things worse, so much worse. The muscles in his face tensed and smoothed, then began to shift in a way that I'd only seen in video footage.

"Colt…" I was going for soothing now, all challenge gone, because somehow, Colt was right on the edge of shifting.

And so were his brothers.

The sounds of pain died away as Fen shoved his way through the group, taking up a position front and centre. He grinned then, a sharp, savage thing, made worse by the splash of blood across his knuckles, one that was smeared across his face seconds later.

"Baby girl, you been holding out on us?" he asked, but it was evidently a rhetorical thing. I couldn't breathe, despite the fact my chest was heaving, because his foot slid out, wedging between mine, then forcing them wide, creating a space he stepped right into, hoisting me up and into his arms, my legs wrapping around his waist on reflex.

No, no, that wasn't what I wanted, but any ideas otherwise were quickly silenced as I was slammed into the side of Clayton's car.

Clayton!

I thrashed in earnest then, but what luck would a single beta have against five fucking alphas, especially when they all surged in? Hands wrapped around my wrists, held them pressed against the cool steel of the car, kept me utterly pinned for what was to come.

I'd spent my whole life wanting this, wanting Fen Vanguard to look at me like I hung the fucking moon and I was a delicious treat, ready to be consumed, so I wondered who the hell I'd pissed off that it was all coming true like this. *Contusions,* my mind pointed out accusingly. *Concussion, a fractured skull.* It was creating a laundry list of all the possible ways Clayton could be hurt, seriously hurt, for being stupid enough to cop a feel of me.

"You need to let me go!" I snarled then, my own voice distorting to a growl in that moment.

At that, the five of them went still, so very still, and then Fen grinned.

"Oh, I don't think we will." He leant in, slowly, slowly, but there was no point in prolonging shit. I was utterly at their mercy, and they knew it, which of course meant that this was deliberate. Fen was playing with me like I was an omega, the power dynamic between the two designations all part of their savage foreplay.

But I was a fucking beta.

"I-I'm not the one for you," I stammered out. "I'm not an omega, I'm a beta."

"No…" Colt crooned, his face losing all its usual world-weary cool and becoming something much more feral. "Not smelling like that, you aren't."

"You're the one." Blake's head jerked like it'd been slapped, but he recovered way too quickly. "All this time, and you're—"

"What the fuck are you doing to that beta?"

And just when I thought things couldn't get worse, everyone's heads snapped around at the sound of an alpha bark.

The Williams pack stood there, only four of them, but they had several years of strength, height, and muscle on the Vanguards and they knew it. Keith Williams, the unofficial leader, stepped forward, his boots planted firmly apart, his arms crossing a massive chest.

"Is this what the famed Vanguard pack does? Attacking beta guys when they're on a date and sexually assaulting beta girls?"

None of this was for my benefit or Clayton's, but I managed to find a silver lining in it. I was free, sliding down the car when they wrenched themselves away from me to face the Williams pack, then crawling free through their suddenly tensed legs.

"Shit, Clayton…" I hissed, scooping him up and then using my top to wipe the blood trickling from his eyebrow.

"Fuck, Riley…" he said, pushing at me weakly. "I can't be seen with you. I thought they were done, that they'd be finding their omega—"

"We have," Ryan said in a deathly serious tone, growling at the two of us. I got to my feet, then slung Clayton's arm around my shoulder, despite his complaints, and hauled him out of the way, the crowds only willing to take him from me when I'd gotten well out of range.

"We need to call a doctor," I told the crowd. "An ambulance? Does anyone have a phone?" But as I said it, they just stared, wanting to see the battle unfold. I remembered belatedly that I did, digging around in my pocket, when a scream ripped through the night air.

Cheryl, Valerie, and Cyrus all stepped forward, their eyes shining as pale as the moons, their smiles sharp. They watched what was unfolding with a kind of alien glee, because the Williams were yanking off their clothes, going to fur with a fluid, well-practised grace.

One my guys were yet to achieve.

"Fuck!" I hissed, grabbing my phone with shaking hands, unlocking it, and then making an emergency call.

"Triple zero," the dispatch person said in a bored tone, "police, fire, ambulance?"

"I need the alpha residence. This is Riley Taylor. I'm up at McDonald's Point, and the Vanguard boys are about to go through their first shift!"

"Oh shit!" the voice on the other end exclaimed. "Patching you through."

"Riley?" John Vanguard was the highest ranked alpha in the whole town, and his voice was firm, a little abrupt, but containing a calm confidence that was somewhat reassuring.

"The guys are about to shift up at the point. They've challenged the Williams, or they challenged them? I don't know, it's all a fucking mess!" I sobbed out the words, my grip on the phone, on reality, slipping.

"Take a breath, Riley." His command resonated all the way through me, my lungs filling and then emptying without any input from me. "We're on the way. Are the omegas there?"

"Yes, Cheryl screamed when this started."

"Silly little girl," he hissed, something I wasn't entirely sure I was supposed to hear. "Trying to egg on a dominance battle and bring on the omegas' heats early. Hold tight, we're on our way."

I ended the call, my hands hanging loosely by my side, but didn't feel any of the usual reassurance that came from speaking to the alpha. I had one guy sitting on the ground, hurting for committing the heinous crime of making out with me, and five guys going through hell, who I'd spent my whole life loving.

Because any scream the omegas might make, it was nothing compared to this.

Chapter 6

This was not supposed to be.

The first shift of an alpha pack was supposed to be a moment of great pride and celebration, particularly the sons of the ruling pack. They should've been doing this surrounded by people that loved them, that would help them through the brutal first shift, protect them from anyone who would seek to try and take advantage of the moment. But the Vanguards weren't here, and four silver grey wolves prowled closer as Colt, then Haze, then Ryan all fell down onto their hands and knees. Right as the Williams pack dropped low, stalking forward, preparing to attack, the night air was split by the sounds of their voices, ragged, hoarse, as they howled out their pain.

Fen and Blake were all the defence they had, standing between the wolves and their brothers, fists at the ready, but even they were losing the fight with their own bodies. Their muscles seemed to jerk on their bones, forcing them to twist and turn in response to forces bigger than any fight for dominance. Keith's big animal snarled, his haunches coiling, ready to leap, when the big black SUV roared up.

"Stand down!"

Every man in the Vanguard pack was an alpha, but only one was a title. John dropped out of the car, ambling closer to the shitstorm before us, refusing to be hurried. Especially when his voice lashed the crowd, radiating throughout the whole of McDonald's Point. The Williams wolves were pinned to the ground now, frozen statues of wolves rather than prospective threats, the only sound coming from them now a high-pitched whine.

"Keith, shift," Alpha Vanguard said with a snap of his fingers, and the Williams boy found his skin instantly, keeping his head down as he scrambled for his clothing, yanking on at least his underwear and jeans. "What the hell is going on here?"

"We got word that your boys were beating the shit out of the guy that was making out with Riley Taylor—"

"Riley?"

Oh fucking shit. Pretty much everyone took a massive step back then, leaving me out there on my own to face the full brunt of the alpha's ire as he turned to face me. John's eyes narrowed, and then he gestured for me to come forward, not even watching to see if I did. He didn't need to, of course, my feet moving all on their own, walking towards him before stopping at a respectful distance.

I hung my head then, because I knew I was in the shit, because this was a clusterfuck, and because no matter how it came out, I'd be seen as the instigator. Now adrenalin was clearing my head, I could see the logic. I had a right to date, to see other guys and do all the usual shit that other girls my age did, but the expectation would be that I prepare the guys for that fact. Dad's fucking promise… It was a life sentence, something I was sure he'd been unaware of at the time, or maybe not. Maybe he would have seen this as worth it.

"Riley…" Fen panted, slumping down onto all fours now, the sounds of his brother's pants and groans filling the air. "She's our—"

"Shift," the alpha said, silencing his son, ending all conversations but giving them this—a travesty of a first shift. This was supposed to be the final step Fen's pack needed to take before being considered adults in the eyes of the other alphas. They'd be awarded a seat at the alpha council table, and that milestone shouldn't have happened in a carpark full of broken glass.

But when I saw their wolves, it was hard to care. It was like a huge hand wrapped itself around my heart and squeezed with all its might, and I didn't even mind. Tears pricked my eyes as I saw them, saw the other side of them. Blake was the massive black wolf, Haze the slightly smaller, less heavily built black wolf beside him. Colt was a dark grey, his fur densely tipped with black. And Ryan and Fen? They had that heavy blonde under-coat that was turned grey only by the light tipping of their guard hairs. They were so bloody beautiful, I took a step forward, but that was a mistake.

"What are you doing?" the alpha said with a frown at me, before shifting his focus to those much more worthy of it. The frown faded, and a smile formed in its place as he gestured for the omegas to approach. "The omegas can step forward, let the boys' wolves get their scents. Who knows, maybe we might even find out who their mate is today."

"That's how it was for me," a feminine voice said, and I saw Omega Vanguard appear. A small woman with waves of long blonde hair and bright blue eyes she shared with Haze, she was soft and sweet and all mother, but one with a spine of steel. "Come, don't be shy," she coaxed the omegas. "You'll be doing this quite a lot, now that you've finished school."

As the omegas, the alphas, moved forward, taking their preordained place by the packs' sides, I stepped away. The alpha had been right to remind me of my place, and it sure as hell wasn't here. I needed to get home, get the hell away from here. I'd lie low until I was ready to leave and then—

But literally nothing was going to be easy today.

I was trying to slink away like any other teenager caught in the shit, and instead, every eye turned to me. The wolves had shied away from the omegas' outstretched hands, rejecting them in a way that was hard to misconstrue, though no doubt there'd be attempts tomorrow. The sounds of the omegas' discontent filled the air as I shook my head, hoping that would change what was happening, but it didn't.

"They follow you everywhere," Nik had said about the boys, *and I'd just shrugged.*

"It's just the promise they made to Dad."

"But it's not. It can't be. They follow your every move, have eyes on you the whole time," she said, *and I saw a familiar concern on her face.*

No one wanted this for any of us, because this was the road to pain and anguish. But the first step was being taken on it now.

"Boys..." rumbled Malcolm, one of the other Vanguard alphas. "Don't do this."

"No..." I whispered as they pulled away from the omegas. "No, no," as they wove through the gaps in the loose circle of adults. "Fuck, no..." I hissed as they reformed into a pack, every single one of them tracking me.

"What the fuck is going on?" another Vanguard alpha said.

"Permission to speak," Keith said, keeping his head bowed as the rest of his pack shifted back, getting dressed with well-prac-tised rapidity.

"Granted," Omega Vanguard said, even as her alphas shot her heated looks.

"This is what we saw when we turned up." I kept backing up slowly, so as not to trigger their hunting instincts, but the wolves kept coming, trotting when my pace picked up. "The girl, Riley, she was making out with another beta when they caught them together, but..." Keith swallowed hard, daring a glance at the ruling pack, then dragging his eyes down again. "They weren't being protective or making sure she was safe. They acted like she was their—"

"Enough!" John said, and everyone went very quiet and very still. "Eloise, get Riley in the car and take her to her mother's."

"John..." The ruling omega of our town stepped forward, but he cut her off with a sharp shake of his head. She sighed, then turned on her heel and bustled over to me.

"C'mon, honey," she said, using that soothing purr only

omegas seemed to possess. When she took my arm, I sagged into her grip, my alcohol sodden brain not able to take a single thing more. But of course there was more.

Low growls built into harsh snarls, then rabid barks as she hustled me over to her car, then even those sounds were cut off by an order from their father. To make it even worse, some continued to growl after he had given them the command.

"In the car, quickly."

There was real fear in the omega's voice, one that didn't seem to stop, even when we pulled rapidly out of the carpark, driving at speed towards my place.

"I'm so sorry…" I said, not even knowing what I was sorry for right now but feeling like it needed to be said.

"It's OK, Riley," she assured me, even as she shifted gears like a raceway driver. "None of this is your fault, love." Before I knew it, we were parked out the front of my house. "Now come along, we need to let your mum know what's been happening."

Mum was at the door waiting, obviously having recognised Omega Vanguard's car when we pulled up.

"Change of plan, Alice," the omega said as soon as we got inside. "The boys shifted for the first time tonight."

"Tonight?" Mum's hands rubbed at her temples. "I thought we had more time." Her focus switched instantly to me. "Riley, go and pack your bags. You don't need to take everything, the movers will take care of the rest. Just pack whatever you'll need for the next couple of weeks until the rest of our stuff arrives."

"What?"

I was being rude and disrespectful. I'd been given a direct order, it was on me to follow it, and I would, as soon as I understood. I just blinked, staring at them and unable to stop, hearing the sounds of the boys' wolves as—

"Things have progressed with your scholarship," the omega said with a warm smile. "When we heard how amazingly you'd done, we wanted to help your family out. Your mum was worried about you being in the big smoke all by yourself, so we decided to relocate the both of you to the city, but things are progressing faster than expected. The university approached us tonight about getting you into a kind of pre-med bootcamp for really capable students. It's an ideal opportunity."

I knew exactly what she meant, having applied for the program when I heard word of it, but I'd had no expectation of getting in. It was for the best of the best, and I in no way considered myself part of that elite.

"The fast-track program?" I asked in a thin voice.

"That's the one. Someone dropped out, so a spot opened up, and they asked us and your mother whether you'd be interested and we said yes," the omega said with a warm smile.

Part of me wanted to interrogate this, to find the flaws in the story, sort the falsehoods from the truth, but I took a deep breath and let that go. Whatever the fuck was going on in Bordertown, it was none of my business anymore, hadn't been the minute I put that pencil down at the end of my exam. I'd been reminded over and over, and now it was incontrovertibly true.

"Thank you, Omega Vanguard," I said, sketching a small bow.

"Eloise, silly," she said with a playful pat on my shoulder. "Always so polite."

That rang in my ears as I went to my room, assessing my stuff with dispassionate calm, picking some stuff over others and packing it quickly but neatly into my suitcase before I carried it down the hallway.

"So you think there's an issue of latency?" Mum asked.

"What else could it be? Jim was always so sure it was Riley for…"

I walked into the kitchen and saw that two of the Vanguard alphas had joined us as well as the omega.

"Hey, Riley," Malcolm said with a warm smile. "Thanks for making the call and bringing us up to the point. I know a lot of kids don't like to snitch…" Christ, could the guy come across more middle-aged if he tried? "But that was a seriously dangerous situation. The boys shouldn't have shifted so early, but we've got them sedated now until we can establish whether or not they're stable."

"Are they going…?"

My voice trailed away as all the warmth in the room cooled somewhat. Not my place to ask. I'd been told that plenty of times, and now it was truer than ever.

"I hope they're OK," I amended, and everyone smiled.

"Well, c'mon, miss future doctor!" Eloise said, linking her arms with mine. "We've got a charter plane waiting on the airstrip, just for you!"

Questions, so many questions, swelled inside me on the ride over. Even more when Mum and I got in the otherwise empty plane and strapped ourselves in.

"You'll be in the big city in less than an hour, ladies." The pilot's voice crackled through the PA system, making us jump slightly before it was drowned out by the whine of the engine. I stared out the window as we moved down the runway, getting faster and faster, until it felt way too fast.

I felt a wrench, an actual physical ripping away of my breath as my heart felt like it skipped a beat. Make that several. My heart felt like it hung in that awful space where it was going to thud, but it just hadn't quite done it when the plane levelled off. I felt my ears pop, and then a familiar beat inside my chest. I searched the darkness, seeing so many tiny little lights twinkling, knowing one of them was our house. *Was.* And the guys?

Don't think about them. Don't worry about them. Just let them be. It'd been my mantra for some time now, since the alphas had sat me down and very calmly and very clearly outlined how things needed to be.

"You're a talented girl," John Vanguard had said, his voice like a heavy hand pushing me back against my chair. *"You have a great future ahead of you, just not one with our boys."*

"This is for your own good," Malcolm had said, leaning forward with an earnest smile. *"Who knows more about the differences between alphas and betas than you, Riley? You've been such a good friend to the boys, but this is just biology."*

"The way things are headed, it'll only lead to broken hearts all round," Graeme Vanguard said. *"Contrary to what some people might think, we care a lot for everyone in our town and we want them to have a chance at happiness."*

"This will make you happy, right?" Eloise asked. *"Studying medicine?"*

I'd just nodded, then, and I nodded to myself again now, because what else could I say?

That I dreamed of their sons every bloody night? And padding through those dreams was a mysterious wolf with reddish tinged fur that ruffled in the breeze, her howl still in my ears when I woke in the morning?

The future, I told myself, even as my eyes filled with tears. *Think about your future.*

Epilogue

So I did.

They could've called. Someone, anyone, could've, to fill me in on what had ended up happening, but they didn't. Not even Nikki, and when I stared at my phone, my thumb hovering over her contact, I found I couldn't. I'd left, they'd stayed, and so we were nothing to each other. At least that was what I told myself as it felt like my heart was being torn slowly from my chest, ripped out further with each day of radio silence.

But I'd escaped into my studies all the way through high school to deal with the unendurable shit of being around the Vanguards, so I did the same now. Each time a massive wave of pain rose, threatening to swamp me, I pulled out one of my new textbooks. I read the dense descriptions with eyes that blurred and a heart that just ached and ached and ached, but the longer I read, the easier it got.

The fast-track program started, and very quickly, I had enough lectures, exams, tutorials, and online study groups to fill my days and my mind. Studying medicine was notoriously difficult, but this? This was elite level shit, designed to stretch us or crush us. I might have walked into lectures in a trance, needing to see Haze lolling in one of the lecture theatre seats like my next breath, wanting to feel Blake's arm around me or Fen's, but pretty quickly, it became clear that I could focus on my future or them. If I had to choose one, I chose me.

As I progressed through my studies, I found that I was much more interested in the research and science of medicine than I was in treating broken bones and concussions. I made the shift into genetics, focussing on that old desire of mine to find out what made us omegas, betas, and alphas, while trying not to think too hard about why that drew my focus.

Because I couldn't open that box. It rattled, deep down inside me, filled with everything I'd experienced, everything I remembered about home, everything about them. Whenever I thought of them, the box was opened just long enough to shove that in too.

Until finally, I didn't need to try anymore. I forgot them, forgot the pack, Dad's promise, all of it. I'd achieved what everyone said I should do—I moved on.

Away from my hometown, I'd achieved everything I had hoped for. I'd graduated with an honour's degree, had some early papers published, and found myself a job straight out of university in a reputable and well funded medical research facility. I had a life, a purpose, to help those people who didn't clearly reveal as alpha, beta, or omega, to explore what was going on when people didn't reveal at all. We were part the way through developing a gene therapy for people who got stuck halfway through a shift and never any further, caught between beta and omega or alpha. Every day, I woke up feeling like this was what I was supposed to do, and that put a spring in my step.

Which brought me to now.

SEVEN YEARS LATER.

I breezed in the door to our business unit, carrying a cardboard tray with three coffees in it.

"Morning, Riley!" Janet, our receptionist, sang out as I

entered, making me smile. She was a cheery, mumsy figure who seemed intent on looking after everyone in our business unit, and we secretly loved it. I deposited a mocha latte with two pumps of caramel in front of her, and she flushed. "You've got to stop doing this! I'm already questioning whether the structural integrity of this office chair will hold up if my arse gets any wider, and it's my job to get the coffee, remember?"

"Pfft…" I replied. "You get more than enough crap coming from Il Duce over there."

Both of us looked guiltily over at the director of our business unit's closed office door. Robert Windsor was a very effective seller of our ideas. He just couldn't claim to be especially personable.

"Don't I know it! I'm cold calling about a million alphas and omegas today to see if we can find some crash test dummies, I mean subjects for your current study." She shook her head slowly as she scanned the list, then glanced hopelessly back at me. "We're getting a few possible nibbles but…"

"You deserve all the coffees," I said, "and the cakes—"

"No."

"And a cruffin from the place on the corner."

"No, definitely not," she said, even as her eyes rolled back in remembered pleasure.

"Good morning, bitches!"

Our remembrances of pastries past was rudely interrupted by my colleague, lab partner, and general pain in the arse, Candy.

"Ooh, is that coffee for me?"

She swept in and took a sip from the nearest cup, then spluttered when she realised that was my perfectly roasted single origin long black. My drink was plonked back in the holder and swapped for the other one—a froufrou mix of milk, sugar, vanilla, and cinnamon, with just a dash of coffee to legitimise its existence. I was kinda glad for its low caffeine content because she had much of the mannerisms of a rabid Chihuahua without adding in stimulants. Janet was less pleased. She handed Candy a cloth with a long-suffering look so she could clean the mess she'd made.

"So, I was thinking, we should all go for lunch today," Candy said, wiping up every droplet of coffee. "My shout."

"Not that male revue place again?" Janet asked with a sigh. "A man waving his limp sausage in my face puts me off eating my own sausages."

"Or that medieval themed theatre restaurant with the guys making jokes about the contents of their codpieces," I said, wrinkling my nose. "Or the all-you-can-eat seafood restaurant where you ended up licking seafood sauce off that guy's—"

"OK, that's enough out of you two," Candy said, shoving her hands in front of our faces and waiting for quiet before sucking in a dramatic breath to make her announcement. "How about The Caledonian for a pub meal?"

Our eyes narrowed as we looked Candy over closely, trying to work out the catch. The Caledonian was a perfectly serviceable pub down on the west end of town. Typically, it catered to the tradie crowd—guys looking for a beer and a hearty feed before going back to work.

"Are there strippers?" I asked.

"Nope."

"Some kind of naked sit-in for better wages and conditions?"

"Nope."

"So why The Caledonian? You got a hankering for chicken schnitty?" I asked, waiting for the other shoe to drop.

"Well, you know how I like my meat," Candy said with a smug smile. By god, she did. The woman was a veritable wizard at Tinder, seeming to be able to find every free-range hottie in town and getting together for bed breaking antics that she then recounted to us. Janet and I lived vicariously through her. Well, I did. Janet had a husband to go home to. "But no, it's time for another mission."

And there it was, the fucking catch. Janet and I groaned simultaneously.

"Operation Riley Catches a Dick, Part… What number are we up to?" Candy asked, scratching her head dramatically.

"We are not doing this again," I said, pulling away from the desk. As I did so, I heard the door open behind us, which should've made me a little more circumspect, but in my defence, it was usually just the post guy or someone from another department who came through the front door. "You are gonna butt out of my personal life, Candy, or I'm gonna lace your coffee with laxatives."

"Well, that sounds unpleasant."

Sometimes, you heard voices, actual voices, and they created a rip in the space-time continuum, grabbing a hold of you and pulling you back to some moment in your past. I froze where I was, still hearing the vague babble of my colleagues, but they were being drowned out by the now cacophonous beat of my heart. I was forced to set my coffee down, my fingers now slick and shaking.

"Any reason why you've taken to stealth feeding your workmates stool softeners, Riley?"

He said my name. He said my fucking name, so I can't just scuttle out of here and pretend I'm not here, I thought furiously, then took a deep breath before turning around. That box inside me, it rattled now with a violence I hadn't felt in so long, but I swept some loose hair back behind my ears, then rested my elbow on Janet's desk hutch as I faced him down.

He smiled, just a little, a tiny twist of those full lips, but that restraint only magnified the delighted twinkle in his eyes. *Eyes do not and cannot twinkle,* I told myself firmly. Glistened, then, or shone, full of a lazy good humour I knew all too well. And that feeling of familiarity rushed through me right now. Those green eyes, like chips of jade, the deeply tanned skin, the sweep of too long dark hair, and a couple of days' stubble gracing his strong chin.

Fen Vanguard.

Alpha Vanguard now, I corrected myself. He and his brothers had taken over the running of Bordertown, which did not explain what the fuck he was doing in my office, forcing me to stare at him like I was some kind of gormless twit. Candy noticed, her eyes flicking from me to him and then back again before she pointed to my mouth, gesturing to the drool forming at the side. I wiped it away and then straightened up, ready to be the smart, professional, well put together woman I knew myself to be.

Of course, that was the moment the rest of them came strolling in.

"She here?" Haze asked. His hair was longer, his piercings gone, but his tattoos now covered both arms from shoulder to wrist, something that was easy to see as he was wearing an old T-shirt with the sleeves ripped out paired with a beat-up pair of jeans. Those pale blue eyes found mine, and he grinned then, all mischief and fangs.

"Fuck, she is here…" Ryan hissed out the words, walking blindly to take up his place behind Fen. Still the second-in-command, but the way his skin paled, his eyes burned as he stared at me… My thought trailed away at the appearance of Colt and Blake.

Hard, that was my first impression. Colt had been the one I'd spent hours with, sitting side by side leaning against my bed as we studied together, his shoulder touching mine. His hazel eyes had always been so soft and expressive, but they weren't anymore. He stared me down without blinking, one hand coming to lock around his other wrist.

And Blake? What the fuck had happened to Blake? Dark circles ringed his eyes, his hair ruffled and haphazard and some-what lank. He still had all that muscular bulk, having grown even bigger in the time we'd been apart, so why didn't he look any better for it? His eyes were wide, staring, but somehow empty.

"Well, well…" Candy said, stepping forward to offer her hand. Fen shook it perfunctorily before his focus shifted back to me. "I take it you know our Riley?"

"Know her?" Colt said with a harsh snort. "She's—"

"Shut up, idiot," Ryan hissed.

"Our pack house was contacted about a study you're conducting?" Fen said, and that was when the ice-cold knife slid up and through my ribs, expertly finding my heart. "The email we got was you were looking for samples."

"It says here…" Haze said, unfolding a folded piece of paper. "'Blood, hair, nails, and semen.'" He looked up and surveyed the room with a grin. "I dunno about these fellas, but I've got plenty of semen to supply. Oof!"

Ryan slammed his elbow into the ribs of his brother, forcing him double, while trying to maintain a civilised veneer as he stared at us.

"We are looking for alpha samples," Candy said with exaggerated glee. "We were just talking about the lack of suitable candidates."

"Suitable candidates?" Fen said with a frown. "You've been handling other alpha's samples, Riley?"

And here we were again, with these chucklefucks getting all possessive and growly again. But why? There had to be an Omega Vanguard by now, so this kind of shit was inappropriate at best and an abuse of their mate at worst. I reached behind Janet's desk, the receptionist's eyes as wide as saucers as I rifled through the folders to find the alpha sample admission forms, before grabbing a handful of pens and slapping them down on top of it.

"If you're willing to supply us with some baseline samples for a typical alpha subject, we'd much appreciate it. Remuneration is not exactly generous, but you'll get something for what is essentially a fairly small amount of time and effort on your part. Fill in the forms and then give them to Janet, and when you're done, my colleague, Ms Baker here, will take your samples and authorise your payments. It's been lovely to see you all, but I've got a million things I need to attend to."

I turned on my heel, ready to stalk on out of here, thanking god I'd worn the tailored slacks that made my arse and legs look fabulous. If you were going to give your childhood crushes your back, you might as well make them rue the day they followed their instincts and did what all alphas did.

"Wait!"

His voice, ragged, broken, coarse, that was what stopped me. The others murmured, but Colt pushed his way forward, scraping his hair back from his face, then moving closer.

"We're not really here for the study."

"Fuck, Colt," Ryan said on a groan. "When are you gonna get some chill?"

"Shut the fuck up," Colt shot back, and that shocked me. My Colt was moody, introverted, but he had a heart of gold. This Colt? He was like a beautiful broken vase—all cracked and spiky, yet somehow, you found yourself still moving closer to take a better look. When he focussed back on me, I saw some of the boy I knew in his eyes, in that hot, desperate gaze. "You help people who are…damaged, right?"

"What do you mean?" I asked, much more gently now.

His eyes darted around. He didn't want to have this conversation here, but he forced himself too.

"Alphas that can't shift, omegas who can't take a knot, people that are stuck in between."

That was a fairly comprehensive list of my life's work so far, which made me wonder.

"Is there someone experiencing designation difficulties back at home?" I asked, Colt's fragile grin making clear my error. "Sorry, in Bordertown."

"You could say that," Blake drawled.

"Are we doing this?" Ryan asked, then shook his head, glancing at Janet and Candy for a second, making me feel bad about conducting this interview in the lobby. "Fuck, I guess we are. Riley, we're the ruling pack at home. We took over after our dads, did everything that was expected of us, but…"

"We can't find our mate," Fen said with a long sigh.

"Can't?" I bit off the word. "Don't you mean won't? There were three omegas for the three packs."

"Cheryl ended up with the Williams, Cy with the Mitchells,

and Valerie left when we rejected her too. Last thing I heard, she found a cashed up pack in the southeast," Fen said, rubbing those big, strong hands over his face.

"But you could have taken any one of them as your mates," I said, hearing a faint ringing in my ears. "There's nothing broken. When they went into heat—"

"Our wolves wouldn't respond," Haze said with a grin that suggested that this was the best possible outcome. "There were shouts, crying, recriminations, and some very impolite comments made about our manhoods."

"Fuck, why am I surrounded by complete fucking idiots?" Ryan asked the ceiling as he threw his head back.

"So, what do you want me to do?" I said, hearing the hysterical whine in my voice, and didn't that grab their attention? They stiffened as a pack, their eyes taking on a silvery cast as they stared. "I'm not a relationship counsellor or a matchmaker."

"We don't need them," Colt insisted.

He reached out then, and the tentativeness in his gesture hurt me physically. Whatever had happened, however shit had gone down, he was my friend. I grabbed his hand, trying to mask the way my body stiffened, the way my lungs had to work to suck air in, and failing. Because touching him? I'd been to plenty of uni parties, gotten drunk, sat up all night drinking red wine and smoking dope, talking shit about life, the universe, and everything before falling into bed with someone, but no one, literally no one had made me feel like this.

It was like touching an electrical current, but instead of a harsh pulsing thing that disrupted all the natural rhythms in your body, this was a gentle throbbing sensation that felt like it set everything humming together perfectly. I remembered then why I'd fought them so hard when they persisted in wanting to touch me and why I'd given in every time.

"We decided to go back to the only woman our wolves have ever responded to," Colt said in a low voice, his eyes completely silver now, his beast watching me as much as the man did. "You're our mate."

"What…?" My voice came out slow and creaky, like a rusty door.

"But you're a beta," Candy said, just as bemused. "And they're alphas."

"It's only ever been Riley," Ryan said quietly, chancing a sidelong look at me. "Our dads made it clear when they were still running the pack that we needed to find another mate, but…" He shook his head then, his lips thinning, but he stared at me, not willing to look away now all of our sordid history was out on the table. "There was only ever you, Riles."

"What in the star-crossed lover fuck?" Candy hissed, her eyes going wide. I fought the urge to slap my hand over her face because one, I wanted to do it every day and that would create a hostile working environment, and two, I was supposed to be a professional and a visit to HR wouldn't look good on my resume. Her mouth formed an exaggerated O shape, and then she jabbed a French manicured finger at me. "This is why you're allergic to hot beef injections of the penile variety!"

Well, fuck.

Part II

A Wolf in Sheep's Clothing

Chapter 7

"You're our mate."

I was still standing in the foyer of my workplace with the boys, no, the men now, I'd spent my life growing up with, all staring at me like I hung the moon or something. Teenage me had grown used to their intrusive stares, but adult me had never found anything close to it. I'd dated, even had short-term relationships, but any guy that came along always seemed to pale in significance, nothing he did comparable to them. But I stiffened, because I realised everyone was staring, including my workmates.

"I need—" I started to say.

"Dick, she needs lots and lots of dick, and you five look like just the dudes to give it to her," my 'friend' Candy said. "Don't let her take no for an answer, either. Well, within reason. No rapey shit, but—"

"If you don't shut the fuck up, I'm going to put everything up on the high shelves again and take away all the step ladders, you rabid little troll doll," I said, fixing her with a steely gaze.

"What was that?" Haze asked with a characteristic purr that had been hot in teenage Haze and was fucking well near sinful in the adult version. He sidled on up to Candy, and even she looked slightly flustered as a result.

"Don't answer him," I told Candy. "Do not fucking answer him."

"Your girl Riley here can't seem to catch a dick," Candy said with a glee so apparent, I was going to melt a whole block of laxative chocolate into her next coffee.

"And why would that be?" Haze asked, but his attention was on me, the forms set aside with a click on the desk.

"She's always been a catch and release kind of girl," Candy said, twirling her finger in her hair. "Like, she'll reel them in. With those legs, how could she not?" A series of deep masculine grunts at that seemed to perfume the room with testosterone. Even Janet was fanning herself lazily with a letter. "But when it comes time to land those suckers, something always gets in the way."

"Does it indeed?" Haze asked, his focus shifting to me.

I took a step back, because fuck, he was intense. Had I forgotten that, or had he just gotten worse? It didn't matter, it was past time to nip this in the bud.

"Well, considering my love life is absolutely no one's business but mine," I told the room primly, "I'm going to go into my special, highly secure laboratory and start working on what I'm supposed to. Candy, you could always try that as well. Guys, I'm sorry to hear you're having such a hard time finding the right omega, but I guess all I can say is that she or he has to be out there."

I smiled then, letting some of the affection I always felt for the pack filter in, but not too much. That locked box inside me might be rattling, but I wasn't opening it up again.

"I'm sorry you got your hopes up, but we don't handle that kind of issue here. If erectile dysfunction is the problem—"

"Not right now, it's fucking not," Haze muttered.

"Fuck, I thought that was just me," Blake shot back.

"Well." I blinked, trying to brain bleach away the mental

images I was getting right now. "If everything's medically sound, can I suggest a psychologist?"

"Why do you think we're here?" Colt asked, then he laughed. No, another word needed to be devised for such a humourless sound. "She was the one who suggested this. I told her it would be a waste of time."

I didn't know what the hell to say or do, but I was saved from having to say anything as our boss swung in through the door. He stopped, taking in the uncharacteristically full reception area with just a cocked eyebrow.

"Robert, we've had an alpha pack present to give us some samples for our database," Candy said smoothly. "This is the Vanguard pack."

"Ah yes, Fen Vanguard?" Robert said, finding Fen with unerring accuracy and offering him his hand. "It's good to finally meet in person."

"Well, I'll leave you to process the paperwork, Candy," I said with a meaningful glare. "Conflict of interest and all that."

"You grew up in Bordertown, didn't you, Riley?" Windsor asked.

"Her dad was an enforcer for our pack. A bloody good man," Fen said, real emotion colouring his words. "We grew up together, were thick as thieves, which is probably why she doesn't feel comfortable taking samples from us."

"My staff is perfectly capable of behaving professionally in every circumstance, but if Candace has some free time…?"

"Of course," she said brightly. "Let's grab those forms and come through here."

SHE SMIRKED at me behind Windsor's back as she swiped everyone in, Haze mimicking her shit-eating grin as I watched the pack file into my lab. I was forced to hustle after them, going through the door before it slid closed, and when inside, it felt like the lovely sterile peacefulness of it had been somehow sullied. I shook my head, dismissing that feeling, and instead marched past the chaos, retreating into my office. It wasn't until I had unlocked the door and shut it behind me that I felt I could take a full breath.

She moved inside me. She'd always been a slight presence, just something…extra I felt every now and then, rising at inopportune moments, usually when strong emotions were in play. An instinct that told me, 'no, not that guy' when later reports came back that he'd been accused of date rape. Like a ghost, she haunted me, appearing and disappearing at will, but in the quiet of my office, I heard her low whine inside my skull.

My hands clapped over my ears, as if that would stop the sound, but of course it wouldn't. Her pants made a mockery of my attempt. I forced my hands down, made myself straighten my spine and then walk over to my desk, firing up my computer.

I knew what I was—a latent. The discoveries I'd made during my studies and then my own research painted a horrific picture for me. Latents contained recessive alpha or omega genes, giving us the capacity to shift, if not the ability.

The accounts I'd read feverishly at night during uni had horrified me. Sufferers told of feeling haunted by a wolf that they could never let free. Some even tried and… It was safe to say that the video footage I'd seen during lectures, the phases of an unsuccessful shift discussed in clinical detail, had been enough to stop me from ever getting in touch with my inner wolf. It did however pique my scientific interest. I never wanted another person to go through that, let alone me. It was that, that bone-deep feeling of purpose that I clung to as I opened up my emails and started sorting through my inbox.

Papers sent by our librarian, along with data sets and, even as I clicked on it, a computer model of a prospective therapy. I twisted the 3D model of the adrenal system using my mouse, consulting the accompanying paper as well, to explain what they were proposing. Messing around with the adrenal, or fight-or-flight system, was risky to say the least, but what they were posing…

I played around with the sliders in the model, showing the

responses to higher levels of adrenalin. What they were suggesting was a massive spike of synthetic noradrenalin to replicate the cascade that went through an alpha or omega's body prior to a shift. It was suggested that a latent's inability to shift had something to do with a beta's much lower levels of the hormone. Trouble was, alphas and omegas had much more robust systems to counter that incredible rush. Their hearts wouldn't go into arrest or develop tachycardia, their blood pressure remained relatively stable, and... I tapped a pen against my lips and started to knock out some notes.

And just like that, any thought of the Vanguard pack was shoved completely from my mind as I began to dig in. The modelling seemed promising, but we needed to find a way to keep a subject stable and healthy throughout the process. We would never get human trials past an ethics committee until that was proven. I began trawling through different databases, looking for medications, existing or in trial, that might help us counteract the dangers of adrenalin overdose...

I frowned when I heard a sharp rap at the door, looking up as it was thrust open.

"I knew you'd be hiding away in here!" Candy announced.

"Go away," I snarled, turning back to my monitor.

"It's lunchtime."

"Don't care. I'm busy."

"We talked about this, Riley, remember?"

At her much softer tone, I finally looked up. Candy Baker could be a bossy, manipulative, pushy fucking bitch, but she was also my bitch. I tended to neglect myself, getting lost in what I was studying, pushing myself harder and harder until... Well, basically Robert stepped in and forbade me from working through lunch hours and spending too long in the lab after hours.

"You're no good to me dead," he'd said brusquely. "I've had to watch way too many promising minds collapse due to burnout, and I told myself no more. Candace, can you remind Riley to take breaks? You don't seem to have quite the same focus issues that she does."

"Nope, my eyes are on the prize," she had replied, "and the prize is food."

"So, The Caledonian?" I asked, looking for my bag.

"Nah, I figured you'd be a bit overwhelmed by this morning, so I ordered in."

"Yeah?" I took a deep breath in, smelling now the savoury scents coming from the break room. "What did you get?"

"A few things. You looked kind of mad before, so I didn't want to ask."

"Mad? You pull that kind of shit again, and I'm going to break into your house and fill all your body wash and shampoo bottles with depilatory…"

I didn't complete my threat because my brain was too busy thinking of new ones as I stood in the doorway of the break room, looking aghast at the contents. She had somehow managed to put on an impressive spread of food on the shared table. I could see Thai and Chinese, Mexican and some sandwiches from the amazing place down the road, but that wasn't all.

"I knew you were *thirsty*, so I got you a drink, and then I decided you might need a little *snacc…*"

A plastic cup filled with my favourite juice blend was shoved in one hand, a muffin in the other, but that was probably because if my hands were full, I couldn't slap her. All around the table were the small team of people I worked with, but they'd been joined by the Vanguard pack.

"Riley! Good to see you joining us. Your friends decided to put on lunch for everyone," Windsor said, "which was incredibly kind. After all the questions you've just been through, it should've been us feeding you."

You're dead, I mouthed at Candy as she skipped away, sitting down between Windsor and the bane of our existence, Suck Up Evan.

"Come and have something to eat," Fen said, getting to his feet and ushering me forward, that light hand on the small of my back burning through my blouse. "What are you hungry for?"

"I know what I'm hungry for," Haze muttered, then shot the table a polite smile before his eyes slid to me. I was slotted into a seat between Fen and Haze, who without a care for the rest of the room, leaned in and sucked in a big lungful of my scent. "Fuck, I forgot how you smell. You left a shirt around our place after a swim one day, and I kept it under my pillow for so bloody long…"

"Calm down," Fen hissed at him as he surveyed the table. "Eat your food and shut the fuck up."

"What he said," I told Haze with a cock of my eyebrow, and he just grinned in response, plucking a spring roll from a tray and eating it with gusto.

I tried to do the same, taking the plate handed to me, even if I paused for a second, struck by those long strong fingers, but as I piled it up with food, I realised everything here was one of my favourites. *Don't think about that*, I thought. *Don't get sucked in by this.* I shook my head and started eating.

"So did you come to the city just to assist us with data collection, Fen?" Windsor asked. "Or are you here on pack business?"

"Pack business—" Fen started to say.

"We're here for Riley," Colt stated baldly. Ryan let out an unhappy little hiss, then looked over his burger at me.

"Oh, wanting to catch up with childhood friends?" Windsor asked.

His tone was affable. He was trying to make some connections, ensure he had support from a reputable alpha pack, to make it easier to call upon them when we were looking for more subjects. He was also a good person, tough but fair, so he probably did actually care about how they were doing. It's just no one was prepared for the truth.

"Yeah, we were—" Ryan started to say.

"We still haven't found our mate," Colt continued, and I was beginning to feel some of Ryan's frustrations right now. I leaned over my plate, staring desperately at Colt, hoping that whatever psychic bond we might have developed, he'd feel me, know that I did not want to be outed in front of my workmates.

"And you think Riley will be able to assist?" Oh shit, a gleam rose in Windsor's eyes. "You've been alphas for how long?"

"We took over from our fathers five years ago," Fen replied proudly.

"And you have a deficit of omegas in your town?"

"No," Blake replied.

"So you've been exposed to omegas in oestrus and never found one your wolves would accept?"

Windsor had the scent in his nose, and he was going to run it to ground.

"The guys just haven't found the right person yet," I replied. "They heard about the work we do here, and we were going to have a chat after work, discuss if there's anything here that can be done to help them. It's a bit of a long shot. The breeding records in Bordertown were meticulously kept. The alphas of each generation were very careful to avoid inbreeding, so there's unlikely to be a genetic basis for their issue, but I said I'd take a look for old time's sake, do some basic screening, just to make sure."

When I saw Windsor's shoulders soften, his body falling back against the chair, I let a little shuddering breath out.

"You'll keep us posted, of course?" he asked me.

"Of course. I hadn't even intended to run the tests until I had your approval, but I'd be happy to forward all the results to you."

That was a no-brainer. I knew deep in my gut that I'd find nothing especially unique in their genetic makeup, because it wasn't them that was the problem, it was me.

"I'd appreciate that," Robert replied. "I don't mean to keep tabs…"

I waved my hand, indicating it wasn't an issue.

"Well, if I'm to get those samples screened and back to the pack so they can make their way home, I better get a wriggle on," I said, picking up my plate with a polite smile.

Everyone watched me go, the silence in the room super freaking awkward, but I didn't care. What I did care about was the fact that for the second time today, I was forced to beat a hasty retreat. I ground my teeth together as I strode away, feeling an impulse to dump the plate of delicious food in the nearest bin when I heard him.

"Riley!"

I stopped at that because he injected a degree of alpha command in his voice. Probably unintentionally, but… I turned around slowly, and there was Fen, standing before me.

It was a fucking crime that he looked so good. The sheepish smile, as if he just realised what he'd done and was sorry for it, but not that sorry. Those fucking dimples that had captivated our whole high school now given an edge with that designer stubble. And the fact that he'd grown into a man. He'd always been tall, always had the powerful build of a Vanguard, but Jesus fucking Christ, did he have to look like this?

He was wearing country boy chic with a pair of bone-coloured moleskin pants, a navy shirt, and a pair of well polished RM Williams boots, but what was overwhelming was the way he filled them. My eyes couldn't help but slide down, catching the hollows of his collarbones, the sprinkle of hair on his chest poking up from behind his open collar, the thick muscles of his forearms, revealed by rolled up sleeves. I forced myself to tear my eyes away, because this wasn't helping.

"Look, I'm sorry. This shit did not go to plan," he said, scratching the back of his neck.

"When does it ever with you and your brothers?" I replied, and for a second, we both snorted in amusement. "Bet you weren't expecting to jizz in a fucking cup when you waltzed in here."

"Didn't worry me." He took a step closer then, towering over me, casting me and my bloody food into shadow, his own masculine scent competing with the savoury one. "We're in your space. We can smell you everywhere. You work long hours here. It was good being in a place that smelled like you again."

"And I'm going to need to put in some extra hours if I'm to get your test results back to you in a timely fashion." I took a step back, trying to put some space between us. "You could head back to Bordertown now. It'll take me a few hours to isolate the DNA, but once I've got the samples ready, we send them off to a lab to get the analysis done. No point hanging around in town."

I said this all cool and collected, except that shit only worked with betas. A beta couldn't scent me, couldn't tell that a single drop of sweat was sliding down my spine with more to follow, wouldn't catch the rapid pant of my breath, not unless I was noisy with it. A beta also couldn't detect the traitorous response of my body to him. My skin was flushing, my pupils dilating, and my nipples felt like they were in the movie, *The Great Escape*, doing their damndest to burrow through my push-up bra. And then there was the increased blood flow and congestion in my vaginal region.

In layman's terms, I was getting turned on.

He put his hand down on the bench closest to us and then leaned in, breathing me in.

"No, Riley, that's not gonna work at all, and if you keep backing away like that, things are gonna escalate way faster than I want them to." His tongue slid across his lips, and I followed its trajectory like it was the first moon landing or something equally momentous. "He's been waiting for you, Little Red. Clawing at my insides when any woman comes close, worse if she's an omega. Snarling, growling, a savage thing. Until he's around you."

My breath had become so shallow, I was feeling slightly dizzy from hypoxia, because I couldn't seem to fill my lungs properly while he was near. It was like coming face-to-face with a wild animal, but for some reason, I didn't want to run. Fen's eyes blazed pure silver, not one hint of his customary green.

"Now I hear him howling, and that's just about all I hear. Howling in triumph that we're finally in the same room again, in pain that I've let us stay separated for so long. Tell me I can see you after work. Just me if it's too much dealing with the rest of the pack."

No, no, no, no…

"The Cumberland Arms," I gasped out, then sucked in one big lungful of air, and then another. He was smiling when I glanced up at him. "It's a pub by my place. I'll meet you there, all of you, at seven."

Why the hell did I feel a sense of loss when he pulled back, with that smug bastard look on his face? I didn't get time to ponder that as he reached out, stroking the side of my face, just like he used to. My eyes dropped down, and I felt the warmth of his touch long after he withdrew.

"I'll see you then, love. Now eat up before your food goes cold. You need your strength."

And with that, one of the only men I'd ever loved walked out the door. All those feelings I locked down inside me rattled, rattled, and then came bursting out twice as hard, twice as hot. *Fen....!* something screamed inside me as I watched him disappear, like he was walking away never to come back again, my heart unable to rationalise that I'd see him again in a few short hours. I wanted to run after him, drag him closer, down into my office and—

I jerked my train of thought like a rough handler would a dog to heel, then rubbed at my breastbone, wincing at the ache, before turning and walking back to my office. I dropped my plate on the table, my hands sinking into my hair as I rode it out, wave after wave of pain. His animal howled for me? Fuck, whatever was inside me screamed.

But it eased up. It always did. Then I turned back to my work, eating methodically as I consulted my research, finding the answers to the questions I could deal with, while trying to forget about the ones I couldn't.

Chapter 8

I got through the day, fobbing Janet and Candy off when they asked about going for drinks. I think even they knew I'd had enough by then. Yet I still had to face the Vanguard pack. I jumped in the shower when I got home, scrubbing my body until it was red and stinging before getting out. It was getting close to seven, and I wanted to get to the pub first, take control of neutral ground, so I flicked through my wardrobe, not sure what to wear.

There was my 'cocktails with other young urban professionals' bullshit wardrobe, but even a little black dress couldn't save me today, so I went with something a bit more basic. Skinny leg jeans with a rip on one knee from the time I had tripped over, drunk on a uni pub crawl, a pair of beat-up old Converse sneakers, and a band T-shirt an old boyfriend had left behind, worn soft and kinda grey. I dragged a brush through my hair, not bothering to style it, and figured my salute to grunge would set the right tone. This was not a date. I was not the girl they were looking for. They could go about their business. So I jumped in the car, pulling into the carpark in no time, and strode on in, only to be hit by the scent of beer, sweat, and old wood.

"Biaaaatch…"

That was the only warning I got as a body slammed into mine, skinny arms and legs wrapping around me like a manic spider monkey.

If you've noticed there's a theme in my choices of friends, believe me, I have too.

"Fucking get off, Spider," I said, giving one of the fine barmen of this venerable establishment a shove and getting a flash of a grin and a whole lot of guyliner for my trouble.

"What the fuck are you doing here?" he asked, dancing back when I took a swipe at him, then raking his bleach blond hair out of his eyes. He was a picture of raffish charm, all the way down to his black painted fingernails. "It's not Fri-yay. You don't drink on a school night. Shit, I'm not convinced you don't, like, sleep in a coffin, drinking the blood of those poor people you study all day."

"Are you finished?" I asked.

"Ahh…no? You still haven't answered my question."

"Who the hell is he?" a deep voice said.

"Whoa…" Spider's reaction and mine were in complete sync, which worried me greatly, but a freshly washed, much less drawn Blake towered over the two of us, and he wasn't looking happy. "What the fuck, bro?" Spider said, the speed of his chattering always a sign of impending doom. "Are you gonna go all Hulk smash or what? Because you really need to do that shit outside."

"Who. Is. He?" Blake bit off each word, and then Spider smiled.

His narrow face lit up like a Christmas tree right before he launched himself at me, wrapping me up in his embrace before lightly dry humping my leg.

"Do you mind?" I said, jabbing my elbow into his ribs, and it took several times to dislodge him.

"Now I know why you're here," Spider said, slapping me with the cloth he used to clean tables. Yuck. "You're meeting your lurver." He turned around and winked at Blake. "Don't worry about it, big boy, you're more my speed than Flame Princess here, if you know what I mean." He gave Blake a big wink, which somehow seemed to make the guy happy, a slow smile spreading across his face. "Like if you wanna go down the alleyway for a little sucky sucky, people have told me I've got a mouth that can suck the chrome off a tow ball…" He eyed Blake speculatively.

"And one that won't stop dribbling shit when he doesn't have a dick in it. Spider, this is Blake. Blake, Spider works here, in theory. Speaking of which…"

"Gin and bitter lemon for your sour arse face?" he asked me with a wide grin. "And what're you having, handsome?"

The idiot fluttered his eyelids manically at Blake. Spider was a hot fucking mess, but he kept the drinks coming, so I tolerated him.

"Riley," he said, reaching out and hooking his arm around my waist and dragging me close. His nose dropped down to nuzzle into my still damp hair. "I'm having Riley."

"Bitch, we are talking about this later," the barman hissed at me.

"No, we aren't. Drink, stat, and keep 'em coming," I hissed back. Spider flipped me off, then sauntered away, hopefully to get me a bucket of gin to drown my sorrows in. "You can let me go now." I wriggled in Blake's grip.

"No, I can't."

And with that, I was steered out the back to a booth in the dingy end of the pub, right near the pool tables, where I saw their eyes before I saw them, all glowing silver in the low light. I sighed as we got closer.

"He's the barman," Blake said, ushering me into the booth, then sitting so I would have to climb over him or the table to get out, Colt sitting on my other side.

"He's fucking dead—" Colt started to rumble.

"He's into dudes."

Colt settled back at that, seeming to collect himself at his brother's words, and that was when he seemed to finally see me.

He blinked, just staring wide-eyed, like he was sure I would slip away any minute.

I wished.

"So," I said, surveying the table, then nodding to Spider as he hustled over. There was a reason why I low-key loved him. He placed beers in front of the guys and a big schooner of gin and bitter lemon in front of me, even with a slice of lime on the rim. The guy could read my mood like no one's business. He winked then and disappeared off to create mischief elsewhere. "You obviously came to the city for more than just providing samples for our study."

"I dunno," Haze drawled. "Part of the process was very…satisfying."

"Shut up, Haze," Ryan said, then looked at Fen.

"You're right," his brother said. "We did come for more than that. You know how we always felt about you."

"We were friends, really good friends," I said, then took a sip of my drink. Juniper, quinine, and sharp, sharp lemon. Yum. "Like siblings, almost."

"Jesus, Riley, is that what you believed?" Ryan stared at me then, like he wasn't entirely sure what he was seeing, his blue eyes narrowing. "We didn't walk around protecting our sister."

"The promise to Dad—" I started to say.

"Don't try and hide behind that," Colt said, that edge back in his voice. "Riley, you know."

"What? We're gonna talk about this now?" I asked, and fuck it, I heard my voice break. I took a breath, then another sip of my drink, before shaking my head slowly. "The thing we were never supposed to admit?" I flopped back against the back of the booth, but that had both of my shoulders resting against Colt's and Blake's.

Did they watch my eyes close then, for just a second, feeling the warm pulse that I'd always felt when I was touching one of them? Because that was what had me so sour. When we were kids, it was just the same friendly, loving feeling I got from my family when they gave me a hug. They were a part of the warm cocoon I grew up in, until it was all ripped away.

Dad died, for one. That had sucked so hard, I was still trying to find a way to get past it, but along with that came the gradual withdrawal of that support base I'd relied on for so long. Mum had…faded. Betas didn't have fated mates, but people theorised that Mum and Dad were, because their love was so strong. When Dad died, she'd kept on caring for me, making sure all my needs were met, except one.

The cuddles became much, much fewer, and I think that was because when I touched her, I felt it—a whistling hole inside her, where Dad had been, and nothing would fill that up, so it had come as no surprise when she too died after I finished my degree. But right when I turned to the guys for that same source of warmth, our bond changed too. My eyes flicked open, every single man there watching me, like I watched them. Rather than soothing and safe, their touch had become something else, darker, more intense, initially bringing with it emotions I wasn't ready for, and when I was…?

"They're not for you, Riley."

I remembered those words as I put my elbows on the table, welcoming the cool distance that came with it when I pulled my body away from Blake and Colt's.

"You need something from me," I said bluntly. "I've been gone seven years, and we haven't talked once, not since… I can't think of anything you could need, but—"

"You." Colt's manner was so blunt, like he just didn't have the energy for niceties anymore. His hand slid over my spine, bringing with it a wave of heat. "We need you."

"What…?"

Colt grabbed me then, dragging me onto his lap, tucking me into the corner, his body sheltering mine, even as the other guys began to growl. My head rested against the wall as he stared into my eyes.

"I know what's going on in your head, because we got all the same bullshit too. Every damn day, our dads said, 'Watch Riley, but keep your hands to yourself. She's not the one for you.'"

I flinched at those words, and his brows creased as a result.

"They also said it would be different when the omegas came into heat. It wasn't. I watched Cy and Val and Cheryl all go through it, writhing and begging for…" He swallowed hard. "Something we couldn't give them. I felt sorry for them, felt a sense of responsibility for the position they were in, but nothing more." He leaned in then, closing the gap between us slowly, oh so slowly. "Not like I do when I'm near you."

Colt was so close, I could feel his breath fanning over my lips, smell the mint on his breath.

"This, this is what I needed. To touch you again and see if anything has changed." His head tilted to one side then, his eyes entirely on my mouth. "To know, once and for all, that it's only you that makes me feel this way."

A hand went to the back of his neck, grabbing his collar and pulling him back, and Colt's eyes flashed as a result.

"We said we were going to take it slow," Blake told his brother.

"Why? It's her. I can fucking feel it," Colt ground out. "I feel alive for the first time in—"

I scrambled to my feet then, scooping up my drink and climbing on top of the table, the pool players checking me out as I walked across the top and then jumped down onto the ground.

"That's what this is about?" I asked and took a great big gulp of my drink, then thought fuck it and swallowed the rest. "Some teenage crush?"

"Now, Riley…" Fen said, getting to his feet and holding his hands out in surrender. "We haven't handled this well."

"Y'think?" I snapped.

"We had this all planned out," Ryan said between gritted teeth. "How we could reconnect first, get to know each other again, then see how you felt about us and vice versa."

"I don't need to take it slow!" Colt snarled. "She's the one!

I've always said it and I'll say it a-fucking-gain—Riley's our fated mate."

Was I feeling light-headed because I'd just skulled a double shot of gin on an empty stomach, or was it that finally someone had spoken the words we were never supposed to say? One of them saw me wavering obviously, so I was scooped up and placed on a chair, facing down the rest of them, and that was when I felt the gut punch.

I'd spent the five years at university working out what the half whispered conversation meant in our kitchen before Mum and I left Bordertown for good, but these guys hadn't had that heads-up. If I knew the old alphas, they probably had never even spoken about it. Being a latent was a shameful thing in small towns, where insular perspectives still reigned. They thought it a sign of bad breeding or lack of strength in their lines, whereas I knew exactly what it was.

Omegas came from us betas. Alphas produced more alphas, not omegas, and for good reason, otherwise the breeding pools would get smaller and smaller. Packs tended to have vague ideas about what produced an omega. From the gods deeming it so, to Mother Nature having a hand in the continuation of the species, but what modern science had found was much more concrete.

Omegas were like recessive betas, the product of tricksy little latent genes, like the ones for blue eyes. Those omega genes were lurking out there in the beta population, only to come together randomly when betas had kids, producing omegas every now and then. The fact there always seemed to be just enough omegas for alpha packs was obviously seen to have mystical import, but we theorised that those genes may have a switch that turned on when needed. So a girl or boy growing up as a beta in the city might actually reveal as an omega if she or he were in the presence of an alpha pack. That was still to be proven, but…

I raked my fingers across my cheeks, then scraped my hair back from my face, winding it up into a messy bun, and the guys followed my every move.

"I'm sorry your parents never spoke to you about this," I

said. "If it makes you feel any better, mine didn't either. I just…"
I straightened up, sitting back in my chair. "I overheard
Malcolm, Eloise, and Mum talking before we left." A little growl
at that. "I'm a latent." I smiled as I said the words, though I felt
no joy in that. "That's what's got you all…" —I waved my hand
around— "whatever this is. Part of you can sense her…"

Their focus picked up then, each one stiffening, their eyes
hot on my skin.

"Part of you can sense the omega I might have been, but I'm
not." I threw my hands in the air. "My omega genes didn't
switch on. Studies suggest it might be because the three omegas
in town were stronger candidates and mine remained repressed
as a result. Or I had enough omega mojo to pique your interest,
but not enough to become what you need in a mate. I don't
know. But what I can tell you is your parents did the right thing
keeping you away from me."

"Riley—" Fen started to say, but I shook my head. I was
going to get this out and then go home, maybe via an Uber.

"I didn't become a doctor, I became a medical researcher. I
study exactly what happens when people are latent, when they
can't shift, when they've got one foot in the beta world and one
in the omega or alpha world. They didn't want that for you,
because it's an ugly thing. Patients sometimes committed suicide
from the strain of it, feeling these instincts but not being able to
act on them. Some get frozen half shift, trapped in this half wolf,
half human form until enough muscle relaxers force them to
come back into human form, only for them to try again as soon
as they come to. Some people have gone into a form of low-
grade heat, experiencing all the increased sexual receptivity and
low inhibitions, but with no alphas to claim them or help them
through it…"

Their eyes went very wide at that.

"I'm really sorry this is the way you found out. You're adults
now, you should've been told, to save the drive up to the city."

I shook my head and then dropped my hands down on my

knees, ready to leave, but of course, it was never going to be that easy.

"They did," Haze replied, peeling the sticker of his beer bottle off with single-minded attention. "They tried to redirect our attention not long after you left, burying us in work until we were too fucking exhausted to keep asking questions. That's why we fought the Williams and the Mitchells and then our dads for control." His eyes slid my way. "We were the youngest fucking alphas in the district, so they couldn't keep secrets from us then. Then it all came out. Jim knew what you were and was pretty sure it didn't matter, but we already knew that."

"Jim told us you were a latent omega on his deathbed," Ryan said, his eyes shining stark in his face. "He told us so we could make sure you were kept safe, and he told us to…"

"Give us hope," Blake finished. He chanced a sidelong look at me. "He knew we weren't compatible with the omegas in town, and none we'd met on visits to other towns had any effect on us either. He seemed to think if we looked after you, spent time with you, then maybe whatever was there inside you would come forth."

"Jesus Christ…" I hissed, feeling like my stomach had dropped through the floor.

"We tried things Jim's way," Fen said. "Then we tried things our dads' way. We've attended so many bloody omegas' heats that the whole damn world knows what our situation is, and that's why we're facing a challenge."

"What?" I asked.

"We come back to town in a month with our omega, mated, or the town gets turned over to whomever the strongest mated pack proves to be," he finished.

And now I knew why they were here.

Chapter 9

"So that's what this is about."

I got to my feet, feeling my head spin again, which made me regret downing that drink, but not more than I regretted coming here. It'd hurt, physically hurt, to leave home, but I'd adjusted, found my place, and ended up feeling that being in the city was better. We had an elected government here that betas could be a part of, not the alpha fiefdoms of the small towns. Alphas never really seemed to care much about what was happening in the world as long as their little patches weren't touched. It was also reassuring that our elected officials couldn't be displaced for not finding the right mate.

"Riley…" Fen said as he rose.

"The Vanguards need to hold Bordertown, no matter what…" I muttered, then shook my head, making a beeline for the door.

"Riley," he called after me. "Riley!"

That last shout stopped me in my tracks. Spider frowned and threw down his tea towel before vaulting over the bar and rushing to my side. He took one look at the way my body was quivering, fighting Fen's command, and then scowled at the alpha.

"What the fuck, man? You don't compel a girl! I don't know what passes for foreplay in whatever bumfuck town you're from, but this shit will get you arrested in the city."

"Jesus, we're fucking everything up."

"Ya think?" Spider said.

I felt the point when my body softened and my autonomy returned, and when I whirled around, that famed red-haired temper was fully in effect.

"What. The. Fuck?!" I stabbed my finger into Fen's chest to punctuate every single word. I felt some satisfaction as the great Fen stumbled back, eyes wide. "Don't you ever do that to me again!" I paced back and forth, raking my hair back from my face before throwing my hands down. "I'm not yours anymore. Not to be walked to class, or picked up and placed on someone's lap. Not to be cradled in someone's arms, not fed or given drinks or all the other shit you guys used to do."

I stopped moving then, staring at him, even as I knew I was making a horrendous scene, but I just couldn't seem to stop, and that made me madder still.

"Your parents put me on a plane."

"They shouldn't've—"

"Yes, they should've." I nodded hard for emphasis. "They did the right thing. I might've resented them at the time, but I've seen it, just how it works, or rather, doesn't. You need an omega."

"I need you, Riley!"

He was there, up in my space, not touching, but not letting me walk away or anything. Just like he always did. His hand hovered in the air, but it didn't touch me. He didn't dare, and that was progress.

"All I fucking want is you. Gimme drugs, try experimental therapies, do anything, Riles, anything that gets me you. I know they sent you away. I knew some of the reasons why, but it just doesn't fucking matter. My wolf, he just wants you." Fen shook his head then and backed off a little. "And if he can't have you, then he doesn't want anyone at all."

I blinked then, shock, alcohol, and just good old-fashioned surprise making me stare openly.

"You OK, Riley?" Spider asked, much more quietly now.

That seemed to bring me back to earth. I turned to Spider, fishing out a few bills from my wallet and slapping them in his hand. "Thanks, Spider, and keep the change."

"Bullshit," he replied with a soft smile. "I'll put your tab in credit. You OK? Neander-dude here's not causing you any trouble?"

"Oh, he's causing plenty," I said with a wry grin. "I'm gonna head home, grab an Uber—"

"Lie back in your coffin, sated by the blood of your enemies?" he finished with a grin.

"We were having a moment there," I said. "An actual moment when I didn't want to drown you in a barrel…"

"Oh my god, you're being sweet. Stop!" Then he gave me a straight-armed shove, but neither of us was the other's enemy, so both of us swung our eyes back to Fen.

"Riley, we just need some time—" Fen started.

"So wine her, dine her, and sixty-nine her," Spider instructed. "Actually, do a lot of that, because this girl is repressed." He threw up his hands as we glared at him. "Looks like both of you are repressed," he muttered as he ambled away.

As he left, he freed up the space next to me—space that Fen stepped into.

He pressed his forehead to mine like the last seven years were nothing. His fingers pushed into my hair, stroking through the strands like he couldn't help himself, then kept going.

"Tell me that you've got everything you need, that there's no place in your heart for us. Tell me you don't feel set alight every time your body brushes mine. Tell me that some beta guy…" — he swallowed hard, then carried on— "has your heart. That he's what you need to be happy. Tell me it's just gonna be me that goes to bed aching for something we were told we can never have."

My eyes fell closed then, and it felt like I could feel every brush of my eyelashes as tears formed, matting them together.

Because I couldn't say any of that.

There was a reason why I buried myself in my work, and it wasn't one I thought too much about in the cold hard light of day. Going over and over something painful doesn't help, it just cements those neural pathways, strengthening that feeling. So I focussed on what was good in my life, as if that were enough to gloss over what my heart knew.

I edged closer then, my mouth and his just hovering over each other's before I darted in, letting my lips touch his, just for a second, a hopeless little groan escaping my throat.

It's a terrible thing, when you're forced to deal with an uncomfortable reality. I'd kissed a whole lot of men, searching, searching for something even a quarter as powerful as this. I didn't know if it was just the emotional build-up of being essentially cock blocked all through high school by our parents and my designation or if it was just Fen, but…

This kiss hurt, like a knife stab to my heart. Old wounds I thought I had patched over were ripped open, emotion, sensation, everything swelling up, threatening to swallow me whole. I kissed him again and again, because there was no one to stop me, because he made this desperate little sound in the back of his throat when I did, because I fucking needed it. His taste was a drug, my tongue flicking out to slide against his, to capture it, before I jerked myself free and opened my eyes, and when I did, they were all there around me. I frowned, then shook my head at the sight of them.

They blocked my view of everything, made it all about them, them, them, and I couldn't let that happen again. Honestly, I wasn't sure I'd survive it. Because what I haven't told you was how many nights I'd lain, sobbing, in my university accommodation.

Back at home, they'd made my life about them, filling every

minute of it, and then it was all ripped away. No friendship, no relationship could ever fill the void that was left. No matter how well I got on with someone or how compatible I was, my heart was stubborn. It wouldn't accept any substitutes. So I'd been forced to live without one.

"This was a mistake," I said, wiping my mouth with the back of my hand, needing to scrub Fen's taste away. "I…"

I knew what I needed to do, I just didn't want to, but I knew I had to force myself. I turned then, one last time, walking down the hall and out the front door, the chill of the night air welcome on my skin. I glanced at my car, wanting to take it home, but knowing I'd be stupid to do so, I shoved my keys deep in my pocket and started walking.

Every stride confirmed what I knew to be true, as every step took me farther and farther away from them. It hurt, fuck, it hurt, so much so I was forced to breathe through my clenched teeth, but I did it, walking down the main street of my suburb, past shops and takeaways, past crowds of people out for the night. Then I turned a corner and started up the hill to my place.

But I didn't do it alone.

I turned once the sound of the main street died away, seeing those dark figures following a respectable distance behind, but close enough they could swoop in, look after me if anyone gave me a hard time. Just like old times. I shook my head and then put on speed, lengthening my stride. I walked faster and faster until she took over.

Run. The impulse was perfectly clear, my buttocks tensing, my stride lengthening. *Run,* she pushed at me, driven by some instinct I didn't understand. So I started at a jog, but soon found my feet were flying over the pavement. *Run,* she insisted, even though that was what I was doing, her voice a persistent beat inside my head, along with the thud of my heart. *Run and let them prove themselves worthy of catching you.*

That slowed me down, but by that time, I'd reached my place—a little duplex buried in the suburbs. I threw my legs over the fence, then strode up my driveway, sucking in air, but they had no such struggles. As I fished my keys out of my pocket, I heard the little gate open and close, and then they came rushing toward me.

A hand slammed down on the screen door as I hurried to unlock it, their breath on the back of my neck, lifting the small hairs there until I was forced to turn around. The pack stared at me then with eyes that matched the moon behind them. A low whine started to rise in my throat, but I swallowed it down. Fen darted forward, breathing in my scent before smiling sharply.

"Don't run from us, Red, not unless you want the big bad wolves to hunt you down."

Keys were snatched from my lax fingers, one slotted into the lock before it was opened, then the front door. We spilled inside, shadowy figures in the darkness. I stumbled back, but they moved as one, herding me into the lounge room, not stopping until the backs of my knees hit the couch.

"Grab her a big glass of water and some painkillers," Fen said, nodding to the others, who moved to do his bidding. Ryan placed a glass in front of me and then handed over a card of ibuprofen, watching to see me pop a couple and then swallow them. "You can head to bed now. We wanted to make sure you got home safe. Give Blake your keys, and he'll run your car back here for you so you've got it in the morning, but, Riles?" Time felt like it ticked by then, so damn slowly. "You're ours. You've always been ours, and we are done pretending that's not true. One of us will come by your office tomorrow and pick you up for lunch."

And without a fucking word from me, my keys were retrieved and then used to lock the door behind them, leaving me in an empty lounge room, not entirely sure what had happened.

I couldn't seem to work out if I was disappointed or relieved to see them file out of my space, so I just shook my head, then drank down the water before taking the glass back to the kitchen.

Chapter 10

I couldn't sleep for shit. Alcohol, while being a depressant, will make you feel tired, but often has the opposite effect on your sleep, but I knew it wasn't the impact of the booze. Stripping down and slipping naked under the covers was something I did every night. But now? Somehow, it felt different, strange, almost decadent. I felt the cool cotton on my skin, and it didn't take a huge amount of effort to imagine something else doing the same —big, masculine hands sweeping across my body, touching me in all the ways I'd thought about feverishly as a teenager and not allowed myself to do since.

God, the five of them walking in my door had brought everything back. Lying in my bed every night in the house I'd been born in, recalling everything that had happened that day. Not the school work I'd revised ruthlessly, nor the conversations I had with Mum, but them, always them.

I'd tried my damndest to stifle my responses, to not let them know what it did to me to feel them touching me, all those endless glancing little caresses that had made my skin sing. I'd frowned all the time, something they'd teased me for endlessly, while I'd hoped that kept them from knowing how I'd longed to

"HEY FANTA PANTS," Candy said when I walked in the door to work. "You're late."

"You're always so punctual," Janet said. "Is everything OK?"

"I'm fine," I replied with a smile. "No coffees this morning, but I'll go on a run down to the café once I've gotten through my emails. Any messages or…?"

My voice trailed away as the two of them grinned.

I'd thought the massive bunch of flowers sitting on Janet's desk was an office decoration or something. She brought flowers in from home sometimes. They were Janet's love language, so when Mr Janet done fucked up, the place resembled a florist shop. But when I looked at the bouquet, full of blowsy looking peonies and crisp grey green eucalyptus leaves, my heart sank.

The two of them sat there like a couple of cats that got the cream, smug smiles on their faces. Janet pushed the arrangement towards me a little gingerly, as if she wasn't entirely sure I wouldn't snap, and there was a good reason for that. I eyed the flowers like one would a massive venomous spider.

"What are these—?"

"'Thanks for the explosive night, Red'?" Candy said, obviously reciting something she'd read. My fingers delved into the delicate blooms, retrieving the card and then reading through it.

Thanks for the explosive night, Red. I can't get your taste out of my mind, and I need more, the sloping words on the card read, right before I crumpled it in my hands.

Fuck.

I looked at Candy, then Janet, my heart rate thumping so hard, all I could do was stare.

What the fuck. What the actual fuck?

My terror came from the fact that the flowers were from Haze and the contents of the card meant…? My scientific brain rebelled at the assumptions I was making, but…

Was Haze there in my dream with me? Did he actually taste my—

Information, my scientific brain said, when it finally kicked in. *Get more information, then we can work out what's happening.*

"I need the admission details for Haze Vanguard," I snapped.

"Do not give her that information, Janet," Candy said before turning to me. "Don't chase those boys! They're like those poor bloody greyhounds racing after the electric bunny, and you're the robot rabbit. They'll run after the rabbit until their legs fall off, but if it turns around and starts begging for the dick it so desperately needs?"

"I'm the robot rabbit in this picture?" I asked. "I'm a dog lure?"

"Alphas need to pursue their chosen mate, you know that," Candy replied, slapping me on the arm. "It's Omega 101."

Which was, of course, the point where everyone went quiet. I stared meaningfully at my colleague, not totally wanting to grind her face in the reality of the situation, but I wasn't above giving her a little shove.

"Shit, Riley—"

"It's fine," I replied tightly. "Just email me the admission forms, please, Janet."

"Of course, but—"

"The card was a joke," I lied in an even tone. "I grew up with these guys, was like their sister, sort of. Haze was always one to push buttons." My eyes narrowed slightly as I looked at Candy. "Maybe I should set the two of you up? It'd be a match made in hell."

I knew how bad my friend was feeling when she just gave me a weak smile with no stinging retort, but I couldn't stand around there for that.

"I've got work to do. I'll let you know when I go on a coffee run."

"Let me," Janet said, her voice like a warm blanket wrapped around your shoulders. Trouble was, I didn't need one.

"That'd be…" I went to grab my wallet, fish out some money, but she just shook her head gravely.

"On me, love."

Oh god, kill me now. They'd finally put two and two

together, coming to the same conclusion that my mum and the guys' parents had come to—that my relationship with the pack was doomed. Which was fine because we weren't having a relationship, and I needed to set whoever had sent those flowers straight.

It was Haze, my brain said. *You know it was Haze.*

You'd think the fucking smartarse incapable of a romantic gesture like that, but you'd be underestimating the man, just like everyone else did. Because those flowers? Someone had bought a huge number of peonies for Dad's funeral, and after it was all done, I'd collected the flower arrangements set up in the chapel and brought them home, shoving them all in a big jar of water and leaving them on my desk.

"You should throw them out," Haze had said one day as he was hanging out in my room. It was his day for Riley watch, the unofficial round-the-clock schedule the guys had set up after Dad… "They're starting to die."

I'd just looked up at him then, and he'd paled but didn't apologise. He knew words made no fucking difference, so he just stared and stared, then wrapped me in the tightest hug known to man.

Deep, bone-deep positive feedback, it helped ground me in the moment, bringing me back to here and now, not in that damn chapel with the stiff simulacra of my dad lying in the coffin. Here, with him. He pressed his lips to my cheek, there and gone again, before he pulled away. But the scrape of his boyish stubble? It stayed there long after he'd flopped onto the floor, fiddling with my phone to make another playlist.

I came back to the present day with a jolt, standing dumbly in front of my office door before I unlocked it and went in, sinking down into my chair. I fired up my laptop, and as I was waiting for it, I grabbed my phone, finding the email with the contact details on it before grabbing a pen. I spun it in my fingers, around, around, then tapped it on the desk as I read through the numbers over and over. Then, with a hiss, I scribbled them onto a piece of paper and forced myself to punch them into the phone.

At the sound of the phone ringing, I felt like I was back at uni again, my heart in my throat as I rang some guy I was interested in. While I considered myself an advocate for equal rights between the genders, the actual practice of making a call to someone I had feelings for was so damn nerve-racking, I was ready to go back to the fifties every time. Right as I was about to end the call, someone picked up.

"Babe…" He was asleep still, or half so, his voice scratchy and raspy with it, but I could hear the smile there. "You got my flowers?"

"Yes, and you can't send flowers to my office—"

"So I should send them to your house instead? Well, now that I know where you live, I can do that."

"No, Haze," I said, more firmly now. My teeth were locking down, and we weren't even a minute into this conversation! "Don't send me flowers at all."

"So you're more a wine and chocolates kinda girl? Gotta admit, thought I was on the money with the flowers, but maybe it was the old Riley that loved peonies. What's grown-up Riley like?" I sucked in a breath to tell him that I didn't want anything. "Does she like naughty gifts I can't possibly send to your office? Lingerie and sex toys to slide into that sweet little pussy…"

Which of course brought my attention back to the crumpled up card in my hand. He kept talking, promising me a thousand dark pleasures in a voice that sounded like whiskey and sin, as I smoothed it back out.

Thanks for the explosive night, Red, it read. *I can't get your taste out of my mind, and I need more.*

"The note," I said, interrupting his flow. "Did you write it?"

"Well, it wasn't gonna be Colt, was it?" he replied, and I could just hear the shit-eating grin in his voice. "I get it was a little forward, but I was feeling…inspired when I ordered those flowers last night."

"Last night?" God, I was going to need to be checked out by a cardiologist, because my heart was racketing around in my chest like a frightened rabbit's, which just brought Candy's

"I'll be there at midday on the dot," he said finally, a kind of breathy incredulity in his voice. "Don't be late, baby. You do not want this wolf chasing you."

I hung up without saying a word, turning to my computer and bringing up some of the medical journal databases we had, starting a search going. I tried 'omega + dream,' 'omega + fantasy,' then 'omega + psychic,' but I didn't get much. I tapped my pencil on my lip before getting to my feet, walking out of our business unit, and taking the lift down to the library the whole building shared.

Gideon Crowe, the owner of the institute I worked for, had assembled a medical library that was the envy of most others in the country, and Helen, the chief librarian, was someone I'd decided to befriend as soon as I was employed here. My Google fu was pretty damn awesome, but sometimes, the padawan just needed to go to the master.

"Hey," I said, knocking on the doorframe of her office. She looked up and smiled, her brown eyes warming as soon as she saw me. "Do you have time to chat?"

"For the most promising young researcher in the building?" That was pure hyperbole, but I flushed anyway. "Of course, come in. What've they got you chasing now?"

"Psychic bonds between alphas and omegas," I replied. "Do we have anything on this? Specifically…dream walking?"

Helen looked slightly befuddled at that, which made my heart sink, but she shook her head.

"Let's take a look."

Chapter 12

"The difficulty is the dearth of omega interviews on record," Helen said, flicking through her multiple screens with a rapidity that made my head spin. She was able to skim read an abstract and accept or dismiss a paper based on that in seconds. "Omega psychology is a study still in its infancy, due to the fact they rarely access services. Few experience mental health issues, so we can't even use second-hand reports from psychologists. What happens when an alpha pack takes an omega?" She shrugged. "We're still working that out."

She downloaded a paltry few papers and then put them in an email before turning to me.

"Hopefully, you'll be able to shed more light on the process? Candy said you had an entire alpha pack volunteer for a comprehensive study?"

"Ah yeah…" I replied, feeling torn.

On the one hand, I didn't want the Vanguards anywhere near me. On the other…? Helen was right—the science was patchy at best due to sheer lack of data. The whole process of becoming an omega or alpha, and then mating, was more of a magic than a science with our current knowledge, and I… I swallowed hard, then looked at her screen, imagining my name there as the primary contributor to a paper that revolutionised our understanding of the dynamics.

I was caught in a familiar dilemma between emotions and hard science. The need to understand the bond was clear. All those images and videos of people struggling with the genetic issues I'd seen at uni had made a clear case for that, but… Being near the Vanguards hurt me physically, my hand going to my sternum, rubbing there absently as the ache started again, and… What Haze had said, what he'd indicated was happening… Every time I got close to them, it was like my body and my mind were not my own.

And imagine how that must feel at eighteen, I told myself. Not all omegas went into a mating happy with the process. The ones in my town had been raised to think they were special, treasured the minute they revealed at about twelve or thirteen, but others? There were records of betas revealing as omegas the minute an alpha pack went through the first shift, their previous existences ripped away from them as alien instincts forced them into a situation they hadn't chosen.

Just like mine had.

"Thanks, Helen. I just wanted whatever background information I could get before I start interviewing the alphas," I said finally.

"They're going to allow you to do that?" The excitement in her voice was infectious, helping me get over my own nerves. "OK, well, let's talk data recording, because this is a once-in-a-lifetime opportunity…"

SHE'D GIVEN me a strict set of instructions about how to collect information and what equipment to use. She reconciled herself to the fact I was going to use my phone for a lot of it, but then made clear how I would need to log each item with her.

"If you do this, you'll be making history. We need to preserve that well so others can benefit."

"Got it," I said, then headed back upstairs.

Before I lost my nerve, I strode into Windsor's office to see that Candy was there, along with the bane of our existence, Suck Up Evan.

"Ah, Riley. We were just talking about the alpha pack you brought us and who's going to head up the study," Windsor said.

"I want to." The words were out of my mouth before I could even think, delivered so bluntly, everyone kind of blinked. "I'm sorry, that was rude, but…" I straightened up and stared everyone down. "The Vanguards are here for me, and I'd be willing to bet they will only speak to me." They would if I told them to.

"Hang on," Suck Up Evan said, raking his lank hair back from his forehead. "As senior researcher…"

He wasn't my senior in anything. He'd barely completed his degree and took twice as long to do it as he should have. That was the senior part. He was a few years older than me, that was it. But Suck Up Evan was also Evan Crowe, son of Gideon Crowe, the owner of this whole building that we were a small part of. I think he'd shoved his son in with us as we were a fairly new and experimental side of the research arm of the institute, so he was less likely to cause issues for business units that had actual deliverables that counted.

"Riley brought the first alphas ever to volunteer for a study," Candy snapped, hating Evan as much as I did. "They've ticked every damn box on our admission form. As well as genetics, they've opted for physiology, psychology—"

"I've got good relationships with the other department heads and can continue to liaise with them once you establish the para-meters for the project, Robert," I said to our leader. "You know how amazing this opportunity is, and I brought it to you. Candy and I work well together. We can make this our focus, and our senior researcher can take care of the other work."

"The Vanguard pack did specify that Riley was to head up

the study," Robert told Evan apologetically. "My suggestion? Go and find your own pack that will allow you the same liberties. But until that eventuates, Evan, as Candace has said, you'll be responsible for the work that they are forced to put aside."

So the key to not grinning like a fucking lunatic in an inappropriate situation is to frown just slightly. Not enough to look super pissed off. Slightly constipated will do. So both Candy and I stared at Evan, not wanting to look away for a second as the slimy little prick got his arse handed to him.

His father, Gideon, was amazing. He used his considerable fortune to actually bloody help people and grow our scientific knowledge. He frequently set up little business units like ours, which were more experimental and perhaps not likely to ever return a dividend, bankrolled by the more profitable units with their creation of new heart medications or cures for erectile dysfunction. But his son?

You know how you get the kids of famous people? Like actors or pop stars' kids or the children of certified geniuses like Gideon? Whatever combination of nature and nurture that produced these truly exceptional people, it totally misses their kids. That was Evan. He was slight, couldn't seem to pull his shoulders back, always had hair that looked like it needed a good wash, but none of that was enough for us to dislike him. He didn't even need to be half as smart as his dad.

Instead, he was this pinched-faced, grasping little man, who seemed to feel the need to shove himself forward. He couldn't let his work speak for itself because he didn't do any. He seemed to think his name exempted him from something, that he could get peons—me and Candy—to do all his dirty work, as it was theorised had happened during his degree. The rumours said he got caught paying people to write his papers for him and Daddy put on the thumbscrews, telling him either to shape up or ship out. So when Evan's eyes slid to us, they were full of loathing.

But Candy and me? We were pretty much unanimous in our response. *Bring it, bitch*, was our silent reply.

"So, do you think you could bring the pack in today and get

the ball rolling?" Windsor asked, trying to keep the desperation out of his voice and failing. This study could make or break us, and he knew it.

"I've already organised to meet with Haze Vanguard for a lunch meeting," I said.

"Oh well done!" Robert's relief was palpable. "That's the kind of go-getting attitude I like to see. So you'll be attending as well, Candace?"

My friend slowly turned towards me and then winked slowly.

"Um, I've got some things to finalise and then the handover of our projects to Su—sorry...Evan. I figured Riley's got the prior *relationship* with the pack. She can do the groundwork, make sure they're *happy* and *satisfied* with the study parameters..." My foot shot out and kicked her ankle, but she continued on without a wince. "Then when she needs an *extra set of hands*, I can be brought in."

Her emphasis was subtle enough to go over Robert's head, but not mine, and by the gleam in Evan's eyes, not his either.

"Sounds like a plan," Robert said with a clap of his hands. "Keep me posted, please. Would daily updates be too onerous? Obviously, I don't want to put extra work on your shoulders, but I think Gideon will be very excited to hear about this study."

More slight frowns as I fought the urge to smirk, Evan letting out a grumpy grunt.

"Daily updates should be fine," I assured him smoothly. "I'll send them directly to you."

And with that, the meeting was adjourned. Candy wrapped her arm around mine and dragged me down the hall and into my office, slamming the door behind her and waiting for the shadowy form of Suck Up Evan to pass by. She went and peered at the long slender window of frosted glass by the side of the door to see he was actually gone.

"Oh my fucking god, I almost gave myself an aneurism holding that shit in!" she hissed violently at me before collapsing on the chair in front of my desk. "But what made you change your mind? Like, I'm fucking stoked you are. The thought of that wankstain" —she jerked her thumb in the direction of Evan's office— "getting all the kudos from what should be your study was killing me, but…"

She fell quiet as I sat down, straightening up and then forcing myself to meet her eyes.

"The message you so intrusively took upon yourself to read," I began, and she nodded. "It…alerted me to something I wasn't aware of." I took a long breath in, then let it out again. "The reason why I jumped at the chance to work here rather than in one of the more high-profile business units is because I am a latent."

"No." Her mouth fell open at that.

"I…became aware that I could've potentially revealed as an omega some time at uni," I said, then shook my head. "No, before that. I used to have dreams…" As my voice trailed away, I could see it, hear her—my wolf, her paws slamming into the earth as she raced across it, every muscle working to push her forward. I blinked and saw Candy watching me, suddenly serious. "It doesn't matter, because we have to keep that side of things out of the study."

"But, Riley—"

"I'm serious. I don't want anyone knowing. I know it skews the data and is a conflict of interest. We'll invent an anonymous omega to explain that in the study."

"But why? There's no shame in being a latent. Thousands of people are, most with no idea what they are." Candy leaned forward, all soft-eyed right now, and I hated it, never wanted to see that kind of expression, ever.

"It's not me," I replied. "I'm a beta. I know that deep inside."

Did I? Or was that the message I'd been told over and over, until finally, I'd accepted it? It didn't matter. This was my life now, and I wasn't messing that up for anyone.

"But I've become aware of some…phenomena that I can't

find any clinical records of, and when I spoke to Haze this morning—"

"Bitch, I told you not to call him! How am I supposed to live vicariously through your torrid love affair with five smoking hot alphas if you don't follow the plan?" She smacked the side of one hand against her other palm. "Never call him first. Let him do the chasing."

"He was ecstatic that I called, thanks for asking, told me he was taking me out to lunch today, and then jerked off, I think."

"Oh."

"But that's not the big thing." I shifted uncomfortably in my chair, looking everywhere but at Candy, until finally, I was forced to.

"Something happened last night."

"God, you fucked on the first date? I'm not sure if I should high-five you or slap you."

"Shut up, Furby," I snapped, then let out a sigh.

I told her what went down, sort of, skimming over as many details as I could while still getting the message across. Her eyebrows jerked higher and higher until I swore they were going to pop off her head and run around the room unassisted.

"So…you were strumming the old clamjo, and as you imagined them doing nasty, nasty things to you, they felt it. Fuuuuck…" she hissed.

"Worse. Apparently, they've always felt this," I said, dropping my head against my palm. "Since I was a teenager."

"So every time you…" Candy blinked frantically. "Fuck, I used to flick the bean so damn often during my formative years, my clit was punch-drunk. Damn…" But then that keen scientific mind came back on board. "But this, this is why they think you're their mate. You're responding to them like an omega. Shit, maybe this is what happens before an alpha pack finds their omega? They are psychically linked through sexual arousal, allowing you to acclimate to them before—"

We both jumped when we heard a sharp knock on my door.

"Is that him?" she squeaked.

120

"I don't know," I whispered back. "Open the damn door."

She got to her feet, making a show of smoothing her clothes and hair before approaching the door and pulling it open.

"Well, hello there, ladies," Haze said, leaning his too muscular arms against the frame. "Were you talking about me?"

We just stood there, struck dumb by the sight of him as he straightened, then strolled in. The old T-shirt with the sleeves ripped out had been replaced by a crisp white button-up that somehow made him look more pornographic, particularly since the sleeves were rolled up over thick, tattooed forearms. He wore a pair of black jeans with boots, but his dark hair still hung in a shaggy mess. He swept it back and off his forehead, a crooked smile on his face as he noted our rapt attention.

"You'll have to excuse Riley today, Candy," he said, moving behind my desk and holding out a hand to me, his blue eyes burning into mine. "She's hungry, I can feel it, and I can't relax until that's satisfied."

What the fuck! she mouthed at me as he drew me out from behind the desk and towards the door, his hand wrapped around mine.

"We can't walk around here holding hands," I hissed at him as I jerked my hand free. "I told my boss you guys would actually follow through on the study you lot signed up for."

He paused then, right in the middle of the lab space, getting closer and closer, but stopping himself from touching me.

"You want to know more about me? Put me under that microscope of yours and try and work out how I tick?" His smile was as bright as it was immediate. "I'm all yours, baby. An open book. And on that note, we've got company for this lunch date."

"What?!" I glanced around, then lowered my voice. "I cannot deal with all of you at the same time again. I just fucking can't."

"I know." It was then he stopped being shit-eating Haze and became an alpha, his voice rich, warm, deep, and resonating all the way through me with its calm confidence. "We worked that out after last night. Slowly, surely, we need to court you just like we would an omega."

"Except I'm not a fucking omega," I said, stalking out of the lab, waving to Janet as we passed, but he caught up to me when we got to the lifts. He settled back against the rear wall once I stabbed at the button for the ground floor, his shoulder just brushing mine.

"I think you'll find all of us are absolutely focussed on discovering exactly what you are, Riley." When I didn't reply, he just sighed. "Colt's with us. Him and Blake… Let's just say being apart from you hurt them the most. They knew, right from the start, that you were ours, and they never wavered from that stance. Fen wanted to try things the way the dads wanted, because of course he did, and Ryan is all about keeping the peace. But every time we were brought to witness an omega's heat, something died inside them."

He glanced at me as the lift opened, then ushered me outside to where Colt was leaning against the side of a flashy-looking town car, scowling at the world until we stepped out. Colt took a step forward then, his face transforming as soon as he saw us.

"And what about you, Haze?" I asked as we stepped closer, the look of blind need on Colt's face setting my teeth on edge. I hated that Colt was hurting but I didn't know what the hell I could do to fix things, because I knew what he needed and I wasn't it.

"Me? People tend to overlook me, thinking I'm just the fucking clown, the dickhead of the pack."

I'd told him not to hold my hand, but as the bitter words came, I found myself reaching for him. Haze grinned then, slow and sly.

"When people underestimate you, it's easy to bide your time, go in for what you need, because they never see you coming."

He used my hand to drag me closer, into the side of his body, making his size and his height all the more apparent. He pressed his nose into the side of my neck, then whispered into my ear.

"I knew it was you for us, babe, it just took those other

fucking idiots time, too much time for them to fucking realise it. But now? I've got everyone right where I fucking want them, and no one's getting free until this is done. You, me, Colt, us. It's always been the six of us. Your dad knew it, I know it, and now so does everyone else. You're mine."

Chapter 13

"Candy said you like Thai food, and this place has the best reviews on Yelp," Haze explained when we arrived at our destination, the austere black and red façade of the Jasmine. It was a fancy arse restaurant, which had me looking down at my work clothes in alarm. "Don't worry." He tucked my arm in his and drew us in. "We booked a private banquet room, where I am going to try very, very hard not to imagine recreating what we did last night over Pad Thai." He reached down, conspicuously rearranging his dick.

"You told her?" Colt said, looking from me to his brother warily. "We said—"

"I know what everyone said," Haze snapped, stopping where we stood in the carpark. "But Riley, she brought me in," Haze replied. "Out of anyone she could've imagined, it was me, and you know why. She knew dream me would give her what she needed, and I intend to. If she asks, I'll answer. If she needs something, I'll give it to her. If she fucking wants her drains cleaned or her toenails buffed…"

My eyebrow jerked up at that, but he met my gaze head-on, because this was the Haze that people rarely saw. Behind the bullshit and the dick jokes was a man with an iron will and unquestionable integrity, and I had to admit that I was glad to see that hadn't changed.

"Whatever you want, Riley, I'll get for you." Then his attention shifted to his brother. "And that's the rules for today. It's Get Riley What She Needs Day. You on board with that?"

"I've always been on board with it," Colt replied bitterly. "I just needed you fucks to get a clue."

But when he glanced at me, his eyes weren't any softer. They sparked now with a terrible intensity—one I couldn't seem to look away from.

"Just make sure that whatever you ask for is what you want." Colt took a step towards me, then another, some of his wolf's grace in his movements. "Last night, when you ran?" He stopped so that our bodies were no more than a hand's width apart. "It took every fucking fibre of my being to stop myself from shifting. My wolf's feral. The others refuse to allow me to go to fur, because every time I do, I started running—running towards you."

He leaned in closer, his voice a low buzz in my ear.

"I'll give you whatever you want, love, if it means you run towards me, not away."

I jerked my eyes up, stepping back, seeing the pain that my action caused him but forcing myself to do it, because otherwise, I never would.

"I just want answers, Colt. I want to sit down like we used to, share a meal and a drink, and talk. I want to know what the fuck is going on, because you guys seem to know so much more about this than me. Like, how long has this been going on for? Have you always…?"

I felt a sudden spike of shame, remembering how I used to get myself off after Colt and I had all those late-night study sessions. We spent so many hours sitting side by side in my room, low fi tunes on the stereo creating an intimate space, one filled with his scent. I wasn't as sensitive to it as an omega was, but I'd picked it up plenty, breathing in his woody aroma, feeling the press of his shoulder into mine, staring into those hazel eyes until every thought of science was gone and there was only him.

Just like I did now.

He smiled then, the first real Colt smile since we'd reconnected, and I knew I was completely and utterly fucked. Regardless of beta this and alpha that, Colt and me, we were friends first. I walked towards him, a faltering step, then a much more certain one, my face screwed up in a frown as I threw my arms around him and just felt Colt.

"Oh fuck, Riley girl…" he rasped out, hugging me right back. "I've needed this so damn much."

So for a moment, we just held each other, probably looking super weird to the outside world, but once I started, I couldn't seem to stop, some bone-deep skin hunger rising and rising, screaming for Colt. At some point, I had to pull away before we fused together into one big pod person, but with that distance came a realisation.

Being around Colt all the time had made me crazy horny in a way only a teenager could be. I'd spent hours being bombarded by him, and at some point, something had to give. So when he'd leave, after I'd had a shower, I'd get into bed and…

Colt's smile shifted then, turning into something slow and sensual and utterly at odds with the boy I knew. This was a man now, and a fucking cocky one—one that knew exactly what I'd gotten up to.

"Did I feel you fingering your pretty little pussy as you dreamed of me?" he asked me in a low voice, eyes heavily lidded. "Yeah, love, I did. I thought it was so fucking obvious. Every day, I'd come around to your place rigid. My cock would be trying to bore its way through my jeans, my breath would be all ragged, and you'd just ask me if I wanted a Coke or something. I'd be looking over your damn textbooks, trying to focus on chemistry or physics, anything to get your breathy little moans out of my head and stop me from doing what I needed to."

He reached out and stroked a hand through my hair, looking at me with such tenderness, I felt almost embarrassed to witness it.

"Whenever you're not actively shutting me out, I can feel you."

"And I can feel how damn hungry she is," Haze said abruptly. "Let's take this inside."

WE WERE GREETED at the door by a waitress in a plain, severely black uniform, all in keeping with the restaurant's minimalist interior. There was a whole lot of gloss black, broken only by splashes of scarlet and gold leaf, as we were led to the back of the crowded dining room and ushered into a private space. Rather than chairs, we sat down on thick cushions, richly embroidered in golds and reds, around the low black lacquered table. The waitress took our drink orders and then closed the door behind us, creating a strange space.

It was intimate, with the two of them sitting on either side of me, and because the door was closed, all I felt, smelled, was them. Expensive woody cologne meshed with their own musky scents to create something magical, but there was more than what I could sense. Our history, both ancient and recent, sat down with us, like another guest at the table. When Haze settled back with a cocky smile against the triangular-shaped back cushion, when Colt watched my every move, I was right back at high school. How had I ever mistaken their intent for anything other than romantic? We had been friends, sure, but that was just the tip of this iceberg, and I was about to find out how much more.

"So...you can step into my dreams and my fantasies?" I asked in a low voice, my eyes on the door. "And you see and feel whatever I'm dreaming?"

"It's more like we share the dream space." Haze's hand slid down the back of my neck, feeling so warm, so heavy.

"We co-construct what happens," Colt added. "We can change or add things, and so can you. Ideally, it's us catering to you." His eyes dropped down to my lips. "Working out what you want and giving it to you. Getting you used to the idea of us taking control." I stiffened at that, and he smiled. "Not in a dictatorial way. An alpha's job isn't to force his mate. It's to provide the perfect environment for her to surrender in."

My eyes jerked sideways, catching Haze's smouldering ones. "That's why you brought Colt in."

"You needed more, and he was always the one who featured in your fantasies. We got a look in sometimes, but mostly, it was Colt," he replied.

"Because he studied with me. He spent hours with me…"

Haze's eyebrow cocked up at that, but the door opened and our waitress returned with our drinks.

She deposited them on the table, mine a lemon squash, theirs, beer, and then took our food order. The guys ordered an insane amount of food, but alphas were like that. They burned hotter and harder than everyone else—everyone but an omega preparing for her heat. I passed my menu back once I ordered my own meal, as did the guys, silence reigning until she closed the door again, then my focus, it slid back to Colt.

I watched one of those big strong hands wrap around his beer, lifting it to his lips, the strong column of his throat flexing as he drank it down. There was a confidence there now, a power that hadn't been before. All that jittery teenage energy had been burned off and replaced with something else—something that stared back at me, quietly observing, when I persisted in looking at him.

"I dreamed of Colt because he was the most believable." A small sigh of satisfaction from Haze as the words spilled out. "Fen was the golden boy and unapproachable. Ryan was always trying to keep all of us in line. Blake was distant—"

"Not distant, just useless with girls," Haze corrected.

"And Haze?" I looked over my shoulder at him. "Even in my dreams, I would've assumed you would just laugh at me."

"Guess we both learned something new then," he replied, then nodded for me to continue.

"But Colt… I knew the scent of him—woody with a hint of musk and some kind of amber undertone," I said.

"That was my dad's aftershave," Colt said, his eyes twinkling. "He beat the shit out of me every time he caught me using it, but fuck…" Some of that boy I'd known was back, a small smile forming. "When I felt how much you liked it, that you had to fight the urge to smell me…?"

His words trailed away as I realised something—this room, this restaurant, it was just like the dream. They were making it easier for me to surrender, but not sexually. I was given a private space, but not too private, not one that would push my buttons, but one that would free me. I'd never leaned in and smelled Colt, because fuck, how would I have explained that? But now? He set his beer down on the table hard when I did just that, burying my nose in the overly long strands of his hair and finding the man beneath them.

His hand cradled my skull, not holding me in place, but supporting me, making clear how much he liked this, as if his little groan of pleasure weren't enough to go by.

"That's it, love. Breathe me in. Suck me deep in your lungs because…"

"Same cologne," I croaked out as I pulled back, and he shot me a lopsided smile.

"I bought that shit in the biggest bottle I could find and wore it always, for you." Colt's thumb brushed against my bottom lip, parting my lips. "Even when it broke my heart. Always for you, Riley. You're my girl."

"I knew that, didn't I?" I said, feeling my eyes ache with unshed tears. "That's why I really dreamed of you. You were there, always there, no matter what, hour after hour, day after day. It didn't matter how long I needed you for, you were there. So in the sanctity of my own head, you were the natural choice for me to fantasise about. I imagined you taking care of me…" —I swallowed hard— "sexually, like you did everything else."

Colt reached over, pressing my forehead to his, speaking fast, like the words needed to come out before he thought better of it.

"The others were that fucking jealous of what we had. There were more than a few punch ups over it, but I treasured every bloody moment of it, love. That bond, that trust, the way you felt." He darted forward, pressing his mouth to mine but pulling back before I could respond. "It was heaven. Pure fucking heaven."

"And I ripped it all away."

I pulled back then, just trying to sit with all the revelations, when the doors opened again and a train of waiters brought in the food. It was all deposited across the table with a smile before they disappeared again.

"Eat, Riley," Haze said, rubbing a hand up and down my spine. "None of this shit is gonna get any easier, and starving yourself won't help."

"Is feeding me a big part of this whole" —I gestured vaguely — "thing you guys have going as well?"

Haze smiled down at the table, then shot me a sidelong look.

"Starting to put two and two together, babe? Thinking about all those lunches we made you eat?" Colt let out a low growl, but it wasn't a threatening thing, more a primitive response to the topic. Haze picked up a spring roll expertly between his chop-sticks and then held it out to me. "You wanted to know more about the bond? Feeding our mate is something that satisfies a very deep, very primal part of an alpha. The part that wants to provide you with every damn thing you need when you become ours."

My eyes went wide as I crunched into the spring roll, his smile becoming one of complete masculine satisfaction.

"Now try this," Colt said, offering me something else to eat.

Chapter 14

"Spill, bitch!" Candy said, plopping down in the chair opposite my desk.

I'd floated out of the boys' car and back into my office without being really conscious of doing any of it, and my friend had appeared some time afterwards.

"I just got hand fed Thai food by two men I spent my teenage years fantasising about, who made it clear they'll do absolutely anything to make me happy if I'll just agree to be their mate," I said, staring at my desk, unable to do anything else, because my brain was still chasing its tail.

"What? I take that back. No, you take those words back. Unsay that shit because... Fuck, seriously?" I nodded blankly. "Well, then help a sister out. Where do I get myself a harem of smoking hot, studly alphas that want to cater to my every need because damn... *Damn...*" Candy shook her head ruefully. "I'm over here dealing with unsolicited dick pics and guys wanting to send me money for photos of my feet and you're...what? An omega who's not an omega?"

I'd forgotten about that crucial detail in all that heat today at lunch, but so many crucial details were slipping past me because of *them*. I rubbed at my forehead, feeling like my head was way too full, trying to find that place of cool, analytical calm that I usually looked out onto the world with.

"Nothing's changed," I said, and as I did, those words seemed to settle me. "I'm still Riley. I've always had history with those guys. It's just all of a sudden come to the fore, but I can't let that get in the way of what I need to do. In this place, I'm a scientist first."

"So don't fucking kill me, but…" Candy sat back in her chair and just watched me, carefully, quietly, and that was when I knew I was in the shit. "There's an obvious impediment to you maintaining your objectivity here. You have a relationship with these guys. You had one before and now?" She shook her head. "The flowers, the lunch date—"

"I can nip all that in the bud," I said with a wave of my hand.

"Don't."

"What?" I frowned and leaned forward, peering at her quizzically.

"Don't nip it in the bud, not if this is a chance at happiness. I can't claim to understand the dynamic. I think I'm just having trouble getting my head past a beta having the opportunity to get her hands on all that dick. Like, girl, this is beta spank bank material for days. Five big, muscly dudes who are packing serious fucking heat?" She eyed me for confirmation, then smiled slowly when I flushed. "And they're all obsessed with you and only you? If I were offered half of that, I'd be out the damn door so fast, throwing Windsor my resignation letter and swipe card as I went."

She shook her head slowly, as if giving time for all of this to sink in.

"Don't throw your potential happiness away for a damn job. Trust me, my parents did that, wedded themselves to science rather than each other…or me." Her lips pursed then, and I blinked, seeing a side to my friend I hadn't even known was there. "Gideon fucking Crowe won't be there at your deathbed, congratulating you for your contribution to science. We do good work here and have the potential to do even greater, but that should never, *ever* replace having a life, a family, if that's what you want."

What did I want? My eyes dropped down to my desk surface, absently tracing the shapes of the artificial grain printed on the laminate. I never was able to answer that question, not fully because… Because everyone had stood in the way of the one thing I knew I did want, and then when I'd tried for something else…

I remembered Fen and poor bloody Clayton, the guy being beaten bloody for the cardinal sin of wanting to look at my tits. My jaw flexed, and I shook my head. What had happened at lunch, it blew my mind, got under my skin, made me think and feel things…but the truth still remained—I was a beta, and they needed an omega.

"I can't throw away a study that could make or break my career," I said. "And for what? I'll never be able to give them what they need. They're just responding to some small part of me, some genetic flaw."

Candy let out a long whistling sigh, shaking her head.

"Look, how about we come at it this way. What's going on between the six of you? That's study worthy. You are study worthy. To get it past the ethics committee, we'll have to have your subject status as anonymous and hope the fuck they never work out your role in this, but…" Her jaw firmed then, her eyes flashing. "Girl, you need to know. C'mon, you know your scientific method. You've been told about what you can and cannot have, what alphas are, what you are. Accepting unproven opinion is not what we do. We identify a problem and create a hypothesis—"

"Test the hypothesis. Perform an analysis, and then refine the original hypothesis," I finished for her. "So that's what we do? We study them…and me?"

She nodded sharply, a familiar look of determination in her

eyes. She might act like a fucking idiot most of the time, but Candy, she was damn smart.

"We should've gotten clean baseline data, tested your hormone levels etcetera before you got back in contact with the pack, but there was no way of knowing this would happen. We'll just outline that as a limit in the study. To be blunt, the novelty of what we're describing is probably gonna be enough to garner some serious attention."

Candy got to her feet.

"Now, I need to draw some blood and record as many of your stats as I can before you see any more of those alphas. Are they coming by to see you tonight?"

"They didn't say," I said, remembering the heated way I'd left the restaurant, their focus on feeding me, on making sure I tasted every dish I liked and then giving me more until I was forced to stop them, my stomach groaning.

"Yeah, you'll see at least one of them," she said with a smug grin. "Those boys, they've got you in their sights now. Not much is gonna stop them. C'mon into the pathology lab. I promise not to stick you too hard…" Her toothy grin warned me of what was to come. "Though I guess you're gonna need to get used to getting hammered by a series of pricks."

"And just when I thought we were having a moment." I sighed, getting to my feet. "You gotta go and ruin it." But I followed her out and down the hall towards the room we used to take samples from subjects.

"Speaking of ruined. Your pussy, babe. You ever seen an alpha's knot?" She formed a small fist that was probably about the right size. "Because dayum. You need to train your vagina to be like a python's jaws or something. Maybe temporarily dislocate your pelvis to swallow that knot down…"

I WAS TREATED to a running commentary on my prospective sex life, right up until she started taking samples. I sat down in the cool vinyl seat, my arm resting on the long arm, my hand making a fist to help make the veins pop. We discussed the right tests to get done, even after she inserted the needle, using a numbered identifier on each. My number, I thought, taking a photo of it later for my own records.

"What're you doing in here?" an irritated voice asked, and the two of us froze. Evan walked in, looking at the samples we were taking, and his frown only got deeper.

"Just getting some baseline beta data," Candy said in a bored tone. "Use it as a control for the study."

We shouldn't need that. Most of our current scientific knowledge was a picture of a typical beta, so why would we bother, but this was Evan. He just sniffed at us, unable to find anything in what we were doing as potentially useful, so he just wandered on out, no doubt to find someone else's work to pass off as his own.

"Gods above, I hate that man," Candy hissed between clenched teeth. "But we are gonna need to be more bloody careful about this. Cloak and dagger isn't really my kind of thing. Now, do you want a lollipop?"

"I'm not a…"

My voice trailed away as she plucked one from a jar that we usually kept for when we had kids through, unwrapping it and popping it in her mouth.

"It's time to go home," she said, pulling it free, "where no doubt, you've got boys lining up to give you something to suck."

But I wasn't so sure. Colt and Haze had deposited me back at work with no indication of doing anything tonight, in that high-handed alpha way, and when I checked my phone, there were no messages. So I drove home, anticipating a quiet night in, until I walked up my front path.

There was Blake, sitting on the doorstep, his massive bulk blocking the entrance, several shopping bags and a six pack of beer by his feet. He blinked at me as I stopped and stared, not saying a thing until he got to his feet. I was forced to look up, up, up at the big man, and then he snorted, treating me to the smallest of smiles.

"You're hungry and tired," he said.

No *hello, Riley, how was your day?* But I guessed he didn't need to. It was hard to imagine him and his brothers sitting down on the bed in their hotel room and gossiping about how lunch went, but I guessed they did in whichever bro dude form made sense to them.

"Yes," I replied, not sure what else to say.

Chapter 15

He walked forward, plucked the keys from my limp fingers, and placed a huge hand on my shoulder blades, using it to move me forward. He took my bag and his, then unlocked the door to usher me into my own place. Inside, the bags were dumped on the kitchen benches, a bottle of Gordon's Sicilian lemon gin and some tonic retrieved, and in a series of practised moves, a drink was made. I reached for it, but instead, he carried it while directing me into the lounge area of the big open plan living room. I was sat down on the couch, my drink put on the coffee table, the TV turned on, the remote placed in my hand, and then a big hand rubbed the back of my neck before he turned and walked into the kitchen.

Blake caught me staring at him, a slight flush colouring his cheeks in response, but then he just smiled and started working on dinner. I tried to focus on the news. The daily breakdown of disasters and political machinations was usually a great way to decompress, but as I sipped my drink, I had headlines of a whole different kind flashing in my mind. *Mysterious Man Cooks Dinner for Woman! Smells Delicious, but What Could He Be Cooking?* Or *Woman Allows Man She Hardly Knows into Her Kitchen. Is This a Date or…?*

Blake and I had grown up together. I'd seen him grow from a spindly-limbed little boy into this massive man mountain, but somehow, I'd never really learned much more. He was always the quiet one, hovering at the back of the pack, ready to throw down at a minute's notice in defence of any of us, but beyond that? I was staring openly now, something he just kept acknowledging with amused little glances but nothing more.

Study him, my brain suggested. *Not all data has to be collected in a lab.*

So I was up and off the couch, draining my drink in one swallow before taking my spot on a stool under the kitchen island.

"What is this?" I asked, the question applying to so many potential contexts, and I would have been happy to have any of them answered.

Instead, he spooned up a small taste of what he was cooking, then pressed it to my lips without a word. I took the sample warily, but that was soon shoved to one side at the rush of incredible tastes.

"Oh my god…" I groaned, making sex noises, but I just couldn't stop. It was an explosion of spices, herbs, meat, umami, whatever makes something delicious because, damn.

"What the hell is that?" I asked, barely able to stop from craning my neck and opening my mouth to be fed, just like a baby bird.

"Bolognese," he replied, saying it as though it were some kind of victory.

"No way. No fucking way is that spag bloody bol. That's… That's…" He stared at me expectantly, but his eyes slid to my lips pretty quickly, that small smile faltering until I continued. "You're a freaking amazing cook."

"That's why I got sent next," he answered, grabbing my humble ten-dollar special butcher's knife and using it to chop parsley into a fine green powder. "You need pampering, and I'm good at that. I also know how to shut the fuck up, unlike my brothers." He paused, staring at me then with those warm dark eyes, yet somehow, it was a friendly, easy thing. There was intensity there, but he was holding it at bay, for me.

Fucking alphas, I thought. He didn't really fit the stereotype of what an alpha was in most betas' minds, but in some ways, he was much more an alpha than they could understand. He took control, of my house, my kitchen, me, in a gentle but firm way, and he provided me what I needed, because my stomach rumbled. The Thai food before was amazing, but the lack of breakfast meant it didn't hold me for that long.

In response, he grabbed a tea towel and a wooden chopping board, retrieving hand sliced sourdough drenched in garlic butter from the oven, the savoury scents assaulting me the minute he pulled the garlic bread out. I started to get grabby hands when he placed the bread on the board and slotted it into the space between us, but he snagged a piece first and then offered it to me.

Big strong fingers, nails neatly cut short, held bread that lured me closer with its aroma, like you see in cartoons. When I leant forward, this felt insanely intimate, especially as I now knew what feeding me signified to alphas. As I stared up at him, not willing to move any further, he just smiled.

"They said you'd want to analyse this, work out what it all means, but you've gotta experience something first before you can understand it. Take a bite, Riley."

Somehow, I was Eve in the Garden of Eden and Blake was an unlikely snake, but I felt no guilt as I surged forward, biting into the garlic bread. He watched me chew, listening to my weird little groans of pleasure, as the bread-butter-garlic ratios were perfect, with exactly the right degree of crunch. He fed me another bite, then another, watching everything I took from him with complete and utter fascination, and when I was done? A thumb reached out, wiping away a small dab of butter before he licked his finger clean.

What the fuck…?

He snorted, then pushed the bread board towards me, grabbing himself a piece and chewing it as he continued to add to the sauce, then turning the heat down so it could simmer.

"Ask," he said, settling against my kitchen bench, bringing his head down to my level.

"What?"

"There's a million questions in that head of yours, Riley. There always was, so ask."

"What…is this?"

Apparently, we were back to this again. He grabbed my hand in answer, my skin beginning to tingle at first contact, before he pushed my sleeve up, revealing the softness of the inside of my wrist. My heart was already starting to race, a soft feeling of pleasure pulsing through me, even before his lips landed on my skin.

"Fuck…" I hissed, the pulsing growing tighter and more intense, building and building until…

He pulled away, throwing his head back and letting out a gusty sigh in response, his eyes fluttering closed for a second.

"That?" His voice was kind of raspy, like he'd just woken up or come or something. "That was everything I fucking needed. It's what you need too." He raised my hand and Gomez Addams'ed my fucking forearm, and now I understood Morticia's smug smile.

I'd had people go down on me for a lot longer and with a lot more gusto, and they hadn't got half the response Blake got from one simple little caress. He stood there now, my hand cradled in his, a knowing smile on his face that said he knew exactly how I felt.

Because he feels it too, I thought intensely.

In the spirit of science, I jerked free of his hold, jumped off my stool, and walked around, Blake backing up until his butt pressed against the sink. My eyes ran up and down a body that completely dwarfed mine, but his body language, his eyes, were wary. I reached out, my hand hovering in the air before I dared to make contact. He watched my every move, a small grunt escaping him when my palm came to rest on his chest.

Somehow, it was reassuring to feel him sucking in breaths, his heart rate just as accelerated as mine, but it was about to get faster. I could've done a visual check, because a guy like him? There was never going to be any way he could mask his reaction to me. Instead, I placed my hand over his groin, hearing a low, stuttering moan from him as I did, finding him big, hard, and thick inside his jeans.

I was scooped up in response, then turned around, my butt perched on my kitchen bench, my thighs spread wide when he surged in. Blake's hands cupped my jawline, his eyes staring into mine as he moved closer.

"You want to know how I'm responding? What you do to me?" His voice was kind of harsh now, his brows creasing as he stared into mine. "Well, that" —he shoved his hips forward, grinding his cock into my now dripping seam— "is just one part of it. Don't get shit twisted, Riley. I'm hard for you because I've always been hard for you, but that's not the whole picture."

He watched me as he slid my hand through the open neck of his button-up shirt, moving my palm across his chest until it came to lie over his heart.

"This will tell you a lot more, and so will this."

He nudged my lips with his at first, testing me, making sure I was cool with things before brushing them more firmly across mine, which parted in response. A sound, a tiny little grunt of satisfaction, of need, of desire, gave me a hint of what was to come, but not the entire picture. He sucked at my bottom lip, only letting it go reluctantly because his tongue wanted to sweep in, collecting mine and sliding against it. I didn't know if I'd ever had such a slow, sensual kiss, one that seemed to go on and on at a completely unhurried pace, even as my fingernails started to dig into his shoulders. I just wanted more, a whole other hunger rising, but he pulled away, grinning when I tried to reconnect our lips. Instead, I was put back down, another drink poured for me as he uncapped his beer and clinked my glass now held between limp fingers.

"You want to study us?" he said. "Well, go right ahead, but

there's a reason why no one has before. What goes on between a wolf shifter and his mate, it defies definition. It's instincts that pulse deep down inside you." His hand landed on my stomach and slid down. "Ones that are hard to quantify but impossible not to feel. I just want you to feel me, Riley. Feel me within you, like I've always felt you."

And at that, I was given the sweetest of forehead kisses before I was patted on the arse and sent on my way.

"What the fuck was that?" I muttered, utterly befuddled. "What the fuck *was* that?"

"A sign of things to come, love. Now sit down and relax. Dinner will be ready soon."

Chapter 16

OK, I was beginning to see why Cheryl et al used to walk around school like their shit didn't stink, because if I were looking down the barrel of a life of alpha pampering, I might've been a little smug too. Blake returned with two bowls heaped high with pasta and sauce, a small sprinkle of parsley applied to both before he set smaller ramekins of freshly grated parmesan cheese and chilli flakes on the coffee table. Then he sat down, right next to me. I watched him when he grabbed the remote, flicking through the channels until he found what he was looking for.

"*10 Things I Hate About You?*" I yelped. "I freaking loved that movie!"

"I know, now eat."

He wasn't exactly being bossy, but there was just a tiny little bit of alpha bark in his words that had me grabbing my fork and twirling the pasta around it. Weirdly, it didn't leave me feeling harassed or pressured. I felt…cared for. He was right though—I needed to experience it to understand it, because if I had picked up anything like this in an interview with a subject, I would've been spikier than even the very irate Julia Stiles in this movie.

But as I slumped back onto the couch, the soundtrack punctuated by the comforting sounds of us eating, I wondered.

When I'd first watched the film, the shrewish Kat's insistence on rejecting Heath Ledger's attempts at courting her seemed ridiculous. Playing Patrick Verona, Heath brought as much alpha charisma as a beta could to the role. He was gorgeous, funny, and his song and dance act, even if it might have been a little calculating, was enough to win teenage me over, so why not Kat? But as my eyes slid sideways, as Blake caught me at it, I started to get a better understanding of her character.

She wanted to protect herself, her ambition, her needs, her desire to be something more than the mould she was supposed to be cast in, and guys didn't respond well to it. So she treated them badly in response, pushing them away before they could even reject her or say anything at all. It was only the persistent Patrick Verona who managed to weasel his way past her sky-high boundaries, finding a way into her heart.

"Am I supposed to be learning something from this?" I asked, having demolished half my bowl of spaghetti and unable to fit another bite in. Blake sighed and grabbed my bowl, finishing this off as well before turning to me.

"You loved this movie."

"Yeah, but—"

"You used to go on and on and on about the main dude and how hot he was, though you liked him with blond hair, not dark."

"Right, though—"

"And after…" He went silent for a second, those dark brown eyes meeting mine. "After your dad died, we watched it over and over on rotation, tangled up in a big puppy pile."

Fuck. It felt like an icy knife had been driven into my chest, because I'd forgotten all about that. The empty bowl was set aside, and then Blake's arm went around my shoulders, pulling me in close.

"You fell asleep more times than I can count curled up into my side, watching this movie."

As he said the words, my hands rested on that massive body, able to see in my mind exactly what he meant.

"You didn't touch me much, or talk to me. I always struggled with girls, and you… I dunno if you even saw me or heard me over all those other dickheads." He let out a long sigh. "Haze wanted to come tonight. So did Colt, so did everyone, but I said no. We pushed all your buttons at once last night, and we have to work hard to undo that."

He pulled me closer still, so I was half sprawled across his lap, and then I felt a gentle kiss pressed to my hair.

"We fucked up, forgot everything we'd ever learned about taking a mate. If you were an omega, you'd be flighty, scared, wondering what the fuck would happen with all of us and there being just one of you. Our job is to create a space that you feel safe enough to relax in, because it's only then that you can let us in."

I looked up at him then, feeling like I saw the strong planes of his face for the first time. I moved until I was straddling his lap, his hands coming to rest on my hips, even as he held his body very still. My fingers found the severe planes of his cheek-bone, tracing down that slope until I reached the squared off shape of his jaw. The result of a lot of testosterone, I knew that academically, but in reality? This was a hard face with no softness in it, but for his eyes and his mouth. I traced his full bottom lip with my fingers, frowning, then said, "If I let you in, then what?"

"I'll be where I know we need to be."

"I'm not an omega. I can never give you what you need."

"Says who?" He pulled my fingers closer, kissing my knuckles. "Says who, Riley? I've had omegas bent over and presenting, begging for my knot…" I growled at that, and he grinned in response, the expression transforming his face. "And I never felt anything but a sense of responsibility and pity. What are you worried about, Riley?"

"That I can't give you what you need."

"And what do I need? Someone to take my knot?" He shook

his head at that. "We wanted to make sure there wasn't someone out there, the mythical omega who would complete us, just like everyone said, but she's not. We spent seven years searching until even the dads gave in. Whatever happened, whatever this is, it's real. When we took fur for the first time, where did our wolves go?"

"That's not—"

"Who did they seek out?" he insisted.

I saw it then, that summer night, the concrete of the carpark illuminated by headlights. And them, I saw them pouring out from between the cars, pushing past the omegas, their parents, coming for me. I wanted to deny this, like everyone had always denied everything. Like Kat denied Patrick on the TV behind us. But just like Kat, I totally hated how much I didn't hate him.

"So that's what it was?" I asked, never really having been given the chance to process that night. "After Fen beat up Clayton and the Mitchells took fur, you walked away from all of that, and what, came to me?"

"Always." His arms tightened around my waist when I went to pull away. "As soon as I found my wolf, all the human bullshit fell away. He knew what he wanted, and it was you." He let out a little sigh, his eyes dropping down. "I wish the bond went both ways, that you felt what I fucking feel, because there'd be no need for any of this if you did."

"Well, I am only a beta," I said stiffly.

"That's not it and you know it. Omegas don't feel what their mates feel until they formalise the bond, so it would make no difference at this point." His grip tightened, forcing me to lie flat against his chest, and I had to admit, I hated that I didn't hate this either. "What you don't seem to get is this, right now, kinda like what we used to have when we were kids, if that's all I can have, it's a million times better than what I did have. If you decide you want more, want to try taking my knot—"

"Th-That's not possible!" I spluttered.

"Yeah? You need to look at porn, love, for science, obviously.

There's some enterprising betas taking fists in every hole, and that's a whole lot bigger than me."

"I'll tell Candy she needs to start watching porn for the study. She'll be freaking stoked," I said, but I snuggled down against his chest, and he seemed to relax at that.

"If you want to have sex, if you want to try taking a knot, if you want me just to sleep beside you, curled around your body, I'm yours, love. You seem to think you can protect someone— protect me, protect us guys…protect yourself. But Colt and me, we aren't moving, not while you're here. The others had it their way, but it's our time now." He buried his nose in my hair. "My time with my girl. Now can we stop talking about my damn dick and just watch the movie?"

And just like that, there was something completely familiar and unfamiliar about this. I ended up lying sprawled across the couch while Blake took care of the dishes. If I wasn't half in love with him before, that sealed the deal. When he returned, he lifted my head and placed it back on his lap, his hands stroking through my hair as the movie finished out.

I didn't mean to, but the combination of alcohol, good food, and a glorious head massage had me nodding off.

At some point, I was vaguely conscious of the fact he picked me up like a doll, carrying me through my house and setting me down on the bed. But when he went to pull away after drawing the covers over me, my hands reached out blindly for him. I felt the prick of something, a pain I'd shoved deep down, but my conscious mind wasn't online to stop me from responding now, and my inarticulate little cry stopped him in his tracks. I started to rouse, wake up, deal with whatever this was, when a heavy weight settled down beside me, a limb slung across my waist. I let out a satisfied little sigh, then fell back into darkness.

Chapter 17

So despite whatever unconscious Riley thought was a good sleeping arrangement, I woke up in the wee hours of the morning, even before my alarm went off, and found myself pinned to the mattress by a man. The heavy weight of his arm across my waist was enough to have my eyes jerking open, but that was quickly followed with a blind nuzzling, then that hand swept down, running down my entire torso to settle on holding my hips still as someone ground their very large dick into my arse.

"Oh fuck…" I whispered, quickly putting two and two together—Blake, dinner, movie, bed, me whining like a little bitch when he tried to leave. I tried to pull free of his grip, but he had biceps the size of my head and a sleeping need to rut against me, so I wasn't going anywhere.

"Ah, Blake…" I said tentatively. A low grunt, followed by a growl, then another thrust of those hips. Jesus, was he gonna…?

"Blake? Dude, I totally appreciate dinner but—"

I let out a little yip as I was rolled under him, that massive body pinning mine to the bed as his eyes flicked open, eyes of pure silver staring down at me.

"Hey, big guy," I said, pretty sure it was his wolf I was talking to right now, not Blake. "You in there? Riley really needs Blake to come out and play right now. Oh!"

When he smiled, I noticed briefly that his incisors had gotten longer, but that was shoved rudely to the side by a flush of pleasure. Damn, this boy knew what the fuck he was doing, grinding against my pants covered groin with just the right pressure and at the perfect angle.

"Fuck, Blake…" I slapped at his shoulder, but my voice sounded all breathy, any attempt to get his attention quickly abandoned.

My body was liking what was happening right now a real lot. Getting myself off, even with my dream helpers, wasn't the same as this. An actual person, real and in the flesh, with a body so much bigger and heavier than mine, making me feel helpless and needy, was next level. His wolf eyes caught my every response, changing the angle of his thrusts, then rocking against me with tiny little movements when he felt me squirm.

"Blake…" I gasped out. Was that a last-ditch effort to bring the man back online or a plea for more? I didn't know, but it achieved one of those possible goals. I was in the perfect position to see the man get back in the driver's seat, his eyes blinking madly, then taking in everything that was going on as they returned to a reassuring dark brown.

"Shit, Riley, I…"

His nostrils flared, taking in my scent and his, and whatever he caught, it made him happy. His face flushed as he smiled, slow and sexy, another little gasp escaping me as he shifted his hips.

"Fuck, Blake, I'm sorry but I—"

Any explanation was cut off as I was rolled over again, this time with him at my back, his hands sliding all over my now overheated body.

"What happened?" he asked in an urgent growl. "What did I do?"

"Um, so you were… Oh!" His fingers made short work of my pants, undoing the button, the zipper parting easily. But what ground my clothes gave, Blake claimed as his, that broad palm sliding to cup my pubic mound possessively. "Fuck, what're you doing?"

"Nothing, not unless you tell me otherwise. Now, what happened?"

There wasn't much of a story to tell, but I told him how we'd woken up.

"I made you needy," he said, nipping at my neck when I went to politely demur, his teeth finding Colt's mark.

"It's OK," I said in a falsely light-hearted voice. "Girls are just as able to rub one out in the shower as guys are." But as I said that, his middle finger pressed back ever so slightly, just beginning to part my folds.

"That's not how it works, Riley," he said in a low, dark voice. "If you accept us, if you take us for your mates, we would claim the right to administer every possible pleasure. There'd be no 'rubbing one out' while we were around."

"So what, you guys would become the masturbation poli— Oh shit!"

His middle finger slipped deeper because I was basically dripping slick. My clit currently felt like a marble coated in oil, the pad of his finger finding it with ease, two sliding either side of it to rub back and forth in a most distracting way.

"Fuck, Blake…" I hissed. "Fuck!"

"Tell me if you want me to stop," he said. "If you don't want me to get you off, just say."

But I couldn't, could I? Because it felt like I'd never had a lover like this—one who didn't need to learn my body, who seemed to just understand it better than I did. He knew when to tease me by not touching my clit directly, sliding his fingers either side of it until I fucking needed him to take a direct approach. Then that was exactly what his middle finger did, light as a feather, then as I started to shift in his arms, a terrible intensity building, his finger pressing down harder, moving faster, becoming little more than a blur as I panted out my pleasure.

"Fuck…fuck…fuck, Blake, I'm…"

"That's it, baby. Come for me. Come all over my fingers."

He used his alpha bark on me then at just the right moment, shoving any concerns or worries I might have away and allowing me to just feel this—the breath taking wave of pleasure that was just building, building, making me wonder if I would ever come back down and keeping me exhilarated for the ride. But as I reached my peak, I came crashing down again, jerking in his arms as the waves washed through me, taking with it all my tension, until finally, I went limp against the bed and him, utterly wrung out.

God, this is perfect... I thought idly as he stroked me through the afterglow, my skin so sensitive, it felt like I was floating in this sensual haze, right up until my alarm went off.

"Shit!" I reached across, grabbing my phone and turning the clarion call off, then slumping down on the bed, when reality came rushing back in. Blake watched me from where he was propped up on his elbow. My eyes slid down his body, taking in the fact he'd ditched his shoes and shirt in the night and was just lying there like the biggest damn slice of beefcake. His muscles flexed under my inspection, but he needn't have bothered. He was so big, his muscles were already prominent when he relaxed, let alone now, but that wasn't all of him that was rigid.

I pushed him on his back, yanking my pants up so I could straddle his lap, then dared to run my hands across that massive chest. He lay there looking oh so pleased with himself, right up until I reached his happy trail. When my finger slid across the dark line of hair leading to the waistband of his jeans, his hands slapped over mine.

"I don't have a huge amount of time before work," I said, wriggling my fingers, feeling him hard and ready for me.

"Riley—"

"If we work together as a team, maybe take this to the shower, I could—"

"Stop."

He didn't say the word loudly or harshly, but I got the message. I pulled my hand away, respecting his limits.

"I was just going to—"

"I know what you were thinking," he said, staring up at me. "You were thinking you owed it to me to reciprocate or something."

Weird. That was exactly what I was thinking.

"Maybe that kind of tit for tat shit works with beta men, but alphas, we provide. Food, shelter, comfort, pleasure—whatever it is our mate needs, we'll move heaven and earth to provide. That's who and what we are. My wolf is chewing me a new one for not doing just that for the last seven years, so trust me, a little morning…tension relief is just helping me to get things back where they're supposed to be."

"And what about your 'tension'?" I asked, turning my fingers into speech marks. "Do omegas just lie back and think of the multiple orgasms, never actually taking it in their heads to please their mates?"

"Of course not." He moved me off him so we could sit on the bed facing each other. "Just as it's in an alpha's nature to provide, so it is in an omega's to nurture. She or he would take great pleasure in seeing to ours…"

His voice trailed away as I went very still, then threw myself away from him, scrambling off the bed.

"Riley…? Riley!"

"It's OK, I get it," I said in a tight voice, ripping at the towel hanging off my wardrobe door and heading towards the bathroom. At least that was the plan. His arm slammed down on the wall beside my head, the other doing the same, effectively boxing me in. I let out an irritated sigh and waited for whatever this was to go the fuck away.

"I didn't say that to make a comparison."

"Right. Cool. I rescind all offers when it comes to your dick, and I need to get to work."

"Love."

His voice was so deep and warm, I just wanted to pull it around me like a soft blanket, and the fact that I couldn't just taunted me, reminding why this was all such a bad idea. But as I tried to wait Blake out, he did something that shocked me. He jerked his hands back, and they went to his jeans, undoing the button and the zip, my eyes unable to do anything but stare as he pulled his cock free.

Whoa.

Like whoa.

I'd seen diagrams and shit, but…whoa.

He let out a frustrated little hiss, then grabbed my hand much more gently and pulled it closer. I could've resisted. His grip was so light, it would've taken little more than a twist of my wrist to achieve that. When I made contact, he felt so hard and so hot in my hand, I almost expected to hear a sizzle. He leant in then as I wrapped my fingers around his cock, explaining stuff in a voice corded with pain. Or was it pleasure?

"You wanna know how many women have gotten my cock hard, love?" I made an anxious little sound then, ready to pull away, but he charged on. "One. Just you. You're the only one to make me feel like this. Only you. The feel of your little fingers…" He shuddered as I began to move them, stroking up his length, marvelling at the way he throbbed against my palm, my fingers unable to even go all the way around. "Fuck, Riley…"

He dipped in closer, brushing his lips against mine, and they parted for him immediately. He surged in then, utterly confident in what he was doing, his hands cradling my face as he kissed me.

"I don't want you to feel obligated to touch me," he said, silencing me with more kisses between his words. "You don't owe me fucking anything. We're the ones that owe you… Uh!"

My hand had slid down, down, to the part of his physiology I'd heard so much about but never encountered in the flesh—the mighty alpha knot, feeling like a swollen lump towards the base of his cock. His breath came in rapid little pants as I swivelled my hand around it, testing its texture. It was softer than the shaft but still distended and taut, and most importantly? It seemed to drive him fucking insane, his words gone, his reactions intense, and right then, I felt like I had him in the palm of my hand, figuratively and literally. Right up until his hand wrapped tight around my wrist, preventing me from moving an inch.

"Babe, you keep going, and shit's gonna get real messy." He let my hand go, stepping back and making quick work of tucking himself away again, buttoning up and zipping his jeans. "Squeezing a knot," he explained almost apologetically, "that tells my body you're ready to mate. Jerking off generates about the same amount of cum as any other dude, but my knot?"

"The super seminal response…" I said, belatedly remembering my alpha physiology class.

"Squeezing down on it creates a helluva mess. It tells the wolf in me that you want to be bred. I'd shove it inside you and flood you with my cum, everyone working to keep you coming the whole time I was locked down in your tight little cunt."

"That's why you're born as a pack?" I asked, looking up at him. "You…coordinate things?"

"We're hard-wired to want to please our mate," he said with an almost apologetic shrug. "All of us. Getting knotted takes time, and we want that to be as pleasurable as possible for her."

Ohhh fuck… Blake had done such a good job of getting me off, so why the hell did it feel like there was a deluge in my knickers right now? It wasn't hard to see in my head. Rather than a clinically described scenario with 'alphas' and their 'mate' doing what nature dictated, instead it was them and me. I dared a glance up, saw Blake staring down at me intently, wanting, needing me to understand, but I did, my whole body feeling like it'd been set on fire as a result. Then, right as whatever throbbed between us felt like it was gonna jerk me closer, my second, *oh shit, get the fuck up, bitch* alarm went off.

When we jerked apart, when I switched my alarm off, I felt like I'd lost something precious, even as he still remained standing there. Probably because practical Riley, rather than panting Riley with slick running down her leg, was taking control.

"I need to get ready," I explained lamely.

"You get on that, and I'll knock you up something quick for breakfast," he told me, daring to dart in and press a kiss to my cheek before turning and walking away.

I had a way too long shower, but I blamed Blake for that. I was forced to shove my arm against my mouth as I got myself off, twice, then scrubbed my fingers extra carefully before getting out.

When I came out into the living area, the place was filled with the savoury scents of bacon and eggs, a perfect B&E sandwich waiting on a plate for me. I scoffed that down, Blake watching me the whole time, wearing a smile of satisfaction and neglecting his own breakfast.

"I've got to go," I said finally.

"Give me the keys, and I'll clean up here," he said. "Ryan's coming for you at lunchtime. He can give them back to you then."

I just shook my head, pulling the spare pair off the ring, unable to believe what the fuck was happening. Was he gonna do my washing and vacuum the floors too? But I found myself moving in closer when I handed them over and kissing him cautiously.

"Thank you for last night. It was…amazing."

Apparently, that was all I needed to do or say, because his face lit up then, looking so different to the careworn man who'd turned up at my office days ago as to appear to be a whole other person. He plucked the keys from my fingers and gave me a wink.

"Any time, Riley."

Chapter 18

"You're late again," Candy said when I strolled into work, her eyes narrowing. "And your face…" She grabbed my arm, yanking me past an alarmed Janet and down the hall to my office. "You got laid. You've lost that pinched thing here and that thing your mouth does."

"Sit down, shut up, and stop going on about my love life, what there is of it," I said, wrenching my arm free of her. "We've got bigger issues to worry about. I found out more last night, a lot more, and it's going to make the study tricky."

I filled her in on what I'd learned, redirecting her the same way you did a cat with a laser. Admittedly, she was much smarter than a cat, but…

"So you mean to tell me that an omega has a fair chance of becoming the queen or king of their town, that a group of super studly-looking alphas with massive cocks spend their lives catering to their every whim, pampering them with multiple orgasms and anything else their heart's desire, and the alphas will never step out on them because they only bone up for their mate?"

I jumped when her forehead connected rather abruptly with

my desk, forcing me to grab a pad of paper and shove it between her head and the laminate. She still managed to crack her head on it and was going back for more. I launched myself across the desk, grabbing her by the hair to prevent even more self-harm.

"Ohh yeah, pull it harder," she said woozily.

"Stop being a bloody idiot," I said. "Like you can afford to lose any more brain cells. But you see the issues, right? We won't be able to get any semen samples without me in the room, and measuring that against a knotted specimen would be invaluable, but… What?"

"Who hurt you?" she said, stabbing the air with her finger.

"What? I—"

"Who fucked you over so badly that when faced with a life of having those stud muffins panting after you, your natural response is to think of the study?"

"Well—"

"Riley, my stupidly tall, ranga best friend, last night you were offered the thing that every straight woman wants. They want to care for you." She ticked a finger off at that. "Look after you." Another finger ticked. "Pamper you. Fuck your oblivious brains out and then fucking breed you with knotted cocks that I just know will do wonders for your G-spot, and you're like 'oh, however will I produce a viable sperm specimen?' Did your dad like to play hide the baloney with his secretary and you walked in on him, or was that just mine? Are you like the Tin Man and we need to go off to see the Wizard so we can get you a heart? Fuck, girl…"

I was well used to Candy's tirades, and for the most part, I zoned out until she settled down again, but this time, I was forced to consider what she was saying. I blinked for a second, then looked up at her.

"Science has been my focus," I replied slowly. "I was told really young that they weren't for me, so I tried to avoid them."

"Making them run harder to chase you," she said, shaking her head.

"I tried to brush them off, to keep things friendly, just like they told me. I knew…" My voice broke on this, old pain rising, but I stuffed it right back down again. "I knew there was no future for me with them, because the ruling alphas and omega told me that over and over. I didn't want to get hurt, get crushed…" I grabbed my bottle of water and took a mouthful, trying to dislodge the lump in my throat. "But it didn't work."

Candy was blessedly quiet, because she seemed to realise that input now would be disastrous.

"I finished high school, aced my exams, got one of the highest tertiary entrance ranks in the state at the time. Mum and I moved here, then I started the fast-track program and…" I smiled then, but why did it hurt so much when I did? "I was busy, so damn busy, with the study load, all the assignments, and trying to maintain some kind of social life as well, but…" I shook my head, then glanced up at her. "It didn't make any difference. Like, it did in a way. It was exhilarating and exciting. I learned so many new things every damn day, my brain was completely and utterly engaged. But when I went back to my room, it was just me."

My fingers clawed at the edge of my desk as it came rushing back.

"Colt was always there, studying with me throughout my whole final year at school, and then suddenly, there was just me. Fen and Ryan were always fussing about whether or not I'd eaten. Haze and Blake escorted me to and from class, to keep the omegas from lashing out at me. Every damn moment of my day was spent with them, and then…"

I shrugged.

"It wasn't. I was all on my own. I made friends, but never ones like them. I met guys, but they were never as interested as the pack was. The Vanguard pack cast a massive shadow over my life, one I hadn't even realised was there until I left, and then there was nothing I could do about it except adjust to it being gone."

I leaned back in my chair, folding my hands in my lap, and

stared at Candy now, hoping she'd fucking understand. If she didn't now, she soon would.

"At the end of my first year I had a kind of… 'Breakdown' is too grand a word for it, but something in that ballpark. I finished my exams, handed in my last assignment, and yay, everything was done. The counsellor I saw said I'd lost the last framework I had to hold myself together. I hadn't let myself think of the guys during the term because I couldn't afford to, but then…when it was all over, there was nothing, absolutely nothing to think about but them. I moved out of my college room and went back home to a place Mum had found, and we were like two ghosts. She was mourning the loss of my dad, her mate, and me?"

I snorted then, eyes narrowing, mouth forming a grimace.

"I mourned the loss of men who were never, ever going to be mine."

I stared at the desk as I saw myself, curled up in my bed in a room that wasn't mine, in a house that I had imbued with no memories. In a lot of ways, it was more anonymous than my uni room. Mum had made no attempt to turn the house into a home, most of our stuff still sitting in the boxes the removalists had delivered. The house had been, still was, just a waiting place between one thing and another.

"Every day, I stared at the window in my room and longed for them, and every night, I dreamed of them. I ached and I ached and I ached, until I just couldn't anymore. I didn't get suicidal or anything, but it made me understand why people do. That's when I saw a counsellor. I realised I hadn't left my room for most of the holidays and had barely showered. She helped me to accept what I needed to—they weren't mine, and I needed antidepressants."

"Jesus, Riley."

That was all the warning I got before Candy launched herself at me, wrapping her arms around my shoulders and grabbing me in the hardest of hugs. After a few seconds, I hugged her back, because the Borg had nothing on Candace Baker. Resistance truly was futile.

"But you're OK now?" she asked, holding me at arm's length and studying me closely. "They're not triggering anything for you."

"They're triggering a whole lot," I muttered, but then smiled when I looked up at her. "It's been a long time since then. I've developed a lot more coping skills, got Mum help too, and I've built this." I gestured to the room. "You know how fucking lucky we are to be this young and working for Gideon Crowe. You'll have to forgive me if I don't want to screw that up. The guys, what they're proposing…" I threw my hands in the air. "Maybe it's real, maybe it's not. Perhaps if I just stripped off and threw myself to the wolves, they'd get their taste and be able to move on. Regardless, the one thing I can trust is this."

I tapped my head, and Candy pulled back, sitting down in her chair.

"This study could catapult us to levels we wouldn't have dreamed of in the first ten years of our tenure, but it's not just the professional boost it would give us. We'd inform future scientific understanding of alpha and omega genetics, physiology—"

"You want to study the pack, study the impact being around you is having," she said, and I nodded. "Fuck, that's gonna be a tough one."

A sharp knock came from the door, and then it opened to allow Robert to stick his head in.

"Morning, ladies, just popping in for an update." His keen senses seemed to pick up the mood in the room, so he stepped inside, closing the door behind him. "Is everything OK?"

"Just some stuff going on, Robert," I said to reassure him.

"Nothing to do with the study?"

He flushed as soon as the words were out, even his impaired social perception letting him know he was crossing a line.

"No, and on that. We're going to need to put together a complex proposal to the ethics committee. The reason why the guys are in town is they're pretty sure they've found their mate, and I've managed to talk them into letting me take some data through the process, beyond simply the genetics. Hormonal responses—"

"Physiological changes, psychological evaluations." The words rushed out of Windsor's mouth, his excitement palpable. "My god, the list is almost endless. And they'd permit a team to evaluate them during this process?"

"Ah, not a team," I said. "Me. This is obviously an incredibly personal time and—"

"You're the one they feel comfortable with. Yes, of course, that does make sense. I'll put it to Gideon immediately, but there would have to be a workaround. If you were prepped sufficiently on the protocols and given all the relevant equipment… Any word on their mate and his or her thoughts on this?"

"She," I said, "and she wants to remain anonymous, obviously. The whole pack does. We're about to release incredibly sensitive information to the scientific community, and—"

"Yes, of course," he said with a wave of his hand. "Leave it with me, though if the two of you could work out the different potential threads for the study and put them to the pack, see what they're amenable to, and email that over, it'll make the process much easier."

He smiled then, a spontaneous, bright thing that I knew set aflutter the hearts of quite a few of the older staff in the building.

"Of course, we'll get right on that," I replied.

At that, Windsor ducked out again, no doubt about to crash Gideon's office with news of the broadened scope of the study, as Candy grinned evilly. She plucked a whiteboard marker out of my packet and then created a circle, and in it she wrote, 'Riley's pack.'

"Candy…" I all but growled.

"If this is the way you want to go, if you just want to focus on the science, then let's focus on the science. Let's do what Windsor said and explore exactly what we might be able to get permission from them to study. You're having lunch with one of the alphas today?"

"Probably, but—"

"So let's get a rough proposal together, and then he can get the rest of his brothers in here to see what they're on board with."

She drew the first line from the circle and wrote 'super seminal response and mating' as the first point. I sucked in a breath, feeling the cool, hard, analytical mindset settling in again before firing off my own ideas, and we kept going until a sharp knock on the door broke our flow. Candy grinned like a manic howler monkey and then opened the door to a much more circumspect Ryan standing there.

"Hey, I was after…"

His words faded away as his eyes locked with mine, a small smile forming.

"Hey, Riley." Silence stretched on and on, Candy looking like the crowd at a tennis match, her eyes flicking from me to Ryan and back again, waiting for someone, anyone to say something.

Finally, he shook his head and then said, "I'm here to take you for lunch."

Chapter 19

"So how are you holding up?

Ryan's question caught me off guard, my eyes sliding sideways. He looked down at me with a slow smile as we walked down into the carpark beneath the institute.

"No one's talking to each other about…well, fucking anything," he went on. "Once we all decided to have a tilt at this separately, so as not to overwhelm you, lips got sealed. But I feel things." My steps slowed, and he turned around, walking backwards as he watched me. "Blake made you happy last night, then happier again, then he hurt you." The smile faded at that.

"Is that how this works? You have a Riley emotional radar going off inside you?"

"Of course." He stopped while I was still walking, waiting until I came abreast of him before his arm reached out and hooked me around the waist. "Fuck, we used to drive you nuts at school. As if those pretty green eyes didn't flash at the best of times, but when we were pushing you…? Why'd you think we hassled you on the bus so much?"

I could feel his strength now, his warmth, see every little quirk of his lips.

"You had every eye on you, which you hated. We were making a scene, which you hated more, but then we'd get you sitting down with us, perched on our laps or wedged between us." His hand reached out, cupping my jaw. "There'd be this brief moment where I'd feel it—a rush of pleasure, a need that looked like the one inside me." He brushed his thumb against my jaw and then pulled his hand away. "Then you'd be back to hating it again."

"I hated it because I had to," I replied.

"I know. Just makes me wonder how you'll respond now, without all the chooks of Bordertown clucking. So what did the big fella do that pissed you off so much this morning?"

"Looking for hints of what not to do?" I asked, cocking an eyebrow.

"Maybe. Maybe I just want to know what to kick his fucking arse for when I get back to the house."

He wasn't quite the smartarse boy from school, but there was a slight hint of mocking challenge there still, like the rough edges of the boy had been rounded off, though not smoothed entirely. No matter where his head was at, though, I was a calm, rational woman and I would remain that, even around the Vanguards.

"Blake started feeling me up in his sleep. I tried to wake him up, but he wasn't in the driver's seat, his wolf was." Ryan stiffened then, his expression becoming thunderous. "He came to, realising what he was doing and…" Fuck, did I do this? "That he'd turned me on in the process," I said with a shrug. "He proceeded to…deal with that." A little huff of breath from Ryan. "That was probably the happy part. But when I turned around and tried to reciprocate… He was explaining about alphas and omegas, all useful stuff, but…"

I hissed out my breath, staring up at him, wanting to look away but unable to, so every bit of my anger, frustration, and need poured into that.

"I watched the omegas strut around the school like they ruled it. Fucking Cheryl tried to take me out several times because I was always with you."

"I know, Riles," he said, thrusting his hands into my hair and moving closer. "It's why we were always with you. They knew. On some level, they had to have. We had no connection with her or with any of them."

"But you weren't told every day that you weren't the right person," I said, pulling free of him. I couldn't say this if he was touching me, his look of concern enough of a stumbling block, but he kept coming and I kept backing away, and wasn't that an analogy for whatever the hell this was? "As soon as I worked out what I was, that I wasn't the omega everyone had been waiting for, they told me. 'Not them, Riley, they're not for you.' It'll be Cheryl or Valerie or Cy. They were the right ones, and I was the wrong one." I let out a short bark of laughter. "That has to fuck with a girl's head, y'know?"

"Riley—"

"No, just stand there and listen. Blake made a comment about how omegas and alphas are supposed to go together. He was just trying to answer a question I asked, but all of a sudden, everything that was hot and sweet and sexy was hard and painful."

I shook my head, but in the time it took to do that, he had his arms around me and was holding me close.

"Thanks for telling me," he forced out, the sound of his voice muffled by his tight grip on me. "I'll tell the others. We'll be more careful. I know we're a bunch of fucking dickheads, but on this, I think you'll find we're apt students."

"Trying to keep the peace again?" I asked, eyeing him when he finally pulled away.

"Trying to find my way, love, and hoping that we don't fuck shit up again." He held out a hand to me, and I took it, just like I had back then. As he drew me closer, wrapping his arm around my waist and walking me over to the ute he'd brought here, I couldn't seem to turn my back on the comfort of it, not even now.

. . .

"I KNOW the guys took you out somewhere fancy yesterday, but I was thinking of something a bit more basic," he told me as he got us out on the road.

"Basic sounds fine. There's a sandwich place…" I watched him flick on his indicators, then take a right, obviously with some destination in mind. "You've got a plan. Of course you have a plan."

Even though all the sons were born alphas, there was often an internal hierarchy within the pack. One would emerge as the ultimate leader, making the hard decisions if the pack couldn't. Others would focus more on the relationship with the omega, the child rearing, certain aspects of the day-to-day running of the town that called to them. Then there were those like Ryan—strong enough that in another pack, they might have been a leader. He was quickly designated the role of problem solver, so while Fen made decisions, the details were often left to Ryan to work out, to ensure they were acted on.

"And you still fucking hate surprises. I couldn't believe you let Haze take you to a restaurant without it being pre-approved," he said, glancing at me with a smile.

"So you are getting some details, then?"

"Had to. Who do you think gave him some decent clothes to wear and worked out what restaurant to book?"

"So where are we going?" I asked, scanning the city streets, looking for clues.

"I could tell you, but…" When I glanced over at him, I saw that familiar grin, different now on a man's face, not a boy's, but some of that same mischievous energy was there.

"You're baiting me?" My eyebrow shot up. "You're still baiting me for kicks."

"For a reaction," he corrected, his eyes becoming heavy lidded before focussing back on the road. "Winding you up so that cool façade of yours cracks for just a second. I'm sorry, love, but you got me addicted to that shit. So no, I'm not gonna tell you, and if you sit there and stew, it's just gonna encourage me." His eyes remained trained on the road, but his voice? It was a low buzz that made me feel all shivery. "I think you'll find there's not a lot I won't do to get a reaction out of you."

HE GOT one when we finally arrived.

"The jetty?"

It was a sunny day, not too blowy, and the sky above us was the perfect shade of cerulean blue, something I didn't realise would lighten my heart until I saw it. For a second, I just stared at the gentle waves, the few fluffy clouds scudding across the sky, but when I turned back to Ryan, I caught him watching me with a look of utter satisfaction.

"You knew…" I couldn't articulate what it was, just that as soon as I was here, I felt myself letting a massive breath out. "How did you know?"

"Don't go reading too much into it," he said, putting his arm across the back of my seat. "The others won't say so, but it's a guess, always a guess. Whatever I get from you right now, it's really heightened. I had something else planned, but…I could feel you were having a tough day and I didn't want to add to it. So low-key fish and chips down the jetty it is."

I frowned slightly, feeling a rush then of complex emotions that just got more complicated when I realised he'd be catching some of them too. I blinked furiously, wanting to hold it all in, but of course, he had to say something.

"Hey…Riley. Love. Oh fuck." He reached across and undid my seatbelt and his own, moving until he was about as close as he could get, his arms going around me. "Jesus, love, I fucked up. I'm so—"

"No."

That's all I could get out, my shaking fingers going to my eyes. Thank god I never bothered with makeup, because otherwise, my face would be a mess.

It would be anyway, I realised. While I didn't have freckles like many redheads, I did have that kind of skin that went red and blotchy when I cried, so I tried with all my might to stop them coming. I drew in a big breath, then let it out, just focussing on doing that for a second until I got my shit together.

"Sorry," I said. "You must think me a fucking madwoman."

"Of course I don't. I'm just kicking my own arse over here and my brothers'. We weren't supposed to handle it like this, just landing in your life like a fucking bomb blast. We talked it through the whole drive up here, getting it all straight in our heads, and then…"

I remembered his frustration at his brothers when they'd first arrived and snorted then, shooting him a watery smile.

"Did you get all frazzled when shit didn't go to plan, Ryan? Did you feel like everything was out of control?" His face was a picture of surprise, right up until he made the connection. "Did you have a really clear idea of how it was supposed to go and then none of it did?"

"Jesus…" Ryan shoved the key back in the ignition, then went to start the car, when I put a hand on his arm to stop him.

"This is a good idea. However you worked it out, being outside and getting some fresh air is exactly what I need. Let's get a feed and talk."

Chapter 20

Walking into the fish and chip shop was all very familiar. There weren't heaps of people here because it was a weekday, and the customers they did have looked like they were down at the jetty for a day at the beach, sporting board shorts with towels hanging over shoulders. We stepped up when it was our turn, and Ryan remembered my exact order, making me smile, the chick behind the till looking at the two of us with a bored expression. She took our money, giving us a small slip with a number on it, and then we waited, leaning against the pinball machine.

"Do you remember—?" he started to ask.

"Yep."

As I stared into his eyes, I knew we were both thinking of the moment he beat Keith Williams' high score on the pinball machine inside the fish and chip shop at home, the older alpha coming by and noting the achievement with a scowl and a sniff. But teen Ryan? He felt like he was on top of the world, that had been plain to see. Before he could consider taking a tilt at PNR's score now, our number was called and out we walked with the warm package wrapped in butcher's paper under Ryan's arm.

We moved across the road, down the footpath that ran along

the beach, and towards an empty picnic table. I brushed my hands across the coarse concrete surface, tracing the shapes scrawled on it with paint and pens. Ryan sat down, unwrapping the food, already waving a hand to get the seagulls that had amassed to piss off. I took a seat opposite and stared at him, not the food.

"I think the reason why this is so hard is because it feels like no time has elapsed."

Ryan froze mid squeeze of his lemon slice, those deep blue eyes flicking up to meet mine. He put it down carefully and gave me that thing that so many women crave from a man—his undivided attention.

"We could be at school. Haze might have just walked me out of English lit. You and Fen could be hovering around, making sure I ate. Blake could be scowling, Colt could be working out when to come around and study with me. I could be right back where I was, surrounded by you."

He watched me patiently, waiting for me to go on.

"You probably think that would be a good idea, that you could just pick shit up where we left it. Pretend Fen didn't beat the crap out of Clayton. Pretend I didn't have to spend seven years getting used to not having you around, learning to be independent, to stand on my own two feet and regulate my own damn food consumption."

I picked up a chip then, as if to contradict everything I'd just said, and crunched it defiantly.

"And how'd that work out, Riley? Was it a good life without us?"

His voice was so gentle, I could've ignored his questions and just gorged myself on deep fried goodness, but of course, I didn't.

"That implies a choice, Ryan—one I thought I didn't have. You've had time to work this out, to get to the point where you were prepared to pull up stumps and come and find me, but I didn't get that. We didn't keep in touch. I forced myself to never Google you, never stalk you on social media to see which omega you ended up with. I was told to forget you, and I did." I stared at him then. "Just like you forgot me."

I stiffened then, wanting to push my chair away from food that didn't smell appetising anymore. I believed in communicating, in getting your thoughts out there, adding to the discourse, but…when I did that with the pack, the usual rules didn't apply. Everything got so fucking intense.

I jumped when he settled down beside me. I hadn't even heard him move. He wrapped his arm around me, sheltering me with his body, and it felt so good. I hated that and the way my body wanted to automatically lean into him. It was as if we slotted together like two puzzle pieces, made to fit. I hated that my stomach instantly settled, then grumbled for some food. So I focussed on grabbing another chip and then another, chewing them mechanically.

"Hey, I get it now…" he said in a soft hush of a voice, his arms going around me. "This is the shit we needed to know."

"What, so you can revise your plans?"

"Too right. The first one is this, if you'll listen to it." I didn't reply, so he took it as tacit approval. "We're not going anywhere, love, no matter what happens. You reject the bond, we'll still be here. We were friends before, and we can be again. We were a part of your life, and that's gonna continue going forward."

Damn, wasn't that tempting? In just a few words, he'd created a mental image I couldn't resist. We'd have to spend time together after work and on weekends, but it could be just like before. But instead of hanging around at school or in my room, we could go anywhere we liked—cafés for brunch, pubs for a drink, or even the clubs when Candy was done pestering the shit out of me. Which reminded me of what usually happened when I went out with her. She took her self-appointed status as wingman seriously, trying to find me a guy to take home that night.

"So what, you'll wave me on my way when I go out on a date with some nice beta dude?" I asked.

That was when he went rigid, a low growl escaping his chest.

He fought it, I could feel it in the slight shake in his arms, but it came out anyway. I might not have been an alpha or an omega, but I knew what I'd find when I turned around.

His eyes blazed bright silver, his lips drawn back from teeth that had lengthened, and his focus? It was entirely on me.

"Just…don't talk about other guys, OK?"

I wanted to taunt him, rub it in his face that this was our reality, but I managed to bite my tongue, for once not digging myself a bigger hole. I did care about him. He was my friend, and friends had lunch together all the time. So I picked up a chip and offered it to him as an olive branch.

He just stared at it for a second, making me think this had an alternate meaning, especially with what I remembered of Blake last night. I went to pull my hand away, but his wrapped around my wrist, holding me still as he swooped in and took a bite of the chip. He bit off pieces until he got to my fingers, then his lips parted around them, his tongue sliding between my fingertips to retrieve the last bit, swiping away grease and salt as he did.

"This is one of those mating things, isn't it?" I asked.

"Fucking oath it is. Do it again."

"Ryan—"

"My dick feels like it's taken on a life of its own and is deter-minedly burrowing its way through my jeans to get to you, so feed me again, Riley."

The dark urgency of his tone had my eyes flicking around, as if we were about to get caught doing something truly salacious, rather than just something slightly intimate.

"Worried people will see?" That mocking tone was back. "Scared people are gonna see you feeding the big bad wolf?"

I broke off a piece of fish with a hiss and then offered it to him with a glare.

"You haven't changed a bit," I shot back. "Still the fucking shit-stirrer."

He grinned, right before he took the fish from my fingers, cleaning them up all too thoroughly, but when I went to start in on my own food, he was there. Apparently, I was to eat only from his fingers, his smile growing with every bite. When we were finally done, wiping the grease from our hands, I turned to him.

"So the food thing, it works both ways? An omega feeds her mates, alphas feed their omega."

"Food is about survival," he replied, staring into my eyes, his almost the same colour as the sky right now. "When you give up your immediate need for food for the other person, it's an act of love." His thumb brushed against my bottom lip. "It says right now, they're the more important ones, that you feel the need to care for and nurture them. To us, that's pretty heady stuff."

"I need to know more about all of this. You've obviously been schooled in everything alpha and omega, but no one bothered to tell me, for obvious reasons," I said.

"Anything you want, babe."

"Anything?" I smiled then, and I saw his grin falter slightly, as if he was worried about what he'd just committed himself to.

AND FOR GOOD REASON. When we returned to the institute, his brothers were all waiting for us in the undercover carpark, leaning against their car. The minute I was out of the ute, there they were, forming a loose circle around me.

"So Ryan explained?" I asked them. "This is a meeting with one of my colleagues and me to determine the scope of the study—what you're comfortable with, how far we go."

"I think you'll find we're open to anything you suggest," Fen said, pushing forward, that all too familiar cocky grin on his face. "We're all yours. Take what you need."

"So you'd be comfortable with another woman taking samples from you?" I asked coolly, seeing his face fall. "Or a man? If we needed to gauge your responses to different sexual stimuli—"

"You," he corrected. "You can study whatever you like, Riley."

I let out a frustrated little hiss, because this was going to look bad, like I was using my friendship with them to completely dominate the study, pushing everyone out. There were plenty of type A personalities in science, but blatantly coming across as one, particularly in a low-level researcher like myself, was not desirable. We had to maintain the illusion that we all worked together as a team, even if we didn't actually.

"All right, come up and talk to Candy and me, and let's get the finer details sorted," I said.

When we got in the elevator, that feeling of déjà vu started again. It was a small space, and they were so big… Having their bodies pressed against mine, it was all too familiar, and yet, it wasn't. My eyes slid down Blake's spine, taking in the broad flare of his lats, then the way his body narrowed down around his hips, remembering just how he'd felt this morning. He turned around slowly, as did the others, their nostrils flaring, low growls filling the lift, right up until the door slid open. Another person waiting for the elevator stood there and blinked, then instinctively took a big step backwards to let us out.

"Hey, Janet," I said as we came inside the foyer. "Does Candy have the boardroom booked?"

She took a moment to respond, just staring at the guys before nodding furiously.

"I set up some drinks in there. Tea, coffee. Just let me know if you need anything else."

"We've got everything we need right here," Fen said, wrapping his arm around my shoulders and steering us out again and into the hallway.

I pulled free with an irritated look at him and then said, "Down this way."

I directed us to the boardroom, opening the door to where Candy sat on her phone, kicking her heels, but she was on her feet as soon as we walked in. She just stared, then started fanning herself slowly.

"Damn, Riley, you've gotta be the luckiest bitch alive."

Chapter 21

"So basically, in terms of the scientific community, what you're offering is a godsend," I said, trying for cool and clinical. "From what you've told me, all the emotional difficulties betas experience in relationships aren't a factor between an omega and his or her alphas, so we get few willing to let us test them. Most of our awareness of alpha or omega physiology comes from where there's an issue—a difficulty bearing multiple children, someone getting cancer, etcetera. Even getting access to alpha or omega cadavers has been difficult, with few willing to donate them to science."

"We have to go back to the earth," Fen replied, serious now. "It's not like we're trying to hold out on you, but wherever a pack settles, the ancestors that died on that land are tied to that place."

I glanced at Candy, and she frowned slightly.

"That's the kind of stuff the sociologists would study, but I don't think we're going to go that broad. We could potentially have the department heads of every university in the state banging down our doors. Gideon is going to have to insist on radio silence for this study."

"I'm sure Windsor will push hard for that," I replied before turning to them. "What we're trying to work out is how far we can go. What are you comfortable with? Where are your limits? Usually, we set them out in a study and then invite betas to volunteer, but this is different."

"We have no limits when it comes to you, Riley," Fen replied.

"Holy co-dependent bullshit, Batman," Candy said to me. "Girl, you need to be careful. Maybe we need Windsor in on this as a supervisor, to stop shit from going too far." Then she faced the pack down. "You need to put boundaries on what you're offering, otherwise they'll keep you locked up in this place for years, studying you through a microscope. Blood samples, hair samples, skin samples, urine, faeces—"

"Why would you need a sample of our shit?" Haze asked with a frown.

"The gut-brain axis has shown us that a hell of a lot of what we assume is in the heart or the brain is actually determined in the gut," Candy replied. "Now you're around my girl, you might find that there's a whole cascade of changes going on in you. Raised serotonin, flushes of dopamine whenever you're close to her, your bodies pumping out oxytocin to help you to bond. Pregnant women have elevated levels of relaxin, a hormone to help their bodies adjust to having a baby grow inside them. It's often been theorised that omegas might have much higher levels of relaxin in their blood to allow them the physical flexibility to take a knot."

"And if we participate in this study, will you look at Riley's levels too?" Colt asked.

I looked at Candy, and she looked at me, both of us wincing at the implications of that.

"In our field, messing with the line between subject and scientist isn't a great idea. Some people have famously done it. Our understanding of how stomach ulcers are caused was revolutionised by a guy who tested infecting himself with a bacteria to prove its cause was a completely different thing than we thought, but…"

She sighed then and stared up at me.

"Riley, I think this is the focus of the study. We can offer to collect samples for other departments where it doesn't become onerous, but…what's happening here, between you six, that's what we need to focus on. I dunno if we tell Windsor about the relationship—"

"No," I said firmly, already able to see the look in his eyes. "I'm not doing that. That would destroy my reputation."

Her breath whistled through her teeth, because she knew what I knew—not declaring my own involvement in this study would potentially discredit it. It was accepted that we all brought our own crap to the table, our prejudices, our upbringings, our worldviews. The only way around that was to declare any potential conflicts of interest so anyone reading our papers could then account for that when they examined our data.

"It could destroy it if you don't," she replied much more gently.

"You'll do the analysis," I said. "We'll make you the primary contributor—"

"Riley…"

"This will be your paper, and we'll be your subjects. Windsor and Crowe won't care, as long as they get the data. We've still got those samples we took of my blood. We can do an analysis, see if there's been any shifts with some new samples."

People incorrectly assumed that genetics were a fixed set of things you were born with, that they were simply a blueprint used to create you. While I wasn't going to be able to change my eye or hair colour, some genes switched on or off depending on environmental factors. My latency for one. If Valerie or Cheryl hadn't been born, I might have revealed as an omega. At that thought, my eyes slid to the pack.

"You want to try and understand why a beta is our mate and not an omega?" Fen asked, stepping closer now. "Yeah, I think you'll find that we're completely on board with that. Whatever you need, we'll get it for you."

"Please say sperm samples," Haze muttered, putting his hands together in prayer. "Please, please say sperm samples."

"Better," Candy said with a cackle. "Our girl here will have to invest in a raincoat or something, because she needs to get up close and personal with your knots."

"Fuck…" I hissed as the guys erupted in a series of incomprehensible sounds, making clear just how on board they were with that idea. "If this is just some elaborate scheme for you to get me covered in pack spunk, I'm gonna kill you."

"Who, me?" She fluttered her eyelids furiously. "But seriously, you know how this has to work. Is there any genetic glitch creating that bond? Are you changing? Are they? If any genes are switching on or off, what's that doing to your bodies?"

Her focus shifted abruptly to the guys.

"We have no idea what's going on here, and if we're going to find out, we'll need to look at everything."

"I would like to volunteer as tribute," Haze said, stepping forward and raising his hand.

"Shut up, idiot," Ryan hissed.

"So I guess while we're here, we'll take some more samples. Not semen," Candy said firmly. "Did you want to do that while I chat to Windsor?"

That ruffled my feathers, I wasn't gonna lie. Candy was just as smart, had graduated with honours as well, from just as reputable a university, but I tended to naturally assume the leadership role. Probably because someone had to stop her from talking complete shit all the time.

"Sure, I can take care of that," I replied.

"Good, so you give the lot of them a little prick and something sweet afterwards, and I'll see you on Monday, because I get the feeling I might be up in their office for some time. Gotta admit, I had hoped if I was ever working late on a Friday night with Gideon Crowe that I'd be wearing a trench coat, some thigh highs, a pair of Manolo Blahniks he'd just bought me, and nothing else." She sighed dramatically at that, then headed for the door. "The things I do for this job."

"Is she for real?" Colt asked as Candy sashayed out.

"Who cares about that? I want the pricks and the sweet stuff," Haze replied.

WHICH WAS how I ended up with all of them seated in the pathology lab. I was aware that some people enjoyed a medical kink, sexualising a medical context, sometimes enjoying fantasies in one, getting a thrill from medical procedures. It'd never really resonated with me, but right now, I was beginning to get an inkling of it.

I knew my procedures, the filling out of forms, creating identifying numbers, assigning them to the different blood specimen tubes I'd need, and then dropping them into separate trays for each man, but when I walked over, Haze was already in the chair, muscular forearm lying on the long armrest, ready for me to draw his blood.

"Make a fist for me," I said as he stared up at me, his lips curling into a smile as he did just that, both of us conscious of the way his muscles popped in response. "I won't have any problems finding your veins."

Like most alphas, his body fat level was crazy low, so I saw exactly where they snaked along his body, just under the skin. He smiled at my inspection, then waited as I grabbed the tourniquet and the needle. I briefly felt around his inner elbow area, making sure everything was where I thought it should be, and then leant over. He watched my every move, those pale blue eyes burning into mine, his smile getting wider and wider.

"Just a little prick," I said as I inserted the needle.

"I'm not gonna be able to tell you the same thing when shit gets real, babe."

I grimaced, shaking my head as I watched the blood fill the small cannister, repeating the process over and over, until finally, he was done. I used a cotton ball to press down on the injection site after withdrawing the needle.

"Press down for me," I said, moving to pull away, but his

fingers covered mine, the two of us staunching the tiny flow of blood, my heart beating frantically in my ears until I finally pulled my hand away. I put a small bandage over it to keep the site clean and then went to move on to do Blake's, but an arm wrapped around my waist, tugging me back down and onto a lap.

"I was a very good boy," Haze told me, gripping me tighter when I squirmed, trying to get free. "Don't I deserve something sweet?"

"Haze!" He released me then, and I snatched a lollipop out of the jar and handed it to him with a huff. "This is my workplace. We're not doing" —I waved my hand in the air— "whatever this is here."

"Really?" Colt asked. "So where will we be conducting the knotting experiments? At your place?"

"Well, no, but—"

"You know how that's gonna have to go, right?" As he stepped closer, all deadly intent, I wondered where the hell the boy who'd spent all those hours studying with me had gone. "Like, I can pull my dick all day—"

"And he does," Ryan said with a snicker.

"As if you're any different, especially since we got to town," Colt shot back. "Is there a clean sock in the whole house right now?" There was silence in response to that. "But I can't engage my own knot—"

"Only I can," I finished for him. "Blake gave me a little lesson about that this morning."

"Little lesson, big fella?" Haze cackled. "Aw, is that what we felt down the bond with Riley? A whole lot of disappointment when she worked out you're not proportionate?"

And that, of course, started a virtual torrent of ribbing about dick size, because if men are given the opportunity to discuss it, they will, ad nauseum, and I was the one feeling the nausea. I was fairly sure there was a big—or not so big—juicy study for a team of psychiatrists to undertake, but thankfully, that was outside my wheelhouse.

"If we could stop talking about penises for five minutes while I finish taking the samples," I said. "I want to get this over and done with. Spider has a bucket full of gin big enough for me to plunge my head into, waiting for me at the pub."

"About that," Fen said, and everyone went quiet. He jerked his head to Haze, ousting him from his seat, and then rolled up his own sleeves, revealing an even more muscular arm. I went to work, taking his blood as he spoke. "We want you with us this weekend."

"What?"

I nearly pulled away, which wasn't smart when you were on the business end of a needle.

"We've got a house. It's a big place. If you really aren't feeling us, we set up a room for you. It's got a huge bed, with its own TV and en suite. You could sprawl out there, watch movies until your eyes roll out of your socket, and just relax. You gotta admit, you're wound pretty tight."

"I wasn't until you lot rolled into town," I muttered to myself.

"Just hang out with us," Colt said. "Honestly, we could just sit and read and I'd call that the best fucking weekend I'd had since high school."

"Pfft…" Haze said, "I figure we could go for a long walk on the beach—"

"Or we could go for a drive up into the hills," Ryan said.

"Guys—" I started to say.

"I could cook."

Blake's comment was short, sweet, but as I removed the needle from Fen's arm, having got everything I needed, his input was what had me turning around.

"That's what gets her attention?" Ryan asked in a hushed tone. "Damn, Blake, you bloody dark horse."

But it was the slow flush of his cheeks, that small secret smile that felt like it was just for me, that snagged at me, but I wasn't about to confess that to the others. I turned back to Fen, ready to tape his arm up, when he rose to his feet, towering over me.

"You didn't hear what I had planned."

"OK."

The word escaped me without thought because I might have been just a teeny tiny bit intimidated by Fen. Back then, the Vanguard boys had been heirs apparent, ready to take over their dads' thrones, but Fen was the king. He always moved like he did now, with absolute confidence. He stepped away from the chair, forcing me to back up, the others rumbling in response.

"You're too tight, Red." And as if to illustrate this, he put a hand on my shoulder and I jumped. Those iron hard fingers dug into my muscles, forcing them to unclench and go loose. "I figure we put on one of those bloody awful rom-coms you always liked, you can sprawl out on the floor, and I'll work every muscle in your body until you're all soft and relaxed. Would you like that?"

Would I like that?

Would I like that!

I was fairly sure every straight woman and gay man in the near vicinity would've liked to pick up what he was laying down.

"That won't be necessary," I said, my voice sounding ridiculously prim, and the guys chuckled in response. "I'll get my chill on in the usual way—through dysfunctional drinking, followed by lashings of carbs, fat, and salt."

"You want to get drunk, baby?" Haze asked with a cock of his head. "There won't be any goon this time and no little beta boys with big crushes."

"No interfering bloody parents, either," Colt added darkly.

"Yeah, all right," I said. "I'm not saying I'll stay for the entire weekend, but yeah, having a drink with people who aren't likely to shove me into the path of a dude just because it looks like he has all his teeth would be a nice change of pace. But we're not going anywhere until this is done."

Blake moved forward at that and sat down in the chair, just waiting for me to attend to him.

Chapter 22

"I'm riding with you, Red."

I had everything bagged up, numbered, and stacked in the fridge, ready for the pathology couriers, when Fen walked up to me.

"And why's that?" I asked him.

"This was going to be my night." He moved in closer, so close we were almost touching, but not quite. "We were each supposed to get some one-on-one time to reconnect."

I didn't want to burst his bubble, but I needed to connect with him before we could reconnect. I'd always wanted to, always found my eyes straying to him when we were together as a group, but that just made it harder, not easier, to approach him. So I guess the part of me that was still seventeen responded to him like he was asking me out on a date or something.

"OK, but I'm bringing my car to your place. You can give me directions."

He smirked at that, like he knew there was more to it. There wasn't. I was determined there wouldn't be. I went to my office, shut my computer down, and grabbed my bag before saying goodbye to Janet.

"Not coming to drinks tonight?" she asked me, treating the guys to a warm gaze.

"Candy's gonna be stuck with Crowe for ages, and I've…had a week. I'll see you on Monday."

"DIDN'T WANT to tell her what you would really be getting up to?" Fen asked, putting his hand on the small of my back as we walked into the carpark.

"What, that I'm hanging out with some old buddies, catching up over a few drinks?" I said when I got to my car, forcing him to remove his hand. "I guess I didn't see it as that big a deal."

He grinned at that, his teeth flashing white against his heavily tanned skin before he nodded and then got into the passenger seat of my car. I put my key in the ignition, but my eyes slid sideways, seeing how he propped his elbow up on the armrest console. The car was just a little hatchback, fine for me, but with him in the car? It was too small, he was too big, too near, too… He watched me shake my head, force myself to turn the car on, and pull out of the carpark.

I couldn't afford to focus on him. We had to get through peak hour traffic on a Friday night, and that was going to take all my attention. As we wove our way through the darkening streets, past people walking to the bus or train stop, to pubs for a drink, a dense silence fell over the car.

I glanced his way, wondering how the hell he was being so quiet, and caught a glimpse of his catlike smile. This was the stillness of a predator, sitting in wait for its prey, endlessly patient, yet its intent was clear. I let out a frustrated little sigh, flicking on the radio, letting the familiar tunes fill the car. When we got to my place, I was up and out of my car as soon as we stopped, feeling a need to put some distance between us.

I opened the gate, walked down the path at a brisk pace, but there he was at my back. When I unlocked the screen door, when I reached for my keys, he crowded me in, placing a hand on the wall above my head.

"Settle down, Red," he said in a low growl. "The pheromones, the vibes you're throwing off right now? They make my wolf antsy, and he's already on edge around you."

I spun around at that, being forced to back up as his body hung over mine.

"If you're struggling with control, maybe coming over isn't a good—"

I was silenced as his hand covered my mouth, my eyes going wide as a result.

"What we've got here is the best I can do," I was informed, his eyes shining greenish silver in the cool half-light of dusk. "It's taking all I've got to keep him from sneaking into your house, stealing you away, and locking you up in a room until you realise what we know." He moved closer then, stroking my cheek with his thumb. "That you're meant to be with us. Now put your key in the lock, open the door, and get us inside like a good little girl, or instead of massaging your arse later, I'll put you over my knee and spank you."

I blinked, staring mutinously at him, but he just grinned as he removed his hand, daring me with his eyes to scream, shout, anything. That's what he wanted—a reaction. So I turned on my heel and did exactly the opposite, strolling into my house without a word, pleased to see the kitchen was spotless. Blake must have put in some time there this morning, because it was the cleanest it'd ever looked.

"There's a bottle of gin in the pantry," I said as I walked down to my room, kicking off my heels. "If there's anything you want, grab that too."

But of course, he didn't listen to a word I said. As I grabbed a duffle bag from my wardrobe, he wandered in. I stopped midway through grabbing a few T-shirts, straightening up to stare at him. He made a show of inspecting the room, his nostrils flaring.

"I said grab—" I started to say.

"You said grab what I wanted," he replied, prowling over to my drawers. He sniffed once, twice, sorting through my belongings until he found what he was looking for. "Mm…" Just a little grunt, and then a pair of green lacy undies and a matching bra was tossed on the bed, then a red pair, followed by a purple pair…

"I'm not wearing those," I said, grabbing them all and shoving them back into my drawer. "They're date night underwear. Usually on the weekend, I don't wear any at all if I can help it."

When I went to grab a few pairs of more basic underwear, he shut the drawer abruptly, staring down at me.

"Well, we wouldn't want to interfere with your routine."

"Fen…" I said in irritation, trying to open it, but he wouldn't let up. I tried again, but he still stubbornly refused to let me open it, so I stalked off to my wardrobe, pulling out yoga pants, T-shirts, and a jumper, maybe a pair of jeans, just in case we went somewhere, and shoved them in a duffle bag.

"Oh, this we are definitely taking."

Here's the thing. Teenage Riley would have just about wet her pants to have Fen Vanguard in her bedroom. Like, sacrificing small animals to dark gods would not have been too much in that regard. But right now, if I could make him disappear with just one look, I would've without a thought, as he'd transferred his attention to my bedside drawers.

"For fuck's sake, that's none of your business!"

Vibrators were tossed down onto the bed with gay abandon, a few he examined more closely as if trying to work out what they were used for, which pretty much sent me into a fit of hysterics. I swept up as many pink or purple silicone implements of self-pleasure as I could and sought to drop them back into the drawer, when he got right up in my face.

"You're gonna need something to take the edge off," he promised in a dark voice.

"No, I'm fucking not." I knew what alpha hearing was like. Even though I had a very good selection of discreetly quiet vibes, they wouldn't be quiet enough for them.

"The first night you let Haze and Colt come into your dreams to satisfy you," he said, flicking up one finger. "The second, Blake helped satisfy you." He herded me back against the wall, grabbing my wrists when I went to jerk away and staring down at me. "You're gonna get all hot and wet—"

"Fuck, Fen, would you shut the fuck up?"

"I'm an alpha, baby. It's my job to see to all your needs. Do I want to be the one to do it?" His eyes slid down my body, and then he grinned that slow, toothy thing of his. "Fuck yeah, I do, but you're not ready and I'm not letting you go without until you are. We don't have to take any of the fun toys with us, but we all smell how you respond to us, know how you feel." He moved in closer, so close, I could feel his breath on my face. "You want Blake to look after you again? Or Colt? He wouldn't stop smiling for a week if you let him do that."

"So what, you want to feed me, fill me full of alcohol, and then get me off so I sleep the slumber of the well sated?" I asked, a crazy little edge coming into my voice. "Are you for fucking real?"

"An alpha sees to his mate's needs, all of them. Right now, we're looking after your body, because that's what you'll let us do." He shifted closer so I could feel the heat of his body. "Then, when you're used to that—"

I jerked my hands free and slid down the wall and out through the small gap between us, scuttling backwards in my own damn room. I picked up Mr Buzzy, my most trusty of vibes, held it up, and conspicuously dropped him in the bag.

"There. Needs taken care of. Now for the love of god, can we move on?"

"Well, I was going to ask what this—?" he started with a grin.

"The internet," I snapped, grabbing something to change

into before heading to the bathroom. "It's a magical thing that will show you exactly what you do with each one of them. Just put them back in the drawer when you're done."

When I switched on the light in the bathroom and looked in the mirror, I saw a woman on the edge. The wolf inside me paced back and forth, whining meaningfully. My face was flushed, my hair was a mess, and my eyes were wide and unblinking. I shook my head, turned the taps on, and splashed my face, hoping to get my shit together before I went back out there.

As soon as I took a deep breath, I could see what an incredibly privileged position I was in. Most women would literally kill to be in this situation, but… As I gripped the sink, consciously slowing my breathing, I knew what was happening. I closed my eyes for just a second, my head hanging low, because the pack, they were wearing me down.

I could easily imagine putting on one of my date night sets of lingerie and nothing else, stalking out into the lounge room of wherever they were staying, and just watching their eyes flash silver as they set upon me, ready to devour me. I lifted my head, staring into the mirror. What would that be like? And that was the most dangerous thought of all.

This was when the scales began to tip in the pack's favour, when I stopped trying to fight all the damn time. My defence mechanisms were able to be dismantled with such ease, needing only a few nice words, some hot kisses, yummy food, and a truly amazing hand job. I'd worked really hard to keep them at a distance, but the walls, they just came crumbling down.

I got out of my work gear and pulled on my clothes, the cotton of this shirt worn so smooth, the weave of it was semi-transparent. Well worth going into the rag bin, but I could never seem to bring myself to toss it. I marched out into the bedroom to the sight of Fen sitting on the end, his eyes taking me in like I was wearing couture or something.

"Damn, Red—"

"Ring your boys and see what they want on their pizza," I ordered.

"We were gonna—"

"Sunny's Pizza is the best pizza in the city, and it's my Friday ritual. It's gotten to the point that they'll probably send the cops around for proof of life if they don't hear me order in tonight."

He nodded and then fished out his phone.

"Meat lovers for me, and I'll check with the guys."

As he sauntered over, I rifled through my drawers, pulling out the green set of lingerie and then stuffing it in my bag, just in case, before zipping that sucker up. When I came out, he rattled off a long list of pizzas, and I made the order. Joe, the owner, and I indulged in a little chit-chat before I hit him with the list.

"You got a party going on, Riley?" he asked me with a chuckle. The guy was in his sixties and had big dad energy, always checking up on his regulars.

"A bunch of friends have just gotten into town, so we're celebrating," I replied, my eyes locking with Fen's. "Really good friends I haven't seen in a long time."

"We'll make your food with a little extra love and care then. See you in thirty?"

I agreed and disconnected the call, but when I went to carry my bag out, Fen took it. He also snatched the keys, putting my bag in the boot before heading for the driver's seat.

"No, no, no, no!" I yelped. "You're too tall and you'll mess with my seat and…no."

He paused, then tossed the keys back to me.

"You're in control, Red, right up until the point that you don't want to be. Just remember that."

I tried not to read too much into his words as I got in the car and turned on the ignition.

We went to Sunny's, then he gave me directions out of town and up into the hills that looked down on it, up the driveway to a very large homestead style house on acreage. The guys spilled out of the house the moment we arrived.

"Ready for the best weekend of your life?" Fen asked before he opened his door.

I considered him, the house, the approaching pack, and wondered, right before I pushed the door open, what I was doing.

Chapter 23

Right now, it was easy to pretend that we had never been apart. Unlike the terrible scene at the pub, everyone was relaxed, full of good food, discarded plates with pizza crusts strewn everywhere, empty boxes piled high. I was lying on my stomach on a foam mattress they'd laid out on the floor for just this purpose, watching a movie.

The room was warm, the lights dimmed to create a cosy atmosphere in what turned out to be a freaking huge house. But right now, it didn't seem so big, as they were all clustered around me. Blake was sitting by my side, his leg pressed against my ribs, while Ryan was moving around on clean-up duty. Haze was sprawled across the mattress too, watching some superhero bull-shit movie, and the others were on the couch.

I felt someone move, then strong fingers grabbed my foot, and before I could say anything, a thumb pressed all the way up my instep, digging deep into the arches, forcing the ligaments to soften.

"Ohh…"

My response was muffled as my face planted into the mattress at the feel of it.

"Jesus, Riley, did you just make sex noises over *Captain America*?" Haze asked me, pushing aside my hair to try and get to me. I just waved him away vaguely as the thumb went in for more, two of them now. As one swept up, the other started, burying themselves in the soles of my feet. I made pitiful little sounds from the rush of sensation that came with each stroke.

"What the hell are you doing, Colt?"

"Her feet were aching, so I'm massaging them."

I let out a mournful little sound when he left off, but it was only to start on the other one. Then more groans into the mattress.

"You can feel that much? Down to exactly where she hurts?"

"You know I've always been bound tighter to her than the rest of you. I think I started the process of making her my mate before she even left."

They were saying important things, while the crash and booms from the TV meant that we were no doubt at a big action scene in the movie, but I couldn't seem to move. Colt had me pinned to the mattress as surely as if his foot were pressing down on my shoulder blades.

Which seemed to egg someone else on.

I felt the mattress depress either side of me, a heavy weight dropping down over but not on top me, then hands going to my shoulders.

Oh god, kill me now, because I was in heaven.

They could've tried so hard to seduce me this weekend. Fine wine and lovely food, expensive gifts and glamorous locations, but all I wanted was this. Muscles held tight all week were pummelled into submission, and I was each pair of hands' bitch if this was what they could do.

"Fuck, listen to the sounds she's making!"

Then, right as I threatened to dissolve into the mattress, another set of hands went to my skull, raking their fingers through my hair before digging them in along my scalp and down my neck.

I was floating then, each individual movement unable to be

detected anymore, but the symphony of sensation they created had me completely and utterly captivated. Time felt like it stood still, because there was only pleasure now.

"Have we broken Riley? She's just making these little kitten noises."

"She's feeling good." That was said with a kind of reverent shock. "All the pain and frustration…"

I rolled over when I came back to myself, conscious I was sprawled now like some kind of starfish, and when I did, I took in my current state. Ryan and Colt had each ended up massaging a foot. When I looked up, Blake was looking down at me, so it'd been his fingers that had been massaging my head, and Fen? He was still straddling my hips, having worked on my back. Haze was, of course, still watching the damn movie. They stared down at me, and I stared up at them, blinking.

"That was amazing," I croaked out. "I feel" —I lifted my arm, and it fell limply to the ground— "so good. But why would you all jump in to do that? A four-person massage? That's not something beta dudes would do."

"That's nothing," Fen said with a cocky smirk. "Wait until we get the massage oils out."

Colt rolled his eyes at his brother, but answered my question. "We feel your pleasure like it's our own Riley. Making you feel relaxed makes us feel relaxed. Just like…" His words trailed away as his eyes slid over my body, making me aware of how else I was responding to them.

Because that was a thing men often didn't realise—when a woman was truly at ease, most of the time she'll be much more responsive to anything else on his mind. Our sex drives were choked by worries, responsibilities, and pressures of life grinding us down, which was why the stereotype of a woman thinking about her shopping list while having sex existed. It wasn't that we didn't want to be present and experience the throes of ecstasy with someone we cared about. It was that we found it hard to surrender to that while all this menial shit buzzed around insistently in our heads.

Surrender…

My eyes scanned the lot of them, taking in the way they watched me so damn closely, waiting for just that.

"Mm…you smell creamy," Haze said, rolling closer to me and burying his face in my hair. "You gonna let me come into your dreams tonight? I've got some ideas I'd like—"

"Sleep with me," Colt said abruptly, his mouth thinning down when he realised how intense he sounded. "I know it's not my turn, but…" He stared at me, and I found myself moving to go to him, patting Fen's thighs to get him off me. When I came to kneel before Colt, he reached out and straightened the sleeves of my T-shirt. "You wore my shirt."

And this was why I could never throw it away. It was airy, comfortable, the shirt I wore when I just wanted to relax, but it was also his. It'd been hot one summer night, and Mum had refused to allow us to turn the air con on, so he'd stripped down to just his shorts, leaving the T-shirt on my floor and forgetting it when he left. I'd collected it up afterwards, burying my face in the folds of fabric to smell him.

"It's my favourite," I said with a nonchalant shrug.

He grabbed me then, pulling me up and depositing me on his lap, my legs straddling his hips.

"You've got a whole lot of T-shirts, and you wore this one." He smoothed his hands over my ribs. "You've worn it a lot. Over and over, you've worn my clothes."

"You…like that?" I asked.

"Yeah, I like that," he replied. "I like it so fucking much, I'd like to break into your house, toss out all your other T-shirts, and replace them with mine."

I snorted at that, then saw that he wasn't totally joking. I slid a hand through his hair, just feeling those silky strands passing through my fingers.

"OK then, take me to bed, Colt."

I let out a little yip when he stood us up, but I needn't have worried, as he carried me easily through the lounge room.

"Say goodnight, Riley," he instructed.

"Goodnight, Riley," I sang out as we swept out of the room.

I WAS CARRIED into a darkened room, and he didn't bother putting the light on, just flicking on a lamp before laying me on the bed. My muscles felt all long and loose, right up until the point he pulled his T-shirt off. I rolled up on my elbows, seeing the boy that he'd been and the man who was here right now, and something clenched hard inside my chest. I studied him, glorying in the ability to just do that.

Bringing me here was perfect, I realised, because they'd taken away everything else, all of the audiences of work or the pub, and removed me from the trappings of my life. Which allowed me to admit this—Colt was fucking beautiful, all nut brown skin, lighter brown hair, and those eyes that wouldn't look away from me for a second. I didn't look away from him, either. I couldn't, and I wasn't sure if I'd be able to again after this weekend.

"Fuck…" he hissed. "The way you look at me."

"You can't blame me," I said. I'd had a few drinks over pizza, so my tongue was looser than it could've been. "Like…"

I rolled up and off the bed, coming to stand before him. Our size difference was so much more apparent now, with him towering over me. He was big, broad, though not quite as big as the others, and there was an elegance to his body as a result, but for all that, he waited so still to see what I'd do.

"I used to sneak little looks at you like this," I said, tracing one finger along the sharp line of his pec. Every single one of his muscles were clearly defined, popping out as my finger moved. "My hands itched with the need to touch you, all the while knowing I couldn't."

"I wish you fucking had," he said in a low, hoarse voice, covering my hand with his and moving it so it lay over his heart. "I ached for you too."

"I didn't know you wanted me to," I replied.

"Yes, you did." I glanced up at him, his head dropping down

195

by tiny increments, getting closer and closer. "You had to have. We were always touching you, always dragging you onto our laps, breathing in your scent." He did that just now, nosing my hair out of the way. "You could feel our need for you."

"Because Dad told you to."

"No."

"Because we grew up together."

"No, you know that isn't true. The Mitchells grew up with the Whites and Amanda was best friends with those boys until they revealed." His teeth locked down tight. "Then they dropped her like a stone."

"Because…" My brain, that buzzed with feel-good hormones, fought to find another reason, even as I knew he'd demolish it just as swiftly as the others.

"Because you felt so good in our arms. Because your body fitted against ours. Because we watched your perfectly formed arse in those damn skirts and shorts you always used to wear and jerked off to the memories of it, alone in our beds. Because your eyes flash like emeralds when you're mad. Because you never let anything stop you from becoming what you were supposed to be."

His mouth was almost on mine, his hand tipping my jaw up until I was at the perfect angle, and then he moved closer.

"Because with every fucking fibre of our bodies, we knew that you were ours, Riles. When our beasts came out, when we found our fur, we found you right there with them. I saw our destiny before us."

"Right before it was ripped away…" I said, almost in a whisper.

"But we're back together now. How many people can say that? To have something so perfect when they were just kids and then find their way back to it." His hand went to my cheek. "The guys told me shit might not be the same, and it isn't."

I stiffened then, but he darted in, pressing a kiss to my mouth.

"It's so much more intense. Before, it was like a toothache—

a persistent thing in the background. But now?" He kissed me, slowly parting my lips with his, kissing me again and again, groaning when I started to open for him. "Now, it's like the throbbing of my heart." Another kiss, snatching any response away from me. "The breath in my lungs." Kisses, so many kisses. "The wind in my fur, the ground under my paws." More kisses, more as he pressed me up against the wall, his body surging closer. "And I'd give every single one of them away for just this."

The reason why I was the closest to Colt was because he was never one for posturing. He knew what his position was in the town, and he didn't feel the need to deny it or flaunt it. Colt just was who he was, and that had always been focussed on me. So when his lips brushed mine, what came with his touch was a terrible sense of inevitability.

Of course his breath, my breath were sucked in the minute we touched, because we'd been waiting for this for so long. We'd secretly traced the shapes of each other's mouths during class or conversations, on the bus or in my room, not letting the other see. We'd longed to replace the taste of our lunch with the taste of each other. And we needed this, that I felt as sure as my heart-beat. My hands were in his hair, his tightening around my waist, pulling me closer, as he rocked his body against mine and sucked my bottom lip. Then his tongue slid between them, seeking more, seeking me.

"Fuck…" I hissed when I pulled away, although not very far. His grip was like iron, and he wasn't letting me go anywhere. His head was already dropping lower, seeking more. "Colt…"

"Mm…?"

Fuck, Colt's kisses were way more potent than the gin I'd been drinking. They clouded my mind as they got deeper, fiercer, making me ache.

"Colt…"

"Fuck, Riley…I can't get enough."

But it was when his hand slid down, cupping my butt then holding it still as he thrust his hard-on against me, that I forced him to stop.

"Colt?"

He blinked slowly, seeming to need the time to come back to himself, and when he did, his eyes were the brightest of silver.

"Hey," I said. "You know we can't go too far with this, right?"

When he smiled, I found myself feeling ridiculously relieved to see it.

"We can't have sex until you're ready, Riley." He tapped his temple. "We feel it in here. Like, now?" His eyes dropped to my lips. "You like being kissed. You might like being kissed elsewhere…" His smile faded somewhat, something darker and more intense rising. "But that also scares the shit out of you."

He straightened up, the silver receding in his eyes.

"I'm making you feel good and scared all at the same time, and I only want one of those things. Just pleasure. I'm sick to fucking death of pain, and I'll never let you get hurt. When the pleasure stops and the fear or pain starts, I'm done. If you just want to lie down and I hold you in my arms until we sleep, trust me, I'll be fine with that."

"Jesus, I think I know why the omegas were such bitches at school," I said. "If I knew I was supposed to get all this" —I gestured to him— "and missed out, I'd be pissed."

"You don't ever have to be," he said with a grin. "Now, what do you normally wear to bed?"

"Ahh…nothing," I said, watching his eyes flare in response. "I think I'll just ditch the pants and the bra and I should be fine."

"Let me," he said, sweeping his hands up the back of my shirt and undoing my bra clasp with a degree of proficiency that made my eyes narrow.

"You had some practice doing that?" I asked.

"None." He snorted. "Trust me, it's just beginner's luck."

I stopped him then.

"No one?"

He wanted to look away, I could see it in the tension around his eyes, but he forced himself not to. He busied himself drawing my bra straps out through my sleeves before letting the garment fall away. It was intense, just feeling the thin fabric fall over my bare nipples, which were pulled tight and throbbing right now, but the question between us remained the same.

"There was never anyone else for me, Riley. No one who caught my attention. No one for whom I gave the slightest shit about, other than you."

He undid his jeans with one hand, then with the other, he grabbed my hand and pushed it inside, so I could feel the hard throbbing length of him behind the layer of stretchy cotton.

"You're the only one who makes me feel, who gets me responding, who… Uh!"

It was just a little moan as I rubbed my thumb up, then down his shaft.

"So you've never done this with anyone else?" I was going for shock, but my voice came out all husky instead. "No one's touched you like this before?"

"No…" he ground out. "Jesus fucking Christ, Riley, I'm trying to be good. You're destroying my control here."

For some reason, that was the perfect thing to say. They'd been all dark and smouldery, complimenting me, taking me out, making me feel like they had all the power and I was just there to have it lavished on me, but right now, I was the one in control. I was making a man, who I'd fantasised about more times than I could count, shiver at my touch. His whole body seemed to narrow down on my hand, on what my thumb was doing, and that made me feel good.

"So show me," I said. "Show me what no one else has touched."

Chapter 24

"What?" He stared at me hazily, seeming to have to focus hard to bring himself back to the here and now. "You want…?"

"I want to see you," I said. "All of you."

He moved only as far away from me as he had to, stripping off his socks, his jeans, and his boxers, and I watched him hungrily as he emerged perfectly naked. I just stared for a second, unable to stop looking him over, my fingers aching to touch, but where to start? His muscles tensed, the cobblestones of his abs clenching tighter under my inspection, and then there was his cock.

Fuck, it might just hurt a little going in, he was that damn thick, the slightly more streamlined look of his body almost exaggerating his size. Despite that, part of me wanted to find out if he'd force me to feel a little pinch the first time he fucked me, something that would ease as he delved deeper.

"Riley…?"

Even as he spoke, my finger reached out, tracing the same path up the length of his cock that I had before, but now over bare flesh rather than fabric. His hand wrapped around my wrist, dragging me closer but forcing it away from his dick.

"You said you didn't want things to progress too far," he said in a low growl.

"I don't," I said with a wicked grin, sliding my hands down his body as I dropped down to my knees.

"Riley. Riley, you don't—"

It was the sharp intake of his breath as I licked a line up his cock that got me, robbing him of the ability to speak. His hands dove into my hair, balling it up into a rough bun, and he used it as a means to hang on. His eyes closed then, those lashes so long, they cast a shadow on his cheeks. His lips fell open as mine parted, like we were in each other's heads, his brows creasing as I collected all the pre-cum bubbling out of his slit, then sucked it down.

"Riley…" His voice was corded with need, desire, and pain. "Riley…" he hissed as I wrapped my hand around the base of his cock, my fingers unable to even grip him entirely. He didn't seem to care, his whole body stiffening as I covered the end of his dick with my tongue, swiping over it with faster and faster strokes. My name came tumbling out in increasingly jumbled ways, until finally, as I wrapped my lips around the crown, it was just a random set of syllables.

One little flex of his hips—that was all he allowed himself as I sucked his head tight, just an indicator that he wanted more without taking it, his body strung taut as a string. It was when my tongue pressed against that sensitive spot right under the head that the groans really started. I wriggled it furiously as I sucked, beginning to go deeper and deeper, until finally, his eyes flicked open.

My soft-eyed Colt wasn't here anymore. Instead, his beast stared down at me with eyes like the moon.

"You gonna suck my cum down like a good girl, Riley?" he asked in a deadly growl. "Need to mark you, claim you, inside and out. Any man that comes near you will catch a whiff of me, know that he needs to step the fuck away."

He took over now, grasping his cock by the base and pulling it free, before feeding it oh so slowly back into my mouth. He was testing my limits, I quickly worked out, because as soon as my throat tightened, he was pulling out, only to push back in again.

"Feed you our cum, cover you in it, and rub it into your skin. Leave it seeping out of your pussy, only for our fingers to scoop it up and push it deeper. You're gonna take it all, take all of us, aren't you? You're being such a good girl, taking me like this, but it's just the fucking start."

Fear and sexual desire all pumped through the same part of the brain, so it was no wonder one fed into the other. I wasn't scared of Colt so much as stunned. I'd started sucking the dick of a guy I loved, and now? Now I had a wild-eyed beast standing over me, one who was watching me with a predator's focus, edging himself closer and closer, until finally, he pulled himself free.

I blinked, my eyes a little bleary, to find him smiling down at me, the shape of his mouth cruel. He stroked his thumb across my swollen lips and then pressed it inside, my mouth latching on without a thought from me.

"Your mouth is so tempting, sweet mate," his beast rumbled. "But the time for swallowing my seed is later. Your scent fills my nose, and your need rides me." He swept me up in his arms, then dropped me down on the bed, his hands going to my yoga pants, dragging a yelp from me.

"Colt," I said as he peeled them down. "Colt!"

He froze, then rolled his eyes up, alien and metallic-looking, and stared into mine. The pants were removed much more slowly now, and a kiss was placed on the sensitive inside of my ankle, his gaze picking up the full body shiver in response.

"You are not ready to mate yet," he said simply, what I was desperate to get through to him stated as if it were a proven fact, but he went for my underwear, tearing them off next. "You won't be ready for some time. You need to be teased and petted and stroked until you are. We start that now."

"Colt, what does that—Oh!"

He drew a finger through my ridiculously wet seam, sliding it

but… Human brains tended to minimise future pain and maximise current pain, and so right now, it was going to hurt me more to turn my back on Colt, to make this one and done like I should.

So I wasn't going to.

I felt a rush of something incredibly possessive as I raised my shaking hand. *Mine!* my soul screamed. After last night, after everything he'd said and done, surely I could… I frowned slightly as I took in a deep breath of his scent, the amber cologne still not entirely faded but now more a ghost of itself, one I'd be able to chase to ground if I pushed my nose into his neck. My fingers twitched with a need to touch him, the silk of his hair, the satin of his skin. He was my Colt, he'd pretty much sworn that. No one had touched him but me, and that was what emboldened me right now. I stroked his hair back behind his ear with just the tip of a fingertip, and that was when he woke up.

He just stared at me, those hazel depths going to silver and back again, as if his beast fought him for control. He watched me closely, then drew down my hovering hand and placed a kiss on my palm, not realising he was stabbing a knife straight into my heart and twisting it as he did. I wanted this, I fucking wanted this so badly. I wanted all the small little gestures people in relationships have. To lie in bed with your lover, for him to kiss you, mark you with his lips as his, and for it to stop feeling like a stolen pleasure. I kept waiting for someone, anyone, to walk in through that door and—

Knock, knock.

"Wakey, wakey, hands off the snakey," came a muffled voice through the door. "Breakfast is on, and Fen wants you two up. You've got ten seconds, so stop whatever naughty things you're doing, because I'm coming in."

Shit, I looked down at my naked form and then was forced to pull free of Colt, tumbling off the bed and scrabbling around, looking for a T-shirt, any T-shirt. I'd just managed to pull one on over my head when the door was flung open.

"That was not ten seconds," Colt said, still lying there placidly on the bed with only a sheet over his naked hips.

"No, it wasn't," Haze said, looking the two of us over, those pale blue eyes staying on me. "You made it clear last night, brother, that playing fair was not gonna get us anywhere."

I found myself stepping backwards, holding my T-shirt down to try and cover all my bits, and Haze just smiled. He stalked over, dressed in a sleeveless shirt and pair of grey track pants.

You know, lingerie for men.

He walked closer and closer, forcing me to retreat until my back hit the wall.

"Haze…"

I said his name as a warning, a plea, and a question all at once, and he just smiled.

"Well, well, is that the scent of sexual satisfaction I smell?"

He stepped into the small gap between my feet and then widened them with his own, pressing his body against mine.

"Haze, you fucker…" Colt rumbled.

"Don't worry, Colton, dear." Haze looked back over his shoulder at his brother. "I just want to make sure you did right by our girl." Those cool blue eyes came back to meet mine, dancing now with barely repressed mischief. "Did he?" His voice was little more than a husky rasp now, a small smile forming. "Did he do you right? Did you make little kitteny cries as he ate your sweet little pussy? Did you come on his fingers or all over his fa—?"

His litany of questions was cut off as I shoved him backwards, the man landing heavily on the bed beside his brother, and that stopped me in my tracks. The two of them together, in the bed, one naked, one with large swathes of his chest revealed by the long arm holes of his shirt. It wasn't hard to imagine a whole other scenario…

"See something you like, Riley?" Haze asked with a cheeky smile, patting the space between the two men. Colt's expression of irritation at his brother quickly shifted to something much, much hungrier. "Come here, baby. We've got what you need. You already know that Colt boy and me, we'll do you right."

"I thought I told you to get everyone up?" Ryan asked, appearing at the door with a frown at his brothers, but when he turned to me, he smiled. "Hey, Riley. You sleep all right?"

"Um…yeah," I replied.

"Come and have some breakfast then," he said, then turned back to the boys. "Haze, what the fuck are you doing?"

He seemed to be doing his best to look up my shirt, prompting me to jerk it down with a hiss.

"Just seeing if the carpet matches the drapes—" Haze replied lazily.

Colt grabbed his pillow and walloped his brother hard with it, then used his body weight to keep the thing over his head, in the face of Haze's hysterical cries. I smiled then despite myself, seeing a million pillow battles fought when we were kids. While they were distracted, I dropped down and retrieved my yoga pants, wriggling back into them lickety-split, Ryan and Colt looking on.

They stared like they were trying to store every movement, every glimpse of skin, away for replaying later, but my stomach put paid to any idea of working out what was going on there, rumbling noisily.

"Is that bacon cooking?" I asked. "I'm starving."

I WANDERED out into the big open plan living area and found Fen reading the paper while eating his breakfast and Blake puttering around the kitchen.

"Oh my god…" I groaned at the smells coming from it, drawn closer as if under a spell. Blake shot me a sidelong smile, retrieving a small bit of bacon from a plate with paper towel on it and offering it to me. It was the perfect mix of salt, grease, and a tiny bit of crunch, but not so crispy all the moisture was cooked out of the meat. I made the most disgusting noise of pleasure in response, chewing it down.

"Didn't hear Riley making those noises last night, Colt," Haze said as he strolled in, his brothers in tow. "Need to up your game. Or maybe bring food into the bedroom. You could try some fruit rubbed all over her—"

"Quickest way to get a yeast infection," I replied, then placed my hands on Blake's arm, looking up at him adoringly. "Can I please, please have some of that amazing bacon?"

He then said the words every woman wants to hear. "I made it for you. They can have whatever you don't want to eat. How do you like your eggs?"

I put in my order and might have gushed a teeny tiny bit, but damn. Saturday breakfast was usually some dry toast or else something I just put off until I went out at lunchtime. This was luxury.

"Take a seat," he said, leaning over and pressing the sweetest of kisses to my forehead. "I'll bring it over to you."

"This is why I had to wake you up," Haze grumbled. "Julia Childs over there wasn't gonna hand over the bacon until you two lovebirds surfaced."

"I coulda waited," Colt said, taking a seat next to me and then grabbing my hand. My breath hitched a little as I felt that now more familiar pulse of energy between us. "I had every-thing I wanted to eat last night."

He shot me a smug sidelong look, one that was full of heat, but he wouldn't maintain eye contact for long and I understood why. What this was, whatever it was, it was super new and frag-ile, and of course, that brought his brothers circling like sharks.

"Baby ate his first pussy?" Haze asked with exaggerated delight, slapping Colt on the shoulder. "How'd he do, Riles? Were you like one of those traffic controllers, having to use the paddles to show him where to go?"

He mimicked the motions with his hands, but he didn't feel Colt stiffen, didn't feel something inside me go ice cold. My fingers tightened around Colt's, as if he would snatch them away or someone else would, and he looked up then, staring into my eyes easily now, searching my face for answers.

"Shut up, Haze," Fen said in a terse tone, finally looking up.

There was quiet now, broken only by the sound of the bacon cooking, Blake hustling over with a plate full of food and placing it before me. I thanked him but didn't reach for my knife and fork yet, needing to say something and wishing I didn't have to.

"Look, you guys are brothers," I said.

"Much as we might wish we weren't…" Ryan hissed.

"And I've been watching you talk shit about each other for years. I get it's part of your whole bro dude thing you do, but you can't do that about anything that goes on between us. Last night…"

Everyone hung on my words, but I didn't care much about what they thought right now, my eyes finding Colt's, something inside them burning just as hot as what I felt burnt in mine.

"Last night is none of your fucking business for one."

"Ouch," Haze replied in a small voice.

"And two…" I didn't look away from Colt, even though I wanted to. I didn't really want to say this, the feeling inside me so naked and raw, it felt vaguely obscene to bring it to the dining table, but here it was. "What happened with Colt and me? I feel like I've waited my whole adult life for that. Like, I've never ever been more aware of something that I've waited and longed for than I was last night." I forced my eyes down at that, focussing on my breakfast but not really seeing it. "You want me to do this, to be with each one of you? Well, that will feel like this does now. That this is really precious and fragile." I sucked in a breath, my chest feeling tight before I glanced up at the rest of the table. "You can't talk shit about us or what happened. I don't even know if I can talk about it at all."

I was yanked away from my seat then and into Colt's lap, his nose going into my hair, one arm wrapping around me and holding me still when I went to move, the other drawing my breakfast closer.

"Just stay, Riley," Colt said, his voice muffled by my hair. "Please."

"So you're gonna give this a go?" I looked up to see an

awfully pale Blake staring across the table at me. "These fucks need to learn to shut the hell up anyway, but…" He swallowed hard. "You're gonna try things with us?"

I studied them all then, every eye in the place on me, and that was a weird sensation. No, it was a familiar one, but one I could have sworn I'd let go of. But here we were, the adults in the room now, and it was us that had to make the decisions.

"You're going to hurt me—"

"No, Riley," Fen said with absolute certainty, but I held up a hand, indicating I needed to finish this.

"You have an omega out there. Who bloody knows, maybe when you're out and about in the city, some girl who would've become an omega in Bordertown but has been stuck here will go through a late reveal and then you'll find her. But…"

Colt's hand stroked up and down my thigh, his other arm holding me tight, so tight around my waist. I was done fighting, done doing the old alphas' jobs for them. Whatever this was, it'd proven to me that we at least deserved a chance to try things.

So that was what I told them.

"You'll never regret this," Fen said, a gentle smile spreading across his face. "I promise you that. If I have to ride every one of these fucks—"

"And we ride you," Ryan muttered.

"Then this is the way it is going forward. And you should fucking know better, Haze."

The man himself sat back at that, arms crossed, every scrap of amusement drained from him. His skin looked too pale, his eyes too bright as he faced the rest of us.

"I should. I do. I did." He shook his head, then chanced a sidelong look at me. "I'm sorry, to both of you." A series of snorts around the table at that. "I crack inappropriate jokes when I'm bored, uncomfortable, sometimes even when I'm pissed, but today?" He straightened up then, loosening his arms across his chest. "Today I was jealous as fuck. I wanted to be in that bed. I wanted to walk in here half naked and reeking of her. I want her on my lap."

Which to me just raised a whole other set of issues. They might be the only alphas in the world dating a beta, but I had literally no idea how to build a relationship between five men without hurting someone.

The thing was, I might not, but they did.

Colt pressed a kiss to the back of my neck and then loosened his hold on me.

"Go to him," he said.

"But, Colt—"

"Go to him. It's fine." I turned in his lap to look at him over my shoulder, and he stared up at me. "I was walking on air when I came in here, but what you just said?" He pulled me close then, twisting me around until my head rested on his chest. "It means that there's potential for more times like this. So many more. Throw Haze a bone. For all our bullshit, we know how to share, and you don't."

And with that, he pushed my breakfast across the table for Haze to collect.

Getting up and walking away from Colt was hard to do, especially as everyone watched me move, but Haze reached for me, taking the need to make decisions away from me as he pulled me onto his lap.

"I'm sorry, Riley girl," he said, just to me, the usual chatter starting up again across the table. "I'd love to tell you I won't do it again, but…" I snorted at that, knowing very well what Haze was like. "This makes it easier, I'll say that." He rubbed his hand up and down my thigh, then continued, "Now eat your breakfast before Blake twists my head off like a bottlecap."

Eating brekky perched on someone's lap was kinda weird, but I couldn't seem to bring myself to find my own seat. Blake started ferrying over platters of food, placing them on the table, and everyone helped themselves, a much more companionable silence settling over the table, until Fen broke it.

"You're not getting Riley today either," he informed Haze. "I'm taking her out for the day."

"Some would say it would be useful to ask the woman in question first," I said, not daring to look up at him.

The thought of going out one-on-one with Fen? It sent through me a thrill of fear, anticipation, and something else that was hard to define—something he seemed to sense as he caught me taking a sidelong look at him.

"You know how this works," he said, green eyes burning into mine. "It's within my rights to demand you sit on my lap, not Haze's. If we are actually going to do this, as you said, then it means spending time with each one of us, and today is my day."

"The others didn't get a whole day," I replied, and this drew chuckles from around the table, Fen seeming to smile despite himself.

"No, but you know them a lot better than you do me. I'm asking for the chance to do that, Riley. To get to know you better."

That was smart, playing the logical angle, and I nodded in response.

"Sooo…any details you want to share with me?"

I nibbled on my toast, all the guys snickering at that.

"You'll find out," Fen replied mildly, turning back to his paper. "Just wear something comfortable."

Chapter 26

So here I was, dressed in a pair of pants and sneakers that were hopefully casual enough for any context, but also wearing a nice shirt that was passable in a more formal context. My main issue was my bra though. I'd put on the green lacy one, thinking hey, if this wasn't a date bra day, what was, but after being a solid B cup since I became a teenager, apparently, I had grown. Ryan caught me manhandling my breasts, trying to wedge them into cups that were now too small, his eyebrows jerking up as I exited Colt's room.

"Somehow, my tits have gotten bigger," I told him in a huff. "Like, they've stayed the same all this time, but…"

My voice fell away as he pulled my hands back, and then I realised he wasn't just some friend I was discussing this with, he was…a potential lover. That thought had me stepping backwards, but he came with me, reaching in under the neckline of my shirt and running his fingers along the line of my cleavage.

"You look perfect, trust me. Fen's gonna shit when he sees you."

His voice, deep and even, settled me enough that I could leave my damn breasts alone.

"Fen's gonna shit over what?" The man himself emerged from his room, blinked, then stalked down the hall to us, those jade green eyes seeming to take everything in. "Jesus, Riley, you look beautiful." I went to snort at that, but he shook his head slowly. "You do. Maybe we shouldn't go anywhere. I could rent us some movies. We could sit in my room and munch popcorn—"

"You could take her lingerie shopping," Ryan suggested. "She's saying her bra feels too tight."

"Ah, no, that won't be…"

I went to protest, but the two of them shared a look then, a dark one and full of meaning.

"We'll make a pit stop at a department store before we get to where I'm taking you," Fen said with a slow smile. "I want to make sure you're comfortable."

"You want to go bra shopping with me?" I asked with a blink.

"If I get to help choose some of what you try on, I'll find the process very stimulating," he replied, then held out a hand to me. "C'mon, let's go."

I reached out and slid my hand in his, feeling a shiver of something that wasn't there with the others. I might feel need, or ache for them, like I was finally able to do something I'd always longed for, but this was different. Fen had dictated all the ways we'd interacted before, pulling me close, deciding to sit with me, indicating I had to eat. Now, the choice was mine.

So off we went, driving into town in the ute Ryan had taken me out in the other day, Fen just smiling when I tried to pepper him with questions.

"Let's get you comfortable first," he said, his eyes sliding to my bustline. "I can feel how much that bra is irritating you."

And with that, we arrived at one of the big shopping centres.

"CAN I HELP YOU?"

The shop assistant zeroed in on Fen, and why the hell not?

He towered over everyone here, his jeans and T-shirt doing nothing to mask the overt masculinity of his frame. Our actors, male models, even our politicians tried to emulate the way alphas looked. It was our blueprint for masculine perfection, and she was just taking a closer look at something she wouldn't often get an opportunity to. I admit, I did wrap my fingers around his arm possessively, and he just smiled at that.

"I'm looking for some lingerie for my mate," he replied.

Her reaction was just a precursor for the way everyone would respond and I needed to get used to that, but her look of surprise as she then checked me out, looking for what the hell was going on with my poor beta arse that let me catch a guy like him, had me smiling tightly in response.

"So what're we thinking? Just the usual bra and underwear sets, or something a little more exciting?"

Her voice was a purr and pitched at him, not me, something that made his lips thin down. She didn't seem to see the way his eyes flashed in warning, maybe she just figured it was for a whole other reason, but this wasn't going well for her. He turned to me, and I felt that little moment of shock I always felt when I had his attention. The shop assistant was young, gorgeous, and looked much more put together than I did, but his focus was entirely on me.

"What do you think, love?"

Power sharing, that was what was going on here. Alphas deferred to people as a strategic thing, to consciously make them aware that they were now in the driver's seat, when they could so easily take control of things. He did it now because it forced the shop assistant to do the same. She made herself smile as her focus shifted to me.

"You'd be about a C cup, right?" she asked, looking me up and down and measuring me with her eyes.

"What? No, I've always been a B."

"Well, not anymore by the look of it," she said, then bustled through the racks, stopping to select a few things before holding them up to me. "Black would look stunning on you with all that red hair, but I'll grab some white and beige as well, to make sure you have some basics. If you thought you were a B cup, you'll need a new everything, I'm guessing. These are cute, and the lilac will do amazing things to your skin…"

And so I ended up shoved into a change room with fifty million different bras hanging on the hooks, just staring at the new tags, unable to believe what I was seeing.

"How're we doing for fit?" the sales assistant asked. "If they're too tight, we might have to look at some D cups."

D? D! There was no freaking way I was a D. As if to demonstrate exactly that, I tore my shirt off, then my bra, my breasts aching already. When I looked down, I saw that the lace and elastic had left red imprints on my skin, so everything felt super sensitive right now. I grabbed the first bra, a kind of bland, everyday beige one, and slipped it on.

As I looked at the mirror, my heart sank. I played around with the way my breasts were lying inside the cup, but there was no getting around it. The bra fit, but just. There was no spillage out the top of the cups or the sides, yet. I could get my mind around the fact my breasts had suddenly grown a cup size, but something made me think that it wouldn't be long before I'd be right back here, looking for another upgrade.

"Fen…" I wasn't sure where my alpha was, my voice high and thready, but he appeared outside the change room curtain in seconds, making me wonder if he'd been there all along. "Is there a reason why my body is changing?"

"Just get something you feel comfortable in," he said. "We'll talk in the car."

I heard him talking in a low voice to the shop assistant, but I couldn't seem to bring myself to listen in. I pulled the bra off and then stared at my topless body for a second.

I'd always been fine being on the smaller bust side of things. I got that a large percentage of the dude population wanted his girl's cups to runneth over, but literally everything was easier with smaller tits—cute bras, going without a bra, running and any other sport, no back pain. Looking like Venus with arms was hard damn work, Candy had informed me of this many times, and as I stared, I was beginning to realise that somehow, I was going to join her in the ranks. My hands shook as I brought them up, but when they cupped each breast, my breath sucked in so fast, it felt like my lungs would collapse.

Having my nipples touched, stroked, plucked, pinched, sucked... All of these were things I enjoyed a lot. It wasn't something I did much when I was on my own, as it never did anything for me, but now? I gasped, great heady bolts of pleasure rocketing through me at the most basic of caresses.

"Riley?" Fen said quietly from beyond the curtain. "Riley, are you OK?"

I couldn't seem to reply, my fingers moving very, very slowly over my nipples, my teeth sinking into my lips to stop myself from reacting.

What the fucking hell was going on? There was no way I was supposed to be this damn sensitive. Like, sometimes my breasts swelled up a little and got super sore when I was on my period, but not like this. They didn't feel like ouchy bundles of oversensitive nerve endings. This was like my own breasts had been wiped away and replaced with breasts 2.0—bigger, firmer, not a freaking hint of sag, and fuck...so damn sensitive. I dared to pinch one nipple, almost dropping to my knees at the sudden rush of pleasure.

"Riley, I'm coming in," Fen said, ducking through the curtain, then stopping still once he was in.

Those green eyes caught me red-handed, literally. I flushed hot, feeling sweat prickle across my brow as he stared, watching my fingers continue to move, the promise of pleasure enough that they kept testing what frighteningly new sensations could be pulled from my body.

Fen breathed out slowly, a long exhale filling the small change room, then he stepped closer and gently brushed my hands away to the sound of my little cry of discontent, his hand slapping down over my mouth.

"Can you be quiet, Riley girl?" he whispered. "Can you be

oh so quiet, no matter what happens? I can give you a bit of relief before we get you a new bra." I made a small grunt of complaint, and he just shook his head slowly. "I'll explain everything, I promise. Just be a good girl right now and be very, very quiet."

He chose to trust me, pulling his hand away, then dropping both to where I needed them the most.

Fuck, my teeth sank deeper, drawing actual blood, if the little trickle of copper in my mouth was anything to go by, but that small pain was more than offset by the feel of him. No matter how much bigger my breasts had gotten, his hands were larger, those warm, callused palms covering me, giving me the heat and sensation I didn't know I craved. Then they moved, just abrading my nipples lightly, making my breasts feel like they swelled further under his attention before his fingers went to work.

My hand went to his waist, trying to stabilise myself the minute they bit down, as it felt like he grasped the base of my nipples, then drew them out from my body, the stretching sensation sending wave after wave of pleasure through me. My cunt clenched frantically in response, as if to exorcise this intense feeling, and I let out the tiniest of whines, feeling so bloody empty.

He was going to make me come, I could feel that with a deadly certainty. Somehow, Fen seemed to know exactly what to do, how hard, how often to caress me, bringing me higher, higher—

"Everything OK in there?" the shop assistant asked. "How's the sizing?"

"Riley asked me to take a look," Fen replied. "I think we'll need some bras in the next size up. Something in a stretchy fabric, if possible, but still supportive."

"Oh!" I could almost hear the cogs inside the woman's head whirling as she worked to put two and two together—what we were doing, how she should respond, and more importantly, how she could get Fen to do the same to her.

Holy fucking batshit, where the hell had that paranoia come from?

But he just stared down at me with eyes blazing silver, watching my face transform into a snarl, then a silent gasp of pleasure and back again.

"OK," she said finally. "I'll grab the same items in the next size up, and then your mate can take a look."

Your mate. They were the words I needed to hear, but what I really wanted to feel was this. Fen stared down at me with deadly focus, drawing me along now, faster and faster, pulling pleasure from my body with expert precision until my hand slapped over my own mouth and it all came to a head.

I deserved a damn medal for staying silent through this, because when I came, it felt like a sudden explosion of golden light, each separate mote a small burst of pleasure, each one fusing with the other, growing and growing until I started to feel like it was never going to stop. Then Fen yanked me close as my legs gave out, my cunt pulsing, pulsing frantically, trying to clamp down on what was missing inside me.

"Here's some new pieces to try," a voice said, the shop assistant thrusting her hand through the curtain to pass us a cluster of garments. Fen took them and hung them up, pressing a kiss to my forehead before pulling away.

"I'll leave Riley to try them on and see if they fit better," he told her.

I didn't want that at all, something pathetically needy forcing me to reach for his hand. He squeezed it, then let me go, ducking out of the change room.

SO FIFTEEN MINUTES LATER, I ended up walking out the proud owner of a brand-new set of bras. Some were Cs. I couldn't seem to let that go, but most were like the one I was wearing now—a simple number in a stiff beige Lycra. The wired cups seemed to both stretch around me and hold me still and supported as we walked swiftly back to the car, but it was a size D… I waited like a good little girl right up until we were inside the cab of the car before I turned to him.

"What the actual fuck was that?" I asked.

"I thought we had more time," he said, raking his hands through his hair. "Ryan and I had some concerns when you said your bra wasn't really fitting properly."

"That's what the meaningful look was? That I might have bigger tits that all of sudden were super sensitive? Like little fucking clits. I like breast play as much as anyone, but it's *never* done that to me before."

And with that, he fucking grinned, looking so damn pleased with himself.

"This is not something to be smiling about."

He turned in his seat then and regarded me steadily.

"No, it's something to celebrate. Alpha pheromones, baby— that's what this is about. Your body must have been on board with the idea of taking us as mates before you finally admitted it to yourself, because you've been responding to them." He swallowed then, as if aware of the potential shitstorm he was about to unleash. "It's probably because your latent omega genes are switching on."

He was right to be worried, because right now, I just fucking stared. I stared and stared at the man whose very presence was changing my body against my will, my hands going defensively to my chest.

My nipples were still sensitive, but not as much as before, which raised my next question.

"What's happened to me?" I asked through gritted teeth. "What did you do?"

"You're going through what an omega does before his or her heat. Your body… We call it ripening. If we were a mated pack, we'd have you holed up on our territory, tending to you day and night. You've got some time before…we'll need to tend you again."

"What does ripening mean? And what do you mean by tending?"

"In an omega, it's when their body starts to make the changes required for mating. If you had been born an omega, we might have chosen each other but you wouldn't ripen for a few years. We would have been able to have sex, but no knotting would take place. The omega always chooses when they're ready. In female omegas, it's when she's ready to have children, and while male omegas are the same, his mates have to find a surrogate."

Fen actually looked abashed for the first time since I'd known him, his gaze dropping and returning to me over and over, a red stain across his cheekbones showing me how he felt about this.

"And tending?"

He let out a sigh at that, his hands forming fists. "We create this change in an omega's body, so it's our responsibility to help our mate through it." He saw my eyes widen, then reached out and took my hand. "It won't hurt you, not unless..."

"Not unless what?" I asked sharply, the hysterical edge in my voice apparent. "Not unless what, Fen?"

"Not unless you resist our attempts to soothe you through this. What's happening to you, it's designed to bring us closer, allow bonding to happen. We'll stroke your breasts, play with your nipples, sensitise them over and over again and drown you in as many orgasms as you can take." His eyes were purest silver now, his wolf looking out at me, making clear what would happen if I tried to fight that. "But if you keep us at arm's length?"

He shook his head then, as if to displace the beast and bring back the man, but he wasn't successful.

"It'll hurt you, Riley. Nature's a fucking bitch that way, but it will."

And didn't I know it? All our beta preoccupations with equality and considerate, respectful relationships were an entirely human construct. But the animal world? It was brutal.

Cute little dolphins regularly drowned their female counterparts during mating season. So did ducks and geese. A male lion killed all of the cubs in a pride he took over to trigger the lionesses' mating cycle. Female praying mantises bit off the heads of their mates and some spiders famously consumed their much tinier male mates after the deed was done. Male honeybees got to mate once, because the process ripped off their dicks and forced them to explode inside the queen, and then there were the chimpanzees.

Waging a war of terror on females for years leading up to mating, they often hit, bit and charged the females, sometimes wounding them, creating an atmosphere of intimidation that helped ensure the female's submission when it came time to mate.

"How long do we have?" I asked, not specifying for what, but he knew.

"Until you need me to tend to you again? At least a few hours. That'll get shorter the further along things go, until—"

"I get it," I said with a wave of my hand. "We're going to need to think of some way to get through things at work."

"We'll do whatever it takes, Riley. You know that. Do you want to head home? That might be wise, what with—"

"If we've got a few hours, let's use them," I replied with a shake of my head, turning to put my seatbelt on, but I had to be a lot more careful about doing that now. "What did you have planned?"

Chapter 27

"Axe throwing?" I asked with a yelp as we pulled up to the front of a building with the sign listing the place as Maniaxe hanging over the front door. It had bright red external walls, and as we got out of the car, a thumping industrial soundtrack greeted us.

"I figure you'd had a tough week, and throwing some sharp objects around might make you feel a little relaxed," he said with a grin. "If you hate it—"

"Nah, I'll give it a go," I said as I walked in.

The place had a dark wood interior, long lanes screened off from each other by floor to ceiling walls of cyclone mesh and Perspex. At the end, the walls had been panelled with rough wooden pallets, with targets painted there, and big, tall men stepped up and threw axes that spun through the air. Those that landed in the middle of the targets received a shout of approval, and those that didn't? In the universal way of dudes, they got howled down by their friends, much joking and shoving around happening until the next person stepped up.

But I didn't pay too much attention to them. It was the bright silver of the axes that caught my eye, those sharp blades flashing and flashing, right up until they buried themselves into the wood. He was right—something about that, the brutal effi-ciency of the axe and the way it was thrown, it called to me. I started drifting closer to one of the lanes, when a massive man stepped in our way.

"I'm Bjorn," he said, holding out a hand to Fen.

"Fen Vanguard and Riley Taylor," Fen replied, shaking his hand.

"You've got a booking," Bjorn confirmed with a nod of his head. "Though I gotta admit, when you said you were throwing with a Riley, I thought she was a he." My eyes rolled his way, narrowing down at his words. "Hey, no harm, no foul." He held his massive hands up. "I think it's cool that chicks dig axe throwing too. So, did you want to have a go as—?"

"Yes," I replied

"OK then. Well, you're booked in for a couple of hours, so let's get you started."

We were given some forms and typical disclaimers to sign, making sure we were aware of the dangers, then as Bjorn was getting our axes together, Fen sat down next to me.

"Nervous?" he asked with a smile, grabbing a pen and starting to fill out the form, but it wasn't the axe I was thinking about. I watched those long, strong fingers and the way they gripped the pen and was instantly taken back.

"No, just…memories," I said, shaking my head before going to fill out my own forms.

"Oh, you can't just leave me hanging like that," he said, looking at me across the top of his clipboard.

I glanced up and then smiled ruefully back at him.

"I just used to watch you so damn closely when Miss Catherine put you at the front of the class 'to be a role model.'"

"She just wanted to get me away from my damn brothers," Fen said, "thinking that would be enough to get us to shut up, not realising I was the one to keep them quiet when I could." He snorted at that, then reached over and grabbed my hand. "What brought that memory back?"

"Your hands," I said, my eyes dropping to the form and

moving to keep filling it out, but he placed one of those hands on top of it. "You always had such beautiful hands, and I found I couldn't stop watching you writing. We were only kids, maybe thirteen or fourteen? I was crushing on you so bad, so I couldn't keep my bloody eyes off you. It's why I always sat towards the front, so I was forced not to stare, but then Miss Catherine sat you in front of me and—"

"Off to your right," he finished for me, his smile faltering. "You were always nestled into the wall, hidden behind a pile of books." His eyes studied mine. "I was crushing on you pretty bad myself."

"Oh, teenage me would've been so pleased to hear that," I said in a self-effacing tone.

"I wish I'd told her." And just like that, he sucked all the humour out of that moment, something he seemed to realise as he stiffened, but once he'd taken that leap, he couldn't seem to stop. "I wish she'd known how long I stared at her, at the way her ponytail fell against her shoulder blades. At the pull of her shirt across her shoulders. At her hand moving lightning fast, always the first one to get all the notes down. You put the rest of us to shame, but me, I was proud. We always knew you were smart, Riley, which just made me try harder to get your attention, to get in your face. God knows I wasn't gonna be able to go toe-to-toe with you when it came to school smarts."

He reached across and grabbed my hand and gave it a squeeze.

"All I could do was tease her, follow her, be there for her, whether she wanted me or not, because that's all I had to give her."

I blinked then, mentally picking up Fen's version of what had happened at school, turning it around and around, looking for the flaws in the arguments.

"It's all I'll ever be able to give you, Riley. I don't understand science like you do. I've had betas try to explain it to me because I'm not a fucking idiot, but I just find myself zoning out. Maybe we're wired differently. Perhaps you can find something in your studies to explain that. It's like you guys can pick and pick at a thing until all you have are the parts, whereas all I'm interested in is keeping things whole. Keeping us whole."

I smiled at that, then went back to filling in my form.

"Alphas are systems thinkers, so you have more in common with scientists than you think. It's just your focus is on the complex web of interconnected relationships between people, whereas ours is on the building blocks of life itself."

"So what do we have when we're together, as a pack?" he prompted gently.

"I don't know," I said. "And that's got my attention." He grinned at that. "I guess that's what we try and find out?"

"How're we doing here?" Bjorn asked in a chipper tone, both of us jumping as a result. It felt like he'd appeared from nowhere. We quickly finished off our forms and then pushed them his way. "All right, I'm going to take you through a safety and throwing basics tutorial, and then you can have a go. The good thing is axe throwing is more of a precision sport than a strength based one, so you're both on relatively equal footing here."

I snorted at that, then eyed Fen's massive form. His biceps were huge, so how that could be true, I didn't know, but I was about to find out.

"SO THE FIRST thing you need to know is that this is not your usual axe. They have a broad head." Bjorn gestured to the axe he was holding. "And these have much slimmer heads, which allow them to dig into the wood without a huge amount of effort."

He threw the axe with a nonchalant ease, and it spun through the air and dug into the wood like it was no big thing.

"So it's not about throwing an axe with all your might, to try and bury it in the concrete behind the wood. It's about getting your form right and going for accuracy."

Bjorn showed us all of this—how to throw one- and two-handed, how and where to stand, where the onlookers needed to stand for safety purposes, how not to throw too high and too low and what to do if you did. The axes fell onto the rubber mat over and over as he showed us the wrong way to do things. Then finally, he stepped free of the lane and gestured for Fen to have a go.

So he'd picked the perfect date to take me on. I was itching to have a go, as it seemed like a simple activity which didn't require too much skill, since despite my ability inside the classroom, PE had been the death of me.

I wasn't super clumsy or anything, but my body didn't naturally do what it needed to with enough speed, grace, or skill, not like I did in theory classes. My sheer ordinariness when it came to sport kinda infuriated me. Then there was them.

Watching the Vanguards playing sport was a painful thing. While they could be restless or find it hard to focus in the classroom—well, Haze, Fen, and Ryan did—on the field was a whole other thing. They were demons on the football field, the basketball court, or whatever sport we were forced to play. I'd be trying to follow the instructions, thinking if I focussed hard enough, I'd uncover the secrets of how to be good at sport. But then the boys would strip their shirts off, moving like panthers in pack formation, and like every other girl there waiting on the sidelines, I would just sigh.

Like I did right now. One of Fen's boots was planted against the line, the other supporting his weight behind him. His T-shirt stretched over his body, revealing his epic musculature to everyone here, or so it felt, before his hand whipped forward, sending the axe flying through the air.

Thud! When the head buried itself into the wood, Fen turned to me with that same boyish grin on his face, and somehow, that made everything all right. Even if he was Alpha Vanguard now, he was still my Fen.

My Fen.

Sometimes, you want something for so long, you get tied to the wanting and don't really know what to do with the having.

He was my Fen if I wanted him—he'd made that clear. If I went over and slid a hand up the back of his shirt, the way I'd always dreamed, that smile would only grow wider. He wanted me to touch him, discover him, in all the ways I'd thought about as a teenager, and to be blunt, all the ways I'd wanted to since. So when he turned to me with an expectant look in his eyes, my nipples pulsing traitorously, I had to remind myself why we were here.

That's right—throwing axes.

I ambled over and grabbed an axe as directed from the bucket, hefting it slightly to get a feel for it. Not super heavy or anything. Bjorn smiled encouragingly but seemed to sense that he shouldn't get too close, if the sidelong look he shot at Fen was anything to go by.

"You might want to try the two-handed throw first…" he started to say, but Fen moved in, stepping up and then pressing his front against my back, those strong arms going around mine.

"You know you could let me just have a go first," I said, pretending like this wasn't exactly where I wanted to be.

"And where's the fun in that?" he murmured against my hair. "I wanna stay right here for as long as I can. All right, thumbs running along the shaft." I snickered at that word, demonstrating with exaggerated care that I had the proper grip. "Don't hold it too tight. Aim it where you want it to go, and then…"

He didn't direct my throw, just supported me as I made it, my heart in my throat as soon as the axe left my fingers, but that reassuring *clunk* sound as the blade bit into the wood was everything.

"Well done!" Bjorn said. "All right, let's do a few practice rounds, try each of the different throws, and then we can try something a little more competitive."

I'D HEARD about axe throwing before and just dismissed it as some kind of hipster bullshit, but now that I was having a go, I was beginning to see the appeal. In some ways, it was a perfect sport for a beginner, as the learning curve wasn't that high. I snuck looks at the other lanes, saw big men performing more complex throws, but at its heart, it was a deceptively simple activity. Then Bjorn started to make things more challenging.

Our axes were all stowed away safely when he produced some balloons, tying them to different parts of the target, giving us new areas to focus on.

"Five balloons," Bjorn said with a grin. "Whoever ends up with the most popped wins."

"A competition? Care to make this interesting, Red?" Fen asked in a low purr.

"What, you want to create a pot?" I asked, reaching for my wallet, but he just shook his head.

"Money doesn't really interest me," he said, his eyes sliding over me, thankfully with his back to Bjorn. My eyebrow jerked up in response to his innuendo.

"So winner gets what?" I asked, kinda dreading what he would say and wanting to hear it more than I wanted my next breath.

"Winner decides what they get," he said with a slow grin.

Well, all right then. I grabbed an axe from the bucket, forcing him to step away from the line, a new-found determination pulsing through me. My brain had like ten years of stuff it'd fantasised about Fen doing, and I wasn't about to walk away from the chance of getting them all fulfilled.

I took a breath as I stood on the line, trying to do what Bjorn had said and centre myself. Shut out the noise, the guys shouting down in the other lanes, the music, even Fen. Shut it all out and just feel my body, feel the axe in my hand.

I wish I could say that some ancient wolfish ancestor rose up and directed my hand, but it didn't. Instead, I was forced to shove my overly analytical mind to one side and just feel the science rather than apply it. Forward momentum, speed, thrust, angle, grip. I drew the axe back, my eyes entirely on the blue balloon that bobbed slightly, and then I let go.

That same feeling I'd felt when I finished my year twelve

exams, when I completed my degree, when I worked on something really tough at work, rushed through me as the axe went flying through the air, and then *pop!* The balloon exploded.

Admittedly, it was the yellow one, not the blue one, but still.

"Well done!" Bjorn said. "Next thrower up."

Chapter 28

Somehow, I was winning.

I frowned as yet another of Fen's axes got close but not close enough, staring up at him as he turned to me, some of his cockiness gone now.

"You're not choking on purpose?" I asked, scanning him intensely, as if I could see evidence of that on his body, which of course, I couldn't.

"Why would I throw the competition?" he asked, looking faintly irritated. "I had ideas, many, many ideas of what I wanted."

Ulp.

I was about to ask what, needing to know like I needed my next breath, but then I saw that Bjorn was waiting patiently behind Fen's shoulder and thought better of that. My body however… Something was different about today. Apart from the buzz of being given an orgasm just from twiddling my nipples, I felt a spring in my step as I walked up to the axe bucket, a strength in my arm, and a certainty in my body as I lined myself up to take my next throw.

If I got this balloon, then I'd win. Fen had taken out one

balloon, me two, and there were only five in total. I took a deep breath and settled myself before letting the axe fly.

"Yes!" I shouted, throwing my arms in the air as I heard that pop. "Yesssss!" Fen smirked, then shook his head as I did a little victory lap, running around the table he was leaning against. "Winner, winner, chicken dinner and you're the loser, loser, chicken… How does it go?"

"It doesn't," he said, yanking me closer, those green eyes flaring. "You're not supposed to rub it in the loser's face."

"Oh, shit."

"Well done, guys!" Bjorn said, coming over. "I've just got some people I need to get started. We're down a man today, but I'll send one of the other guys over to keep an eye on you. Just remember, no throwing without a staff member present."

As he moved away, Fen's hands slid lower, cupping my arse.

"I'm gonna go and get us some water," he said. "Keep you hydrated. Just sit tight." He lifted me up and placed me on one of the stools facing the lanes. "I'll be back in a sec."

I missed him and the warmth of his body the minute he pulled away, some part of me wanting to reach out, drag him back, and not let him go. I wasn't that girl, I knew that, but… I watched him go, that biteable arse showcased in perfectly fitting jeans as he walked over to the small bar they had set up, then pulled my phone out, tempted to take a photo and show Candy, when something else occurred to me.

The changes to my body. I frowned as it felt like I focussed on that for the first time. I'd been walking around in a haze of post-orgasm bliss since the shopping centre, and it felt like that popped only now. I opened up my texts and sent a quick one off to my partner in crime.

R: Stop sucking dick and ring me. Urgent.

One, two, three…

My phone obediently started ringing, and I accepted the call.

"How the hell did you know that's what I was doing?" Candy said. "Are you stalking me again? Because if I liked girls,

I assure you it'd be your muff I'd be diving on into, but while you don't have a dick, it's a no from me."

"Because the minute five PM Friday rolls around, you're gobbling cockmeat sandwich right up until Sunday night," I shot back. "Now, enough about your predilection for hoovering dick, I've got something for the study."

"Of course you do," she said with a groan. "Repeat after me—all work and no dick makes Riley a very dull girl. Say it."

"How about my tits have gone up at least a size, maybe more, and apparently, I'm so damn sensitive now, I can come from nipple play alone."

"Shut the fuck up." Silence, actual silence, coming down the phone line let me know how much of her attention I had. "Really?"

"Really."

Trying to keep things clinical, I filled her in on our morning's hijinks—the changes in my body, this need for 'tending.' I admit, now I was sitting down and focussing, I was beginning to feel a little…antsy. But hey, I was throwing axes with the guy I'd spent my teenage years fantasising over so…

"So they're going to need to tend to you on a regular basis until you… Shit, when was your last period?"

"What?" I asked.

"When was your last period? They're talking about things escalating, and I'd be willing to bet ovulation is gonna be what pushes you over the edge. C'mon, Riles, you've read the theories about omega's heats. The first one comes not long after he or she chooses their mate, and then at three-month intervals until—"

"They have kids," I said. "But that's not what's happening here."

"Isn't it? We need to get you into the lab, take some swabs. Breasts can increase up to twenty-five percent during sex if a girl's having a good time, but that increased blood flow is a temporary thing. What if this is part of what an omega goes through, your latent genes pumping more and more blood to all your good bits—"

"Keeping me in a state of continual sexual arousal."

I whispered that last bit, turning around to see Fen chatting to the guy at the bar.

"But is this permanent? Will your body go through a second puberty, laying down fatty and fibrous tissue, increasing your milk ducts in preparation…"

Her voice trailed away. No, not really, just my ability to listen to it. Was this what was happening? Was I changing? Was a secret part of me switching on, changing me, making me into—

"Well, well, what do we have here?"

My eyes jerked around to see some of the guys making all the noise down in the other lanes had come over, clustering around my table. The speaker, a massive blond dude that made Thor look like a little freaking baby, leaned over, putting his arms on the end of my table, probably to draw attention to his freak-ishly large biceps. Candy was still talking excitedly, but I wasn't hearing it, because as I took a deep breath in, I was hit with something I shouldn't have been able to smell.

I knew my pack's scents because even though I was a beta, I wasn't anosmic, but all of a sudden, I got a glimpse into what alphas and omegas experience. I was hit by this rich, dense scent. Part wood, part smoke, and was that an earthy, peaty undertone? Kinda like the way Scotch tastes. My mouth filled with saliva then, something I quickly swallowed as my heart began to race.

Run. There was that pulsing instinct again. *Run!* she insisted, deep inside me, but I dug my fingers into the wooden tabletop, hanging on for dear life.

"And what's a pretty like you doing sitting here all on her own?" Thor dude asked. "I'm Mark, and this is my pack." He held out a hand then, something I just stared at, like I was an alien that had no understanding of social rituals at all, while somehow, I understood this all too well.

Don't touch him. That beat strong and true inside me. *Don't let him touch you.*

So I pulled away, wanting to put as much distance between him and me as I could without actually running, because I knew what this was and what that would do.

He was an alpha, though what the fuck they were doing in the city, I didn't know. His scent, his pack's scent, filled my lungs, choking me, and he was looking at me like I'd just announced it was steak and blow job day and I was the one about to administer them.

Like I was an omega.

"Shake hands now," he said in a deceptively friendly voice, the thread of command almost disguised by the tone, and my hand twitched in response. "You don't want to be rude."

But I did, I really did. I wanted to use said hands to flip the guy off, tell him to back the fuck off to his lanes, and leave me the fuck alone, but my lips didn't move and my hand just did as it was told, sliding slowly across the tabletop. He watched it come closer with a satisfied smile, the guys around him rumbling in appreciation.

"What the fuck do you think you're doing?"

Fen's voice was like a welcome splash of water on my face, breaking Mark's hold on me, allowing me to jerk my hand back. I cradled it against my chest like a wounded bird, but as Fen shoved himself between the other alphas and me, I found my shaking hands grabbing my phone.

"...so maybe it's a wholesale shift in your endocrine system—"

"Candy," I croaked out. "I need you to listen. Meet me at the lab. We'll be there soon."

"Yeah, sure, I'll just send the guys home and be there in fifteen?"

Guys? Of course she had guys.

"Done."

"Who the fuck do you think you are, coming near my mate?" Fen snapped.

"Mate?" Mark replied, a mocking edge to his voice. "Didn't see any marks on her, and she doesn't smell mated at all.

Wanting to be mated? Yeah, we got that the minute she walked in the place. You bring an omega that fucking ripe into a place like this—?"

Mark's reply was cut off as Fen's hand went to the other alpha's shirt, gripping it tight as he lifted the other man up, dragging his face closer.

"She's not for you," Fen rumbled, his voice so much deeper and distorted by his beast. "She's mine!"

"Hey, hey, what the hell is going on in here?" Bjorn asked, having rushed over. "Mark, take your boys and piss off back to your lane or you're out." But Mark didn't respond. "Look, if you two are gonna throw down—"

I was down and off my stool in a second, pushing between the two men in the next.

"I don't want you," I said, injecting every bit of anger, irritation, frustration, and yeah, fear into my voice as I addressed Mark. "You're not the one for me. He is." Fen jolted as my fingers did what they'd always longed to—they slid up and under his shirt, touching some of that taut, hot skin. "He's always been the one for me."

"So why hasn't he marked you yet?" Mark jerked himself free of Fen's grip to the sound of my alpha's growl. The stranger alpha slid his eyes over me so slowly, it almost felt like something I could feel. "Pretty little firecracker like you? Me and my boys, we'd look after you so right."

But I was pulled behind Fen, his body a barrier between the other pack and me.

"You don't even know what you're saying," he snapped. "You have no fucking idea what she needs or who she is."

"And you do? How the fuck haven't you marked her yet? She smells so fucking creamy. She needs tending, and we're the guys—"

Thud, thud!

Bjorn contravened all the carefully explained rules of the place, slamming two axes down onto the table, forcing the alphas to jump back or get sliced.

"Everyone needs to calm the fuck down and piss off back to their lanes, now!"

For a beta, the guy had an impressive voice on him.

"Riley, did you want to talk to Mark and his pack at all?" Bjorn asked me.

"Say yes, babe," Mark said in deadly purr. "We'll—"

"No," I replied, injecting every bit of scorn I could into my voice. The other alpha narrowed his eyes then.

"So you need to back the hell off and respect her boundaries, or I'm calling the cops," Bjorn said. "Whatever Neanderthal bullshit you guys pull out in the boonies does not fly here."

"Fine," Mark said, but the muscles in my body didn't relax until I saw them turn their backs on us. When they did, my body began to shake like I'd just escaped some life-and-death situation or something.

Adrenalin was pumping through me, that presence inside me pacing now, whining in my ears, drowning everything else out, but I couldn't afford the luxury of giving in to my emotions right now.

"What the hell were you thinking, bringing an unmated omega in here?" Bjorn said to Fen.

"She's not an omega and she's not unmated, just unmarked," Fen explained as he grabbed my hand and pulled me close. "Anyway, we're out of here."

"That's probably for the best," Bjorn said, trying for polite but sounding irritated.

Likely because we'd brought some kind of primitive love rite into his nice, neat establishment without even realising it.

Fen grabbed my hand, yanking me after him, even as he placed a call. He opened the door, then picked me up, putting me in my seat before slamming the door shut.

"Yeah, you need to meet us—" Fen began to say.

"At the lab," I croaked out, twisting and turning against the seatbelt. It felt wrong, constrictive, and not in a way I craved, my skin so sensitive right now. The fabric of my pants was stiff and artificial, my top coarse and scratchy.

"You sure?" Fen asked me.

"Close. Need samples."

That was all I could say, my eyes boring into his, pleading for him to just do as I said, even as a weird little whine escaped my lips.

"Meet us at Riley's lab. Things have escalated way faster than expected. She's beginning to transition. Yeah, I know, I didn't expect it either, but…" His eyes were blazing silver as they slid to me, just staring at me with this curious alien warmth. "But our girl, she needs tending, and she wants that done in the lab, so meet us there pronto."

The locks on the car doors were engaged as Mark and his pack emerged, eyeing us warily, but Fen already had the motor running, getting us out of the carpark and down the street at speed. He managed to rein that in once we were on the road, his eyes scanning the streets for dangers.

"Go left onto South Terrace," I said on a groan, my body flexing against the seatbelt. In some ways, the restraint was exactly what I needed, pressure on my skin, forcing me to stay where I was, but in some ways, it was the exact opposite. I stared at Fen as he chanced a look at me for way too long, imagining the belt being replaced by his arms, his body pressed hard against mine, but he jerked his eyes away and followed my directions.

"HOLY SHIT!" Candy gasped out when I almost fell out of the car, my hands clamping down on my breasts. They felt hard somehow and swollen—so swollen, I could almost feel the pulse of my blood into the veins running through them. "Jesus, Riley, what's happened?"

"She's transitioning," Fen snapped, scooping me up into his arms, and I didn't even protest. "Breathe me in, love." I obeyed automatically, pressing my nose to his neck and taking big lungfuls that seemed to settle me. "You lot wanted to study how omegas reveal? Well, you're about to see it up close and personal."

They talked about something, but the sounds came out all muffled and distorted, as if the conversation were being held under water, only becoming clear when the others came. My head jerked up as those spicy scents pushed through, infiltrating and meshing with Fen's.

"Hey there, Riley girl." Blake's voice was so soft, so warm, it was like a soothing blanket all over my skin, and I found myself reaching for him, his arms opening in response.

But Fen held me where I was. There was a slight growl, a sound that had me squirming in Fen's arms, but for what? I didn't know, just feeling an awful restlessness that I couldn't seem to shake off.

"What the fuck, Fen?" Haze snapped, shouldering forward.

"She's perfuming," Colt said, breathing in deep, and when he did, his eyelids fluttered shut for just a second. Then when he opened them again? A slow, carnal smile spread, one that reminded me just how good that mouth felt, right on my—

"We need to get her home, on our territory," Ryan said with a frown. "We need to protect her."

"We need to get her upstairs," Candy insisted, my lips peeling back from my teeth at the sight of a woman so close to my mates, but she just shook her head slowly. "This is what she asked for, to study this. Is this" —she waved vaguely at me— "a permanent state?"

"She'll come back online after we've tended to her," Fen informed her.

"OK, so tell me what the hell that means on the way upstairs, because this is what she wants."

When the woman swiped a card and opened up the elevator, the smaller space, the way it compressed all of our scents settled something in me, which would've been perfect, but for her... I eyed Candy suspiciously, even though she kept a scrupulous distance from us. My men, my pack, they were all clustered close, their skin touching mine, helping hold me until we were whisked out again, through doors, too many doors, and into a harshly lit space.

"Riley?" the woman asked, and I growled then because she was coming closer, even though her hands were held up in surrender. "You called me, remember? I was settled in for a long weekend of dick, and you made me send them home. You wanted to document what's happening to you."

It felt like my prefrontal cortex rudely shoved whatever haze I was simmering in to one side, then I blinked, seeing and feeling everything as if for the first time.

"Shit…" I hissed, then fought my way out of Fen's arms, my alpha setting me down on my feet. "Get the blood pressure cuff, the ECG, and some needles for a blood draw. Fuck, what else do we need?" I swiped my hand across my forehead, feeling it was slick with sweat. "A thermometer and some swabs for fluid samples."

"There's my girl," Candy said with a grin, then scurried off to do my bidding.

Chapter 29

"…an ultrasound of my breasts to try and look at what's causing the swelling," I said as I paced back and forth. "Like, are we talking increased blood flow or lymphatic swelling? Mammary gland engorgement?"

"Riley," Fen said, but I waved him off.

"Maybe a… Uh! A pelvic ultrasound for sure," I ground out as I felt a sharp stab not unlike period pain twist inside me.

"Riley," Colt said, moving forward, but I shied away.

"Do we do a brain scan? I don't think I can sit still for an MRI or CT," I said.

"Maybe after…?" Candy nodded to the guys that ranged at my back, her face twisting in concern, and that was what let me know there was a problem. Usually, me fighting a wave of intense sexual need would've had her rolling in the aisles, but right now?

"No, we need to capture as much data as we can while I'm like this," I insisted, because I knew something she would never understand.

Right now, there were two Rileys. One was a beta and a scientist, who was rubbing her fucking hands at the opportunity this presented. I could do whatever the hell I liked with my own body and beg for forgiveness afterwards. But the other? That wolfish whine in my body was just as alien as the deep throbbing need that pulsed inside me. I had to fight my feet to stop them from walking closer, the soft Lycra of my bra feeling intolerably coarse right now. My nipples ached, I ached, for them. It was like that persistent, nagging feeling of a toothache, but this one promised all of the pleasure if I just…

"We need to move fast," I said, the words spilling out so quickly, my tongue tripped over them. "Whatever this is, it's hitting me harder. I feel… I feel…"

"For fuck's sake," Candy hissed, but her focus was them, not me. "Take her into her office." She tossed Ryan a set of keys, wisely not coming any closer, my body feeling like a reddish haze hung over me. "Tend to her or whatever it is that you do. I can't see her like this."

"No," I said when arms went around me, when I was picked up again. "No!"

"Yes." Fen's order was short, sharp, and absolute, pushing my protests down and then obliterating them altogether. "You will experience this over and over until you accept us, so you can plan for it, mapping your responses more comprehensively than any omega before you."

"I'm not an omega," I whined in response.

"Yet." His voice, those cool green eyes, they stilled me then as he waited for me to understand. "Now's the time, Riley, for you to become what you were always supposed to be."

"Our mate," Blake said with a sharp nod. "C'mon, her needs are fucking clawing at me."

"Shh…" That was Haze, and he carried me close to his chest, my eyes searching his as I heard the tremor there. He smiled though, a shaky, sharp thing, his thumb brushing over my cheekbone. "Look at your eyes, baby girl. They're starting to silver."

"I need to document——" I began to say.

"Gimme your phone," Haze said, holding out a hand, but not specifying who should hand it over.

"Camera app is open," Ryan said, slapping his in Haze's hand.

My alpha took photos then, carefully making sure to record everything. This, this small act, helped my body uncoil.

"We've got you," Haze said, sensing my unspoken realisation and addressing it head-on. "We're honoured to be able to help you through it. This is everything we've fucking dreamed of, love. Everything."

"Dream?" I barely breathed the word as I was swept into my office, all the stuff on my desk quickly dumped in one of the cupboards before I was laid down on the desktop. "You've dreamed of this?"

"Blake and I first," Colt said, pushing forward and taking my hands. "Everyone else dismissed it as just fantasy, not a true mate dream, until—"

"Until they got their fucking heads out of their arses," Blake rumbled, shooting a dark look at Fen and Ryan.

"We're here now, and it's time to tend to our mate," Fen said in a voice that would brook no arguments, but when he looked down at me, everything softened. "Riley, we're going to strip you down now." My eyes went to the door, looking with alarm at the strips of frosted glass on either side of the door. Blake pulled away and wheeled my whiteboard over until it blocked the entrance off. "And then we will tend to you."

"Tend?" My question hung in the air. "What is—?"

"We touch you, soothe you," Colt said, dropping his head down near mine and stroking my hair back from my forehead. "We do whatever we can to make you feel good and acclimate you to us."

He said the words gently, but there was a heat in his gaze as it slid down my body, one that conjured an answering one in me. My hands were shaking as I went to the buttons of my blouse, but they were quickly pushed aside, clasped by Colt and by Ryan as the others went to work.

"Let us, seriously," Haze said, silver-eyed and desperate, all of his former humour gone. "We want the privilege."

And so, in my office, at my bloody workplace, I was stripped bare for them.

I groaned, my brows knotting as Fen scooped me up in his arms and then sat down with me on his lap in one of my office chairs. I made an anxious little noise at that, as being naked in my office was a freaking weird experience, especially with all of them standing there, staring.

"I know, love," Fen said, stroking my hair. "I wanted you sinking into our bed for the first time at this. Only the softest of mattresses for our Riley. But this is what you wanted, what you needed, so we'll make this work." His focus shifted to the pack. "Keep your cocks in your pants for this one. This is about her pleasure, not ours."

"I can't fucking wait to start rubbing my cum on your skin, babe," Haze said, staring down at me with that familiar wicked smile, one that widened as I let out an involuntary whine. "But you'll just have to wait like a good girl for that. Kisses first?"

I stiffened, like I could feel their lips on my skin already, but Fen tipped my head back.

"Listen to me, Riley."

This was how an alpha command was supposed to be used. His low, gentle voice kept me pinned just as Mark had, but with such a different intent, a quiet settling inside my head in response.

"Just listen to your alphas, and we'll see you through this."

"FIRST THING we need to do is put you on display," Fen said, turning me around in his arms so I faced the others. I resisted a little, feeling so damn exposed, but that was just the tip of the iceberg. His hands went around my wrists, stroking the sensitive skin there before pulling them wide.

"Oh fuck..." Ryan's eyes were brilliant silver, his mouth

falling open, and that was what distracted me from my discomfort. "Riley, you're even more perfect than I thought."

"They want to see you, need to see you," Fen said, his lips against my neck as my arms trembled, resisting him ever so slightly. "You're the one they've longed for all this time, and now you're so close to being theirs. Let them see those pretty tits of yours. They ache, don't they? Just like they did in the shop when I—"

"When you what?" Colt asked with a frown. "Sounds like a lot has happened in a few hours."

"When I tended to our mate," Fen replied, a slender thread of a growl in his voice. "I wanted to take her home. I wanted to bring her to you. I knew we'd end up here, but she was adamant she wanted to go out. Her breasts were very swollen and sensitive, just like they are now." Fingertips brushed against my nipples, making me shudder in response, illustrating his point. "I touched her like this, just lightly, and…"

Maybe Fen kept talking, maybe he didn't, I couldn't seem to tell. His fingers, his presence, the warmth of his body against mine, it all had me going limp against him, then my back arched as his caresses grew more insistent. My thighs fell open, and that was when I heard their groans, but it didn't seem enough. I needed to be open to them, some instinct pushing at me hard. Fen's thighs moved with mine, giving me more space, but it wasn't enough, not for what was coming. Those frustratingly light caresses had me simmering, but I needed to boil. Then he came.

A hand on my ankle forced my eyes open, and there was Blake.

"It's OK, Riley. Everything will be all right now."

And with that, he lifted my leg and put it over Fen's thigh, splitting me open.

"Fuck, she's dripping," Colt said on a groan.

"Now the other leg, and then you'll be fine."

The contrast between Blake's gentle voice and the position I found myself in was stark and seemed to just add to what I was feeling.

"That's it, love. Good girl," Fen said. "Now, arms around my neck." They moved without thought, wrapping around him, feeling the curl of his hair against my fingers. "Look at how you're displayed for them." He ran a possessive hand down my stomach. "You're everything they've ever wanted, and you're just out of reach." His hands returned to my nipples, his fingers plucking at them, harder now, my hips beginning to pulse in time with each stroke. "You want them to have a taste, right? They want it, need it."

As soon as he said those words, I did too. Everything he was doing was stoking a fire inside me, one that was growing hotter and hotter with each tug. I was empty, needing, the sweetest of aches beginning, but I couldn't bear another. I needed to be petted, stroked, soothed.

"Who do you want to have their first taste?"

My eyes went to Colt, a pained smile spreading across his face at that, but he shook his head slowly. My gaze followed his as he stared down at the man at my feet.

"Blake?"

"You ready for that, Riley?" he asked, sliding his massive hand up my thigh. Those thick fingers, they'd push hard inside me. I remembered exactly how that felt as I followed the slow progress of his tongue as it slid across his lips.

Like he could already taste me.

"You ready for me?" There was something darker, more insistent in his usually gentle voice, all of the deep brown gone from his irises. "I can smell your need, love. You need tending. Let me."

I nodded, just once, and arched my hips up as soon as he moved between my thighs, wanting whatever he had to give. His hands slapped down on top of them, holding me still as he wedged those broad shoulders between them.

"Gonna make you feel so good," he promised in more of a

it. Before, I had been swept up in…what? A sensual haze? A feeling of rightness that came from being near them? Pleasure, more pleasure than I'd ever felt before, but now came something else.

This wasn't me. I wasn't someone who let five guys touch her in her damn office, leaving the whole room reeking of sex. I wasn't an omega. And then the most important one—I didn't lose control.

I scowled at them, although even in this state, I knew that wasn't fair or rational, but I wasn't feeling like either of those things, which was important.

Because I was so used to feeling like that all the time.

Not like this, I thought furiously as I shoved my white board out of the way.

"Riley." Fen said my name, injecting so much into it, yet no command. I was grateful for that. "You want to run."

Yes, yes, yes! That was exactly what I bloody wanted, my body trembling with that need now that my other needs had been seen to, and that made me pause.

It felt like a war was being waged inside me on too many fronts. Dealing with my past with them, finding our way towards each other. Trying to hold down my job, and better, becoming a success. And the impulses that were swamping me, removing any cool, calm objectivity, turning me into this reactive mess.

When I opened the door, I confirmed everything Fen was saying, but even as I spilled out into the hallway, more shit came with it.

Guilt at walking out on them. Pain too, an ache starting in my chest, making me think an ECG might be good for other reasons. I needed to go back to my office and I needed to get the fuck away and I couldn't seem to reconcile either impulse.

"Hey, you OK?" Candy asked as I stumbled out into the lab.

"No," I said, the first honest thing. "Candy, I can't do this."

Chapter 30

"What the hell did you do to her?" Candy asked as the guys spilled into the lab. She moved until she formed a very small but very spirited barrier between them and me. "Like, I know what you did to her and I hope like hell that scream was of pleasure. And if it was, do you guys have another set of brothers or cousins maybe who might be interested—?"

"That's not helping," Fen rumbled. "Riley, I know you're scared—"

"I'm not scared!" I spat as I began to pace back and forth. "I'm..." Words, too many words swelled up, ready to fill that gap, creating a log jam in my head. "I'm not me," I finally ground out.

"Or maybe you're more you than you've ever been and that's fucking terrifying." My head jerked up, my eyes wide as I saw that Colt had stepped forward. He didn't crowd Candy, respecting the boundary she'd made and looking beyond it. "Maybe we all are. When you're a kid, your reality is created for you, told to you by your parents, your family, your school, and your community." His lips thinned down then. "Ours lied. They told us a story about who and what we are, thinking it would help in the long run. Did it?"

I could've shoved off his sweet words. I could've snarled if any of them had come at me, but this? I was never neutral when I was around them. The analytical mindset I craved fell to pieces the minute I was with them, but… He stared at me, eyes stark but still their reassuring hazel colour. He didn't posture, intimidate, or do anything but ask me a damn question, forcing my mind to race to answer that.

"I made something here," I replied, my voice shaky and emotional in a way I fucking hated. "I made something I was proud of. I was starting to build a career, find my feet as a researcher, and develop a good reputation. How am I gonna do that if…?"

My hands went to my breasts, wincing at the warm pulse of pleasure that washed through me, which just seemed a further betrayal by my body.

"Is that what's got you running out here like the hounds of hell are chasing you?" Candy asked, turning to me. "Fuck, girl…" Her eyes shone as she stared up at me. "Who says you can't have both? I am totally a have your cake and eat it girl."

"I know," I shot back without thinking. "You have mine and eat it all the time."

"God, just because you got that super special Black Forest cake with the ganache," she said, pulling a face. "You left it in the fridge for days."

"Hours," I argued.

"Then I'll get you another one, because, Riley, you're about to experience it all. Are you worried about your reputation? You're in here, going through transition, half out of your mind with lust for these guys, and you're still contemplating whether or not a CT scan or MRI is worth doing. You're not letting go of who you are. You're prepared to share what must be an excruciatingly personal process with the scientific community to help us learn more."

"I just had a guy go the growl in my office," I said.

"And I fucked two guys in the copy room at the office Christmas party," Candy shot back.

"Seriously, who?"

"Don't worry about my sex life, because we obviously need to be concerned about yours. You can't come into work."

"No, no, no, I have—" My voice got higher and higher as I considered what she said.

"You can still conduct the study."

"What?"

Candy's cool statement had me stopping still, considering an option I hadn't been able to conceptualise yet.

"We do field research all the time, and I put the possibility of that into the proposal I pitched to Gideon. Seriously, those guys are willing to do whatever it takes to get the data. We'll draft an email, say that things have escalated quickly and that you'll need to be in the field until transition is complete." She put a hand on my arm, which made me jump, but her touch wasn't as repellent as before. "If you're continually funnelling back data to the team, why would they have any reason to be concerned?"

I blinked and then looked past her to where the guys waited not so patiently. I could feel them now, in ways I never had before, their scent betraying their fear and the burning need to control the situation, even as they brutally suppressed it. I nodded slowly, seeing what she was saying, and now it was my mind racing, not my body.

The next few hours were a race against the clock, trying to take as many swabs, readings, and samples as we could before the need started to bite deeper. I refused to go when I felt the cramps begin again, forcing Candy to perform an ultrasound as they did, taking over and running the wand across my pelvis when she stopped.

"Your uterus is swollen," she said with a worried look. "I'll run some panels on your bloods and get back to you, but I think things are changing in your pelvis as well as your tits. You're getting ready to take a knot."

"And she's coming with us, now," Haze said, stepping

forward and grabbing the roll of paper towel, scrubbing the gel off my stomach despite my protests.

"Haze, I need—"

"This is what you need, Riley." He placed a hand over the top of my pubic mound, his palm feeling like a heat pack right now. The cramps weakened and then stopped.

"That eased the cramps, right?" Candy asked, tapping out some notes furiously on her phone.

"Yeah."

"And I'm going to need to do this all the way home, otherwise she'll be screaming in pain," Haze said, injecting all the vehemence he could into his words, trying to make us see. "We know what you need, Riley, and that's why we've tolerated this, but enough is enough. You are not an elastic band that can be just stretched to fit the needs of science. You are a person, a woman." His eyes burned bright blue as he stared at me. "And my mate."

I was helped off the table, my clothes put to rights, all of the guys working together to help or keep hands on me, which seemed to keep the pain at bay, and Candy just shook her head slowly.

"You're a crazy bitch. They just want to take you home and drown you in pleasure and you… I'll draft that email and CC you into it, letting Windsor and Crowe know what's going on."

She went to put a hand on my arm, but I shied away, no longer able to tolerate it. With a nod, she handed me a bag of a million different bits of equipment and sample tubes.

"She's not wrong," Haze said as we walked out, his hand on the small of my back. "But that talk of 'exploring our super seminal response'?" He shot me a sly grin. "I admit, I'm particularly looking forward to that bit."

"It'll help you as well, Riley," Ryan said, looking a little pale. "Our cum… Whatever's in it, it'll help settle your body down, make it hurt less, and make the need for tending less urgent."

"So I need to be hosed down with your cum to function as a human being," I said between gritted teeth. "Good to know."

Then, as we were walking out, someone else walked in.

Suck Up Evan looked at us in surprise, followed quickly by irritation, his face flushing.

"What are you doing here?"

A low growl from the guys had him stepping back involuntarily, but he firmed his stance, then glanced back at me.

"There's been a development in the study, and Candy and I came in after hours to take some samples, to make sure we don't miss anything," I replied coolly. "What are you doing here?"

"My father—" He just shook his head slowly. "I had to come in. You two are dumping everything else on me, so I need to get my head around the mess you've created."

And with that, my already raging paranoia rose several notches.

Evan's MO was to faff around, doing as little as possible, until someone else could be 'persuaded' to take his work on. He would never do weekend work to catch up. There was a possibility he might be under the pump due to his dad's interest in our study, but... I pulled out my phone and tapped out a quick message to Candy, alerting her with our special code that Evan was en route.

Go home. Have doctor prescribed orgy. I got this, was all I got back.

THE DRIVE back to their place was a tense one. I couldn't seem to get comfortable, even though I was wedged between Ryan and Haze in the backseat. The touch of their skin was a bit like a TENS unit, sending low pulses of warm electrical feeling throughout my body, which stopped the pain and brought a realisation with it.

What the pain masked was a deep need that throbbed on the same frequency as their touch. It was like something inside all of us was starting to synchronise, only hurting when it was out of sync. Colt was driving, and his eyes flicked to the rear vision mirror regularly to check on me, but when I had that realisation, they held mine for just a fraction longer.

· · ·

"SO WHAT DO I NEED?" I asked when we got to the house, my voice a little breathy as I felt something tighten inside me. "I have questions, so many questions."

"And we'll answer them as soon as we've tended to you," Fen replied. "Inside and into the shower in the main suite."

"The main…?"

I didn't get a chance to wonder what that was as Ryan picked me up, carrying me down the hall and through the last door at the end.

"What the fuck?" I asked, catching a glimpse of a massive bed and floor to ceiling windows that Colt and Blake quickly jerked closed, creating a warmer, darker, cosier space.

Which somehow made my muscles start to unlock.

Bags were dropped on the bed, then they moved as one towards me.

Run, she told me again, but with no fear this time. Instead, it was a delicious thing, like she was suggesting I gorge on my bodyweight of Swiss chocolate. *Run, and they will catch you.*

But before I could decode that, Fen stepped forward, putting his hands on my shoulders.

"You wanted answers?" he said. "You'll get one of them now." His eyes roamed up and down my body. "The way you respond to our cum. Haze and Ryan, you're up."

"Oh, thank fucking fuck…" Haze hissed, stripping down instantly, Ryan doing the same, though more slowly.

"Fen, we've barely even kissed," he said.

"So take your time, or as much as her need will allow," Fen instructed. He stroked the side of my face with his thumb, then pulled away. "I said I didn't know the science, Riley, and I don't, but I do know this—what's in us, what's in you, it works together through a ripening. We'll lick every drop of your slick away as often as you'll let us, use it to coat our cocks, our fingers, our tongues, but you need to do the same."

"So what, this is gonna be some kind of biologically mandated blow job?" I asked.

He stepped in then, right up into my space, so I could feel

the heat of his body just before he pressed his thumb against my lips. They parted without thought, and he watched with complete fascination as I swallowed his finger down.

"No one will make you do anything. Scientists reliably predict what will happen based on hours of observation." He blinked, then withdrew his thumb, rubbing it against my bottom lip. "Then you can consider alphas among your number. We have observed the care and preparation of omegas for centuries, finding ways to ease the pain and maximise the pleasure. You will bond with us, my mate, when you are ready. You will be locked down, unavailable to all other men but us. We will be together, heart to heart, until such time as it's our moment to return to the earth, so we take the process of mating an omega very seriously."

He took that last step forward, my body pressed against his as his arms wrapped around me, holding me close now.

"We want you to be happy, Riley. Satisfied, fulfilled, but mostly? We want you to come out of this loving us, not hating us, and I think you'll find we're prepared to do almost anything to make that happen."

A kiss to my forehead. That was what I got before Fen pulled away and was replaced by Haze.

"You ready, baby?" he asked me, eyes dancing, like we were kids again and at the fence to Mrs George's prize orchard, ready to raid it for apples. When he held out his hand, I took it, just like I had then, and with that, he drew me into the adjoining bathroom.

Chapter 31

"Wow—" I started to say as we entered a huge bathroom.

"Ignore it," Haze commanded. "This place was built to alpha specs, so it has to be able to fit everyone inside it at the same time. Now, we need to get these off."

He'd started to undo the buttons of my blouse when Ryan walked in, looking around warily at everything that wasn't me.

"I thought we'd have more time," Ryan said, almost to himself. He dared a look at me but wrenched his eyes away again, particularly as Haze revealed more and more skin. "I intended to spend some time to get to know Riley again."

"What's to get to know?" Haze asked his brother but stared at me. He slid his hand down the side of my neck. "She still has that crooked little grin." The pad of his thumb touched the side of my mouth. "She still has that funny little snort when she laughs at things too hard."

"I'm sorry, what?" I replied, knocking his hand away.

"She probably still does those terrible farts when she's had ice cream and blames it on the dog."

Haze's grin was wide now—the one that was always a precursor to some fuckery.

"This is the shit you say when you wanna get laid?" I asked, cocking an eyebrow, but he just spun me around to face his brother, working expertly to keep unbuttoning my shirt.

"You want to get to know this Riley? Kiss her, brother. You can say and do all sorts of shit, but when you kiss her? Something shifts. It's like nothing's changed at all and everything has, all at the same time. I know you fucking want to."

"Of course I fucking want to," Ryan rumbled. He strode over to us, his long legs eating up the distance before stopping just short of me. "But what do you want, Riley?" Haze growled at that, but his brother charged on. "Do you want to kiss me?"

There was a vulnerability now in his face that I'd never really seen before. The Ryan I'd known had loped down the halls with all the cocky confidence of the rest of the boys. Since he was taller, stronger, harder than some of the others, people rarely messed with him, especially when his role as fixer of Fen's problems became clear. He was a power to be reckoned with, one who would rise to prominence in the pack, so people afforded him the proper deference. I wasn't standing here in front of a role, though, I was in front of a man.

One whose face I knew all too well. My hand rose, stroking down the side of his face, feeling the sharp plane of his cheekbone, pressing a fingertip to the small scar on his chin that came from when we'd fucked around in the creek as kids.

We'd been young, too young to be playing down there, as the alphas made clear later, but that hadn't stopped us. We'd brought jars and buckets down to put frogs in for me.

I'd been reading about frog dissections, and it was the only science thing that actually interested the guys, so Fen had the bright idea that we should go and find our own 'specimens' in the creek. Like always, we'd followed him down there, walking through fields of long grass that in hindsight, were likely to have been full of snakes. We'd followed the dirt track, passing paddocks of mildly curious cows, until we reached the creek proper. There, we'd clambered over mossy rocks, clinging to tree roots as we lowered ourselves down onto the banks. We'd pored over the area, too bloody noisy by half for frogs, I was sure, until we found 'the one.'

"Oh my god!" I had shout-whispered, pointing my finger to the big brown frog sitting in amongst the rocks, obviously assuming his dull skin colour was enough to mask him from our eagle eyes. The boys had clustered closer like the young wolves they were, forming a pack once the hunt was on.

"If we come this way, we'll scare him," Fen said, taking one step into the water, and sure enough, the frog moved slightly as a result. *"We'll have to flank him."*

I'd learned what this meant later in history class, but to them, this was essential knowledge. I watched the lot of them, a tribe of ten-year-old boys, fan out across the riverbank, moving like ghosts through the trees and the shrubs, leaping over the creek further upstream before closing in.

"Are you sure about this?" I asked Fen, glancing at him, then the frog longingly. *"He's so perfect. We could—"*

"Shh…"

He had it back then, that alpha command, but he'd known better than to use it. His fathers had been strict as hell about their sons abusing their power. Later, I found out through study that many alpha packs had ruled through barked orders and an oppressive system of coercion, but weirdly, maintaining that level of control over a whole community was as difficult for the alphas as it was for the community to bear it. Right now, Fen deployed his gift as he was supposed to—for the benefit of the pack.

I watched Blake, Ryan, Colt, and Haze emerge out of the trees, moving on silent feet, my eyes narrowing at Haze. That grin of his, always too sharp, too wide, often meant he was about to do something stupid, but in the end, it wasn't him that did.

They glanced at each other, communicating silently, hands held loosely at their sides as they dropped down into the creek as one, forming a semicircle around the frog, which wasn't a bad tactic except for this—the gaps between their slender legs were more than big enough for a wily amphibian to jump through. In his bid for freedom, he leapt with all of his might, and that was when the hunt began.

Boyish voices filled the air as they all shouted instructions, feet and hands slapping in the water, trying to catch the frog. He jumped and he jumped with all his might, not knowing what we intended but fairly sure he wouldn't like it, their grasping hands confirming that.

"Fen…" I said, wrapping my hand around his arm.

"*I know, Riley, I know.*" *His eyes jerked back to his brothers before he barked,* "*Catch that bloody frog!*"

Ryan was just doing as he was told, throwing his whole body after the frog, hands outstretched, fingers closing in, every muscle straining to try and stop it from escaping.

He got it, his eyes going wide for a split second at the feeling of the slimy frog fighting against his grip, but of course, what goes up must come down, and for Ryan, it was onto an unforgiving bed of river rocks.

It came back to me then, that moment where Ryan had to decide—let go of the frog and put his hands out to break his fall, or hold on to the frog for me and let the chips fall where they may.

In that split second, I was faced with a very adult problem my selfish little child mind struggled with. I didn't want Ryan hurt. I knew what falling down felt like and it sucked, but I also wanted that frog with all the single-minded obsession a kid like me could have. What happened next seemed to resolve all of that.

I saw the moment Ryan realised what was going to happen, the world feeling like it slowed down, going quiet as his eyes went wide, right before his chin hit a rock hard.

Blood. Shouts. Legs tensing then springing into action, buckets tossed aside as I went running across the stream, my feet dancing over the rocks to get to him.

"*Ryan?*" *I called out his name as I saw the blood flow, as I saw how pale he was.* "*Ryan?*" *I dropped down beside him, not even sure how I got there so fast, trying to rake his wet hair back from his forehead, then hissing at the steady seep of blood.*

Trouble. *That was my first thought. We were gonna get it, that was for sure. We weren't supposed to be at the creek in the first place, and now, with one of the pack hurt? He groaned then, eyelids fluttering, and that forced everything else out of my mind.*

"*You have to run back,*" *I shouted at the boys clustered around me.* "*You have to get the alphas.*"

"*We can't,*" *Fen countermanded.* "*We can get him back, clean him up, and say it happened out riding.*"

"*No.*"

I never directly contradicted Fen unless I absolutely had to, but I had to right now. I prised Ryan's fingers open, letting the croaking frog go free before sitting down on the rocks and lifting his head into my lap.

"He's hurt, and it could be bad," I said, stroking his forehead. "Moving him could make him worse. Blame me for it if you want to. I can take the punishment, but we're not moving Ryan, not until one of your dads comes here."

Colt settled down beside me then, wrapping an arm around my shoulders, and Blake, he turned on his heel and ran back to town, bringing Malcolm, one of the alphas, back some time later. But Fen and Haze, they crouched down around Ryan, staring at me like they'd never really seen me before this.

"Are you OK?" I asked Ryan, ignoring them. "Does it hurt real bad?"

"Kinda," Ryan answered, his nonchalance ruined by a wince. "You let the frog go."

"I don't care about any frog, not when you're hurt." I felt a flush of something then as I said the words, something it'd take me years to understand. "You're way more important than a specimen."

He'd smiled then, as much as he could, the blood flowing from his chin slowing, and I'd grabbed his hand and squeezed it. He squeezed back, right as Malcolm came storming down the creek bed.

"Are you still the boy that'd catch frogs for me?" I asked Ryan, and he smiled at that, taking my hand away from his scar and kissing my knuckles.

"Always, Red. You know that."

And I did, he had always been there for me, and no matter what happened before, we had that surety between us. Which was perhaps why I leaned forward, pressing a kiss to his scar at first, while Ryan held himself completely still. Warm, prickly, stubbled male skin met my lips, then his head tilted, bringing his mouth to mine.

"Whatever you need, I'll half kill myself to get it for you, I promise."

Other women needed hearts and flowers, but for me, that was a big enough avowal to satisfy me. My hands went around Ryan's neck, his locking around my waist as his scent filled my nose, making me pleasantly dizzy with it until I pressed my lips to his.

I liked the insistent press of his lips, the way his arms tightened around me. I liked that sharp intake of breath, as if I'd somehow surprised him. I liked the way his lips parted, beckoning mine in, the way his tongue slid forward, carefully, experimentally at first, and when I let out a little whimper, surging to claim my mouth. I liked the feel of his hair under my fingers, the broad expanse of his body as I raked my nails across it, the heat of his skin as I shoved up his shirt.

"I need you," I announced as I pulled apart from him. "That's what I need—both of you."

"Stop bogarting the babe," Haze said, wrenching me away from his brother and holding me close as I was treated to the sight of Ryan pulling his shirt up and over his head, revealing all that bronzed muscle. "Mm..." Haze said, nuzzling into my neck. "Her scent shifted as soon as you did that. I don't think you have to worry about wooing our girl."

"After, during," I said as Ryan prowled closer. "We can do that—work on discovering who we are in the gaps between tending. Can't we?"

"I'm gonna have to insist on it," Ryan replied, tugging me back to him. He pushed my shirt off my shoulders as my hands went to his jeans, unbuttoning and dragging down his fly.

"Oh..."

I stopped and stared as it became apparent I wasn't the only one who didn't like to wear undies on the weekend.

"That better be the hushed sound of awe in your voice," Ryan said as I continued to stare at his hard cock.

"More like the sound of doubt and trepidation as I consider letting that beast anywhere near me," I replied. "That's fucking huge."

"Yeah, baby," Haze said, then kissed my neck. "You know exactly what a guy wants to hear."

"It'll fit," Ryan said smugly, then pulled back to remove his pants too. "Now, let's get you naked so we can show you how."

Chapter 32

"What, like now? Are we sure about that, because I'm really not," I babbled, backing away from the two of them. "Like, maybe we need to try and use something to dilate things?"

"Oh, there'll be a lot of that," Haze replied, the two of them tracking after me. "Alphas don't just slam their big cocks in, not until you've shown you can take us. This is part of that process."

"Hormones or chemicals or whatever in our cum?" Ryan added. "It helps that process."

"We rub it into your skin." Haze grinned when my back hit the shower cubicle wall. "We push it into your pussy. Rub it into your tits, let you swallow it when you're ready. You'll know where you need it, but first, we need you out of these clothes."

"How will I know?" I asked, batting his hands away when he went to undo my pants. "I can tell you comprehensively I've never woken up and thought, 'fuck, wouldn't it be awesome to become a walking bukkake for the guys I grew up with?'"

But then I let out a hiss of pain.

"You might not know, because no other man has done that for you," Haze replied, staring at me intensely then, as if daring me to contradict him. "And no other alpha has ever touched you."

"Nor will," Ryan said with a growl. The two of them settled in against me, pressing their hard bodies against mine. "You belong to us, and it's up to us to show you how it can be. That takes trust, and you might not be there right now."

"Shut up, Ryan," Haze snapped.

"No, he's right," I said, and Ryan nodded slowly in response. "I…have trouble letting people take control."

"We can help with that." Haze's voice was dark and sinuous, like a snake in the tree, offering me an apple that would be so sweet to eat. "An alpha's power to command isn't just something to be used judiciously in the running of the community. Primarily, it's for just this."

Ryan's eyes sought mine, his fingertips brushing across the slice of stomach revealed by my open blouse.

"You're being bombarded with foreign sensations," Ryan said. "Your body is changing, and that's frightening. We can help you, but you don't know whether you should let us. Give us control, just for here and now. Let us show you how it can be. We can't stop you from speaking, responding, or reacting. If you hate what's going on, just say so and everything will stop."

My heart was thudding fast in my chest, and I wondered if they had any idea what they were asking. I was the master of my own destiny. I made all the decisions in my life, and right now, he just wanted me to hand that over?

"Just for an hour, half an hour, or ten minutes, if that's all you can tolerate. We'll look after you the whole time until you don't want that anymore. Just let us look after you, Riley. You're our girl, and we can't stand to see you in pain."

As if to remind me of that, a sharp stab sliced through my body, taking my breath away.

"Just until I say stop?" I asked between pants.

"Just until you say stop," Ryan agreed.

I nodded then, unable to bring myself to say the words, and

the two of them, they made low sounds of appreciation in response.

"I'm gonna need you to strip down now, love." Ryan's voice felt like a rope now, thrown out to me as I thrashed around in a rocky sea. "We love it when you reveal yourself to us."

"You're so fucking beautiful," Haze rumbled. "Show us everything we've been dreaming about."

At that, my fingers moved without conscious thought, unbuttoning the rest of my shirt and pushing it off my body, letting it fall to the floor.

"That's it. You're doing so well," Ryan said.

I reached behind and undid my bra strap, the garment falling free almost immediately, and my breasts throbbed in response. This bra seemed better for the way my body was right now, yet still my torso protested at being bound up in it. And now? I felt every slight brush of air against my swollen flesh, my nipples tightening so painfully, I began to stiffen.

"Shh…" Haze's mouth was at my ear, his hands covering my breasts, just cupping them, which turned the pain into something so much better. "That's it," he said as my head rolled back, resting on his shoulder. "Such a good girl. You gonna let Ryan do the rest? You've already done so much. Let him take over."

I just nodded now, feeling like a soft haze had settled over me, partly because touching them removed all pain, partly because my body felt heavy and useless and he was so much better at this than me.

"Look at you, beautiful girl," Ryan said, his fingers undoing my pants button before he dragged the garment down my legs, then staring up at me as he pulled them off over my feet. His fingers then went to my underwear, hooking into the sides but not yet pulling them down. He just stared, making me start to shift restlessly. All that intense connection we'd shared as teens was still there, but it was so much more now. He moved forward, slowly, then pressed a single kiss to my hip before peeling my underwear away.

"Now there's nothing between you and us," Haze said, moving in closer, grinding his naked body against mine, making me gasp at how hard he felt. "Just the way it should be." His hands swept over my breasts, the palms abrading my sensitive nipples, and that just started my clit throbbing. "We need to give you our cum, Riley. It's what's gonna help you, but there's no reason why this needful application can't be a pleasant thing for everyone."

He nipped at my ear now, chuckled when I jolted in response, then soothed the bite with a lick of his tongue.

"You're scared, wound tight, not sure of what's to come, but any good scientist understands that knowledge comes from going out into the field and doing hands-on research. Get down on your knees, Riley."

"Haze, we shouldn't—"

Ryan's voice was a growl of warning, but it was choked off as I found myself obediently dropping down. The tiles were cold on my knees. They were so tall, and now I was entirely dwarfed by them. My world was narrowed down to just them.

"Put your hand around Ryan's cock and give it a lick," Haze said, and I did just that.

Haze wasn't controlling me. His voice, his alpha command was like a hand on my shoulder, giving me a little push. I was just as capable of pushing back, but I didn't want to. That was what his mild compulsion freed me from—the feeling that I should want to resist. When I put a hand on Ryan's hip, he hissed, staring down at me like he couldn't believe this was happening, hands reaching out for me. He bundled my hair up in his hands, unable to bear anything in the way as I reached out and gripped his cock.

"Fuck..."

I liked Ryan's groan. I liked Haze's dark chuckle as well, as if he felt like his plans were all coming to fruition. I liked the way Ryan's cock flexed in my grip and the breathy little sounds he made as I swivelled my hand up. But it was what happened when I pulled the head closer, when my tongue flicked out, that pleased me most.

You would've thought this was a classic power exchange. That the alphas were in charge and I was the poor little berated beta, forced to do their will. But in some ways, Haze was right— I needed to experience things to understand them. As Ryan watched my tongue flick out, his eyes silver bright as I moved closer, it was his breath that came in rapid little pants, his hands tightening in my hair in response. His body was iron hard, tensed completely against what was coming and craving it with every breath.

I had him literally and figuratively in the palm of my hand as my tongue slid along the crown of his cock.

"Fuck!"

Ryan's cry echoed off the hard tile walls as his taste exploded in my mouth. Sweet, that was the shocking part. None of the usual salty mucusy thing that was going on with beta men, I found myself going back for another lick because pre-cum bubbled up and out of his cock with each swipe, summoned by my tongue, then my mouth, as I took him deeper.

"Riley girl, that feels so fucking good." Ryan's words came out in a growly babble. "You feel so good. Your mouth is like velvet and—" A low groan as I sucked harder and harder, rewarding me with a burst of sweetness.

I had a sweet tooth, but this was something else again. The ache that Haze had banished rose inside me, but in quite a different form. It was that delicious feeling when you were craving chocolate so bad and you just so happened to be in front of one of the best bakeries in town, some chocolate covered monstrosity staring back at you from the window. You wanted something desperately, and you were just about to get it, all of what you needed. As if sensing my thoughts, Haze moved closer, putting his hand on the back of my skull.

"You need more, don't you? His taste, it's awakened some-thing. Don't be scared. Take it, take him." And with that, he placed a gentle pressure on my head, encouraging me to take Ryan deeper, alerting me to a need to do just that.

I'd always had a relatively touchy gag reflex, but apparently, that was gone now. My hand gripped the base of Ryan's cock tighter, my mouth sliding lower and lower with every stroke.

"Fuck, you feel good. Gonna give you everything I've got, baby. Never felt anything like this. Fuck, Riley, fuck!"

As Ryan got harder, his hips flexing with every stroke, some-thing else rose. It swelled in my hand, growing and growing, until finally, I pulled my mouth free with a pop, going to consult it. Swollen and red, his knot looked angry, painful, resulting in me covering it with my palm and squeezing it.

"Jesus, don't do…"

I was rewarded by a large spill of pre-cum, though now it was more white than clear, and when I licked him clean, a low growl formed in my chest. I squeezed harder then, licking him again as more oozed free, going back for more and more.

"Riley, no, you can't—" Ryan started to protest.

"She has to," Haze interjected. "She's our mate. Our knots are hers to take in any way she wants. Give her what she needs, brother."

Ryan dragged me free of his cock then, his expression dark and alien with those moon filled eyes. He smiled then, showing me his fangs when he did, his thumb moving to scoop a small trail of pre-cum that had slipped out of my mouth and then push it back between my lips.

"You need me, love?" he asked in a feral voice. "You need all of me?"

I didn't know exactly what that meant, but I found myself nodding anyway.

"You can't suck down my load if you play with my knot. If you squeeze it when I come, you'll get a lot more than you bargained for." But he angled his dick down, brushing it across my lips. "But you're gonna suck down everything I've got, right up until that point."

His words settled over me like firm hands, directing me

Chapter 34

I dreamed of a wolf with reddish brown fur.

Initially, it was a calm dream, a prosaic one, like a wildlife cinematographer had left their B reel running in my head. I watched her nose the ground, snuffling at the scents there, hit somehow by blasts of dirt, grass, flowers. She jerked her head up then, snorting to dislodge the dirt before trotting on, over the grassy scrublands. She was an interloper here, yet she made her way through the bushes and the few trees like it was her place to call home.

Until she heard them.

With all the vigilance of a predator—or was that prey?—her head jerked up when she heard the first howl, faint, distant, just a slight noise carried on the wind, but she picked it up immediately. Her nose was thrust into the air, sniffing the breeze to detect who or what that was, and what she found had her turning tail. Her feet engaged as quickly as she worked it out, trotting, then loping, then running with the long, earth eating gait of a wolf, but rather than put more distance between her and them, it seemed to bring them closer.

Their howls grew louder, more of them now, and if she

strained, she could hear their paws thudding the ground along with her own. She didn't. Any effort she had to spare was directed at her legs, her haunches, powering the dense muscles to keep them striding forward.

But no matter what she did, no matter how hard she ran, they caught up to her. She could hear so much more now—the rapid rasp of their pants, their claws raking the soil, and most of all, their hunger. How did that sound? It was the harsh whines that escaped their chest, the faintest sounds of jaws being opened, ready to bite. It was the whip of the wind, working against her and with them, bringing her to ground.

She knew what was coming, what she needed, what was supposed to be, but she also knew she couldn't just lie down and take it. She had to run, and they had to prove themselves worthy of catching her.

My view shifted abruptly as I emerged, standing in front of all of them, watching the she-wolf run towards me, seeing the pack slaver behind her, one I knew all too well. I'd seen these wolves before, picking their way across a darkened carpark, walking on up to me, but they weren't making their way towards anyone right now. They were hunting something down.

I was frozen, unable to move when she leapt. She treated them to a brief glimpse over her shoulder at the pack as they closed in on her, as she made one last jump to try and keep out of their jaws. My eyes flicked open as I jolted awake the moment her body hit mine.

"HEY, BABY," Colt said, looking down at me, reaching up to stroke the side of my face as I blinked. "You sleep well?"

I couldn't answer him immediately, my brain struggling to come online. Part of me was still there, with those wolves. Part of him was there too. But my eyes closed for a second, just feeling his caress, my lips falling open as something shifted inside me.

"Are you getting needy again, Riley?"

The sweetness was fading out of Colt's voice, replaced by something harder, more insistent. His fingers buried themselves in my hair, grabbing a hold as he searched my face for an answer, but that wasn't where it was to be found. I reached up, taking a handful of his hair too, using it to pull his lips down on mine, something he gave me all too gladly, covering my body with his in moments, grinding me down into the softness as I kissed him with everything I had.

"Not yet," I panted out finally, and his head jerked back, his eyes quizzical until he worked out I'd belatedly answered his question. "Soon." I slid a finger down his bare chest, loving the fact he only had a pair of grey track pants on right now. "I'll need you soon."

"Whatever you need, you know that," he said, grabbing my free hand and kissing the back of it before pressing it against his chest. "Now, come and eat while you can."

I STUMBLED out into the main house and saw the sun was setting now, and spread out on the table was an apt metaphor for whatever the hell was going on in this house.

There was food everywhere. Cakes, chocolate, soft drink, and chips, but in amongst that was actual food. Thai, Mexican, all the many choices Candy had recommended for them on that first day. I looked up, and they all watched me, Haze and Fen nursing beers, but they all noted where I sat, at the very end of the table.

"So, this is how it works?" I asked, reaching out and trailing a finger through a bowl of whipped cream garnished with chocolate shavings, then licking the sweet glob off the end. "You feed me whatever I want, fuck me in anyway I'll accept, until what?"

"You've got it wrong," Fen said, leaning forward, depositing the bottle on the table with a clunk, his muscular arms and bare chest on display as he rested his elbows on the tabletop. "We give you what you want, all of it. Every damn thought, dream, or impulse—it's happening. You're changing, and that's likely to be harder for you than someone who revealed as an omega." He watched me shift restlessly at that. "But that just means we need to treat you sweeter, ease you through this."

I snorted at that, my mouth falling open as I studied the lot of them. Like, academically, I kinda knew this was the way it worked between alphas and omegas, because why else were the bastards so damn smug, but…? *Not me, not for me.* That pulsed inside me like a heartbeat, which just made Fen smile.

"For you," he insisted, his grin widening. "All for you. Everything we dreamed of and everything you did. Now…"

He moved around the table, pulling me out of my seat and replacing himself in it, then drew me down on his lap, treating himself to a brief nuzzle to my neck before he pulled the nearest dish forward. His arm tightened around me when I went to move, and this time, adult Riley was all too aware of the way he was responding to me. He was thick and hard in his pants, but he didn't let me focus on that.

"Have something to eat. Have several somethings, because, love, I would very much like to hand feed you morsels of everything here, but you're not ready for that. Eat, or I'll have to help you do that."

So here I was, right back where I'd started—unable to sit on a seat by myself, unable to dictate my own feeding schedule. But y'know what? Part of me fucking loved it, and I was kind of sick of denying that. Fen's hand rubbed up and down my spine as I began to eat, a sigh going out across the table when I did. I picked my way through a disgusting mix of foods, some kind of hunger burning inside me, building with every stroke of his hand, until I couldn't eat a thing more.

Fen straightened up as I licked my fingers clean, a little savage now.

"Are you ready now for us to tell you how things will go?" he asked. "You promise that you won't run?"

I frowned slightly, thinking of the wolf running in my dreams, but then said, "Would it make a difference?"

I could almost feel him smiling into my back, his arm tightening around my waist.

"Only if you want to make things more interesting."

SO WE ADJOURNED to the lounge room, but as we went that way, Blake snatched me away from Fen, dropping down onto the couch and bringing me with him. His brother's eyes narrowed right up until I curled up against Blake's side. He was so damn big, I kinda wanted to burrow down into one small corner of his body and hide because the others, they all took their seats on the floor or on the lounges and stared at me.

"An alpha's job is to help his mate through the transition until she accepts his bond," Fen said, trying to keep shit educational. "He might know she's the one, but she…" Those green eyes fixed on mine. "Often, she needs some time to get there." He grinned then, teeth too white against his tanned skin. "That's all part of the chase. We help her manage what she's going through, and then…"

"Then she admits what she knows is true," Colt said. "That she's ours as much as we are hers."

"But that's the emotional side of things. Right now, we're focussed on the physical. Obviously, you know about the cascade of events that happened when your body went through puberty."

"Yeah…" I replied.

"In some ways, this is like an extension of that. I can't tell you the science of why this happens. Maybe you will be able to."

Oh Fen, you wily dog, dangling that lure in front of me.

"But you are going through a sensitisation process." My arms moved at that, feeling my nipples boring through the T-shirt I'd picked up off the floor, the cotton abrading them in a way just enough to make me oh so aware of them. "You'll pick up our scents more." I moved then, looking back at Blake, who gazed down at me with amusement. I took a reflexive breath in and caught a lungful of his woody scent. "But what we're worried about is what's happening here."

He moved then, sliding a hand under my shirt and placing it over my pelvis. I let out a little gasp at the flare of heat that came as a result. Blake's arm went around my waist, and that just added to the heat, my lungs stuttering as I fought to take a full breath.

"You are opening for us." He moved his hand in a small circle now. "Your cunt, your womb, your hips, your whole pelvic region. When your heat hits, you'll want us deep, hard, and everywhere we'll fit."

My eyes flicked open then without me realising I'd closed them, and I studied his face. Those green depths bore into mine, willing me to understand.

"Everywhere?"

In my mind, I had a stereotypical view of an omega—on all fours and begging for alpha cock, or at least that was how it was shown in porn. And they'd give them to her, in her mouth, in her cunt, in her…

"Dude, I cannot take your dicks up my arse."

The guys all spluttered at that.

"Well, if you want some help preparing—" Haze started to say.

"Shut up, Haze," Colt said before turning to me. "No one's putting anything anywhere without your permission." His eyes shone then as he straightened up. "People don't get what being an alpha is really like. It's not about barking at people and forcing them to carry out your will. At its heart, it's about caring for people."

He shook his head, then looked down at his hands.

"When we took over Bordertown, that's what we tried to do, the same as our parents. Keep the community going, maintain peace and harmony, solve problems, settle disputes. We did that for them, and that's what we'll do for you." He stared at me now. "That's all we've ever wanted to do—care for you and make you happy, give you everything you need. Now, that's what's going to happen."

"And what, make me Beta Vanguard?"

My voice was small, scared that they'd say yes, but equally scared that they'd say no.

"You don't get it." Colt's voice got sharper, harder, like he couldn't believe we were having this conversation again. "We looked after everyone else as best we could, continued the Vanguard legacy like everyone wanted, until we couldn't anymore…"

"There will be a dominance fight at the end of the month," Ryan said, his lips a thin line. "We haven't rented this house. We bought it. If the dads want Vanguards to continue to rule in town, they'll have to jump in, because we won't."

"We're done." Blake's voice had me turning in his arms to face him, and he ran his fingers down the side of my face when I did. "We tried to be what they wanted us to be, and now we're done trying. Are you done trying, Riley?"

You had to guess at what that meant, which was totally Blake. He used the least number of words possible, and the ones he did use made you think. What could I be done trying to do? Trying to be the best possible beta? Trying to contribute to science? Or was it something else? Trying to be what my parents and their parents had told me to be—their friend, then not even that, shoved to one side the minute they shifted. Given the means to build an impressive life, the Vanguards had definitely helped me with that, but the message was clear. You are done in this town, done with the boys, done…

"You mean am I done trying to keep away from you?" I asked, but I knew the answer.

"Are you done trying not to be what you are? You are brilliant, beautiful, strong, but, Riley, you're also ours."

The guys all made clear their approval at that statement, and somehow, I found the courage to nod just then.

"Yeah," I said with a little frown, "I guess I am done pretending this isn't exactly where I want to be."

Chapter 35

We all worked together as one then, putting the food away, cleaning the table, putting the dishes in the dishwasher, and even though it was the same shit going on in a million households across the country, it felt weird. This wasn't just a place they were staying in now, it was their home, and by extension…

Don't think too far ahead, Riley, I told myself as I slid a tray of enchiladas into the fridge, seeing that wolf running in my dreams. As Ryan filled the sink, washing off the big platters that wouldn't fit in the dishwasher, as Colt set the machine to run, as the guys walked through the kitchen, carrying stuff and calling the others foul names when they got in each other's way, I was catching a glimpse of a future my mind wasn't ready to accept. *Stop thinking so fucking hard*, I thought, paraphrasing my psychologist's advice in probably stronger terms than she would have used. *Just let yourself be.* As if in response to that, Blake appeared at my shoulder.

"They'll take twice as long as they should doing this," he said with shrug. "They can't fucking help it. C'mon."

"Where are we going?" I asked, and he just smiled in response.

"Come see," he said, grabbing my hand and leading me out the sliding doors, flicking on the lights as we went.

I let out a little gasp at what I saw—a big deck along with an outdoor setting, then beyond that there was a firepit set up, filled with wood ready to light. He walked us further out, over to a huge tree, little lights marking the pathway up to it, and there, hanging from a massive bough, was a swing seat. He sat down on the whitewashed wooden seat, then patted the space beside him.

I sat down, of course I did, because the air was cool but not too cold, enough to make me comfortable snuggling into him as he pulled me into his side. I let a long breath out, then his legs pushed us off, sending us rocking back and forth.

"So what are we doing?" I started to ask.

"Shh…" he replied, holding me close, stroking my hair.

Telling me to be quiet didn't actually change things at first. My brain still raced, taking in the landscape of the huge gardens before us. Noticing the big pond beyond and all the trees that were growing around it. Noticing the moon as it rose, casting its silvery light over us. Noticing the massive shed, the paddocks beyond, and him.

Blake was the one I felt like I knew the least about, yet why did I feel so comfortable here, nestled up against him? Why did I feel tension leaching away the moment we touched? Why was—?

"Bloody hell, I can almost hear the cogs inside your head turning," he grumbled. "Just take a breath, Riley, a big one, then let it go."

His grip tightened slightly, and I did just that, feeling like something emptied out of me when I let that breath go.

"Why wasn't it like this before?" I asked him, the real question I needed answered.

"Why didn't I touch you like this?" he asked, rubbing his hand down my side. "Why didn't I pull you onto my lap and cuddle you, just like the others did?" His grip tightened then. "Because I was shit at it. Because I didn't have the confidence of my bloody brothers. Because I was terrified if I reached out for you, you'd push me away and go sauntering over to Fen or Ryan."

"Blake." I frowned slightly as I looked up at him, and he just smiled.

"But really, because if I took you in my arms, I knew I wasn't letting you go. You didn't dream of me." I stiffened at that, feeling irrationally guilty. "But I dreamed of you, over and over. I knew you were mine, and while I was never a very good boyfriend, I am very good at being a wolf."

His eyes shone now, growing lighter, more silvery, competing with the moon for its brilliance.

"If I couldn't be the fun guy or the guy you spent hours studying with, I could be the guy who plotted and planned. It probably sounds crazy stalkerish, but when I'd come by and pick you up from class and take you to the others, I played different scenarios in my head, ones where you turned to me and looked into my eyes the way you looked into theirs." I made a small sound of distress at that, having had no idea that was how he'd felt and feeling weirdly guilty as a result. "That's why I pushed hard for us to buy this place when we came up here. Fen wanted to rent. Ryan wanted to see how the market was going, get your input first, but I said no. I found this place and made sure we bought it."

"You wanted to go all in," I said in barely a whisper.

"I was all in, the whole time, Riley. I argued fucking hard every time we were put in front of yet another omega I knew we wouldn't be able to bond with. It made us and her unhappy, but we did it over and over. I knew it was you for us. How could it not be? Everything we'd been taught pointed to you, except for one thing."

"That I'm a beta," I finished for him, my head dropping down at that as I forced my mind to focus on the swaying motion of the swing. Anything but my words.

"Are you? Roll onto your back and put your head in my lap."

"What? Why do you—?"

"Just do it, love."

Blake's alpha command was so much lighter than the others', but I still found myself following his dictates. The swing bucked slightly at my movement, then corrected itself as I settled. His hand slid down my body then, casting a warm shadow as it came to rest on my stomach.

"We don't know what you are, love. The people who should've been there to help you with this, they didn't, but we're here now."

I was about to say something, to ask questions, but right then, under his hand, I felt a sharp ache twist inside me.

"You...knew?" I asked between pants.

"You will too, when you accept us. You'll feel our responses and needs like they're your own, but right now, that's all one-sided, so you have to content yourself with letting us look after you."

Blake's fingers pulled up my shirt, then worked their way under the yoga pants slowly enough that I could stop him if I wanted.

"If you don't want to make a mess of your pants, you might want to take them off," he said as his hand moved lower.

"What? Uh!"

At every point where my body touched Blake's, I felt a warm glow, one that helped settle the twists and turns inside me. As his hand slid down, the warmth grew, bigger, more expansive, radiating all the way down to my bones and melting me. I was limp now, on the swing, in his grip, because I was capable of nothing else. His heat had turned me to an overly responsive goo, right up until his finger found my clit.

I let out a helpless little groan, feeling a tiny vestige of beta shame at letting a guy finger me outside, but that was shuffled to one side. He chuckled as my thighs fell open, his fingers seizing ground so quickly surrendered. I could see how this worked, why alphas were so essential to omegas. They took away the pain and replaced that with pleasure, making you cling to them with everything you had.

And what pleasure.

"Blake…" I gasped out as he rubbed his finger slowly, purposefully, over my clit.

"I know, love. I know. You're feeling needy again, and I'm going to take care of you. If you need me to, I can make it quick, or…"

My eyes flicked open then, finding his, the silvery glow and the glint of his fangs making clear exactly who was in the driver's seat right now.

"Or?" I gasped out.

"Or I edge you for a bit, get you close, so close." My body stiffened at that, as if his words were reality and that was where I was right now. "Then let you settle back down again before getting you close again."

"And not coming?" I complained. "That sounds like hell."

His grin widened.

"But imagine how intense it will be when you do come."

I could imagine it all too well, the bastard, and he knew that.

"And what about you?" I asked, moving my head slightly, feeling the thick, heavy weight of his cock under it. "Aren't you all supposed to be hosing me down with cum right now for my own good?"

"It helps hold you for longer. You were able to sleep for hours, then have a meal, and you've only just started aching again when I brought you out here. Whatever is in us, it helps settle the changes in you."

"So you'll fuck me," I said, trying to be brash, but my voice just came out all breathy, his fingers moving slightly faster.

"Riley—"

"You'll put that freaking huge dick in me."

"Riley—"

"You'll have to ease it in, because damn, you're fucking huge."

"Dammit, Riley. We're trying to do things right here."

"Right?" I got up then in a series of shaky movements as the swing moved, Blake forcing it to a stop before I tipped myself

pleasure, pampering, pleasing me until I felt like I couldn't bear any more, and then they'd do something else super sweet.

Flowers from the garden. My favourite breakfast prepared just for me. Movies from my childhood played on the TV, and them, always them. Holding me, pulling me onto their laps, stroking me, which quickly led to other things, as they seemed to stoke the fire burning inside me until it felt like I couldn't burn any higher.

The thing about dreams though? At some point, you have to wake up, and I did one morning to find a strange woman at the end of the bed. Eloise, Omega Vanguard, stood there, staring down at me, a small frown forming.

"I wondered where they'd got to, and now I know," she said, her voice corded with pain. "I thought... I hoped..." She shook her head sharply. "Hello, Riley. I really hoped I'd never find you in this position."

Chapter 36

Suddenly, I was right back in Bordertown, the only adult in the room looking down at me with disappointment, my heart racing as I tried to work out why, but it was no great mystery, obviously. I was here, in her sons' bed, alone.

"I thought we'd talked about this?" Now she looked affronted as well as disappointed, her eyes seeming to take in my dishevelled state and the fact I was naked under the covers in an instant, her brows furrowing further. "I thought we made the realities of this situation clear to you. The boys, they're—"

"Not for you, Riley," I said in a low whisper, repeating that phrase I'd heard over and over. It was mantra I'd lived my life by, a prison sentence that had been slapped on me without proper process, but when I met Eloise's eyes, I saw for her it was doubly true now.

"I always wanted you for a daughter-in-law," she said, obviously trying to soften the blow, and when she stopped frowning, I felt a weird sense of relief. "I wanted you for my sons just as much as your father did, but you can't beat biology."

As if summoned by her words, a sharp slice of pain had me

wincing, and then that frown was back, but that was just a tiny precursor of what was to come.

"I don't know what they've told you, what they've done, but…" Her eyes went distant then, containing a world of pain, one she was about to drag me into. "The boys left the town without warning, with a message that the running of Border-town was to revert to the alpha council until such time as a new ruling pack could be established via a dominance fight. I stepped in as pack omega, forced to look through the paperwork and business transactions to try and find where my sons had gone, because none of them were answering their phones or emails, and guess what I found?"

She blinked then, her eyes taking on a slightly accusing cast, but I couldn't work out why. I didn't do this, couldn't tell her boys to do a single thing, as was evidenced by me lying here in their bed.

"A huge purchase of a property just outside the city and an email for a request for subjects for studies run at your work-place." She glared at me now, drawing herself up with all the fractious power of an omega. "You were listed there, in the email, as one of the researchers. We paid for you to go to medical school, to become a doctor. We pulled some strings to get you into the fast-track program, thinking you'd use that to go out and help people, and instead?"

She was talking too fast, her words jumbling up in my head, the growing sense of dread that came with them thwarting my ability to decode them.

"Latents used to be…removed from my old pack, for just this reason," she charged on. "Not enough beta to know your place, not enough of an omega to be what they needed, but Janine is."

"Janine?" I said with lips that felt numb.

"They found their mate," she snapped. "Did they tell you that? Whatever little…farewell this was…" She looked around the room, the crease in her forehead only growing deeper. "It was a bloody expensive one, though I guess if Janine wants a holiday home…"

"Janine?" I said again, unable to get past the name.

Eloise hissed at that, pulling out her phone and swiping until she found what she was looking for. She turned the device towards me, and just like that, whatever vague twinges that were building inside me were completely and utterly obliterated. There, on the screen, was the future I'd grown up to believe in. She was sweet-faced, cute, and had the same outrageously curvy body of an omega, but that wasn't evidence in and of itself. It was the way she was centred in the photo, five familiar bodies clustered close around her, in a protective way I knew now all too well. My eyes felt as sharp as knives as I caught the way their hands rested on her shoulder, the way they smiled at the camera, at the warmth in their eyes.

"They found their mate," I mumbled, needing to say the words to process them.

My response was immediate.

"Get out," I snapped, clambering out of the bed.

"Riley, I'm just—"

"Fine," I said. "You get to see my tits then." I ripped the blankets away, grabbing a bra, a shirt, some pants, and then proceeded to wrench them on at rapid speed.

"Oh, well, I'll just…"

She said something, no doubt important to her but not to me, not right now. I saw that wolf running inside my mind, in my dreams, and her frantic lopes made perfect sense to me now. I grabbed my bag, my phone, shoving everything into the bag before my fingers closed around the thing I actually needed—my car keys.

"Riley!" she yelped as I shoved past her, but I didn't have time for niceties right now. I'd bow and scrape and offer my apologies if and when I saw her next, but right now, I had other priorities.

The mess in the lounge room, the mattress we'd lain on, the bowls of stale popcorn taunted me as I strode past them. They spoke of a familiarity, an intimacy that I had fought so hard to resist, but they'd… I scanned the living room, hearing Eloise splutter something at me, but I didn't bother to listen. I had belongings scattered through the whole living area, but none that I'd miss too much if I lost them. And I would, because I wasn't coming back here, ever.

Then we both froze when we heard the key in the front door turn the lock.

I moved fast then, adrenalin helping me to move with surgical precision as I flicked open the sliding door, one foot out of it, when they came walking in.

"Mum, what the hell are you doing here?" Fen asked, his arms laden with groceries, but it was Colt that saw me.

"Riley?"

"Who's Janine?" I asked, my voice containing an alpha's bark of its own, just this once. I studied their faces, watching their expressions like a hawk, looking for the evidence to support the hypothesis I was testing like the scientist I was. I found surprise, alarm, fear, anger, but all of them were ones I could've worked with. There could've been reasonable explanations behind them, but it was Fen and Ryan's expressions that sealed their fate for me because I knew them, knew what they looked like when they knew they'd fucked up. Knew what a flush of guilt looked like on them. My mouth thinned, my jaw locking down before I nodded and then turned on my heel.

I slammed the door behind me but chaos erupted as I did. *Run*, she told me inside my head. *Run away from these unworthy mates. Run!*

So I did, my feet feeling like they were sliced open by the gravel, but that didn't slow me for a second. I heard my name shouted out at me as my hand slapped down on the driver's seat door handle of my car, my finger depressing the unlock button on my keys. Then I was inside, my bag shoved onto the spare seat, my finger locking down the car right as Colt's hands slammed down on the bonnet. He was mouthing something, his voice muffled by the glass and the thumping heartbeat in my ears, then the roar of my car's engine as I turned the ignition. He protested, cried out some kind of plea or something, but I just stared into his silvered eyes as I put the car in gear, watching him forced to jerk himself away and out of my path as I turned the wheel and drove out of the property.

At first, I couldn't think or do anything other than focus on keeping the car on the road. Trees, paddocks, cows, it all whipped past, but I just kept my eyes on the road, just driving and driving until a familiar buzzing sound started up. I tried to ignore it, keep driving and just…get away, but I couldn't be allowed that privilege, could I? The sound of calls coming in felt like a drill was slowly boring into the side of my head, one I couldn't ignore, until I was finally forced to flick on my indicators and pull over on the side of the road. The sound only got worse now, the quiet invaded by the regularly pulsing buzz. I ripped open my bag, pulled out my phone, and then looked at it.

This was when I would answer the phone. This was when I would speak to the men I'd known half my life and get their side of the story. This was when we would talk things out like adults, where they would break the news to me about what was happening, what they'd done, and why they'd done it. But as my thumb hovered over the answer call button, something stopped me from allowing the call to go through.

If you stop and think about it, you'd know what it was.

It was that moment when you felt like you totally connected with someone, whether on a date or when you met them at a party. You went from wondering if there was anyone out there for you to being filled with that magical feeling of affinity, all the more extraordinary because it was with someone you'd only just met. Yet once you'd parted, when it came time to make contact, when you were buoyed up by a sense of optimism that was almost dizzying, nothing. Ignored texts or DMs, calls that went unanswered, it all slowly had you realising that at least for him, none of it was real.

It was those many, many small moments of unease that built when you were in a relationship. Initially, the lessening of attention and affection could be put down to a relationship settling into a comfortable groove, but then…it got worse. He was always pulling away first, had absences he couldn't properly explain. He smiled all the time but it never reached his eyes, and he was always busy, always skating around serious queries about how he was doing, until he was ready to have the final one.

Or the lack of that final conversation altogether. Coming home and finding him gone, every trace of him carefully removed from your life and letting you fill in the gaps the best you could.

Or not. They just didn't care enough either way.

I didn't want to talk to the guys, didn't want to hear what they had to say. It was listening to them that had gotten me where I was right now. I hadn't wanted to do this, sure that they had a mate out there, and they'd heard my arguments, nodded along, and then systematically worked to get under my defences, dismantling all my protests until I was here—half-dressed, bedraggled, pressing my thumb on the reject call button, only for another call to come through seconds later. They were going to insist, demand, use that alpha bark to get what they wanted, and what would that be? A beta mistress to keep in their pack house, away from the public eye and their true omega, but trained now to take alpha cock whenever they wanted? I rejected the next call and the next, then put one of my own through.

"Biaaaatch…" Candy said. "Can you talk or have you randomly clit dialled me and have a mouthful of alpha dick going on?"

"Candy…"

"Shit," she said, her tone changing completely. "Hang on for a sec, I'm heading to my office." I waited until she came back down the line, and when she did, I let out a long breath. "What did they do?"

"They have a mate," I forced out.

"Yeah, you." But her voice bristled with indignation.

"No, they have an omega mate."

I couldn't say any more after that, feeling my eyes burn as I tried to hold it all back, but what I refused to let out felt like it multiplied exponentially inside me. What Eloise said had felt like an ancient prophecy, one I'd been warned about long, long ago, but I'd just persisted, thinking somehow, I was exempt from its conditions.

Only to find out I wasn't.

"Meet me at my place if you can," she said. "They'll come looking for you at yours. Or I can come and get you. Where the hell are you anyway?"

"I'm fine," I forced out, even though everything about my voice said otherwise. "I'll meet you at yours."

After we ended the call, I turned my phone off, unable to cope with yet more calls coming through. I was going to need to use every damn scrap of focus I had to get me across town to Candy's, so I did what I did when I first came to town—everything that had happened since they came back was shoved down in that box, the same one I'd stuffed full of memories last time. It rattled and shook as I drove, but I felt much more clear-headed, right up until I got to her place. She was sitting on her doorstep, a bag full of tubs of ice cream on one side and some Jiffy firelighters on the other.

"Eat ice cream first, then burn their place down, or arson first, then empty carbs?"

"Empty carbs," I replied, stumbling on inside and slumping down on her couch.

A tub of ice cream was put in one hand, a spoon in the other, and I peeled off the lid and stuck the spoon in, taking a mouthful as she settled down in the opposite arm chair.

"So they have a mate? How is that possible?"

At that, the ice cream was left to melt in my mouth, then trickle down my throat before I set the tub down on her coffee table. I took a deep breath, and then I told her.

Chapter 37

I'd spent the rest of the afternoon eating my body weight in ice cream and then drinking the shitty sweet red wine Candy had in the house. She'd offered to get something that I actually liked, but I hadn't been up for that. I needed support more than a good bottle of gin, so we'd hunkered down in the lounge room and dug deep.

"Are you going to talk to them?" she asked after my verbal diarrhoea had stopped. I'd vomited out everything that'd happened in great big lurid chunks, and she'd winced around her ice cream.

"If I talk to them, they'll just suck me in like before," I said, a hysterical edge to my voice. "Maybe they've been using their alpha commands the whole time."

"Riley…"

"No, you don't get it. You haven't heard the way they talk. Sometimes it's like a whip crack. Do this now! But half the time, it's this sneaky thing. It sounds like a suggestion, but really—"

"Fuck, girl, I'm not saying for a second that this situation isn't completely shit, but seriously? You're trying to tell me that you had to be ordered to fall on their dicks and let them hose you with cum like your bush was on fire? C'mon."

I blinked, then shot her a filthy sidelong look.

"I thought you were on my side."

"I am on your side. Not mentioning whoever the hell Janine is, that's a dick move of epic proportions and one they need to explain and provide verifiable facts to support their answer. Even then, I'm pretty sure they all need a collective junk punch."

I snorted at that.

"But you can only ghost them if you don't give a shit, and you…?" She shot me an empathetic look. "You care about them." I hated her voice, soft now with none of its usual acerbic edge. "And that's the problem, isn't it?"

"Shut up."

"You never stopped."

"Shut up! Seriously." I frowned then, my head aching in response, so I took another slug of wine straight from the bottle.

"Oh, so we've gotten to the 'glasses are a bourgeois affectation' part of the evening? Good to know." She pulled the bottle from my hand and took a big gulp from it without even wiping the lip, and that's when I knew we were truly besties. "Then if we aren't gonna talk about the guys, we need to talk about you. 'Round-the-clock sexual care, with liberal dosing of sparkling alpha ball juice' I believe was the prescribed regime, and I'm assuming you're all out of wolf boy spoof. We don't even know what's happening to you, what the dangers are, or how to mediate them."

And that was how she managed to pull me out of my funk, at least temporarily. Problem solving was my jam, so I pulled over a pen and paper and started drawing a cross section of a uterus and vagina.

"So they kept talking all this bullshit about something in their jizz helping me," I said through gritted teeth. "Probably a total scam and a means to keep me letting them baste me with broghurt." Candy snorted at that, then forced her expression to become solemn under my inspection. "What *is* happening is I feel like someone's scraping the inside of my uterus with a rusty spoon and my tits are like bombs ready to go off."

"I did notice the chest enhancement," she said. "Welcome to the D club…" She held out a fist for me to bump, but I just stared at it.

"These are involuntary changes to my body that I didn't sign up for at all," I informed her.

"Yup, but on the plus side, when you are ready to get up on the baloney pony and ride, those tits on that frame? You gonna get offers."

She meant it as a consolation, but it just felt like something was dying inside me. In some ways, this was a very protracted, long overdue end of a key relationship. Beforehand, we'd just disappeared from each other's lives, but now? Now we were breaking up, for good this time, but where the hell did that leave me? I'd been fucking with my latency like it was no big thing, knowing what I did about it. My fingers tightened around the pen, the tip boring into the paper until Candy said, "Prostaglandin."

"What?"

"Prostaglandins," she said. "As per usual, you've got your head up your ar—I mean, in the sand, and don't want to deal with what's going on emotionally, because feelings, ew. You want to focus on what you can have some sort of impact on. Science."

"I need to get my body back online," I said sharply. "I've just done…fuck knows what to it and now… I need to get back to work, to try and recover from this shit, because I'm gonna have to tell Windsor the study is off."

"Or you don't." She looked at me steadily. "They're not the study, you are. We'll get their DNA analysis reports back tomorrow, but…"

She shrugged.

"I'd be willing to bet you whatever you like that they don't show up anything interesting, that they're bog standard alphas with all the usual genetic markers. We include them in the study, compare them against the DNA of other alphas to illustrate that point, but you… Your reports will come back tomorrow too. Prostaglandins make our uterus contract during childbirth and a period, relaxin helps the ligaments in the pelvis stretch to take a baby. We'll head up to endocrinology tomorrow, see if they can run some tests for us, maybe even inquire about some synthetic relaxins they're trialling and see what they do. In the meantime, we'll get you on some Midol and see if that eases things."

I nodded slowly then, seeing the wisdom to what she'd said, but my fingers were still tapping the pen on the pad over and over.

"So if that solves the immediate issues with your career, what about everything else?"

I gave her an unfriendly look then. Candy had dealt with all the issues I'd raised as a means to bring me back to the ones she thought I should deal with.

"I need to order some clothes and underwear if I'm to front up to work tomorrow. None of my old stuff is going to fit."

She let out a sigh, then shook her head.

"Drinking away your sorrows and doing a makeover. Usually, these are my tried-and-true means of getting over someone. Well, aside from getting under someone else. I can't interest you in Tinder?"

"Tinder's full of sociopaths and fuck boys," I grumbled, grabbing out my phone and navigating over to a website where I bought a lot of my work clothes from.

"Yeah, but if they have a rough tongue and can breathe out their ears, who fucking cares? Now gimme. You have literally no idea how to dress for your new figure, and it has been a personal mission of mine to get you out of the *school marm with a stick rammed up her arse* bullshit you used to wear."

"Oh please, introduce me to the ways of corporate thot-wear," I replied, but I handed over my phone. The bitch turned into an angry child if her grabby hands didn't get what they wanted.

"Thot? Bitch, please. You need to do a lot more than get blasted in the face a few times by blue veined junket pumpers to become a thot. You need to earn that shit. Now, this is what you should be wearing."

She turned my phone around, revealing a woman in a pinstripe suit. Nipped in at the waist and single breasted, it could totally work. The plunging neckline of the satin blouse she had under it was not quite what I was thinking, but...

THE NEXT MORNING, I stared into the mirror of Candy's bathroom, patting a little more concealer over the massive bags under my eyes until I began to look more human. It didn't really work, but it was the thought that counted, right? My head throbbed, my eyes ached, I'd popped enough Midol to make my gut roil uneasily, and my heart beat erratically inside my chest, but the combination of drugs and wine had eased the pain enough that I got a few hours' sleep. I looked at myself in Candy's bathroom mirror, dressed in the clothes she had picked up just before closing, then swiped on some mascara and lip gloss.

I was as ready as I was ever going to be.

"You don't have to do this, you know," my friend said to me, looking at me blearily over the top of her cup of super milky coffee. "Windsor still thinks you're out conducting the study. You could take a few days, lie around and watch some movies—"

"Did that," I said with a tight smile. "Didn't help me then and it won't now. I need a distraction, and nothing is a better distraction than work. Plus, I want to see those analyses before Evan gets his hands on them."

"Yeah, fuck, C-3PO, you might have a point there." Candy's eyes narrowed. "That little fuck is getting squirrelly due to being 'demoted' to doing our work. It's been a while since he's tried to steal someone else's research, and god knows this is the perfect project for him to poach."

I finally got her on board. She got ready in a scramble then, the two of us going in her car and arriving just in time.

· · ·

"I'M TAKING OVER THE GIRLS' work, so all correspondence should come through me," Evan insisted, but Janet looked over his shoulder, her face brightening as she saw us. She had the mail clasped to her chest like one would an injured puppy, not giving an inch as Suck Up Evan tried to physically wrench it from her grip.

"No need for that," Candy drawled as we entered the reception area. "I wouldn't want you to be exposed to all my plentiful fan mail, as well as my monthly subscription to *Stud Muffins of Science*. I'll take our mail, thanks, Janet." She propped her elbow on the high desk counter and looked Evan over slowly. "You get caught opening something not addressed to you, I will follow up with HR. And you remember how that went last time? Don't go trying to bully Janet either. She has Felicity on speed dial."

Felicity was our HR rep, a total spitfire, and one who had Gideon's full support, especially when dealing with his son. Saved him from doing it, I guessed.

I moved closer, wanting to see Evans' foul expression more than I wanted my next breath, and sure enough, there it was— bottom lip pushed out, his claw like hands scraping his lank hair back from his face as he scowled impotently at us. I was sure he qualified for both meanings of *impotent*.

"What're you doing here?" he snapped at me, the fuck's eyes dropping down to my chest within seconds.

"Eyes up here, motherfucker," I replied. "There's a lull on things at the moment, and I wanted to come in and look over the analysis and any preliminary reports that have come back from pathology."

"Those are here," Janet said, passing them over. "They came via special courier."

"And where's the other samples you should have been taking?" he asked with a sneer. "Or have you just been too busy rolling around like a bitch in heat, hit by all those alpha pheromones they're producing for their omega, to bother to take any?"

I had been doing exactly that actually, though I'd collected plenty of samples. Not grabbing them when I ran out of the pack's house was a rookie mistake. Unfortunately, Eloise breaking my fucking heart had created a lapse in professional judgement. Before I could answer his shitty question, the door opened and exactly the man I didn't want to see stepped in.

Colt looked like shit. Eyes too wide, skin too pale, and the dark pouches under his eyes rivalled mine and Candy's, because like the Louis Vuitton website, he had bags for days. He also had a plastic bag in his hand.

"You left some stuff at the house," he said with the voice of the undead. "There's some personal stuff, but I figured you'd need the samples."

"Man, you look wrecked!" Evan said with some grotesque approximation of bro dude bonhomie. I winced as he raised a hand, waiting for Colt to fist bump him or something. "The little lady keeping you busy? Omegas, amirite?"

So this was like watching a very slow, very horrific car crash happen right before our eyes. Colt's eyes went bright silver in a flash, his lips peeling back from his teeth to reveal sharp fangs, an almost inaudible growl making Evan snatch back his hand and take a step away. I almost smiled as the weaselly beta withdrew, shooting the three of us heated glares, but after we watched him beat a hasty retreat back to his office, no doubt to do nothing other than play endless games of spider solitaire, I was left to face down Colt.

Janet made herself busy. Candy deserted me with a slap to my shoulder, taking possession of the mail and pathology reports.

"Thanks for bringing these in," I said.

Like most women, I could plaster on a professional smile when I needed to, hide my feelings behind my mask. I did that right now, even as it felt like my face would crack with it. Colt just eyed me, his wild silver eyes and vicious-looking fangs as out of place in this beta ruled territory as his actual wolf form.

"Riley—"

"Did you want to come through to my office? I know you need to get back to *your mate*."

I bit those last two words off, just slightly, but he nodded, and it seemed like Janet only took a full breath when we walked into the lab. I knew the fucking feeling. I stalked through the lab and down the hall to my office on fucking heels because Candy had assured me everyone felt kickarse in heels. I actually felt off balance and unsteady, but that seemed to be a good metaphor for my life, so I went with it. I unlocked my door and wrenched it open before ushering him abruptly in.

"Riley—"

"Don't," I said, with a bright vicious edge. I wasn't going to cry or rage or do anything. I was going to survive. That was it. "You're just going to talk at me, like everyone always does. Bamboozle me with bullshit, have me believing up is down and red is green." I sat on the edge of my desk, hoping I looked like a fucking suited badass, but was pretty sure I just looked tired and worn in comparison to my crisp new clothes. "Who's Janine?"

"She's an omega," he replied, his fingers twitching before he shoved them in his pockets.

"Of course she is." I glanced at the smooth white walls, their blandness soothing on my eyes. "It's always a fucking omega. And you didn't tell me about her." He stood there, not moving, not looking away for a second. Fen was hard at work, as per usual, having sent the alpha most likely to be the sacrificial lamb. "And that's why you're here. Not Fen, not Ryan, not Haze. You're the one I'll feel safe enough to lash out at, unload all my anger onto. You're the one who'll stand there and just take it."

His nostrils flared, his gaze unending as I stepped closer and closer. I watched the hope war with pain in his eyes, right up until I removed the bag from his fingers and then scooted on out of his reach, somehow disappointed when he didn't try to stop me.

I rifled through what was inside there, seeing crumpled

clothes, toiletries, my phone charger, and then the precious pathology bags crammed full of samples.

"So if words won't do, what will?" he asked, his jaw firming, his gaze sharpening.

I sucked in a breath, ready to fucking tell him just how bloody futile all this shit was, when there was a sharp knock at the door. Candy poked her head in, glancing warily at the two of us.

"Endocrinology will see us any time this morning. They've reshuffled all their appointments when they saw we were interested in coming up. So, do you guys need time to tear into each other or tear off each other's clothes? Fight or fuck, you tell me."

She eyed the two of us like a small child would their fighting parents, but I wasn't going to do either of those things today. I pushed myself away from my desk, keeping my distance from Colt.

"Evidence," I told him. "I've heard what you said, what they said, what your mother said, and I'm done listening to opinions. That's the freaking point of science—it goes beyond emotion to the actual hard evidence."

The muscles in his jaw flexed before he nodded, then drew a specimen jar out of his pocket and thrust it at me. It was full to the brim with a milky liquid I just knew was cum. I frowned slightly as I took it from him, then gazed up at him quizzically.

"If you start hurting too much, apply that. It's fucking gross, but I don't know what else to do for you."

And at that, he turned on his heel and walked out of my office.

"Man, kids these days, vaping Tide pods and giving girls jars of their own semen…" Candy said, trying to laugh and failing. "Endocrinology?"

"Endocrinology," I confirmed.

Chapter 38

"So, what can I do for the ladies of genetic disorders?"

Simon was a big guy who had the manner and the physique of a bear, just a gentle one. He flopped down into his well padded office chair, us doing the same across from him.

"You've been kept in the loop about our study?" I asked.

"Candy filled me in. Damn, I wish the subjects had answered our call for participants. You've got a latent responding positively to a pack of alphas?"

He might be all honey blond hair and a big bushy beard, but those brown eyes were sharp and shrewd, skewering us on the end of his gaze.

"It looks like she might transition," I said. "The alphas seem absolutely sure about that."

"Hormones," he said with a dismissive snort, but he was nonetheless hanging on our every word.

"The latent has gone through considerable physical changes," I explained. "Breast size, widening of hips—"

"A second adolescence?" Simon leaned forward, then his fingers started to fly over his keyboard as he pulled up papers. "Lemme guess, the latent didn't so much reveal as a beta as plump for the designation? And the changes only began when in the presence of the alphas."

"Now she is. She was known to the pack during childhood."

"Including during adolescence?" he asked, scanning the literature.

"Yep."

"Hmm…that definitely is intriguing. So talk to me. What do you need from us?"

"There's some concern about what this is going to do to the woman, obviously," I said, forcing myself to keep my tone cool and clinical, as everything else rattled around in that box inside me. "The dangers for latents have been well documented."

"And overemphasised," he replied, shooting me a genial smile. He was a nice guy and everything, but there was a little *pat the hysterical woman on the head* in his tone. "I know they love to do the cautionary tale bullshit at university, but honestly? We've seen a lot of latents come through here, and only about one percent of our patients need medical treatment. Every beta is a latent in some way or another, which you should know as geneticists."

I smiled and nodded then, even as I gritted my teeth.

"Well, what's brought us to you is some alpha mating rituals," I said. "They call the phase the latent is going through right now 'transition.' She's being readied for mating with them through near constant physical contact, a lot of emotional bonding, as well as what appears to be a regular schedule of sexual interactions focusing particularly on the application of sperm orally, vaginally, and on her breasts. They explained that this eases the pain of transition."

"And now we get to the good stuff." Simon leant forward, resting his head on his arms. "Sounds like quite a job you got going there." There was something just a little sleazy about his smile then, or was I being too sensitive? "You must have an excellent relationship with the pack and their prospective mate to get this close to the purpose."

313

I smiled tightly in response, leaning back in my chair and staring back at him coolly.

"I don't actually see any of this, obviously. Omegas are notoriously touchy about other people getting close to them and their packs during transition, and the subject is the same. I instructed the pack on how to collect samples for us before things went too far, and they've been quite diligent about it. I think they're hoping we'll be able to help if things go pear-shaped during transition."

"I bet." His eyes shone, then he straightened up. "They want her to shift from being a beta to an omega. There might be more examples of that happening, but we don't hear about them. They're strangely close-lipped about it all, caught up in some kind of fucked-up racial purity bullshit. OK, so what do you want from me? To brainstorm what to try with this latent? And what tests to get done to try and narrow down what might be effective? Adding hormones like relaxin or adrenaline isn't a simple thing. The body produces different hormones in complex cascades within the body to keep the endocrine system healthy, so slamming this latent full of one or the other probably won't have the desired effect. Let's get some baseline stats and then work out a plan from there."

We walked out of Simon's office with a handful of pathology forms, both of us quiet until we got in the lift.

"Riley?" Candy asked when we saw the carriage was empty, the elevator jerking as it took us down several floors. "You OK?"

"Hormones," I said, flashing her a smile I didn't feel. "Just hormones."

AND WEIRD GENETIC DEFECTS.

When we got back to my office, we retrieved the DNA analysis reports I'd kept locked in my drawer. As we pored over the films and the reports, the guys were all exactly as we expected—grade A Australian alphas. But mine?

"Shit," Candy said, her eyes widening. "No wonder they've been responding to you." She dragged over my computer and then pulled up some of the textbook omega DNA samples people had taken from sick omegas admitted to hospital. "Look, here, here, here…" Her voice faded away and was replaced with a high-pitched white noise buzzing inside my head as I saw all the points of similarities.

We'd been made to run our own DNA samples at university to learn how to extract DNA using the equipment. I'd resisted looking too hard at my own, trying not to analyse what was there for fear of first year medical student syndrome. People were constantly lampooned for their tendency to assume every single rare and horrific medical condition was one they now suffered from. By this point, we'd all learned that there was a whole lot of genetic diversity that just floated under the radar, rarely identified unless there was an issue. I knew I was a latent, I knew I didn't have issues, so I didn't need to analyse it.

But a big part of it? It was what rattled in that box. I was given a simple way of explaining things, that I was a beta and the guys were alphas and never the twain should meet. If they'd come and found me at university, burst into a lecture and claimed me before everyone, just like I'd often fantasised about, then maybe I would have taken a second look. But while population level aberrations were of interest, individual quirks? They were just outliers until proven otherwise and not worth the mental energy to look at.

Until now.

"Riley," Candy said in a hushed tone. "In any other community, you would've been an omega for sure."

I frowned at her words, rubbing at my temples, feeling a now familiar ache start up inside me, but this time, it was joined by something else altogether.

Riley Taylor was the great pretender. I'd faked hating the guys' attention back at high school. I'd faked being OK with leaving them when I went to university. I'd faked being OK as I studied, right up until I hadn't been. Even then, when I broke down, I'd learned what I was supposed to look and act like from my psychologist and then I'd faked that too. I'd faked so fucking well, I believed my own lies. My fingers scratched at the desk, Candy watching me in alarm, as I tried very, very hard right now to fake keeping my shit together and not scream.

For seconds, minutes, hours, I couldn't tell which, I just focussed on my breath, loud and rasping, rattling in my chest, fighting to get in and get out, right up until my claws dug into the desktop.

"Oh, fucking shit…" Candy said, peering closer, catching like I did the minute my ragged nails shifted. They became hard curving claws sprouting from human fingers, with small smatterings of reddish fur along their lengths. "Riley… Earth to Riley, because fuck, girl, I am not down with getting up close and personal with your fursona. Um…keep taking deep breaths, just like that. Good girl. Such a good girl."

"Are you talking to me like I'm a fucking dog?" I all but growled, and felt a pang of fear as it came out distorted and guttural.

"Nooo…and, bitch, you need to stay fucking calm. You've got eyes like twenty-cent coins right now, and that ain't no French manicure you're rocking. Stop thinking about whatever fucking omega bullshit—" I bared my teeth then, wanting her to shut the fuck up, pleased when she did, but it didn't last. "You've also got a little thing right here…" She pointed to my canines, flinching when my tongue flicked up and felt the sharper points.

Of course that was when someone knocked on my door.

It didn't feel like it was my eyes that stared at the door. I couldn't exactly say how, but it felt like I saw more, scented more as I took in a deep breath, catching the stale Cheetos and Diet Coke stink of Evan, along with Candy's bright taffy sweet scent.

"Riley," came Evan's whine. "We're supposed to report to a meeting of department heads. Don't be late."

"Down, girl!" Candy hissed, slapping a hand down on my arm, right up until my focus shifted down to her grip. She yanked it back, then held a wavering finger in front of my face. "Sit. Sit and stay."

"I can hear you in there," Evan whined.

"Of course you can," Candy shot back. "We're just finishing off our hot, hot lesbian scientist make out scene. As soon as I can get Riley to leave my clit alone, we'll be there, but this girl just can't get enough."

"Fine," he grumped, then stomped off.

"OK, so we need human Riley back right fucking now," Candy said in a low voice. "Like if jizz cures what ails you, then you'll get a whole lot of it as every department head spontaneously ejaculates when they realise they have an actual latent transitioning into an omega in the building, with a fully functional wolf to call. But you'll be on the other side of the microscope, girl, the subject of some fuck's study, an anonymous footnote in their paper."

Candy knew me so well, the sheer disgust I felt at that scenario forced my claws to recede, my teeth becoming reassuringly blunt again.

"Department heads?" I asked. "What the hell will this be about?"

She let out a hysterical little laugh at that, pointing at me and shaking her head.

"What the fuck? What the actual fuck? You just… Then you…" Another frenzied laugh as she raked her hands through her hair. "Like, I am convinced five days out of ten that you aren't actually human and are just some kind of android that Crowe plonked down here to troll us, but fuck, Riley."

"Fuck Riley has a meeting and so do you," I said, getting to my feet and somehow feeling more certain about what I was doing, not less. My head felt clearer, my eyes had stopped aching, and my steps seemed longer, taking me to the door and out of it, leaving Candy to lock up after me. She hustled to catch me up, jumping in the lift with me, where Windsor was waiting.

"Good to see you, Riley," he said. "I wasn't expecting you in today, but it's fortuitous that you are. Gideon has a proposal for the team."

I took in his smug smile, the way he stood tall, and nodded graciously in response. This was gonna be good, I could just feel it.

Chapter 39

When Gideon walked into the boardroom, it was hard to see how he wasn't an alpha. He had that kind of presence that drew every person's eyes to him, and he just nodded slightly in recognition before taking a seat at the head of the table.

"Thanks for joining me at short notice. Recent developments in a brand-new genetic study I have no doubt you've already heard about led to me calling this meeting," he said.

Candy reached under the table at that, giving my hand a squeeze, because Gideon turned all that intense focus on me.

He was a good-looking guy, that was for sure. He'd been featured in as many magazines for his good looks as for his scientific and business achievements. His suit did everything it could to emphasise his broad-shouldered frame, but it was those eyes that made you feel like you were sinking into them. Dark cornflower blue and twinkling with a magnetic combination of intelligence and charisma, they made you feel like you were the only person in the room.

Which unfortunately reminded me of some other eyes that had done just the same. I frowned slightly, then straightened up in my chair, holding my head high. This, this was a much better situation to find myself in, one I actually had a chance to succeed in. So I inclined my head in recognition of Gideon's attention and then listened hard to what came next.

"We are about a year out of the big symposium being held in New York. We've already identified several studies we hope to present there." He listed each one of them, acknowledging the department heads they came from. "But I think the Crowe Institute's keynote address needs to come from genetic disorders."

A slight murmur of discontent there, but I just allowed myself a small smile. I'd heard the brief descriptions of the other studies, but c'mon. Anyone with half a brain had to know ours was what was gonna get bums on seats.

"Candace came to see me late Friday and pitched the idea to me." More mumblings, because damn, that took some balls. I shot my friend a quick sidelong look, but she just smiled serenely, staring down the table. "The study entails looking at the attempted transition of a latent omega into a functioning one, due to her exposure to a pack that believes she's their fated mate. And Riley Taylor will be the keynote speaker."

Right then, all the exhaustion and pain were blasted away, because I couldn't feel a fucking thing. The room got whiter, brighter, any sense of my body left as whatever was left of me seemed to just float, amorphous and strange.

What the hell had Candy done? Had she stalked into Gideon's office in just new Manolos and nothing else, promising Gideon a thousand decadent pleasures? Because if she was using the power of the thot for my benefit…

I came back to my body abruptly and found my heart was pounding, my head aching with it as everyone in the room stared my way. But me? I tried to swallow the lump in my throat and utterly failed as I turned to look at Candy.

I knew she was a good friend. We were an unlikely pairing, but she was relentlessly, endlessly supportive, whether I wanted her to be or not, but right now… Her eyes sparkled right now, a smile forming, a look of the sweetest pain on her face, one I recognised because I felt the exact same thing.

Gideon was going to put forward whoever presented this study as a keynote speaker. Windsor probably hoped it was him, but I'd given Candy carte blanche to claim the study as her work, to prevent the conflict of interest of me studying myself. But damn her, she'd gone on up to the top floor and argued for me, for me to present at one of the most prestigious medical conferences in the world, as the keynote speaker for our company.

"Riley? I hope that's OK with you?" Gideon prompted gently.

I let out a little laugh then, which was half sob, half snort.

"Ah, yeah, of course. Of course it is, and thank you so much for this opportunity," I said, trying to play it cool and utterly failing.

Gideon kept talking then, about the plans for the conference and the progress of the different projects, but everything just washed over me. I couldn't seem to listen, think, or feel anything beyond this.

I was being given the greatest possible opportunity someone like me, especially at this stage in my career, could get. My mind raced as I thought furiously about all the angles to take, how to present the information, which sources to reference, until finally, the meeting came to an end.

"Windsor, contact my secretary and set up the first of what will no doubt be many progress meetings around this study," Gideon said with a smile as we all got to our feet.

"Dad!" Evan pushed his way forward, the people exiting the room not really giving way to him, so he had to fight against the tide to get to his father. His face creased in irritation, growing darker and darker until he was positively fuming by the time he reached Gideon, though he took the time to smooth his face into a more acceptable expression. "So, about this study. I was thinking as senior…"

I had to give it to Evan, he persisted way past the point I would've. Gideon stared at his son with the kind of implacable look that had your words dying in your throat, just like Evan's were now. His was a watchful gaze, one that waited for you to prove that this interruption was warranted, but also made clear that anything frivolous would not be tolerated.

"Evan, my answer remains the same," Gideon replied quietly. "You want a keynote address? Earn it."

And with that, he nodded to the three of us before stalking out of the room.

CANDY and I held it together right up until we got out of the elevator, and then, as soon as Windsor's back was turned, I punched her right in the arm.

"Ow! What the fuck was that for? I just gave you exactly what you wanted, Tin Man," she spluttered, and I just stood there, staring at her. "Ohh…that's right—you're that emotionally repressed that you don't know how to deal with that." She peered up at me and then started speaking in the kind of tone you use with small children. "Now, Riley, I need you to use your words."

"Thank you." That was all I could get out right then. It was manifestly inadequate, but that realisation just made my throat lock down harder. "Thanks for everything."

"I got you, bitch, I told you that. Now c'mon. We're gonna need to work our arses off if we are…"

We walked down the hallway to find my office door open, and an ice-cold finger slid down my spine in response. It shouldn't have. We knew who would be there, and of course, there was fucking Evan, pawing through the reports we'd just left lying there on my desktop, due to my little furry incident before.

"What the hell do you think you're doing?" I snarled, and Candy shot me an alarmed look, because it wasn't entirely Riley who was speaking right then.

And Evan knew that.

His head jerked around, his eyes wild as he saw that he'd been caught, but he didn't care. If all the times before were anything to go by, he wouldn't be reprimanded, and in any case, he'd get what he wanted. But right now, my precious paperwork slipped from his fingers as he just stared at me.

"What the fuck...?"

He was staring at my eyes, stammering some bullshit out as he pointed with shaking hands, but mine didn't shake a bit as I grabbed the front of his shirt and dragged him closer.

"What the fuck are you?" he asked, eyes flicking everywhere, as if that would tell him what was happening. "What have you...?"

As his words trailed away, his eyes went to the desk, the papers, and the very deep furrows I'd carved into the desktop with my claws. Evan wasn't stupid, just really, really lazy, so it didn't take him too long to put two and two together.

"You're the latent," he said, the jubilation palpable in his voice.

"And you're fucking dead if you breathe a single word of it to anyone."

My body coursed now with a kind of power I'd never felt before, my muscles like iron as my grip tightened around his collar. His hands went up, scrabbling at the fabric, at my fingers, but got nowhere with it. His breath started coming in wheezes, the sound soft and pleasant on my ears, then his face went a fetching shade of purple.

"Fuck, down, Cujo!" Candy snapped, and that seemed to break whatever spell this was. My grip instantly loosened, dropping the man so he ended up sliding down the wall into a gasping mess at my feet. "Remember, the first rule of Candy and Riley club is we don't kill Evan, no matter how much he might deserve it. Gideon will miss him, I think."

"You fucking crazy bitch!" Evan tried to shout, but his voice just came out as a hoarse whisper. "You tried to kill me!"

"And you just broke into my office, into my turf, and went through my stuff."

Any indignation he might have felt was quickly wiped by my expression.

Was this what the alphas felt like as they moved through the world? Was this why the omegas at my school had ruled it with an iron fist? Because right now, Evan's eyes went wide as it finally sunk in what he'd done. He thought he'd discovered a trump card, but instead, he'd found something with sharp teeth and claws.

When I spoke next, I was fairly sure my eyes were shining bright silver, and Evan, he couldn't seem to look away.

"You will not speak to a single soul about this," I said in a voice that was part wolf, part woman. "You won't ever enter my office unless it's with my express permission. You will not try and fuck with my study or do anything that might piss me off."

"Or Candy," she added at the end of that.

"Or Candy. Do I make myself clear?"

He didn't want to, but he gave me a sharp little nod.

"Then get the fuck out of my office, now."

I watched him scuttle on out, not entirely sure there wasn't a wet patch on his pants as he did. When he was gone, I walked over to my door and shut it with a decisive click.

"Oh my fucking god," Candy said in a faint little voice. "Riley, you're a badass now."

Chapter 40

I felt like one, right up until I got home. I decided I was going to try and stay at my own place tonight. I'd turned my phone back on, and while there were a bunch of missed calls, voicemails, and texts waiting for me, none came after I'd spoken to Colt. I admit, part of me was disappointed, but the rest? I was sure this was the right way to do things, until I walked up to my front door. There, sprawled across my doorstep, was a massive freaking wolf. I took in the buff-coloured fur tipped heavily with grey and knew exactly who it was.

Fen.

"Well, you can bugger off home," I said, but his wolf, he just stared back at me with eyes of jade green. "I mean it, Fen. You hang around here, and the pound or the police will turn up." His lips pulled back from his fangs slightly as a small growl rumbled in his chest. "OK then, your funeral, but you're not coming inside."

As much as a wolf could acknowledge my words, Fen did. He got to his feet, the sheer bloody size of him hitting me hard, looking way, way bigger than a natural wolf. But even as he stood there, a picture of feral power, he stepped back and away from my door, letting me unlock it and go through before he took up position by the door again. He whined as he looked through the security screen, but that just made me angry all over again.

What the hell was he doing here? Where was Janine, and how did she feel about her mate lying in wait outside my place? I admit, when I thought about the opposite, of them staking out this mysterious omega's place, I was nowhere near as cool. My fingers tightened around my mail, shredding the edges of my gas bill, forcing me to take a long, steadying breath until I was able to smooth the paper back into some semblance of order. I stared at my fingers, hearing the sounds of Fen's whines through the door as my claws receded again, returning to my normal nails.

The problem with being home was it was haunted now, and not just by a bloody massive wolf lolling around on my front step. When I went into the kitchen to grab a drink, I saw the ghost of Blake as he'd moved around the space, using it to perform culinary magic. Something I could do with now, if my stomach's rumbling was anything to go by. But as I picked up my phone, punching in Sunny's number to get them to deliver me a pizza, I saw Fen and his investigation of my underwear drawer.

I'd have to pretty much toss it all out now, I thought darkly and then placed the pizza order.

As I walked into the bedroom, I saw the phantoms of Colt and Haze, entering my dreams and my heart, then as I went into the en suite, I felt Blake pressing me up against the wall, telling me exactly how he felt. But I brushed past him and all the ghosts in my heart, and after peeling my new clothes off, then stepped into the shower. I scrubbed away the makeup, the bullshit, the highs and the lows of the day, finally walking back into my bedroom.

My first thought was yoga pants, because they were stretchy enough to cope with whatever was happening with my body, but those were forever tainted now. I ended up squeezing into what used to be a roomy pair of sweatpants, groaning at my now gigantic arse. Initially, I rethought the idea of pizza, but based on what I knew of omega physiology, this was happening no matter what I did. So I threw a T-shirt on over them and walked out into my lounge room, ready to wait for my pizza and just watch some damn TV for a bit, try and recentre myself, when I was faced with yet another problem.

Johnny, my usual delivery boy, carried a big stick torch with him when delivering, just in case the local dogs were feeling frisky, but I imagined him coming up to my gate and being confronted with Fen in wolf form. I let out a long sigh and then walked up to the front door, jerking it open and forcing Fen to scramble to his feet.

"I've got pizza on the way," I said, not even sure wolf-Fen could comprehend what I was saying. It was yet another aspect of alpha physiology we didn't really understand. "I need food. Like, really need it." Fen-wolf whined as my stomach growled in response. "Johnny is not going to come down the front path if you're sitting there, which will deprive me of delicious, delicious pizza-y goodness." He just blinked at me then. "Aren't you supposed to want to provide for your mate?"

That was a mistake. His body went stock still, letting out a low-pitched whoo sound in response.

"Fen, I need you to fuck off home and do whatever the hell it is you do there. If I don't get this pizza—"

"Hey, Riley…" I looked up to see Johnny was already standing there. Sunny always reckoned he could hear when I was hangry and would get the pizza out to me in half the usual time. "Got a new dog?"

"Um, yeah," I said, then walked over to the gate, Fen following on my heels. I'd paid for the pizza on my card, so he just handed me over the box, eyeing the wolf.

"Good doggy…" he said, reaching out a hand, only to snatch it back when Fen let out a sharp bark. "Not real friendly."

"And not here for long," I assured Johnny. "I'm just minding him for a friend."

"Right, well, enjoy your night."

I waved goodbye to Johnny before deciding I would do

exactly what he said, walking back to the house and opening the front door. Fen danced around slightly then, his nails clicking on the concrete as he eyed the pizza, the door, then me.

"No," I said firmly to all of it, and he sat back on his heels abruptly at the sound of command in my voice. I'd learned something important through all of this.

The popular image of an omega was a smaller, weaker, seductive creature who ensnared his or her alphas in a web of dense pheromones that none could resist, but that was bullshit.

Eloise was Omega Vanguard. She might tend to focus on the welfare of women and children rather than the big decisions about how things should go forward, but she was still a real power in the town, and not just as an adjunct of the alphas either. She might not have their musculature, their presence, but she could bark orders like the best of them and expect to have them obeyed. I'd seen her throw down with other omegas, fight in bloody battles to maintain her position as ruling omega in the pack or to hold off those who thought they might like to become Omega Vanguard themselves.

I'd been worried about what tapping into my latency would do to me, fearing that one day, I'd become one of those pitiable creatures shown in slides during a lecture on genetics at university. Instead? I set the box down on the coffee table, then popped the lid, grabbing a slice of pizza before switching the TV on. I felt like I'd tapped into a source of hitherto unknown power.

If only that was the feeling that stayed with me.

I'd thought I was sleepy, full of food and awash with good feelings of being warm, comfortable, full, but as I stood up, things went sideways, almost literally. I heard Fen's whines first, followed quickly by an incredible wash of dizziness. "Whoa…" I said, my hands flying out to steady me, but how?

It felt like the world had lost all solidity, tipping to one side, then the other, sending me staggering after it. Paws raked across the metal security grill of my screen door, the sound like a cacophony inside my head, but that was quickly drowned out by the rapid skitter of my heartbeat in my ears. Sweat broke out all over my skin, forcing my fingers, my claws to slice across my clothing, ripping it into shreds, but freeing my body didn't help. There was a crash as a body slammed into my door, then another, right as I pitched forward onto my hands and knees, and then I knew what the fuck was happening.

"Nooo…" My voice was distorted, part cry, part howl, coming from a throat no longer entirely human.

Because that was the thing about power—it always came at a cost.

"Now, I realise this will be a distressing sight for many of you," my lecturer said. Can't remember what his name was, just that he'd been wearing a thick Arran knit jumper, the collar of his white shirt poking over the top, along with a pair of tweedy pants. "But we can't shy away from uncomfortable things in our field. What is usually an almost magical confluence of physiological and psychological forces, the shift into wolf form."

He'd turned to the screen, where we saw a naked man on all fours. The video slowed down then, showing what was usually a swift transformation from human to wolf form, instead giving us a blow-by-blow view of the process. Of bones snapping and reforming. Of fur sprouting from hair follicles. Of muscles shortening, lengthening, shifting with the man to become that of a beast. Finally, the clip sped up again, showing a panting wolf where a man had been.

"Sometimes, that gets disrupted. The person in question is missing the key elements of a successful shift, yet feels impelled to try by instincts we're still trying to understand," the lecturer continued.

He pressed the button on his clicker so a new slide appeared on the screen, and then we were treated to the sight of the same transformation, just in a very different process.

The woman's lips were pulled back into a snarl before she even went down into a crouch, her teeth bared as every muscle locked down. If you've ever seen fasciculations before, they are strange things. The muscle seems to jump on the body without any conscious effort from the person themselves, twitching and jerking in response to something else altogether, and that was what happened here. Her flesh seemed to…ripple? There was no better word for it. A wave of fur appeared, then disappeared, bones cracking to initiate a shift, but then reverting back.

The only thing that seemed to progress was her pain. She screamed at the start and kept on screaming, a small titter of defensive amusement starting up in the lecture theatre, but the lecturer didn't bother trying to calm us down because the video did the work for him. We were watching some kind of torture porn as part of a learning experience, her agony apparent as she fought and fought to try and make the change, only to end up collapsing down onto the floor, and that silenced everyone. We all watched the woman fight a battle she could not win.

When the medical staff came forward and injected her with a sedative, we all let out a sigh of relief. I just wished I had something similar right now.

I was sucking in oxygen in great noisy gulps, my sides heaving like a bellows. I wanted to cry and scream as the first shots of pain started, my fingers becoming claws as they dug into the floorboards. My first shout came out choked off and mangled, my head thrown back as my throat warred between human and wolf form, my tongue feeling too big in my mouth, then too small as I did, but that was minor compared to what was happening to my body. It felt like someone was systematically breaking every one of my bones, then when I managed to reset them, they went back and broke them again. Agony, so much agony, flooded my body, narrowed down my focus, and locked me down inside a dark hole I knew now I'd never escape.

Everything I'd ever feared was coming true. Trapped in my body, I was forced to admit the truth—I was a latent. I didn't possess all of the elements of a successful shift, which was why my beast had always been a weak presence inside me. A true wolf shifter's beast made itself known, springing forth on call or when it decided it needed to intervene, and mine had done little more than whine in my ear, just as she did now. I heard her anxiety, her fear, but it was a grinding sound, further emphasising that I was fucked. I might become locked like this, always reaching for my beast and unable to find her, my mind racing faster and faster until…

The slams on the door stopped because he burst in, wearing human form now.

"Shift!" he ordered, using his alpha bark to command me, every muscle in me straining to do exactly that and failing. "Shift, Riley! So fucking help me, you have to get out of her way. She's trying to come through, and you keep fucking blocking her. Your fear, your anger, your…" He paused then, something I meant to ask him about later, but always forgot. "Jesus Christ, shift, now!"

Afterwards, I realised what I'd been going through was like banging my head over and over against an invisible ceiling. I couldn't see the barrier keeping me stuck, so I couldn't fight past it, not until Fen reached down and yanked me through. Everything happened so fucking fast now, my body shifting, changing, breaking, and remaking until…

I stood there now, on my own four paws, panting frantically as I tried to catch my breath, my muscles shaking with the effort. Slowly, so slowly, I came back to myself, flicking my tail, then throwing back my head and letting out a godawful howl to mark what I'd just been through.

"Riley girl," a voice said, dragging my focus back to him. "You're beautiful."

Chapter 41

For a minute, I just was in a way only animals can be. I breathed, existed, my new form hit from all sides by stimuli. I'd never realised how harsh the detergents I used on my tile floor smelled, and drool formed in my mouth at the ripe scents of my pizza box, even as my stomach informed me very clearly there would be no more consumption of food without consequences. The tiles felt too hard, too smooth under my paws, my claws having nothing to dig into for traction. The artificial breeze from the fan slowly cycling above ruffled my fur and pushed wafts of different scents at me in waves that were confusing. Then there was him.

My head jerked up, my eyes taking in the tall man above me and then the mess he'd created of the barrier into my den. Then he made the mistake of crouching down, close, too close, a low growl forming in my chest as a result. He ignored that with an arrogance that just made my anger flare hotter, harder, that had me shying away when he reached out with a hand, snapping at the air when he persisted. With my fangs and my snarls, it became apparent what I thought of his offer, until finally, he pulled his hand back. I moved restively then, seeing the silver light rise in his eyes, eyes that looked just like mine, I was willing to bet. His beast stared at me, and I stared back, making it clear nothing had changed. *Stay away, leave me*, my gaze said clearly, and I didn't look away for a second until he did just that.

"I'm going," he said. "Text me in the morning, or I'll come back, assuming you need help to shift back." Fen nodded then, his eyes scanning me with a kind of possessiveness that had me growling again, but he didn't attempt to get any closer. "You wanted evidence? It'll be coming your way in the morning, via your workplace. You'll want to be there for it."

My wolf couldn't relax until he was out of our space. Fen was too big, took up too much room, his scent perfuming the air, filling our nose, and he hadn't earned that right. In this form, I wasn't exactly clear about the complications that had me unhappy with him, I just knew I was, and when he walked out, shutting the front door behind him, my muscles unlocked. So why did we trot over to the entrance, scrambling to place our paws up on the front windowsill to watch him go? He turned when he reached the gate, noting this with a smile before leaving.

Left to my own devices, instincts roared up now and my nose went to the ground as soon as I put my paws down, snuffling at the tiles until I had trotted back to the bedroom. I was up and on the bed in one smooth leap, pawing at the blankets, pushing some aside with my nose and others into a pile until I formed a loose kind of nest. I took a long whiff of the fabric I had approved, smelling him there, seeing that massive body, those dark eyes in my mind for just a second before I circled around and around, three times in total, then settled down in amongst them.

Sleep came easily. I hadn't had enough lately, and the deficit was weighing heavily on me. Wolves didn't experience insomnia, so as soon as I closed my eyes, I was sucked down into slumber, into a darkness as black as a wolf's throat.

· · ·

BUT NOT FOR the entire night.

Fen wouldn't be needed in the morning, I quickly realised, right as I woke up. I was in my human body, I got that first, then it all came rushing in. I stiffened, shaking with the pain that ripped through me, my screams stifled behind clenched teeth. If he thought finding my human body was going to be the issue, he was much mistaken. Losing fur was easy, but this?

I'd thought I was doing OK, thought I had this under control. I hadn't taken any of the medicine I'd used last night, nor availed myself of Colt's homemade remedy. No, I'd lain down a wolf and awoken with a body on fire. I'd had period pains in the past, so intense, it had honestly felt like a knife was slowly being inserted into my uterus, but not like this. It felt like everything inside me clenched down, like it was trying to expel my insides out, and at that thought, waves of nausea did rise. I couldn't throw up though, not yet, not while I was panting, sucking in air frantically.

There was nothing lonelier than being crushed by pain on your own. I couldn't scream, couldn't cry out for help, and there was no one to help if I did. I couldn't call someone, Candy or even 000. I couldn't do anything but be pummelled by wave after wave of punishing pain. I couldn't do anything other than feel this agony, without a soul to at least mark the occasion. Then, as if summoned by that thought, by my frantic aborted howls, as I was strangled by my straining body, they came.

"Riley girl," they said.

Interlopers that slipped in via the bond we still shared or some other process I didn't fucking understand, they forced me to experience the indignity of their touch, and worse, each time a hand landed on my body, it uncurled. Like the rush of potent painkillers, the warmth that exuded from them washed through my body, unlocking muscles, smoothing ligaments, until finally, I went limp on the bed. For a second, all I could do was pant and experience that most seductive of pleasures—the loss of pain. They weren't really here, each one of the Vanguards, but it felt like they were, just as it had when Haze and Colt entered my dreams.

"So fucking stubborn," Colt said with a shake of his head.

"Well, she was hardly gonna douche with cold cum, was she?" Haze snapped. "You should've stayed, Fen, or let one of us."

"Her wolf would have ripped me apart if I did," he replied.

"So?" Blake's question was blunt and to the point.

"Next time then," Ryan said, then faced me. "This can't go on, Riley. We can't let you keep hurting like this."

"She won't," Fen said in a definite tone, staring down at me. "Not after tomorrow."

I should've interrogated that, but I was beaten, by pain, by the changes they'd wrought, by finding my beast. Whatever it was, it pulled me away from consciousness, a wave of pure exhaustion rising up and then swallowing me down.

"RILEY!" someone shouted the moment I walked into the lab.

Dear freaking god, why was everyone so damn chipper when I felt like death? I turned around slowly, my body feeling like lead, my joints, my muscles, everything aching, but here I was, at work, reporting for fucking duty.

Windsor hustled over with a pretty woman in tow, her and a hulking beta by her side. My eyes narrowed slightly at the sight of them. The exaggerated curves of her figure made clear what she was, the challenges of being an omega something I was now becoming a whole lot more sympathetic too.

For one, it was impossible to find good clothes. I'd picked up some more after work yesterday, but everything was either too big around the waist or too small around the arse and thighs. This omega, she had to have been shopping at some special boutique that I needed to find the name of, because she looked perfectly put together.

"I was just telling our new volunteers about our star

researcher," Windsor said in a warm tone. "Riley is currently working with another pack dealing with an unusual mating situation. I think she'll be the perfect person to look into your case."

The omega smiled politely, then regarded me steadily in a way that had my own wolf shifting restively. Extended eye contact, so prized in Western society, was often seen as a sign of aggression in every other culture and species, and I wasn't sure if that was what was happening here. I returned her smile and her gaze, waiting to get the details on what was expected of me.

"This is Janine Evans," Windsor said, the penny fucking dropping, and so did my stomach, it suddenly feeling like I was in a lift during freefall. "And this is her mate, Blue Walker."

I moved through the requisite pleasantries, offering my hand, telling them it was nice to meet them, all the while hearing a high-pitched whine inside my head. Windsor kept assuring them I'd be the person best placed to help them, and for now, I was grateful that he was doing the talking because I had literally no idea what my role was here. Whatever I had become now, it looked beyond what was said, to what I could see, because being a wolf was excellent for sniffing out evidence.

The two of them were mated, I knew that. It took me a few seconds to work out why. He kept his hands on her at all times, seeming to be unable to stop from touching her, and Janine? She leaned into each caress with a subtle shift of her body weight. Not visibly so, not unless you were really looking, but it was there. He also reeked of her and vice versa, until it was difficult to get the individual scent of either of them. They'd become... meshed somehow, but it was more than that. Perhaps deliberately, her hands went up to the neckline of her pretty silky blouse, running a finger along the collar in a way that was pure alpha bait.

If you weren't already wearing someone's marks.

She nodded and smiled along to everything Windsor had to say, but her fingers were all I could focus on. A lurid red mark, not too new either, was there on the creamy skin of her neck, and when my eyes darted to Blue? He was a big guy, looked a lot like my dad, down to the reddish hair that had earned him his nickname. He wasn't paying too much attention to the conversation, instead watching me. When he caught my eyes, his hand went to the collar of his plaid flannel shirt, scratching his neck with exaggerated care so I saw the bite there.

"All right, I'll leave you in Riley's capable hands. Thanks so much for coming in, Ms Evans."

"Let's go through to my office, shall we?" I suggested. "Can I get you tea or coffee?"

I kept up the pretence right up until I had my door unlocked and I'd ushered them in, shutting the door behind us.

"Fen sent you," I said flatly, gesturing for them to take a seat, then taking my own behind my desk. I stared blatantly now at the both of them.

"Fen recommended you," Janine corrected. "You've heard of us?"

"I've heard of you. Eloise said you were the boys' mate."

I watched her face fall at that, her fingers going to her brow and rubbing the small line that formed. Blue was at her side in an instant, picking her up in a way that was all too familiar and impossible to fake.

Well done, Fen, I thought, trying to hold onto my anger, but I felt it fraying between my fingers.

Blue ended up hauling her up into his lap, the much smaller omega fitting in the crook of his arms in a way that seemed perfect for the two of them. They slotted together like jigsaw puzzle pieces, making it hard to see where one started and the other ended. My brain rebelled at the idea, but my gut told me something loud and clear.

Together, they were complete.

"So...how do you think I can help you?" I said, much more gently now.

"I'm an omega mated to a beta," she said, her fingers scratching restively at Blue's chest, the beta holding her tighter.

"We want to have a family, form our own pack. But there's literally no one who will talk to us about this."

She pulled away from Blue's chest then, just enough to look back at me.

"You've seen how people respond, how Eloise responded. She's bad, but my family are worse. They see our marks…" Her fingers reached up, tracing the shape she'd left on Blue's skin, and he shivered in response, then took her hand and kissed her fingers.

"They just laugh at us when we try and talk about it," Blue said, to Janine, not me. "Neen's been kicked out of her pack until she 'comes around.' Eloise has told me my services are no longer required as pack enforcer. No one talks to us or is willing to even countenance that what this is, is real."

How? I wondered right then. I'd spent about thirty seconds in their company, and I could see the evidence as clear as day. I could smell it, feel it. Blue felt…subtly wrong to me, like I didn't want to get too close or something. Not because he was a bad guy or anything, just that he was…taken. Something about him said *no, no, no*, inside my head, like a subtle warning.

"And no one is willing to talk to you about potential pregnancy?" I asked with a frown.

"Omegas bear alphas," Janine said in a way that told me she knew those words by rote. "It's why…" She straightened, then kissed Blue's cheek, but when his arms tightened around her, she climbed free of them. She sat down in her own chair, facing me now, that same steady gaze back. "It's why the Vanguard boys offered to act as surrogates initially. We discussed whether or not they could trigger a heat in me, whether or not artificial insemination might be needed."

She stopped right then, eyes widening as my claws formed, making yet another mess of my desk. I stared at her hard, Blue getting to his feet and putting himself between his mate and me.

"They couldn't," he said bluntly. "They wanted to help, but they couldn't, because in trying to help us, it all became clear. If they could accept that Neen and I were mates, destined to be together, despite me being a beta and her an omega, well…"

He smiled then, just a little, then shook his head slowly.

"Then five alphas mating a beta didn't seem like such a stretch," I finished for him hollowly.

Chapter 42

I promised them nothing, because in good conscience, I couldn't. I knew fuck all about omega fertility, the process all shrouded in mystery, and that was now a way more pressing area of research for me. I did scribble down as many notes as I could, getting as comprehensive as possible a background on each one of them. There was nothing in their family histories that suggested anything different about them, no weak expression of their designation. Blue was big, but Dad had been as well, as were many betas. I doubted I'd find any significant latency in his background, but I explained I'd look into it. Janine was obviously all omega, and that pricked at me a little. I could see why Eloise had fixated on her, chosen her, and refused to see Janine as anything other than her sons' mate. If Janine wasn't pushing them away, looking like she did, Eloise saw that she had exactly what she wanted, right there within reach. All she had to do was...

The two of them blinked when I let out a growl, Janine jumping slightly as my pencil snapped in my hand. I raised a shaking hand to my forehead, saw that my claws were out again, felt the prickle of my fur against my skin.

"I'm sorry…" I forced out. "I…"

"You shouldn't be here." Janine chanced sitting forward, staring at me with eyes as soft as a cashmere blanket. "Excuse me for saying this, but you look like shit." I gave a hysterical little snort at that. "And so do they."

That had my eyes locking with hers, with Blue's, like the answers I needed could be found there, but of course, they couldn't be. No one else would have the right answers, not them, not anyone here, not Eloise or the boys' dads. They'd always said they did, but that didn't make it true, did it?

Evidence, I'd said. *I'm sick of words, of people telling me what they think. I want to know.*

But the thing was, no one could give me that evidence, because I had all I needed inside me. If I thought back to the pack, to us, to the way we'd lived before the parents came blundering in, it was all there.

Sunlit days of lying in the grass in a big puppy pile. Skimming rocks across the surface of the lake. Piling on top of each other in the pool, forcing someone's head under the water, only to cop a nose full of harshly chlorinated water yourself. Running wild like young animals do, just for the sheer fucking pleasure of it. Laughing, spinning, shrieking, climbing, loving…

"Stick with the boys," Dad had said as he gasped his last breath, because that was what he'd wanted me to remember before he went. *"They'll always look after you."*

And they fucking did, every damn day, despite my protests and attempts to keep them at arm's length, right up until our parents had stepped in and forced us apart.

I don't care how old you are, you're never really an adult until that moment when you question the shit your parents lumped on you in a messy pile of well-meant intentions, worries, dreams, dictates, and just plain desperation that you make it through childhood OK. When you realise that at least some of what they put on you doesn't belong there, even if they meant well.

"You're right," I said, nodding to Janine and Blue. "This is important, and I promise to look further into what you've told me." I smiled weakly then. "If there's a medical way to help you form the pack of your dreams, we'll find it, I promise, but right now—"

"Right now, you have to fight for your pack," Janine said with a nod of her head. "You have to take them back, because they need you to do that more than anything else in the world right now. If you'll forgive me, I've got some advice about how to go about that."

I EMERGED out of my office in a rush, striding down the hall, not looking where I was going, and managing to blunder straight into Windsor.

"Riley!" he said, catching me adeptly and then holding me steady. He stared into my eyes, peering at my face as if seeing me for the first time, and a shiver went through me as a result. I glanced surreptitiously down at my hands, balling them when I found them reassuringly human, but for how long? "I've been meaning to talk to you."

"Robert, I can't—"

"Riley, I know what's going on." It felt like someone had upended a bucket of ice water all over me then, my eyes finding his as I went perfectly still. "You are such a driven, hard-working, and dedicated scientist, I cannot fault your work ethic one bit. You show initiative and pursue a project from all angles, often delivering results even I would never have expected, and if I dare doubt you, your documentation and supporting evidence is all there, to give credence to your hypothesis, but, Riley…"

I just stared helplessly, caught in his grip, a rabbit in a trap, not a wolf.

"You stand on the brink of greatness and I feel privileged to witness you take that first step, but right now…" His eyes studied mine, studied me in a way I doubt if anyone here had ever done, except for maybe Candy or my pack. "Don't burn yourself out before you've even had a chance to shine. Go home. Rest. Don't go and take any more samples from the alphas. Just take a day to recuperate, please."

I grinned then, a weird reflex, when all I felt was a wash of the most complete relief.

"You know what, you're right. That was what I was coming out here to check with you. I've taken some notes about the Walker-Evans project, but that's all I've got in me today. I'll be back on deck tomorrow—"

"We'll see," Robert said, patting me on the arm now. "Rest up, and then we'll talk in the morning."

I nodded, pulling away carefully, and then went out into the reception area at a much more careful pace.

"Hey, Riley—" Janet said. She was standing with Candy, her bag in hand, the two of them obviously about to go for a coffee.

"I've got to go," I said, raking my hair back from my face. "I need to—"

"Go get your fucking harem of studly men?" Candy asked, her face crumpling. "Fuck, girl…" She ran over, enveloping me in a disproportionately powerful hug. "Baby's first orgy. Mumma couldn't be more proud. Just remember, two in the hole is always the goal."

"Baby's first dominance fight," I corrected, and their eyes widened as a result.

I EXPLAINED the way it had to be, the way it would always be if I didn't do this. Since I didn't know much about the way omegas worked, Janine had been forced to run me through a quick omega hierarchy 101 class in my office.

"An omega takes a pack from their mother," she told me. "You'll find this out yourself if you ever decide to have kids with them." Her eyes softened then, as if she could see my prospective sons running around my desk. "Though hopefully, you'll do a better job of transitioning. Eloise has ruled Bordertown in one way or other since she was just out of school, first as the elder Vanguards' mate, then as the mother of her unmated sons while they

343

ran the town. She's been in the driver's seat, and like a lot of people who've had their own way for a long time, she's used to it."

Janine shrugged.

"It's not as if she was openly hostile to me taking Blue as my mate as she was dismissive of it. She knew better. She'd run the town for so many years. The boys were strong and healthy. You'd become a success. She could point to so many positive outcomes that came about from her actions, so why question them? Why look beyond the surface? She was worried about the boys finding a mate, but also in no hurry, if that makes sense."

Janine smiled tightly then.

"When I was brought to the community as a potential mate for the boys, I noticed it almost straight away. I'd make decisions, only to have them quietly countermanded. She'd kill me with kindness, all the while removing my personal autonomy, without even realising she was doing it, I think." Her lips quirked at that. *"I'd like to think she just thought she was doing what was right, whether or not it actually was."*

Janine's gaze sharpened then.

"She's not going to take you seriously, or the boys' bond with you, and she won't stop trying to meddle with shit until you put her in her place. You don't have to seriously hurt her or kill her."

Her smile widened then, showing an array of sharp teeth now.

"But you do need to declare your dominance over her. If I were a match for the boys, it's the first thing I would have done—established myself as the power in the town, as the mate of her boys, as the person who came first in their lives."

She nodded to me then.

"Thankfully, I don't have to. Blue's mum is lovely…"

I blinked then, catching Candy and Janet staring at me then.

"Here." Janet shoved a pair of her Ray-Bans at me. "Your eyes are shining as bright as the moon."

I jammed them on, right in time for the doors to open and allow more people inside the lift.

THANKFULLY WHEN WE got to the ground floor, we were the

only ones left, because I burst out of the small space like a bullet from a gun.

"Wait!" Candy shouted, racing over. "Do you want us to give you a ride?" She took a step backwards when she saw the state of me. I handed back Janet's glasses with hands already starting to shake with what was coming, my feet toeing off my shoes, my arms stripping off my jacket. "Ah, Riley, you want to wolf out here?"

Her eyes darted around the carpark, and for good reason, but I couldn't pay too much attention to it because time had run out. Whatever I was now, it was done waiting, done hurting, done being a good girl and following the orders I'd been given. My fingers went to my shirt, trying to unbutton it and failing, then resorting to tearing it free from me, and that was probably what got Evan's phone out.

I couldn't stop what was happening, the girls clustering around me protectively, showing a loyalty that had the wolf inside me chuffing. It was no mean feat, turning your back on a predator, but they did it to try and protect me. Still, he sat there, unremarked and unnoticed, as he often was when he wasn't drawing attention to himself, in the safety of his car, and filmed me taking fur.

I was down, stretched out on my hands and knees, summoning the creature I knew as well as my own heart. She was my heart, the one that beat true and hard and wild, no matter what anyone else said, and now she was going after the thing she needed most.

The ladies shrieked as I tore out of the carpark on paws like springs, streaking out onto the footpath, sending people shouting and crying out, leaping to get out of my path. I liked that, this automatic reduction of obstacles, as I ran out of the city centre, across main roads, down alleyways, and out, out, out, towards them.

I COULDN'T TELL you how long it took or even how I got there.

All I knew was I was panting heavily as I trotted up to a familiar open gate, looking up the rise to a house I recognised easily. *Home*, my wolf heart asserted, then we loped on up the pathway, catching snippets of conversations on the wind.

Deep masculine ones, they drew me closer and closer, creating a pain inside me, but one I ran towards rather than away from, and then there was her.

My jaws snapped shut, and I paced for a second, allowing my lungs the chance to circulate oxygen through my body, my muscles a chance to process the lactic acid build-up. My wolf self might not understand the complex machinations of humans, but she knew this—one went into battle from a position of strength, or you didn't do it at all.

I came back to skin, and usually, the thought of walking into a group of people stark fucking naked would have filled me with horror, but hey, the element of surprise was always useful in battle, right? I strolled round the back of the house, full of studied nonchalance, breathing in the scents of cooking meat, the flowers in the garden, and them. My mates' eyes all jerked up the minute I rounded the corner, their dads and Eloise taking longer, but see me, they did.

"Eloise, Omega Vanguard of the Vanguard Pack," I said, remembering Janine's words perfectly. "I challenge you for your position as omega of this pack."

Chapter 43

"What?" Eloise frowned, looking me up and down with that self-same disapproving look—the *I'm very disappointed* look we were all on the receiving end of at some point, irrespective of age. Janine's explanation of Eloise's self-concept made perfect sense now. She saw herself as the whole town's mother, with all the care, authority, and lack of appropriate boundaries that could come with that kind of relationship. Well, I was done being anyone's kid. "Put some clothes on and stop being ridiculous," she said, dismissing me completely.

But Fen, Ryan, all of my mates, they smiled then, the deep lines in their faces, the dark bags under their eyes clearing in that moment. I snorted in response to Eloise's high-handed bullshit and then took fur, the process as fluid as breathing now. I knew my wolf and my wolf knew me, and we were done pretending we didn't. There was no more need for words, so I dropped my head down, snarling my intent.

"No, Eloise," John, one of the dads, said. "You can't just dismiss a dominance challenge, not unless you're ready to relinquish your position in the pack." I watched her frown at that, eyes flashing silver in response. She put the BBQ tongs on the table with a clack, her lips thinning down.

"Stand down, Riley," she barked, throwing everything she had at me in a deceptively stripped back tone.

I felt the pulse of her will. Of course I did. I'd felt it for my whole damn life, like a whip across my shoulders, cracking over and over, correcting me any time I softened towards her boys, trying to keep me on the straight and narrow, but she still didn't seem to get it. Sending me away from Bordertown had broken me. I wasn't the dutiful little girl I had been. I'd been exposed to a whole wide world who didn't give two fucks about Eloise Vanguard, just like I didn't now.

I roared my answer, my growl growing and growing in my chest, getting so big, it felt like I was my fucking anger, my outrage, my complete and utter disinterest in what had gone on before, and Omega Vanguard, she could not take that lying down. She was out of her clothes and in fur in the time it took to blink, and then she was on me.

If you've ever watched animals fight, it's bloody terrifying, all vicious snarls and raking claws. It's also largely performative. There was a reason it was called a dominance fight, not a battle to the death. Animals killed each other all the time, but when it came to dominance, it was largely just hurting the other and posturing until the other backed down, but I wasn't sure if Eloise had gotten that fucking message.

A massive white wolf came barrelling towards my side, ready to knock me on my arse, but I swept my body out of the way at the last minute, then turned in the air, twisting around to attempt to do the same to her. When my head hit her ribs, when she went spiralling back, something rejoiced inside me just for a second before I gathered myself and attacked, ready to try and capitalise on my success. I got a few snaps at her flailing forelegs, human shouts coming from behind us, but I didn't care. It was her I wanted, but she righted herself quickly enough, a picture of an angry wolf.

Well, I was pretty fucking jacked off myself.

Her ears were laid flat against her skull, her lips pulled back from her muzzle. Her teeth shone in the morning light, but the thing was, mine did too. I lunged at her, not fucking caring if she bit me right now, and my recklessness gained me something. I snapped and I snapped, driving her back, then I darted in, my teeth sinking down into her ruff and her skin, dragging a high little yelp from her, right as my head began to thrash. I flicked it from side to side, tearing at her flesh, even as she fought to bite at me with glancing little bites all over my face, but I just kept going, right up until I released her and snapped again, digging my fangs right into her muzzle.

Her screams rang through the block, sending birds flying out of the trees and forcing the men to cluster closer. I hadn't seriously damaged her, but it would've hurt like a bitch. A dog or a wolf's nose was exquisitely sensitive, and by burying my fangs into the flesh there, I'd caused maximum pain without killing her.

"Stand down, Riley," John said, his alpha command feeling like a hammer beating against my skull.

"No fucking way, Dad," Fen snapped. "This is a fair fight, and it needs to end that way."

"It has ended that way," John said to his son before turning back to me. "Shift, Riley and Eloise, now!"

My skin came rushing back in a flash, and so did Eloise's, the two of us sitting on the gravel blinking for a second, blood pouring out of Eloise's face.

"You bitch!" she shrieked the minute she came back to herself, launching herself at me, but John hooked her around the waist, lifting her up in the air, a flailing bunch of limbs. "You bit me! After everything I did for you!"

"Stop," I said firmly, clearly, as I got to my feet. "This stops now." And just like that, quiet settled over the whole house. "John, you and your pack need to leave now. This is my territory, not yours. You'll be welcome back when we say so, but not before then."

"No! No!" Eloise's shouts were the screams of the heartbroken. "No, this can't happen. John, Malcolm…you need to stop this, now!"

"What are you fighting, love?" Malcolm asked, brushing his hands off on his jeans and scowling at his mate. "What are you working so hard to prevent? The concern before was that Riley was a latent, that she and the boys would be trapped in a relationship that would make them miserable, and we didn't want that for either of them. They've worked out a way. I don't know how or when, but Riley's an omega now."

"More than that," Colt said, eyeing me with a smug smile. "She's Omega Vanguard, just like she was always supposed to be."

"No…" The fight seemed to die in Eloise as she collapsed against her mate's body, dissolving into tears.

"You worked so hard to keep them apart, and for good reason, but those reasons are gone now," John said. "It's time to let go, and we're going to do that, at home."

Malcolm and the rest of the dads nodded to us, readying to carry their bloodied omega from the property.

"When you're ready, come home," John told us. "We'll look after the town until you get back, but—"

"No," Ryan said, blinking as he did so. He paused, as if to make sure that was right, then nodded to himself. "If you'd fucking worked with us, let us do what we needed to in claiming Riley, worked with us to find a solution, we would have stepped up, become the ruling pack of the community, and kept the Vanguard legacy going."

"You killed that with your controlling bullshit," Fen said. "We're not Vanguards anymore. Fuck, we'll become the Taylor pack if that's what it takes, but you forced Riley to build a life here, and we won't be making her give that up for anything. This is our territory, she is our mate, and you need to go now, with no more asides. We're done playing. It's time to claim our mate the way we should have seven years ago."

It was then that the dads seemed to finally realise what they'd done. Belated moments of self-reflection aside, we were finished with them, and I let out a little growl to let them know that, right up until I saw them get in their car and drive away.

WHEN THE QUIET RETURNED, when my heart stopped pumping blood frantically around my whole body, when I took a breath in and then let it out, let all the breaths out I'd been holding for so long, I found I was forced to wipe the back of my hand across my forehead. The sun was beating down on me and I'd run halfway across town to fight another wolf, but… I wiped away the sweat, but more formed and more again, and that drew the others closer. Their eyes shone perfectly silver as they approached, as their eyes slid slowly over every inch of my naked body.

"Welcome home, Riley girl. My mate," Fen said, catching me when I stumbled into him. He stroked a hand down my face, my hair sticking to my skull.

"Fuck, her scent…" Haze rumbled, drawing closer, some of his wolf in his jerky movements, in the way he sucked in breaths.

"Heat," Blake ground out.

"That's right," Fen said with a grin, like I'd managed to achieve the most perfect thing. "Our mate returned to us, fought a dominance battle to claim us, and now it's our turn to claim you."

He moved slowly, so slowly, until I was whining anxiously, needing his mouth on mine, and when he kissed me? Fireworks went off inside my head, exploding within. I'd been waiting for this kiss for so fucking long, I could barely feel it at first, and then it was all I could feel. My mouth took over, plundering his, sucking his bottom lip in, scoring it with my teeth, then tangling his tongue with mine.

"You ready for that?" he asked, pulling free of me. "You ready to take everything we've got to give you?"

"We'll need to be careful," Colt said with a growl. "We didn't get to prep her as much as we should've."

"It'll be perfect," Haze insisted. "We've been waiting for this forever. My body knows hers, just like my heart does. We'll fit together exactly the way we're supposed to, you'll see."

"What do you think, Riley?" Ryan asked, fighting for calm, and I liked seeing him lose that battle. "Are you ready for us?"

"I've been ready for as long as I can remember," I replied, grinning then as I felt a lightness I wasn't sure I'd ever felt. "Take me. I'm yours."

Chapter 44

Strange instincts hit me as soon as we got into that big bedroom at the back of the house. I squinted at the bright light pouring in through the windows, sniffing at the stale scent in the air. Windows were open, fresh air let in, and then the blinds were pulled down, Blake and Colt just staring at me as they did that, smiling in satisfaction as I relaxed.

"I…"

I had things to say, didn't I? Things to discuss, ground rules to establish, but right now, I was so bloody hot. My fingers raked at my skin, trying to dislodge clothes that were boiling me alive, but I didn't have any on, only skin that throbbed with a palpable heat, even at my own touch.

"I need…"

"You need a shower, Riley. That's what you need."

Colt's voice was confident and sure, so when he offered me his hand, I took it, feeling something intense shoot through me at the contact. He waited for me to recover, my eyelids fluttering, my whole body trembling in response.

Delayed reaction to all that adrenalin? I thought, but the part of my brain that analysed and gave me answers was quickly sidelined. Colt led me into the bathroom, the cool tiles helping to soothe my hot skin, and then my Colt, he pulled away from me, just briefly, to start to strip down. That there, I knew what to do as soon as his hands went to the hem of his shirt. I knocked his hands away to the sound of his amused snorts, my own replacing his.

He was mine, that was what I felt as I stared up at him, and I knew then, as I watched his smile falter and something else rose to replace it, that he knew that too.

"Riley?"

He grabbed great handfuls of my hair, balling it in his fists, making the strands pull against my scalp, and I leaned into that pain. That was what we'd always had—so much fucking hurt, over and over, aching and needing and...

"Not anymore," he promised. "Never again. We fought for this. You fought for us." The last bit was said in almost a hushed whisper. "It's you and me, Riley. It's always been you and me."

And that seemed to unlock the floodgates I'd spent my life living under the shadow of. What Eloise never seemed to understand was that while she was trying to help us, she'd done the exact opposite.

Tears pricked my eyes as I shoved Colt's shirt up and over his head, his arms getting tangled in it until Haze stepped forward, tall enough to pull it free and then toss it to one side. My hands went to what was revealed, my brows locked down in a terrible frown. It was the only way I could bear looking at him, looking at them. I glanced over Colt's shoulder to where Haze hovered, to where the guys stood within the doorway, but I could only do this one at a time, my brain struggling to cope with even that.

When I touched the boys before, it had been a whole other thing—heat, desperation, need. I'd kept things about the physical as much as I could, knowing this was coming, because when our eyes locked, when his shone silver into mine, all my carefully constructed barriers fell to dust.

"You're mine," I said, wrapping a hand around the back of his neck.

"Always."

"No, Colt." I shook my head frantically, blinking to try and dislodge the tears there as they formed. "You're mine," I insisted.

"Whose else would I be, Riley girl? Who else was there for me? You were in my heart the minute you were born. I know that, now you do too." He stroked the side of my face, his fingers lingering over the top of my cheekbone. "And I need to show you just how much."

He stripped down then, working with a gratifying swiftness, and me, I was forced to watch every move until my Colt was there, naked and hard for me. My fingers went to his chest, feeling that warm flesh, feeling him, my mate. I could feel that now, and then I felt him. He grabbed my hips, dragging me closer, bending me backwards as he brushed his lips against mine, then took them as his own.

I burned for Colt, always, but before, it was a flickering thing, a little point of light in all this darkness, but not now. Him, he burned within me now, forcing something so hot to flare inside my chest, in my body, and he wouldn't stop until I was on fire.

I was hoisted up into his arms and swept into the shower, the taps slapped on and cool water raining down upon us before I was slammed against the wall, the cool tiles a godsend on my overheated skin. I barely felt a fucking thing, though, because Colt's lips were on mine.

This wasn't kissing, it was devouring. We couldn't seem to kiss fast enough, even with our preternatural power. I needed more, more, and Colt needed the same, until finally, we pulled away, panting.

"You're mine, Riley girl. That's what's gonna happen now. I'm going to claim you, mark you, make you fucking mine." He stepped in closer, pressing his forehead to mine. "I would've done it in the carpark that night, so the whole town could see—that's why they whisked you away so damn fast. I would've made you mine, just like I'm gonna do now."

Colt fell on me like a starving wolf, because what else was

he? I was forced under the water, his hands the only means I had to be made clean because he wouldn't tolerate anything else. He kissed my mouth until it was bruised, pulled away to leave little nipping bites along my neck that made my thighs slide wider. I needed his teeth, moaning something to that effect, and he chuckled in response, pulling back and grinning, showing me his fangs clearly in the artificial light.

"You'll get them, my love. I'll dig my fangs into your flesh as soon as you're ready to take my cock, and you'll do the same, right?" It was supposed to be a question, but it came out entirely as a statement of truth. "You'll dig your teeth into my neck and mark me forever."

I wanted to do that now, right fucking now, and a growl formed in my chest as a result. Instead, his hand went around my throat, pinning me to the wall as he dropped down lower. Nipping little bites made my nipples sting, only to be soothed away with slow, soft kisses that drove me fucking mad, my fingers digging into his hair until he relented. One hand wrapped around one breast, his thumb brushing over the nipple with deliberate emphasis, but his mouth? It closed around my other nipple, drawing it into him with long, slow sucks that just made the fire burn higher.

I felt swollen and heavy with pleasure as Colt fed from me, swallowing down my responses, but something else built inside me as he worked, my hands raking across his shoulders, scratching him up, marking him already, as it came. It wasn't an orgasm precisely, though I kept up a litany of frantic little sounds as he ratcheted me up higher, my thighs rubbing together in response, wanting, needing that friction, but what came was something else altogether. Colt's head jerked away, his nostrils flaring as it felt like something inside me burst.

Even in the shower, I felt a sudden wetness explode out of me, coating my thighs, coating me, and Colt looked at me like I was the most precious thing in the world.

"Your slick..." he said in a low growl.

"What?"

"Your omega slick has come in." The others clustered closer now, watching the two of us with rapt attention as Colt swiped his fingers up my thighs and then jammed them into his mouth, a low groan coming in response. "Fuck, baby, you're ready for us."

"What—?"

I was yanked out of the shower, but no one bothered to dry me, probably because my overheated skin was sucking up the moisture already. The guys moved as one, stripping everything extraneous off the bed before Colt laid me down on the smooth cotton sheets. He followed close behind, pushing his knees between my thighs, widening the space between them, the others groaning as he did.

"An omega is physically different to a beta," Colt explained between kisses that worked their way down my body. "Your slick has changed now. It's thicker." He slid a finger along my seam, and it came away dripping, something he licked away with a grin. "There's more of it to keep you lubricated as we take you, and it tells me something else."

At first, he just played with me, letting his fingers trail featherlight through my folds, a ghost of the kind of caress I craved.

"Colt…"

"I know. I know exactly what you need. I'm your alpha, and I can feel all of it." His palm covered me possessively, claiming my cunt as his. "You ache deep inside."

"Yes."

"You feel it clawing at you, a need to be filled."

"Yes," I said, shifting restlessly on the bed, his words seeming to conjure that need or just draw my attention to it.

"Because you feel more empty than you've ever felt before."

My head jerked up as I felt exactly that, right as his fingers pushed ever so slightly deeper, hovering over the exact place I ached.

"An omega's slick helps her to take an alpha's knot," Colt informed me, rising up to kiss my lips, even as his fingers brushed against my sodden cunt. "But when it first comes in? It tells him that she's ready to accept him, that she needs him deep inside her, just as he aches to bury himself in her."

I had questions, thoughts, and they tumbled around in a jumble inside my head, but Colt settled them all with his kiss, a slow drugging thing that seemed to settle me, right up until his fingers pushed in.

It wasn't enough, I felt that immediately. It was a pleasant enough sensation, but it was ruined by the knowledge that I needed more. His two fingers slipped right into me without the requisite friction, my body twisting as a result. He laughed and kissed me more, pushing another finger in, then another, but it wasn't right.

"Colt…"

"I know, love. I can feel it."

But he can't have, not really, not when he pulled his fingers free to rub my clit. That was already swollen. I was already swollen, and I needed more.

"Colt…"

"I love your impatience," he said, his voice growing hoarse and growly. "I love that you need this just as much as I do." He pulled back then, my eyes raking down his body, staring possessively at what was mine, but if it belonged to me, it needed to do as it was told.

"Colt, I need you to fuck me…" I started to say in an intense tone, trying to use whatever omega command I might muster.

"What, like this?"

He grinned then, the boy still inside the man, and that reassured me because the man, he took over pretty quickly, his smile dying just as quickly as it formed, my leg thrown up and against his shoulder as he settled down, and that was when I got everything I needed and more.

My body flopped down on the bed as he gripped his cock, rubbing the head against me, making me moan, then remember Blake's aborted attempt to satisfy me before.

"Shh…" Ryan said, lying down behind my head, stroking his

kicked them over the fence." My focus was jerked around to see Blake sitting there against the wall. The lines were there again in his face, even as he smiled gently at me. "I've taken direct kicks to the nuts during footy that didn't hurt as much as that. Nothing does. You walked out. You left us."

"Because of Mum," Ryan rumbled.

"Janine told you what to do?" Colt asked. "Or you just spontaneously felt like now was the time to kick Mum's arse?"

"She told me, everything." I went limp then, Ryan pulling me closer. "I'm sorry—"

"No," Fen said with a definite shake of his head. "Nah, we're not doing that." He glanced at his brothers in confirmation. "That's what this is—moving on from all the bullshit of the past. Our mate wears some of our marks. She won't be leaving this room until she wears all of them." Then his focus switched to me. "And if you give her that, you give her your protection, your love, and your future. The past can go fuck itself."

I snorted at that, then when I recovered, I turned to Ryan with a question in my eyes.

"You want to commit to a bright and glorious future with me?" I asked.

"Fuck, Riley," he responded, much more seriously now. "I can't think of anything I want more."

For a second, he just held me close, and I found myself letting out a breath as a result, sinking into this moment of quiet, just feeling him. It was all so shiny and new, decadent almost, that I could do this, spend this time with him, and so many moments like this if I chose. I chose. I felt him stiffen as my arms went around him, my face nestling into his neck, breathing his woody scent in, just being with Ryan.

"Riley girl…"

I felt that rumble inside his chest, heard my name like a summons, then in the silence, I realised exactly how this needed to go.

With the others, it'd been this tender moment during sex, but

Ryan and me, we were still working out the details of our relationship to allow for that kind of thing to happen. Still, I wanted it, wanted him, wanted his mark on my skin, claiming him as mine. I also wanted to get a reaction from him in return. I grabbed his shoulder and his head in my hands and held him down in the split second it took for me to strike like a viper. I heard his shout as I sank my fangs into his flesh, sucking hard to make sure it took and then pulling free, smiling through a mask of blood.

"Looks like I've gotta get a reaction too," I said, before throwing myself off his lap.

He took only a second to respond, launching himself after me, my laughter ringing through the room as he grabbed at my legs, but I kicked free. Fen just shook his head, moving out the way as I made a beeline for the edge of the bed, sure if I got there, I could shift and—

"Come here!"

I had a big shit-eating grin on my face as he flipped me over, right up until he covered my body with his.

"You marked me?"

There was an accusation, a very real pleasure, an elation, but also a wonder there.

"Of course—" I went to reply.

"No, of course. You marked me," he said again, his tone soft now. I licked my fangs slowly, getting all taste of him from them as he watched with rapt attention. "You marked me as yours."

"Because you are now, whether you want to be or not." God, I sounded so bloody teenaged right now, everything feeling like it came out wrong, so my eyes trailed down, fixating on his collarbone.

"Want to be or not…"

That was the only warning I got as I was flipped over and then spanked hard, once on each bum cheek.

"What the fuck!" I snarled, but Fen was there at my head, tipping it his way as he rose up on his knees.

"You denied him the pleasure of feeling your fangs inside

wellbeing. As he held me, as he pulsed inside me and I squeezed him dry, there was a rush of warmth that felt huge, airy, and expanded out to encompass everything.

"Love you, Riley girl," he said as we collapsed down onto the bed.

Chapter 47

I think I passed out a little after that, but when I came to, it was to the feeling of soft kisses placed all over my body. Initially, just little points of contact, gentle brushes. They reminded me I had a body, had skin, because they bathed every inch of it in delicate caresses that drew me slowly, surely back to the land of the living.

"There she is," Fen said with a small smile, hanging over me now.

"I made her pass out," Ryan said, congratulating himself with a muffled voice, his head buried in a pillow.

"I'd probably reach for unconsciousness too if I had to fuck you," Haze said drily, ambling back into the room and lying down on the bed. "How you doing, baby? Still hanging in there. So close now." His eyes flicked to Fen, then Blake. "You're gonna need to do the work. She's exhausted."

"And needy." Colt rolled over, shooting me a secret smile. "She needs both of you."

"She needs all of us," Fen corrected before those green eyes swung to me.

I was treated then to something all the girls at my school

pulled away from me, I turned to fur. I snuffled at the bedsheets for a moment, getting a much richer banquet of all of our scents, and that seemed to satisfy me. We turned then, saw our pack in skin and the hungry looks in their eyes, right before they took fur as well. We panted, just for a second, and then we were off.

The run from the city to here, the fight, the claiming, none of that seemed to keep me down now. I bolted out of the house, out into the cool night air, running, running, out across the grass, and they followed behind me, hot on my heels. We shot them a quick look over our shoulder and saw them gaining on us, so our body stretched further, our muscles pumping, our heart pounding with the sheer pleasure of the chase. I couldn't even say where we were going, what we were doing, just that I needed this.

When they did catch up, that was when it all slotted into place. We were a pack and we ran like one, together, pace for pace. We'd be doing this our whole lives, and now nothing would get in the way of that.

Chapter 48

I don't remember coming home. I don't remember the sheets being stripped off and replaced by new ones. I don't remember the six of us collapsing into bed, yet when I woke up, there we were. Hands grabbed for me, bodies pressed against me, everyone snuggled in close. For a moment, I just existed in a warm cocoon of sweetness, then the phone started ringing.

"Fen…" someone groaned.

"Unh?"

"Fen. Phone!"

I blinked then, waking up myself, my head jerking up under the covers at the sound of Fen's voice.

"Yeah, she's here. What? No. No. I get that, but…"

Everything had been so good, so sweet, and so nice, but that seemed to all go away now. I fought my way free of the blankets, finding my way to Fen's side at the edge of the bed, and he handed me his phone.

"Hello?"

"Hey, sorry for interrupting wolf-bang-ageddon, but we have a situation here."

"Candy?"

"Who else it gonna be, bitch?" she asked, trying for levity and failing, which made me tense. "Look, I dunno if you can pole vault off their dicks for like, half an hour maybe, but if you can, get down here. I'm doing damage control, but…"

"But what, Candy? What the fuck has happened?"

"Suck Up Evan is now investigative reporter Evan. He filmed you shifting yesterday." Oh fuck, it all came back, the memory of him doing just that. "He's photographed your desktop" —I saw those long rents I'd left in the laminate— "and he's demanding access to the data. A full meeting of the department heads has been called, but…"

Part of me stored the details of the meeting in my head, but the rest? It was in a free falling spiral. A part of me that still felt like a little girl complained that this wasn't fair, I'd only just found my pack, had just spent my first full night with all of them, and… I jumped off the bed and stalked over to the bathroom, and they came with me.

"What's happening?" Colt asked sharply, stepping under the shower spray when I didn't answer immediately. "Riley?"

"You feel scared, angry…" Blake said, his face mobile as he seemed to use his spidey sense to detect my moods.

"Whatever is going down, we face it as a pack," Fen said.

"Damn fucking straight we do," Haze said.

"And I think you'll find us amenable to removing any obstacles to your happiness."

It was Ryan's somewhat sinister comment that had my head jerking around. I could see it then, the five of them approaching Evan, making the weaselly little fuck pee his fucking pants as they—

I stopped then and took a shuddering breath in.

"We need to get showered and dressed. Evan saw me shift in the office carpark yesterday. I saw him film it, but…" My eyes went to the floor, but I forced them back up again. "I didn't care because I was coming to you. He's trying to discredit me. He'll reveal that the study is about me, not this anonymous omega, and that will derail the whole thing. The symposium, the keynote presentation…" I blinked, seeing everything I'd thought I gained through this going out the window. "He'll try and take the study from me, like he always fucking does."

Colt took my hands, and when I looked down, I saw they shook, halfway between claws and fingers. He rubbed his thumbs across my palm, and suddenly, I felt a little better.

"So we know who the enemy is," he said in quiet voice. "We know the objective, and all we need to do is work out a way to get what you need, together."

Just like that, my breath came rushing out again.

"Yeah, I guess that's how it needs to go."

So we got ready, then piled into two pack SUVs and drove back to the city.

WE STOPPED AT MY PLACE, swapping my borrowed clothes for something more corporate friendly, but by the time we stalked into that meeting, I was about to take fur. There, playing up on the screen in front of every damn department head of Crowe Corp, was a shaking video of me stripping naked, then shifting.

"So you can see that Ms Taylor has been lying to all of us— she's been the subject of the study she initiated." A small rumble across the boardroom at that. "She's the one who's been using company resources to try and resolve her own genetic issues. No doubt, if left unchecked, we would have been footing the bill for any gene therapy she might need, or reproductive assistance, all in the name of these precious studies."

I wasn't sure how this was going to go for me as I stepped inside the room, but I did feel like I could see Evan's future clear enough. Everything he'd said about me was damning, but he'd managed to deliver it in a way that made him look like this petty, grasping, sad little man, who could see his colleague was going through something serious and just tried to use it as a means to ensure his own success. There were some amoral fucks out there who would've done the same, but the ones that succeeded were often intimidating as fuck or charismatic enough that you didn't care, and he was neither. My eyes went to Gideon, because everyone else could quietly get fucked, it was his reaction that mattered the most, and when they did, I saw that Gideon had already noticed my arrival.

"Riley," he said, his tone carefully neutral. "Thank you for coming. I wasn't sure you could make it."

And didn't Evan turn pale as milk at that? The little fuck seemed to sink into himself then, arms like a praying mantis, curling towards his chest.

"Dad, I—"

"You've had your say, and without the accused present," Gideon said in that same even tone. "You can sit down now."

The order left Evan no room to do anything else but, so he obeyed then, sitting down all by himself in an empty group of chairs.

"I apologise for my lateness," I said, but even I could hear the growl in my voice. "I didn't have my phone with me, as is probably evident by that video." Gideon frowned slightly, then reached for the projector remote and switched it off. "You want to know if it's true? If I was the omega at the centre of the study?"

"But you're a beta…" someone said, then seemed to realise that outburst was entirely inappropriate.

"I like to know what's happening, always," Gideon replied smoothly.

"I've known I was a latent for a long time," I said. "I didn't think too much of it. I felt my wolf, but she wasn't pressing me to go to fur like some latents experience. She was just…there. She didn't interfere with my work, until they came back into my life."

The guys stepped forward, and it felt like every eye in the room went to all the places they touched me. We had just declared ourselves as a pack to the entire room.

"The Vanguards came here for me. The institute wouldn't have seen hide nor hair of them without me. Alphas and omegas are not coming forward to be studied." I glanced up at the blank screen. "And why would we? You want to know what's going on with us? So the fuck do I, but I knew if I let everyone know it was me, all my rights and privileges would be revoked. I'd be a helpless subject, a footnote in your papers, and I didn't want that because I can tell you with all confidence, I wanted to know what the hell was going on with me more than any of you do. For you, it's an academic interest, but for me?"

I hated that my voice choked then, tears pricking at my eyes, but I would not let them fall, especially as those warm hands clasped my shoulders, my hands. Their power, our power, flowed through me, and as a result, I straightened up and faced the room down.

"I put in fail-safes. Candy was going to be the lead researcher. She'd announce my role in the study once it was complete, and my conflict of interest would be declared in the process." I searched for my friend's face and found it, her eyes shining so bright as she stared at me. "She'd be the one presenting in New York, and the institute would have everything it wanted—the first institution to map out the process of a latent becoming an omega. You would lose nothing and gain everything."

"Better to ask forgiveness than permission?" Gideon said, then snorted, his smile wry. "I understand that, but I understand this more." His gaze held mine for some time, until Fen and the boys got restless, letting out little growls in response. "You were going through something terrifying, life altering, something that completely rewrote who and what you are as a person, and while you did that, you did it with integrity. You meticulously recorded what your pack was going through. You were willing to work with other departments to share your findings. You were prepared to do whatever it took to ensure we understood the process better, so that we might help others in the future."

He sat back then, hands forming a steeple on his chest before he slowly nodded at me.

"Well done."

I let out a little gasp of breath, but it was lost amongst all the others.

"It took an incredible amount of balls to even conceive of that, let alone carry it out, but that's the kind of reckless bullshit I live for." Gideon's grin was wide now as he continued. "The scientific method is there for a reason. Its dictates help us find out what is real, rather than what is assumed, but sometimes, those rules are hard to live by. Sometimes, you just want to fucking know and the only ethical way to do that is to use yourself as your guinea pig."

His focus shifted to the rest of the room now, then settled on Evan.

"I'm guessing you all scurried up here to witness a ritual blood-letting, but that's not what is going to happen today. I'd never have reached the position I'm in now if I wasn't open to some unorthodox methodologies. Are we going to have to work hard to make sure the study is framed correctly before presenting it?"

"We…?" I asked faintly.

"Yes, we. Windsor, Candace, and you and I, we're about to become very familiar with each other, because we will be working very hard on doing justice to the sacrifices you've made to ensure we better understand our omega and alpha brethren."

I thought that the meeting was over, and I admit, I was so fucking numb, I couldn't even feel my face, but I didn't much care. When I turned around, seeking the eyes of my pack and finding them all zeroed in on me, I had everything I needed, and that was so damn heady, I couldn't even process it.

That's what we can do to people sometimes—in our attempts to do the 'right' thing, sometimes we divorce people so far away from who they are and what they need in life, they have moments like this. Pleasure was a dim thing, muffled by a thick layer of disbelief and unworthiness, but that was OK. I knew my pack, knew they would get through to me or die trying.

And then Gideon spoke again.

"As for Evan, this is about to get personal, something I'd

much prefer to have dealt with at that level, but by bringing these pieces of 'evidence' before the management of my institute, you've unfortunately forced me to deal with this in a public forum. Concerns about colleagues are to be dealt with privately through HR. If you felt like they were not dealing with it satisfactorily, you could have brought it to me personally. Christ, seeing as you're still living in the guest house and only eating what your mother cooks you, a conversation could've been had over dinner. Instead, you tried to turn this into some kind of public spectacle to repudiate Riley for the sin of being the exact opposite of you and then assumed that was a point of weakness that you could then use to your own advantage."

I could see the real pain in Gideon's face as he stared into Evan's wide eyes.

"You're done here. I didn't want you working here in the first place. Nepotism rarely brings results, but your mother was adamant. Your 'internship,' for want of a better word, is over and I'm cutting you loose. You know Mum and I will always support you, but I cannot continue to support you working here." Gideon sighed. "The log of complaints HR has against you is reason enough," he muttered. "Collect your stuff and head home."

It was Gideon Crowe, not Evan's dad, who faced the rest of us now.

"Unless there's anything else anyone wants to bring up?"

I FELT like I staggered out of the room on legs made of wet noodles, but they all rushed in to keep me upright, including Candy.

"What the fuck?!" she hissed, shooting a look over her shoulder at all the department heads filing out. "What the actual fuck?! Pub, now, because I need to shove my head in a wine glass the size of a bucket to process what bloody happened, because what the fuck?!"

"Candace, Riley." We turned around to see Windsor

standing there looking all stiff and repressed, but his mouth was turned up in a smile, just. "I just want to say…" The pause was a killer, my guts already sure we were on some kind of roller coaster because I'd been up and down all day. "Well done," he said finally, Candy letting out a gusty sigh, but he reached out and patted my arm awkwardly. "I know now why you were so frazzled, and quite frankly, I'm astonished." He looked from one to the other of us. "The work ethic, the trust, the team work…" He nodded sharply then. "I've been told it takes quite a lot to impress me, but I have to say in this case, I am very much so."

Whatever passed for warm fuzzies in his world, they were quickly shoved to one side.

"Gideon's asked me to mention that you are on paid leave as of now." Robert seemed to notice my pack for the first time, nodding in their direction. "You've formed a pack" —his eyes slid over the bite marks poking above my collar and away again — "and you need time to consolidate that, but you'll continue to collect data? The early results from the swabs you took are very promising. Gideon's paying quite the sum to have them pushed through as a priority."

I grinned then.

"Try and stop me."

"Well, that's good then. We'll discuss whether or not you will need to set up a work from home scenario when you're back on deck, but apart from that, we don't expect to see you back here for two weeks. Now, Candace."

My friend visibly swallowed, looking at our boss with big eyes.

"We're going to need to—"

"I'm going home sick."

"What?"

She coughed then, made it seem quite believable, her eyes watering as she did so.

"I've got a virus, probably just a twenty-four-hour thing. I only came in for Riley because…"

Windsor's eyes narrowed at that, seeming to rake over Candy

with a frankly frightening intensity, so that when he finally nodded, we both let out a sigh of relief.

"I'll expect to see you in the morning then, fully recovered."

That wouldn't happen of course, because the minute we walked out of the institute, we were planning where to go next.

"Pub?" Candy asked with a wide grin.

"Meetcha at the Cumberland," I replied.

"HOLY FUCKING MAN MEAT, BATMAN," Spider said when we all filed up to the bar, his eyes finding my mating marks with ease. "You look like the girl that got all the bones and then they used you for a chew toy afterwards. You OK, or do I need to call the pound to come collect?"

"I'm good," I replied with a smug smile. "This is my pack."

"And you're a fucking omega," he said, then waved his hand at my chest area. "Either that or you had a plastic surgeon pump them titties up with helium, because damn."

"Gin and bitter lemon," I said, then, "and whatever everyone else is having."

"No, nup, nuh-uh," came his reply. "No more bitter old spinster bullshit for you. It's girly froufrou drinks all the time. I'll make you guys some piña coladas with lots of pineapple juice in it. Drink enough of it, and all that spoof you're guzzling will taste as sweet as honey."

"How do you know it's not already?" Haze asked, settling his body against mine. "How do we taste, love?"

"Perfect," I replied and kissed him.

"Fuck this…" Spider grumbled, starting to mix cocktails for us and pouring himself a big glass of bitter lemon sans gin and taking a sip. He winced, his mouth forming a pinched little circle. "Looks like I'm drinking this shit now, because I'm the fucking bitter one." His eyes flicked up to the guys. "Got any other hot packs full of alphas looking for a beta to plunder? Because I can fit my fist right up my—"

I reached across and slapped my hand across his mouth, right up until he fucking licked my palm.

"Ew! I do not want a sample of your DNA, thanks, though maybe we should." I turned to Candy. "Surely there has to be some kind of genetic glitch going on here."

"Fuck, you're never going to stop. Look, you overly analytical robot, it's now time to celebrate! You got the guys and the job and we kicked Evan's fucking arse! Riley." She gripped my arms now. "You did it."

And that was the moment it became real, my brain finally accepting what I knew to be true. We did do it, together, and when Spider put fancy cocktail glasses of piña coladas out, everyone grabbed one for a toast.

I was ready for my happily ever after.

Chapter 49

A year later, in New York.

"Where are we at with Janine's ovulation results?" I asked as I paced back and forth across the floor of the plush hotel room.

"Just pulling them up now," Colt said, tapping away on his laptop. "All right, lemme scroll through…" He nodded then, drawing my focus, making me finally stop still and wait with bated breath for his answer. "Looks like the Collins pack's tests are back. Everything is looking normal." He glanced at me and smiled. "All that tainted blood bullshit is exactly that. I'll send them the results when you're speaking."

"Awesome, now…" I spun my finger in a small circle, indicating he needed to speed up.

"Miller pack… Joneses… Ah, here we are."

My heart was in my throat as Colt started reading. I wanted to snatch the computer off him, but we worked on this as a pack now. Gideon had been more than happy for us to bring the guys into our business unit. Not as scientists obviously, but as Fen had said, they weren't stupid. They were amazing at client relationship management, about going out to communities and introducing us as an institution to the different packs. Problems, inconsistencies and genetic quirks often came out of the wood-work as my guys started talking to other alphas, but Colt? He was right back where he was before—at my side, helping me with my work. It was great having an assistant that was so closely attuned to me. The fact he was smoking hot was just a bonus.

"Fuck…"

His voice jerked me back to the here and now, my heart sinking as a result. Janine and Blue had been trying relentlessly to have a child, and the experience was starting to break them down. We'd had more than one sad moment in my office where the two of them cried, Blue pulling his Neen into his arms. We'd offered tissues and a quiet place to grieve as they experienced another setback in their dream to have kids.

"No…" I whispered the word. I'd been so sure that this therapy would've worked. I wasn't disappointed for us, but for them. I couldn't go back and tell them that this wasn't successful. I just couldn't.

But I didn't have to.

"Yes," Colt said, eyes jerking up and meeting mine and holding them as a slow smile spread across his face. "Yes. She fucking ovulated."

"Are you serious!"

"What's going on?" Blake asked, walking into the room and handing me a lunchbox full of yummy smelling food.

"Janine ovulated," Colt said with a broad grin.

"She what? So she can…" Blake's face transformed then, a flush of pleasure washing through him. "She can have Blue's baby?"

"In theory," I said, grinning myself. "We'll have to look at what needs to happen next, but…"

Blake cut me off, grabbing me around the waist and pulling me close, the lunchbox pressed hard into our chests.

"You did it, Riley. You did it."

Actually, Janine did. We were just trying some therapies using different alpha hormones to see if we could trick her reproductive system into thinking Blue was an alpha. We'd

talked about sperm donation, but they were reluctant to introducing anyone else's genetic material in the mix until they were
forced to, but now... I gave myself just a second to enjoy Blake's
warm embrace before pulling away.

"Call her, please," I said to Colt. "I know it's probably stupid
o'clock over there, but..."

"She'll want to know," he said with a nod, walking out of the
living room into one of the bedrooms with the computer.

"C'mon, milady," Ryan said, wandering out with my suit in a
dry cleaning bag. "Time to get that gorgeous arse into your suit.
It's getting close to go time."

"Right, right..." I said, all the elation going and being
replaced by sheer freaking terror. I tried to hand the lunchbox
back to Blake, but he wasn't having it.

"You need to eat," he insisted.

"And if I do, I'm gonna vom." I clicked the lid onto the box.
"I'll take it with me, then eat something after the presentation, I
promise."

"Riley..." Blake's voice was a low growl, one that vibrated all
the way through me, making me shiver in response. "You
better."

"Nerves getting to you, love?" Haze asked, strolling in
looking very dashing in a suit of his own. "I'll be there in the
audience. Just imagine me below the podium, sliding down your
zipper and working my tongue right into your tight little—"

"How the hell would that help my nerves?" I asked with a
shake of my head.

"It wouldn't," he replied with a shrug. "It'd just be super
hot."

I let out a frustrated little snort, grabbing the clothes, but
Ryan pulled me in close when I did. He held me against him,
nuzzling his nose into my neck, and then said in the most
persuasive of alpha commands, "You've got this. You've always
had it, you just need to demonstrate that to other people today.
Show them what we know—that you're fucking amazing."

"Brilliant," Fen added, walking in wearing his own suit, since he and Haze were the ones to escort me today. "Accomplished, and what did Gideon say the other day? Visionary." He leaned in and pressed a chaste kiss on my lips. "You're visionary, Riley."

"I'm just fucking lucky," I said, the fear creeping back in. "Any other researcher who was given free rein with a pack of alphas would've—"

"But they didn't," Haze said firmly. "You did. You could've lolled around at home, riding the high of endless multiple orgasms without a care in the world, and you didn't. I admit, I'm slightly disappointed by this, but—"

"Shut up, Haze," Blake said with a sigh.

"Yeah, shut up, Haze," Ryan said. "Now c'mon. You've practised and practised this. You know what to do. You just need to do it." It was his turn to kiss me now, just a soft thing. "And do it knowing every fucking one of us is proud of you. You're amazing, Riles. Every day, I'm proud to call you my mate, but none more than today."

A sharp knock at the door broke our focus, and Blake went over to open it, letting in a flustered Candy.

"You're not dressed yet? Bitch, stop pogoing on alpha cock for five seconds and get your arse dressed!"

"You wonder why I'm nervous," I said to the guys as I disappeared into the bedroom.

I pulled my clothes on with careful precision, feeling like a knight donning his armour before battle or something. As I put it on, I wasn't Riles or omega, I was Riley Taylor, one part of the team presenting for Crowe Corp. I brushed my hair, twirling it up into a professional-looking bun, and then walked out.

"So afterwards, I'm thinking we all come back here and get pissed on Gideon's dime, because oh my fucking god…" Candy babbled. "Though maybe we should go clubbing, see if they have any free-range alphas looking for some strange. I heard they don't tend to form packs in the city here."

"Candy, let's just get the presentation done first," I said. "Then we can plan ways for you to land yourself in the A&E for vaginal trauma."

"Vaginal trauma…" she said with a hum, her eyes fluttering like it sounded like the most delicious thing in the world. "If we ever started a punk band, that could be our name!"

"Fuck…" I hissed, looking back at the others.

When I got nervous, I got quieter, but when Candy did, words came flooding out, with little care for meaning or volume.

"Come on now," Fen said, his rich alpha voice rolling over both of us like a firm hand. "Let's get down to the auditorium. The two of you can go over your notes one last time…"

SOMETIME LATER, Candy and I stood in the wings of the stage, Windsor and Gideon standing at our sides.

"You'll be incredible," Gideon said. "You've got this presentation down pat. Now it's time—"

He was interrupted by the compere's voice as it filled the auditorium, transmitted via the speakers throughout the whole place, which was packed with people. I didn't hear much of what he said, my heart pounding in my chest too loud, until he turned slightly towards us and said, "…Riley Taylor and Candace Baker for Crowe Corp."

We walked out onto the stage, our heels clicking in sync, right up until we reached the podium. I took position on the left, Candy on the right, because the mics had already been positioned for her tiny arse. For a second, I just scanned the audience, seeing all those faces, registering interest, boredom, cynicism, and optimism, skating over them until I found the guys. Haze grinned, throwing his thumbs up, even as the guy next to him threw him a disgruntled look, Fen doing the same. Once I saw them, it all came back, because what I was about to talk about? I was going to use big, fancy words and refer to a whole lot of test results and a survey of current scientific literature, but what it really was, was the story of us.

"Good morning," I said, hearing my voice ring out through the cavernous space. "I'm Riley Taylor, and this is my co-author, Candace Baker, and we're going to talk to you today about what we found when presented with the case of a beta with strong latent omega genetics that was able to successfully shift into an omega." I paused for a second for dramatic effect, seeing at least some of the bored expressions perk up now. "It's my story, mine and my pack's."

I then stepped back, looking to Candy, who moved closer to the microphone and began to give an outline of the context for the study.

"OH MY FUCKING GOD!"

Candy, Fen, Haze, and I stumbled into the suite, the other guys getting to their feet where they were huddled around Colt's laptop.

"How'd it go?" Ryan asked. "Fuck, scratch that. It was awesome. It was, right?"

I walked around to see that they had purchased a digital seat to the presentation and had been watching our talk on the screen, but that wasn't all. They seemed to be having some kind of viewing party, because there in a Zoom meeting was the elder Vanguard pack.

"Hi, Riley," Malcolm said with a weak smile. "We've just been watching the presentation with the boys, and—"

"You were amazing, love," John said, his deep voice just like Fen's. "What you went through—"

"And you used that knowledge to help people." Eloise's voice had a tight edge to it, but when she stared into the screen, her eyes shone. "That's so you, Riley. We're proud of you, all of you." Her eyes slid around what she could see of the room, of all of her sons. "We've been getting reports back from other packs, and..." She shook her head. "This is well done."

"So when are you coming back down to Bordertown?" Graeme, one of the pack's other dads asked. "We'd love to have you come and stay. I know the Mitchells were thinking..."

"We'll be coming down once we get back from New York," I replied finally, once he was finished. I smiled then, and it felt like a real one. "We've got some good news for Janine and Blue, and...I think it's time for a visit."

I watched the lot of them flush at that, excitement rushing up that they quickly tried to play cool through. For the first time in a long time, I felt excited about going back to my hometown. I could see the green fields, the sheep, and the cattle on the outskirts, giving away to houses, then commercial buildings as you got closer to the main drag, then there at the centre was the alpha residence. I'd left the place in a shameful rush, but now? I looked around me, at every person in this room, and saw the love there. Now I was returning knowing exactly who I was and who I was meant to spend my life with.

"We'll look forward to it, love," Eloise said in a choked voice. "Can't wait."

What's next?

I have some ideas for some more second chance wolf shifter omega verse books, especially one featuring a secret baby! If you'd been keen to read more, let me know!

Acknowledgments

The amazing Steph Tashkoff did the edit of the novella when it first came out, then super editor Meghan Leigh Daigle, did the rest.

https://www.facebook.com/Bookish-Dreams-Editing-105567517555119/

Cover was created by the team at Damoro Designs

Special thanks to Jayne, Cherie, Dianne, Joanne, Judi, Kayse, Liza, MaryAnn, Saoirse, Richelle and Steph. This book came out of nowhere and I couldn't have done it without everyone's encouragement and awesome feedback.

Stalk me!

Stalk me!

Facebook author group: Sam's Hall of Heroines
Facebook page here
Newsletter sign up here
Instagram here
Book Bub here

CONTENTS

Author   **Jinny Johnson**

why do cats lick their fur?

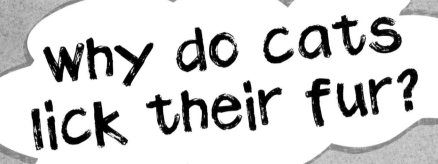

Cats lick their fur to keep themselves clean.
A cat's tongue has a rough surface, which helps
to remove dirt, loose fur and small insect pests. A
mother cat will lick her
kittens to clean them
and to bond with them.

Mother
cat

Kitten

2

what do cats and kittens eat?

Cats are carnivores, which means they eat meat. Wild cats have to hunt other animals to eat. Pet cats and kittens eat special food made for cats, as well as meat and fish.

Kitten

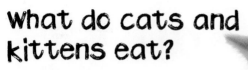

Food bowl

COPY
Watch how your cat arches its back when it stretches. Can you copy it?

How does a cat show it's angry?

An angry or frightened cat arches its back and makes its fur stand on end. This makes the cat look bigger than it really is and helps to warn off enemies.

Playtime!
When a cat plays with a toy mouse it's not just having fun, it is practising how to hunt a real one!

3

why do kittens play?

Kittens play because it's fun! It's also good exercise and helps them to grow stronger. From four weeks old, kittens start to play. Play-fighting with their litter mates helps kittens learn how to get on with other animals.

Kittens playing with a ball of wool

How long do cats sleep?

Cats sleep for about 16 hours a day! Many cats rest during the day and are most active early in the morning and at night. Sleep is extra important for kittens because it helps them to grow.

Sleeping cats

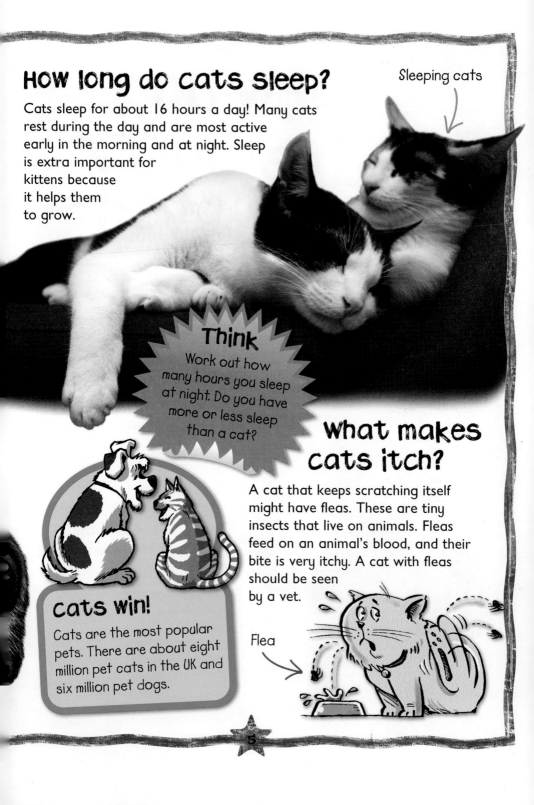

Think

Work out how many hours you sleep at night. Do you have more or less sleep than a cat?

What makes cats itch?

A cat that keeps scratching itself might have fleas. These are tiny insects that live on animals. Fleas feed on an animal's blood, and their bite is very itchy. A cat with fleas should be seen by a vet.

Cats win!

Cats are the most popular pets. There are about eight million pet cats in the UK and six million pet dogs.

Flea

HOW do cats carry their kittens?

Cats can't pick their kittens up with her paws, so they use their mouths. To carry her kitten, a mother cat holds the loose skin on its neck. This is called the 'scruff' and it doesn't hurt the kitten when it is carried like this.

A mother cat carrying her kitten

6

Why do cats purr?

Cats usually purr when they are feeling happy and content. The noise comes from the breathing muscles in the cat's chest. If you put your hand on a loudly purring cat you can feel the vibrations of the sound.

Purring cat →

Speedy cat!

A pet cat can run at about 50 kilometres an hour. Cheetahs are the fastest wild cats and can run at twice this speed.

Are black cats witches' cats?

No, of course not! Many years ago some people believed that black cats were witches in disguise and that they helped witches to carry out their magic.

Purr

Practise making a purring sound. Relax your tongue, curl the end up a little and breathe out.

what do kittens drink?

Kittens drink their mother's milk for the first few weeks of their lives. A mother cat has teats, or nipples, on her tummy and her kittens suck on these to get milk. After four weeks, a kitten starts to drink water instead of milk.

Kittens suckling

Are cats good climbers?

Yes, cats are very good at climbing. They can scramble up anything that they can grip onto. Cats hang on with their sharp, strong claws and pull themselves up. Young cats sometimes have trouble getting back down again!

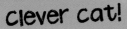

Cats climbing a tree →

Clever cat!

Cats are very clever animals. They can even learn to open doors by pulling down handles with their paws.

How long do cats live?

Most pet cats live to between 12 and 15 years old. Some reach the age of 20 years old – that's nearly 100 in human years! One of the oldest cats ever lived to the age of 38.

Find out

Can you think of some other animals that are super climbers like cats?

How fast do kittens grow?

Kittens grow very quickly. They are born helpless – unable to see, hear or walk. By one week old their eyes open, and at four weeks they can run around. At eight weeks, kittens can eat solid food and are almost ready for life without their mother.

Newborn

One week old

Three weeks old

Four weeks old

Eight weeks old

Kitten's paw

How many toes do cats have?

Cats have 18 toes. They have five toes on each front paw and four toes on each back paw. Sometimes a kitten can be born with seven toes on one paw!

cat flap!

Many cats have their own special doors in and out of their owners' houses. Some can only be opened by a computer chip on the cat's collar.

Why do cats wear collars?

So that people know they have owners. A collar can carry a telephone number so that if the cat gets lost, it can be brought back home. Some collars also help to get rid of fleas.

Make

Ask an adult to help you make a cat mask. Stick straws on a paper plate for whiskers, cut eyeholes and paint it.

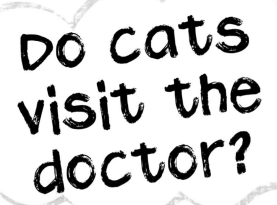

Do cats visit the doctor?

Yes, cats sometimes need to go to see an animal doctor called a vet. They are taken to the vet if they are ill, but also to have injections called vaccinations. These protect them from serious illnesses, such as 'cat flu'.

Vet examining a cat

Owner

Do cats like being picked up?

Some do, but some really don't. You should be careful when picking up a cat. Move slowly and calmly, and handle the cat gently. If it is not yours, check with the cat's owner first.

Lap lap!

A cat drinks by curling its tongue into a spoon shape and scooping up a little liquid at a time. It flicks water into its mouth and swallows every few laps.

Why does a cat rub its head on things?

To spread its scent. A cat will rub its head on its owner, or on furniture and other objects around its home. This marks out the cat's home area and warns other cats to stay away.

Play

Collect some sticks and pebbles and use them to mark out your own territory, or area, in your garden.

Cat rubbing its head against a chair

HOW many kinds of cat are there?

There are more than 100 different kinds, or breeds, of pet cat. Each breed has certain features, such as a particular fur colour and pattern, body shape or eye colour. Some breeds weigh twice as much as others!

Russian Blue

Cornish Rex

Longhair

What does a cat's meow mean?

Meowing is a cat's way of getting attention. A cat may meow to tell you it wants to be fed, stroked or let outside. A loud howl may mean a cat is in pain or upset. An owner quickly gets to understand the sounds their cat makes.

Claws out!

Cats have super-sharp claws. They are perfect for grabbing hold of wriggly prey, such as a mouse, during a chase.

Meowing kitten

What is the cheshire cat?

The Cheshire Cat is a character in the book *Alice in Wonderland*, written by Lewis Carroll. It is best known for its big smile. Alice sees the cat sitting in a tree. Then it slowly disappears, leaving just its wide grin, which vanishes last.

Create

Paint a picture of your own cat breed. Choose the colour and pattern you like and give your breed a name.

what does a new cat need?

It is a good idea to get a basic kit for your new pet. This should include bowls for water and food, cat food, and a litter (toilet) tray until the cat is old enough to go outside. Owners may also buy some toys, a brush and a bed for their pet.

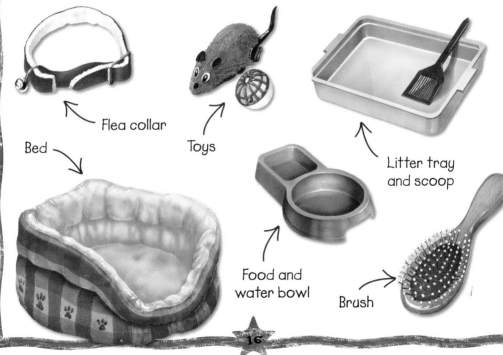

Flea collar

Toys

Bed

Litter tray and scoop

Food and water bowl

Brush

Do cats really have nine lives?

No, they don't. But sometimes it seems that cats can survive dangers that other animals can't. This is because a cat has excellent senses, strong muscles, good balance and super-fast reactions.

Tight squeeze!

A cat's whiskers are very sensitive. They help a cat judge whether its body will fit through a narrow space.

Black cat

Make

Scrunch up some paper and tie it on some string to make a toy for your cat to chase.

Are black cats really lucky?

Some people believe black cats are lucky, but others think they bring bad luck! Some people think that if a black cat crosses a person's path and walks away, it takes the person's good luck with it!

How high can a cat jump?

A cat can jump up to five times its height! Even a champion human high jumper can only jump a little higher than his or her own height. A cat's bendy body and the powerful muscles in its legs allow it to leap so far.

Cat jumping high in the air

Pretend

Imagine you are a cat. See how quietly you can creep up on something – perhaps your own cat!

why do cats bring presents?

No one knows exactly why cats bring mice or other creatures to their owners. Mother cats bring prey for their kittens. Maybe cats bring gifts to show their owners that they think of them as part of their family.

know that nose!

All cats have a pattern of ridges on their nose. Like a person's fingerprints, no two cats have exactly the same pattern.

Are all cats furry?

Most are, but there is one kind of hairless cat called the Sphynx. It looks like it doesn't have any fur at all, but it is covered in very fine fur, called downy hair, which is thicker on the tail and legs.

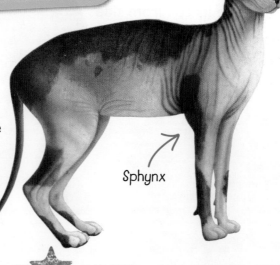

Sphynx

DOES a cat 'talk' with its tail?

Yes, a cat uses its tail to send messages about how it is feeling. When a cat holds its tail straight up it is saying 'hello'. If it is sweeping its tail from side to side it may be about to pounce or attack.

Measure
Gently, see if you can measure how long your cat's tail is using a tape measure.

Kitten holding its tail up

20

How do cats keep their claws sharp?

Cats keep their claws sharp by scratching. A cat will scratch most things, including furniture, so it is a good idea to buy a scratching post. Scratching removes old protective covers, called sheaths, from the claws.

Scratching post

Sniff!

A cat's sense of smell is about 14 times better than a human's – but not as good as a dog's!

Do cats dream?

Experts think that cats do dream. When a cat is asleep its paws and whiskers twitch sometimes. Scientists think that this is a sign a cat is dreaming, but they are not sure what they may be dreaming about!

why do cats love catnip?

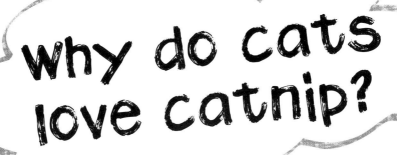

Catnip is a type of plant and it makes cats feel very excited! Many cats behave differently when they come near catnip – they rub themselves on the plant, roll around in it, lick it or eat it. Lots of cat toys contain catnip.

Cat eating catnip

Think
Can you think of some poems, rhymes or stories that have cats in them?

How do cats hunt?

A cat creeps towards its prey very slowly. It moves quietly and crouches low to the ground to stay hidden. The cat gets as close as it can then makes a final speedy dash and pounces on its catch.

A cat hunting in the grass

Mouse

Which cat went to sea in a pea-green boat?

The cat in the poem 'The Owl and the Pussycat', by Edward Lear. The author loved cats and drew many pictures of them. In the poem, the cat goes to sea with an owl.

Puss in boots!

In the story *Puss in Boots*, written by Charles Perrault in 1697, a cat brings gifts to a king so his owner, a poor man, could meet and marry the king's daughter.

index

First published in 2011 by Miles Kelly Publishing L
Harding's Barn, Bardfield End Green,
Thaxted, Essex, CM6 3PX, UK

Copyright © Miles Kelly Publishing Ltd 2011

This edition published 2014

2 4 6 8 10 9 7 5 3 1

Publishing Director Belinda Gallagher
Creative Director Jo Cowan
Editorial Director Rosie McGuire
Editor Carly Blake
Volume Designer Greg Best
Cover Designer Rob Hale
Image Manager Liberty Newton
Indexer Gill Lee
Production Manager Elizabeth Collins
Reprographics Stephan Davis, Thom Allaw
Assets Lorraine King
Character Cartoonist Mike Foster

ISBN 978-1-78209-478-4

Printed in China

British Library Cataloguing-in-Publication De
A catalogue record for this book is availab.
from the British Library

ACKNOWLEDGEMENTS
All artwork from the Miles Kelly Artwork Ban

The publishers would like to thank the followi
sources for the use of their photographs:
Cover Artmim/Shutterstock.com
Dreamstime.com 22 Cvrgrl
Fotolia.com 3 Willee Cole; 7 Fragles;
9 iChip; 18 Mr Flibble **iStockphoto.com** 15 T
Campbell; 20–21 Vladimir Suponev
Shutterstock.com 5 Alberto Pérez Veiga;
12 Monkey Business Images
All other photographs are from:
digitalSTOCK, digitalvision, John Foxx, PhotoA
PhotoDisc, PhotoEssentials, PhotoPro, Stockb

Every effort has been made to acknowledge t
source and copyright holder of each picture
Miles Kelly Publishing apologises for any
unintentional errors or omissions.

Made with paper from a sustainable forest

www.mileskelly.net
info@mileskelly.net

Made in the USA
Las Vegas, NV
09 December 2023

82389051R00223